OUT OF DARKNESS

A novel

Other books by Rex Owens

MURPHY'S TROUBLES
DEAD RECKONING

OUT OF DARKNESS

REX OWENS

CKBooks Publishing

CKBooks Publishing
PO Box 214
New Glarus, WI 53574
ckbookspublishing.com

ISBN: 978-1-949085-47-1
E-ISBN: 978-1-949085-42-6
LCCN: 2018948563

Cover design by Express Creative

Printed in the United States

To my wife Lynette Owens.
You make my writing life a reality.

ONE

23 May 1998

I snatched the revolver off the table, spun the cylinder, and popped it open to check the chamber. There was only one round. Was the bullet meant for me or did Kieran intend it for himself? I wondered. The cartridge dropped into my hand. I put the pistol back on the table exactly as I found it. I walked to the small woods just north of the cottage and heaved the solitary bullet as far as I could. I shivered and noticed, as I scurried back inside, a few rays of faint light appeared in the east, revealing a thin mist clinging to the tops of the trees. I staggered into my bedroom and fell onto the bed face first, fully dressed.

"Ian, coffee?"

I stumbled out into the hall following the pungent aroma of French roast.

"Mickey?"

Taking the cup in both hands, I took a sip. "It's strong."

"I woke with the notion I should check on you this mornin'. Call it my Irish intuition. I found this handwritten note on the kitchen table."

I rubbed my eyes and finished the cup of coffee, then sat down at the table without picking up the note.

"Aren't you going to read it?" Mickey asked.

"I will. I need a moment, if you please. Another cup of coffee would do me well." I poured myself a second cup and took my time drinking it to let my mind clear. I pushed the empty cup to the side of the table and picked up the note.

Help me out. Don't leave your cottage for at least 48 hours. Don't turn your lights on at night. Don't answer the phone. When they discover you're still roaming the earth, they'll snatch you for interrogation. They will figure I couldn't betray you—soft heart, no guts. Ireland will be turned inside out searching for me.

My future will be to lie on a cold slab. Remember the Green Book instructions on surviving an interrogation. Your story will be you asked to get drunk before I pulled the trigger. You passed out. When you woke in the morning, I was gone. After two days, hiding in the open will be your best strategy to being around to celebrate your next birthday. Burn this note.

I turned the paper face down on the table. I wasn't aware Kieran had a flare for the melodramatic, I thought.

"Jesus, Ian, you look like you're in one of your black moods. What is the note about anyway?"

I felt my right hand tighten and hid it under the table. "Just instructions, Mickey. I'd like to share them with you but, trust me, you're better off not knowing. I need to be alone. I appreciate your thoughtfulness, checking on me this morning; you're my rock. I need to sort things out for myself. I'm fine. I need to get back to my writing."

"I know. You always do."

Mickey left without saying another word.

I shut my eyes tight. My head felt like a Welsh miner was setting off dynamite charges deep in my brain. A kettle drum reverberated in my ears. When Kieran and I share a bottle of Midleton, there's always hell to pay the next day.

Memories of last evening gurgled into my consciousness and burst into the morning air.

Jesus, he's gone. I am alone. In the past year my lover betrayed me and now to save my life, Kieran has abandoned me. Is my life worth saving?

One day after celebrating the Good Friday Agreement vote and I was both the most fortunate and the most haunted man in all of Ireland. I buried my face in my hands as tears wet my palms. Twice, twice I've looked death in the face. This was like one of my books. People just don't get two chances in life. I didn't hear the banshee's song last night; I should have known it wasn't my night to die. Why have I been given two chances to live?

I gulped in air as I stood up and went to take a shower, to let the steamy water cleanse yesterday off me. I let the water run until I couldn't see my hand in front of my face. A steam shower was like returning to the womb. The water pummeled my face, forcing me to see the reality of the situation. How long will it take the Provisional Council to figure out I'm alive and Kieran was somewhere crafting a new identity?

He was probably in New Zealand or anyplace he could become the invisible man? Kieran asked me to hide for only two days, meaning he had a definite escape package. He never intended to assassinate me. How had he convinced the Council he was capable of putting a bullet in my head—a fellow IRA provie?

His reputation for being calculating and ruthlessness must have made Kieran credible, though just his display of intense anger with me for abandoning the Cause would have been enough. Kieran was angry with me; he had made that perfectly clear last night. But lifelong friendship was stronger, so Kieran was able to hide our friendship from the Council for thirty years. That was quite a feat. Maybe he was a magician after all; an Irish Houdini weaving illusions every day of his life.

The fog in the bathroom lifted when I opened the door wide. I wiped the mirror with a towel and looked at myself. There were lines on each side of my nose and dark folds of skin under both eyes. My hair was still thick with only a slight receding hairline that disappeared when I combed it just the right way. My famous walrus mustache was laced with white. Maybe a beard would help hide my face. With any luck, it might make me look like G.B. Shaw, maybe even help me get a Nobel.

My first decision on the first day of the rest of my life was to grow a beard? How trivial. No matter, strong coffee and a couple of fried eggs and toast would make me feel like a human being again, and I could begin to sort through a plan to be a prisoner in my own cottage.

Once breakfast was finished, the next job was clearing my head so that I could think through a plan. I checked the refrigerator and pantry to survey my food supplies. My panty was embarrassing: two cans of beans, one can of Irish stew, one can of tomato soup, and a tin of sardines. Having a pantry was a waste of space for me; everything I needed could fit in one cupboard. But my mother used a pantry, so I felt the need to follow her example, even if I didn't use it well. The refrigerator didn't offer much more: package of rashers, a carton of eggs, and grapefruit juice. I had never felt the need to learn how to cook, just to feed myself. I had never associated cooking with feeding myself because there were alternatives, my favorite being pub food. It was filling, satisfying to eat, and could always be accompanied by a pint and a single malt whiskey chaser.

I wandered out of the kitchen to my writing room, not sure how these meager supplies would suffice. I settled into my chair, packed a pipe full of tobacco, drew the smoke into my lungs, and let aimless thoughts drift through my mind.

Jesus, the phone. I darted out of my writing room, back to the kitchen. Just as I went to grab the phone I thought, I can't answer, then it stopped ringing. Who could have been calling? There were only three possibilities: Mickey, Caitlin, or someone from the college. Am I scheduled to lecture today? Did I miss my class? I rushed back to the writing room and searched through my desk for my calendar. I threw papers off the desk left and right and found nothing but created a small mountain of paper on the floor in the process. I searched the drawers—nothing. Where is my briefcase? I found it on the floor of the hall closet, exactly where it is supposed to be.

I flipped calendar pages and today's date had WRITING printed in three-inch letters in the middle of the page. It wouldn't have been the college calling. While I had my calendar, I checked my lecture schedule. I wasn't scheduled for the rest of the week. Mickey wouldn't have been calling so soon, either. He wouldn't be a friend if he had. That eliminated two of the three, so it must have been Caitlin. And Caitlin would keep trying. She told me that sometimes she called ten times a day trying to talk with me. I think she got that trait from our Ma. Me, if I tried to call her once and wasn't successful, I would wait until the next day to try again.

What time is it? I looked at the clock on the wall; half nine in the morning. This was a problem. I didn't want to alert her. If it rang three more times before noon, then I would take the chance that it was Caitlin and I'd answer. She knew I lost track of "real" time so I'd have an excuse. I couldn't risk her making a visit out here.

The phone rang the fourth time at 11:56 a.m. No doubt it was Caitlin. I picked up the phone.

"Ian, you're out of breath." It was Caitlin.

"I ran from my writing room."

It's not that far. You need to start getting regular exercise."

"Is that why you called?"

"No, no. I would like to have you for dinner tonight."

"How kind. Unfortunately, I can't."

"You can't?"

"No."

I couldn't lie to my sister. She would know in a heartbeat.

"Ian, are you being a recluse again?"

"I'm working."

"You're working. That's more important than time with your family? Brianna misses you."

"I was with both of you yesterday. Can it wait a few days? How about our standard Sunday dinner?"

"Ian Murphy, you are impossible."

"Please, Caitlin understand, working on that Peace Accord was the most difficult writing I've ever attempted. The egos involved were astronomical. I'm a fiction writer. I desperately need to get back to my writing. I'm only asking for a few days. Please don't visit, either. Time alone is crucial to me, you know that. Don't I deserve time to recuperate? I've helped draft the Peace Accord. Shouldn't that be enough to atone for my years in the IRA? No, wait, don't answer that. It's just that..."

"Ian, you worry me. Are you all right?"

"I don't know."

"An honest answer. I'll respect your need to be alone a few days. The past few months have been stressful, I know. Sunday it is. Take care of yourself. Don't drink too much."

"Thank you. Thank you, Caitlin. Sunday for sure. Give Brianna my love."

TWO

I settled into my chair in the writing room, flipped on the computer, opened a new document, and began writing. Writing has always been my solace. Writing was what I did – period. That day my writing was what they call stream of consciousness because I didn't have a current writing project. My work on the Peace Accord was exhausting. I had my own editor for at least twenty years and we had a symbiotic relationship. Working with politicians to craft an agreement that Sinn Fein, the Northern Ireland Unionist Party, and the British government could accept was a humbling experience. They fought over damn near every sentence, often words within each sentence. The process was chaotic and drove me to the brink of depression. Many evenings I retreated into a bottle of single malt to dull my senses, forget the day, and ensure sleep, even if it was a restless sleep.

The Peace Accord was my first nonfiction writing, and it would be my last. I lived in a world of fiction that I created, with only the characters I breathed life into to keep me company. My relationship with all my characters was intimate. I understood their history, their motives, what they cared about. It was a very private world. In the "real world" I was considered both a hero and a traitor. Because of my work on the Peace Accord, I was considered a hero, or so it had been said. The Provisional IRA announced months ago I was a traitor for betraying the Cause, which we Irish had shed blood over for the past thirty years. Was it possible for one man to be both? Am I both?

Father O'Connell ordered me to atone for my years with the IRA, and by working on the Peace Accord I fulfilled his order. Yet, I felt empty. What kind of life did I have that I was a target for the IRA, saved only by the bond of friendship that Kieran and I have forged piece by piece. I'm a prisoner in my own cottage for two days so that my friend can implement his escape plan, whatever it may be. God, I would like to know his plan, just to feel…maybe even to know that he is safe, not just for today but for years to come. I'll relinquish having him near me in order to ensure his safety. In truth, the IRA Council would want his death much more than mine. He had made the unforgiveable mistake of letting friendship interfere with business. God, I hated being trapped here. I could spend days here on my own, perfectly content, but to not have the choice to go about as I wanted was maddening.

I wandered about my cottage cell, then settled into my favorite chair in the sitting room. There were two bottles of Midleton hidden under the side table. The ash tray was filled with a noxious mix of cigarettes and pipe tobacco. Our smudged glasses sat on the table reeking of whiskey that sat out all night. I walked over to the table where the revolver sat. Why didn't he take the damn thing with him? I now had the duty to dispose of the revolver that was to end my life. That was the literal definition of ironic. At least I knew it wouldn't be traceable, so if I was careful with finger and handprints, finding a place to dump it should be easy. What do I know about chucking a gun? I had a debate with myself whether to just throw the thing in a river or smash it up into pieces. From deep, deep inside, anger flared in me. I found a mallet in the car park and beat the revolver into little pieces. Sweat poured down my face when I was finished, and I felt relief and peaceful satisfaction. I put the pieces in a small box and threw it in the car. I would throw out the box when I had a chance.

As I cleaned the sitting room, I picked up the two bottles of whiskey and stared at them. You have me in a vice grip. I'm going to swear off you. I've been chosen to live for some reason, God knows why and I need to be sober to figure things out. I can't afford to be drunk again. This is going to be the battle of my life, but I'm going to do it. I am.

THREE

It was nearly 8:30 p.m. before the daylight in my writing room failed me and I was forced to turn off the computer. When I did, my stomach growled, reminding me that I hadn't had supper. Often, time and my cottage disappeared when I wrote. That was the joy of my writing process. I didn't know if other writers had the same experience. I certainly hoped so. My stomach growled again; it was relentless. I didn't think it would be safe to turn the burner on the stove; with my luck the blue flame could be spotted from ten meters away – giving me away. Secrets have been an overbearing part of my life. During the Troubles, keeping the secret that I was a Provie gave me freedom to live both the life of a writer and to search for the dream of reuniting Ireland again. I never imagined myself as a terrorist until Eileen Donohue exposed my secret in the Irish Independent.

Her article actually called me a despicable terrorist – this description from the woman, who a few short months before the article was written, claimed to love me with all of her heart. I know now I was naïve, especially for a forty-eight-year-old man. But maybe it wasn't naïveté, but inexperience. How could a man in his late forties be inexperienced? It happens.

I couldn't open the refrigerator door, that damn light was too bright. That didn't leave a lot of choice. Crackers and sardines for tonight. Not really that much different from most nights, except those evenings that I stopped in at Mickey's pub for a nibble. It would have been such a waste to drive into Cork just to have something to eat, and I didn't like to ride my bike back home in the dark. The roads just weren't made for both vehicles and bicycles. It was a rotten shame. What to drink? I opened the cabinet—three bottles of Midleton. I reached for one, set it on the counter, and popped off the cork. The sweet fragrance of single malt was warm and cozy. I reached for one of my whiskey tumblers. "Stop!" screamed my soul. I had made the most sacred promise possible. A private promise to yourself was both the most difficult to keep and yet the one that must be kept at any cost. I needed to have discipline in my life if I was ever going to find out why I've avoided death's reaper twice. I looked down at my hand. I was shaking but still held the glass. Jesus. This means only one thing. I'm a drunk. I'm an addict; I'm addicted to whiskey. This is going to be a very long night. I shoved the whiskey bottle and the glass back into the cupboard and slammed it shut.

I scoured the kitchen for something else to drink with my skimpy dinner. God, I can't just drink water. Then I saw the electric teapot. Of course, it was so obvious. The sun had fallen below the horizon so finding the Barry's tea bags and a can opener for the sardines in the dark was a challenge. As I had gotten older, I noticed that I no longer saw well at night. What am I going to do tonight? How am I going to get to sleep? The Midleton put me to sleep almost every night and tonight I have to find out how normal people sleep. Maybe this is too much? Maybe I've set myself up for failure.

I had to decide what was important in my life, having a drink, or figuring out why I had been allowed to live beyond the age of forty-eight. It was not fair that a man my age was still questioning his purpose in life. All my adult life I had thought my purpose was to write. I had the best of all worlds, I wrote my fiction and wrote for the IRA to train volunteers and keep the fires of civil unrest burning. Jesus, I did it for thirty years.

I even had to rely on my pen to atone for those thirty years, those years of inciting insurrection, desperately wanting unification. Would there even have been a Peace Accord this year without my pen? My ego soared. Had I no shame. The truth was, without being consumed by guilt and remorse for my years with the IRA, I would never have been part of the Peace Accord. It took Brianna's injury in a Belfast Peace Zone to shake me out of my cozy, self-deluded world.

I put the crackers, sardines, and cup of Barry's on a tray and carried it gingerly to my writing room. I looked around the room. It was completely dark now. Here I sat, in a small room, by myself, in a small cottage outside Cork City, still having the shakes. I was pathetic. How have I arrived here? Maybe eating would help. Sardines in oil with crackers wasn't exactly a gourmet meal, not that I ate very many gourmet meals; I had been raised in Ireland, after all. I put several fish on a cracker and then another on top to make a mini-sandwich. After munching several of my impromptu concoctions, I slurped down half the cup of tea. My hunger subsided, even though I expected it would be temporary. I had no idea how I would make it through the night. I needed to give up drinking but that didn't mean I surrendered my pipe too. Attack only one bad habit at a time. Mark Twain said a person needed to keep at least one bad habit so that when you got sick, you had something you could give up, even if only temporarily. Right now, that sounded like good advice. Any advice from a fellow writer was to be valued.

I grabbed the pipe closest to my tray and packed it tight with tobacco. I reached for a box of matches and stopped myself just as I went to strike it. What the hell? How am I going to light my damn pipe? I can't close the curtain, that would be too obvious. In a flash it came to me. I jumped up and ran into the bath and shut the door. Thank God this room doesn't have a window. Was this ridiculous: a man sitting alone in his bathroom, smoking in the dark because he was afraid to be seen in his own house? I had to do this for Kieran, not for myself. I could risk myself; it was my choice, but I had to protect my friend. Where can Kieran be now? Will I ever see Kieran again? How can I carry on without Kieran's friendship? Being alone in the world and being lonely were very different things. Without Kieran I felt lonely. My other friend had been Midleton whiskey. I have the power to give it up, I do. I must. I don't have any choice but to give up Kieran; both of our lives depend on it. At least his life depended on it. The Provisional Council could always send someone else to assassinate me. I was going to learn what the expression "the sword of Damocles" meant in my life. If I remembered my Greek morality lessons, the sword represented living under threat and peril throughout your life. I'm living with that sword dangling over me by a single thread. I have only myself to blame. It was my decision alone to join the Provisional IRA; it was my choice to fall in love with Eileen Donohue, though I never could have imagined she would be a traitor; it was my decision to abandon the IRA; it was my decision to be the scribe for Sinn Fein to write the Peace Accord. So what? I accept responsibility for my own decisions. I'm not searching for sympathy or even understanding. "Oh God, I need a drink. This is too hard." With a bit of whiskey, I can think better.

"Ian Padraic Murphy, put that bottle back in the cupboard, now!"

"Caitlin?"

"Listen to me, brother. You're overdue for a come-to-Jesus moment."

"Oh please, dear sister, don't ask me to live the Catholic guilt journey."

I closed my eyes, wondering if Caitlin would still be standing in front of me when I opened them again. My head was pounding like a bodhran. I rubbed my temples in a circle to relieve the pain but it was futile. I opened my eyes and Caitlin was still there, her arms crossed over her chest; she was the image of our mother.

"When did you get here? I didn't hear you."

She stared at me without saying a word. She raised her arm and motioned toward the sitting room. "Go, I'll make us some tea and bring you an aspirin. Your face tells me you're having one of your migraines."

I went into the sitting room as I was instructed and leaned back in my favorite chair to close my eyes again. Caitlin can't be here at this time of night. This makes no sense, I must be hallucinating.

Caitlin came into the room without making a sound and carried a tray with two steaming mugs of tea. She set the tea on the table and let me take my cup. She left her cup on the tray.

"Aren't you having tea?"

She shook her head.

"What the hell are you doing here? Did you leave Brianna alone?"

"You need me, even if you don't know it. You need me tonight. I want you to have the strength to leave that bottle in the cupboard. Sobriety is your path to redemption."

The incessant pounding in my head almost drowned out what she said. "Redemption? What the hell are you talking about — redemption. I followed that priest's instruction precisely. I atoned for my days with the IRA; I'm responsible for the Good Friday Peace Accord."

Caitlin continued to stare at me. She leaned forward to pick up the mug of tea. She blew on it and took just a sip. "Your ego is as big as all of Ireland. The Peace Accord would have happened with or without you. Ok, you gave it a measure of elegance, and you influenced the sections on language and culture. You still don't understand the politics and I doubt if you ever will."

"You're harsh."

"I'm honest. That's why I'm here. You need to learn to be brutally honest with yourself, then you can be honest with the world. You don't have a lot of experience with honesty. Your experience is with secrecy and deception. You need to redeem yourself before all of Ireland."

"When did you start pontificating? It doesn't suit you."

"So who do you have in your life now? Kieran will be in hiding for the rest of his life. Eileen betrayed you and damn near sent you to a British gaol for the rest of your life. Mickey is respectable and dependable, but he doesn't have the courage to tell you what you need to hear. The whiskey will kill you and make your life a misguided missile. That just leaves me, brother."

I couldn't believe Caitlin was talking to me like this. She has always had strong convictions and was not afraid to express herself, but this was different.

"Caitlin Maureen Lourigan, you are full of shit. I don't have to listen to you. I'm my own man now and plan to be in the future. Redemption? You have no right to talk to me like that. I may not have a lot of friends, but Mickey is a better friend than you think. Don't count him short. If I remember, he was in the hospital with us after Brianna was injured. It was Mickey who took care of you and Brianna when you moved to Cork and I was in hiding. That Mickey is a rock. A rock I say."

I leaned forward and struggled to lift myself out of my chair. The clock chimed once. "A whiskey will clear my head."

"Forget it. Sit down. The strongest thing you're drinking tonight is tea. Do you need another mug?"

I fell back into the chair and rubbed my face until I could feel it swell with blood. This is not real. This can't be real. What is she talking about – redemption?

"Ok, I'm going to pretend we're really having this conversation. What do you mean I need redemption?"

"I give you credit, you took the priest's advice and atoned for your days with the IRA by helping bring the two Irelands a peace they haven't had in decades, but with your history, you're certainly not going to get nominated for the Nobel Peace Prize for contributing to one document. Redemption is personal. You made your amends with Ireland with the Good Friday Agreement to pay back your hand in thirty years of violence, civil unrest, and death. Are you so arrogant to believe that absolves you for the lives you're responsible for? You haven't even taken the first step on the journey for personal redemption."

FOUR

When I woke, the sun was high in the morning sky. I stumbled into the bath and gave myself a good look over. My hair stuck up in the back—the family cow lick. The stubble on my face was distinctly white, not gray, not black – white. I rubbed my face, the beard didn't scratch, at least not yet. Should I shave it? I admitted to streaks of gray in my hair, but maybe it was white after all. I'm not going to shave. This one minor physical change will signal the new Ian Padraic Murphy.

I didn't drink last night. I couldn't remember a night when I hadn't drunk myself into a sleeping stupor. Of course, I don't remember. With that much whiskey, my memory was like peat bog: thick, dark, and ready for a flame. I didn't know what to think about sobriety.

One day didn't make a life of sobriety, but it was a start. We all lived one day at a time, and that was how I was going to stay sober – one day at a time. I didn't have the discipline or self-control for some grand plan to live a life without my Midleton. It was a miracle that I had even come to the point in my life when I would take on this herculean task.

My eyes had deep red lines and stung when I splashed water on them. Must have been a lack of sleep – it wasn't from a hangover. I had no idea when I collapsed into a dark sleep. I did remember the clock striking two in the morning. I woke this morning in my bed, although how I got there was a mystery. Why would that be? God, I was too old to be learning these simple things about myself.

My stomach cramped and a wave of hunger swept through me. Last night's supper lacked anything close to good nutrition. I still had one more day in my home prison. I needed to take the time to plan what I would be eating today. For now, eggs and rashers would satisfy my famine.

The bath filled with steam as I let the near scalding water cascade over my head and down my shoulders. I lathered up from head to toe, then stood directly under the streaming water until my skin bristled. My head cleared and memories of my evening with Caitlin bubbled to the surface of my consciousness. How did she get here? Did that really happen or was the entire evening a figment of my overactive imagination. I needed to find out. I grabbed a towel, then the phone.

"Caitlin, this is Ian. I have an unusual question to ask you."

"Have you reconsidered my offer for dinner? You're welcome tonight."

"No, no, it's not that. Sunday is still best for me. Listen, did you visit me last night, here at the cottage?"

"What an odd question, Ian. Of course, I didn't visit you. I was home with Brianna the entire evening. Why are you asking?"

"It's hard to explain."

"Well, dear bother, I think you need to explain. Did you have one of your drunken nightmares?"

"No. You wouldn't let me. You made me promise to give up whiskey."

"Oh, but I wish that it was so."

"That's what I was afraid of."

"What are you afraid of, Ian?"

"This is going to be difficult to explain, but last night I wanted a drink, like every night. You stopped me from drinking.

You made me promise to stop drinking. Not sometime in the future but today. I mean, yesterday. So I did."

"Well, Ian, that's quite a story. But if that leads to a life without booze, it's worth it."

"There's more."

"More?"

"You told me I needed redemption, that being part of the Good Friday Agreement wasn't enough."

"Oh Ian, I've never felt that. I'm proud of you turning your back on the IRA and being a part of bringing peace to Ireland."

"That's not what you said last night."

"It wasn't me, Ian."

"I can't imagine why you would put those words in my mouth. This is unsettling, dear brother. One night without whiskey and you've become delirious."

"Forget that I asked."

"I don't think it's safe for you to be alone. You're frightening me. Why don't you sleep over here tonight?"

"I can't leave the cottage."

"Ian, that's ridiculous. You can leave that cottage any time you want to."

"No, no I can't. You don't understand, and I don't have the time or patience to explain it to you now."

"You're scaring me."

"I'll be fine. I just have some things to work out. I'm sorry I called. I didn't mean to alarm you. Just trust me for now. I'll see you Sunday as we planned."

"All right. I'm uneasy about this, but I'll trust you. I don't have a choice, do I? If you need to call again, don't hesitate. I'm always here for you."

"I know, thank you. I'll see you Sunday. Goodbye."

Who would imagine that a sister would take the role of your conscience; it was Freudian. I had two choices. First, I could rack myself trying to understand why my moral guide came to me as Caitlin. Second, I could chose to not wrestle with myself over how I was delivered the message and instead concentrate on the message. I will concentrate on the message. Father O'Connell told me, atoning for my part in the deaths during the Troubles would wipe my cosmic slate clean.

Maybe that wasn't what he said at all. Maybe he simple directed me to atone for the blood I shed. I was trying to remember that conversation and I couldn't recall him saying it would absolve me of anything. He definitely didn't ever say the word absolution. I asked him what prayers to recite and he was lackadaisical on that too. He never mentioned I needed redemption; I would have remembered something that crucial. So was that why I have been spared, to seek redemption? Even if I accepted the need to be redeemed, how to go about that was incomprehensible. I was beginning to feel like Don Quixote, but my Sancho Panza had gone into hiding and left me a raving lunatic on a quest I could not comprehend.

I understood atonement, I didn't understand redemption. A good Catholic should certainly understand what redemption means, but I had never sought to be a good Catholic, at least not since Ma made her journey to eternity. The answers had always been simple and clear. Now I was afloat on a dismal, uncharted sea, alone, totally alone, and loneliness was seeping in.

FIVE

Day Three

rode my bike toward Cork as fast as these old man legs could carry me, in an act of defiance and self-liberation. The wind reddened my cheeks and my hair flew behind my Donegal Tweed driving cap. By the time I reached the outskirts of town, a trickle of sweat ran down both my cheeks. Compared with being a prisoner in my cottage, a simple bike ride felt like sailing a dinghy on Cork Harbor on a clear summer day. I didn't care if someone from the Provisional IRA was laying in wait for me. The Provies expected me to be dead. The ruse would be exposed after I had been in Cork for several hours, but those hours belonged to me.

Breakfast was jam on bread with several cups of tea, and my bike ride brought on a ravenous hunger, so I rode directly to Mickey's pub for lunch.

Mickey O'Shay greeted his friend. "Ian, I've been waitin' to see you. Since the vote, you've been a stranger. How would you like some lunch? Salmon is the special today."

"Mickey, you are a sight. I'm famished. Bring the salmon with a plate of boxty," Ian insisted.

"I'll add a pint to wash it down," Mickey offered.

"A mug of tea will do fine, thank you."

"Tea?"

"Yes, Mickey, tea."

"Tea it is. Think I will join you."

"You are just the man I wanted to talk to."

"So have you been playing hermit the past few days? People come in here asking about you every day. They all want to shake your hand and thank you for the Good Friday Agreement."

"What have you told my well-wishers, Mickey?"

"Well, what could I say? I told them, knowing you as I do, you were hard at work on your next novel. Am I right?"

"Well, I have been writing, but not on a novel, not exactly," Ian explained.

"Well, you were writing. Not a bad guess."

The waitress set the plates with steaming food on the table without a sound

"Here's the food, let's eat."

The plate of salmon and boxty were perfect, like a picture in one of those culinary magazines.

We ate without talking, not looking up until we pushed our plates to one side at the same time.

"A pint will be the perfect finish. Are ya sure you don't want one, Ian."

"Sure."

"Odd, very odd. I'll get one for myself, then."

"Mickey, I have a favor to ask."

"You're like family, Ian Murphy. What can I do for you?"

"What do you know about redemption, my friend?"

"There's a strange question. Why would you be asking me that?"

"Just tell me."

"Well, I'm not a religious man, but you're talking about our Lord Jesus Christ. He died on the cross to redeem all of us – even the feckin' Protestants, as I understand it. You're a Catholic, Ian, why are you asking me a question like that?"

I stared down into my tea mug, not wanting to have eye contact. "Oh, I've just been doing a bit of soul searching, that's all."

"Ian, you don't need a barkeep, you need a priest. Wasn't it Father O'Connell that got you to give up the IRA? Maybe you need to talk to him. This ain't no conversation for me."

"Mickey O'Shay, you underestimate your own wisdom. I'm off to Saint Mary's."

✝✝✝

The sign read Cathedral of Saint Mary and Saint Anne. Growing up I knew it simply as North Cathedral. It was a religious fortress at the bottom of the hill with a view of the harbor. Murphys had attended North Cathedral for its entire 200-year history, although I was not a staunch member. When I met Father O'Connell several months ago, I had to introduce myself and explain which Murphy family I represented. My name was not on the role of parishioners. Yet, it was a safe place for me, even if I was not churched. Father O'Connell didn't judge me or ask for an explanation on why it had been so long since my last confession or since I'd taken the Eucharist. This behavior was rare for a priest, especially an Irish Catholic priest, which was most likely why I was drawn to him.

Since it was midafternoon, I walked in the side door searching for the office where I thought I would find the father. I didn't find the office, and I didn't find Father O'Connell. The interior of the church was a labyrinth, especially since the overhaul it received two years ago. Nothing was familiar to me. Wandering down a hall with no windows, a voice bounced off the walls, "Aye there, can I help you?"

I turned to see a man leaning on a broom, suspenders holding pants onto his scrawny frame and hair going in every direction. He had a red pug nose and matching deep red cheeks. I was sure he deserved a lot of the credit for the immaculately clean sanctuary. "Yes, I have lost my way. I was trying to find the office."

The man looked me over from head to toe. "Ya look like a Murphy."

"That's remarkable. My name is Ian Padraic Murphy."

"So you're Roman Catholic?"

"I am. I was raised in this church."

"Fine, I'll lead you to the office."

He turned, walked down the hall, turned right, then an immediate left. He didn't introduce himself or say another word until we stood outside the office door.

"Here."

"Do you know, is Father O'Connell available?"

"Wouldn't know. He's not been known to check in with the likes of me. I just keep it clean 'round here. That's all. Ask inside for the father."

"Thank you. Thank you for taking time from your busy day to help me."

The man shuffled down the hall, dragging the broom behind him without saying a word but raised his hand in a wave.

"Is Father O'Connell in?" I asked the woman in her early sixties, who was sitting behind a mahogany desk that was too large for her.

"Do you have an appointment? I don't think you have an appointment. I don't recall Father having any appointments this afternoon."

"Sorry, no I don't? Is he in?"

"What's your name?"

"Ian Padraic Murphy."

"The writer?"

"The same."

The woman patted her hair and a smile grew across her wrinkled face. "I think he would want to see you. A short time ago he said he needed a stroll through the garden. I'll show you to the door."

The garden was in a small interior courtyard. In the center was a circle of dog rose planted on a small mound surrounded by clover. Along the edges of the garden was a mix of foxglove, blue-eyed grass, and pansies. At the end of the garden sat Father O'Connell, on a small stone bench. He appeared to either be napping or deep in meditation since he didn't notice my intrusion into his organic sanctorum. I stood as still as a stone, not sure if I should interrupt the good priest.

"Father?" I whispered as soft as the spring breeze. He opened his eyes and took time to focus

"Ian, I've been expecting you. Come, let me show you our little garden." Father O'Connell stood, hooked his arm in mine, and walked down the path just wide enough for both of us.

"You were expecting me?"

"Oh yes." The sun reflected off the gold cross hanging midway down his chest. He took small, deliberate steps. He was a man meant for the priesthood since birth, with a gift for both compassion and empathy. He was also the only person I could share my recent experience with Kieran.

"I need to share with you what I found when I returned home from the craic at Mickey's Pub the night we celebrated the referendum. The IRA sent my best friend to assassinate me. Luckily our friendship was stronger that our allegiance to the Cause so he commuted my sentence and then we drank until we passed out. He's gone into hiding now. The next day I had a vision or hallucination or something telling me to give up whiskey and that I needed to make a personal sacrifice. I was told I needed redemption."

Father O'Connell turned and looked directly into my eyes for a long time. "We are all sinners, Ian; we all need redemption. You share that with all humanity."

"Not you. Not the Pope."

"Oh yes. We are priests, we are not perfect. In the human condition, we all need redemption."

"I did what you instructed. I atoned for my years with the IRA; I worked hard on the Good Friday Peace Accord. Who could have imagined peace in our time?"

"Let me share with you the church's teaching on redemption. Redemption is deliverance from sin and the restoration of our relationship with God. By dying on the cross, our Lord Jesus Christ the Savior redeemed mankind. His sacrifice was an example for us. To be redeemed, we too make a real and personal sacrifice. It is an individual act of contrition and a way of life that alters your path for the rest of your days on earth. You should study the mystics, especially St. John of the Cross. He was a Carmelite. I think the contemplation practiced by the Carmelites will appeal to you."

We walked around the small garden wearing a path into the grass. For me, time stopped. Once again the priest, who was a stranger to me just three months ago, was able to see through me like a stained glass window in the chapel.

"I must prepare for evening Mass. Stay as long as you want. You may want to join me and the congregation for the Eucharist."

"I've not had confession, Father; I'm not able to have communion."

"Oh, but you have."

SIX

Father O'Connell was not your typical Irish priest. Irish priests had a well-earned reputation for giving specific guidance, directives, admonitions, instructions, all provided without expectation of being questioned. I left the garden in a mental haze. The first time, when I tried confession, he refused to give me contrition but directed me to atone for my years with the IRA, instead. Now, he made a suggestion. An Irish priest making a suggestion. The world was unraveling. Should I attend mass? Why did Father suggest I share the Eucharist? I have learned that Father O'Connell was a deliberate man. He didn't speak without having completely thought through both his intent and meaning.

Something automatic in me took over and made my decision. I left the garden, hopped on my bicycle, and pedaled to campus. Many of the humanities programs recently relocated to the O'Rahilly Building, including my own Celtic Studies. I devoted so much time to the Peace Agreement that I wasn't able to participate in the move to the new building. Our administrative assistant arranged everything for me. The religion department also moved into the new building but I had no idea which floor. Even though it was a new building, the campus planners were wise enough to maintain the gothic architectural heritage. I entered through the main door and searched the building directory, which was enclosed in a locked glass case inside the main foyer. The Religion Department library—my first destination—was listed on the third floor in the center section of the west wing. My office was on the east wing of the third floor, and this would be my first opportunity to visit my new home.

The interior of the building was thoroughly modern. I peeked into the lecture rooms on the first floor. They had comfortable seating with all the modern technology a class-room in 1998 should have. The technical features were lost on me; I liked to have direct, open discourse with students and didn't even need a microphone and sound system. I preferred our discussions to be at the level of the human voice.

The sign on the glass door to the library read: Religious Studies Collection 9:00 a.m. – 6:00 p.m., in gold Celtic letter-ing. Early closing for a library. I pushed the door open and walked into a small room filled with oak bookshelves lit by fluorescent lamps embedded in the ceiling. There were only three standard six-foot tables, with three chairs on each side, again, all oak. All the furniture was moved from the old library to this new facility. Funding for Religious Studies was minimal for University College Cork. The big money was all going to research and the medical sciences. Those programs attracted private money like a magnet, and there were always govern-ment grants for applied research—the new direction for UCC. Those of us in the humanities were satisfied with the leftover funding crumbs. It was enough.

I found an oak card catalog in the center of the room and searched for Catholic Mysticism. There was a small list of books, two written by Saint John of the Cross: *Dark Night of the Soul* and *Spiritual Canticle*.

"Oh, Mr. Murphy. May I help you? I wouldn't have ex-pected to find you in our little library," said a thin woman. She appeared slightly younger than me, with light brown hair pulled straight back into a pony tail that draped casually to almost the center of her back. Her nametag read, Mairin McCarthy, Librarian – Religion Department.

"You know my name?" Ian thought out loud.

"You are quite well known."

"I am?"

"May I help you locate a particular volume?"

"I have two, actually, both by Saint John of the Cross."

"Catholic mysticism? I must admit some surprise. Are you researching your next book, Mr. Murphy?"

Light from the floor to ceiling windows struck the librarian's hair, making it appear almost blonde. I found myself distracted by the halo-like affect.

"Mr. Murphy, are you all right? Did you hear my question?"

"Oh yes. Please, we don't need to be formal. I prefer to be called Ian. I even insist my students call me Ian. No, no I'm not researching a novel. A pr...I mean a friend suggested I read St. John of the Cross. He suggested the *Spiritual Canticle* and *Dark Night of the Soul.* Even the title, *Dark Night of the Soul* sounds frightening."

Mairin turned and disappeared into the stacks. I heard something drag on the floor and then steps. She must have been on one of those library stools. I wasn't sure if I should follow to offer my assistance or let her do her job. My experience with librarians was that the library was their turf and they didn't appreciate intrusion, so I walked to the closest table and sat down.

As if by magic, Mairin stood beside me and placed the two books in front of me, one stacked on top of the other. I was surprised that she sat down right across from me.

"Are you searching for something?" she said, nodding her head in the direction of the books. "The article that Donohue woman wrote about you was damning. You wrote the

Green Book, for God's sake? Rumor is the volunteers had to memorize it. Is that right? "

"They did."

"You taught them to be murderers. You taught them propaganda, and you were instrumental in lengthening the war by more than twenty years...twenty years. Are you ashamed?"

Mairin McCarthy locked onto my eyes, never looking away, as if she was due an answer, as if I was supposed to cower to her accusations.

"Can the books be loaned out for a month, like at the other libraries?"

"You can't fool me, Ian Murphy. A person that requests the work of Saint John of the Cross has a burdened soul, as you should. You haven't given me your answer. I asked a very direct question."

Both of my hands tensed up into tight fists, which I tried to hide under the table. I scooted away from the table and cleared my throat. "Is that really any concern of yours?"

Mairin folded her hands on top of the table, giving no indication she would give up on her interrogation. "Well, you've had such a turnabout, haven't you? From Provie to peacemaker. Unusual, quite unusual. There must be an explanation."

I squirmed in my chair, trying to buy enough time to find a way to avoid answering. "Well, you haven't answered my question, either, so we're even. It must be close to closing time. I should be leaving. I'll just check these two volumes out. "

Mairin checked her watch, a smile floated across her lips. "You have a good sense of time, Ian Murphy. Yes, actually it's quarter past closing. I only have myself to answer to and I have no plans this evening. For the books, you're faculty; there is no time limit on how long you can borrow them. I'm only required to record that you took them today."

Mairin McCarthy was clearly an intelligent, bold woman. What did she mean, she has only herself to answer to? I found myself both frightened and intrigued with her.

"I should go about my business." I walked to the door, shuffling my feet, then turned abruptly to face Mairin. "I'm a regular at O'Shay's pub. Mickey keeps a table for me. Would, would you consider joining me?"

"Yes, I'll join you. I don't like dining alone night after night." She looked at her watch. "I need to stop by home; my toy collie could use a romp in the park."

"A toy collie fits you. What is her name?"

"His name is Eltin."

I scratched my stubby beard. "Fitting, traditionally Celtic. Shall we meet at the pub, say half seven?"

Mairin offered her hand in a handshake. "Half seven, yes." We shook hands and I left to find my new office.

SEVEN

I walked down the hall, the floor still spotless and polished. How long would it last? A plastic sign stuck out from the wall at the top of my office door: Mr. Murphy 302. The second line read Irish Literature, History and Culture. Every sign above every door down the hallway was identical. It wasn't pretentious, even though it was boldly nondescript. The appearance was intentionally egalitarian. I flicked the handle. The door was locked, a testimony to the modern obsession with security rather than the open academic environment of days gone by. I searched the hall for the administrative offices in hopes that the department administrative assistant would still be in. I was in luck that her industriousness meant she was in the office past the traditional closing time.

"Good to see you again, Teagan."

Teagan looked up and brushed back dark red hair that hung over both shoulders and ran halfway down her back. A smile raced across her face, her light green eyes flashing recognition. "Mr. Murphy, so good to see you. Congratulations on the Good Friday Agreement. That vote demonstrates how desperate we are for peace. We are all very proud of you here. There's a rumor a special banquet is being planned in your honor."

"Let's have none of that. I thought I should see my new office. I'm in your debt for moving all my personal affects."

"We have the keys safely locked away in a key cabinet in the staff lounge. You will get a key to the cabinet and one to your office. We'll always keep a spare key here for you – just in case, you understand – no judgment intended or implied. Now, follow me." Teagan lead the way to the staff lounge.

"You're sporting a new scruffy look."

"I've decided to disguise myself by growing a beard. I have an unexplained desire to emulate G.B Shaw, at least in appearance."

Once inside the lounge she demonstrated how to get access to the key cabinet. I had to smile; Teagan was an unlikely combination of efficiency, attractiveness, and personality. Every first-year male student was infatuated with her.

"What do you recommend? Should I leave my key in the cabinet or carry it with me? I'm guessing the new policy is to keep our doors locked when not having office hours."

"You're very insightful. Security you know. If it were me, I would leave my key in the cabinet. Who needs one more thing to keep track of?"

I chuckled at her impeccable reasoning. "I wish you would manage the rest of my life Teagan, you would be perfect."

Teagan blushed and hid her face behind her hand. "Thank you, Ian, that's very kind. You appear to be managing quite well."

"My dear, it's an illusion – a total illusion. Now, I should let you go home."

†††

My office door swung open without a sound. My old office had door hinges that were manufactured at the turn of the century and resisted all forms of lubrication. The door announced when a visitor arrived, preventing me from being caught dozing off or staring out the window. This office didn't have a window. Without an advanced degree in my area of studies, I'm sure I wasn't high enough on the academic pecking order to warrant a window. The desk was directly in the center of the room facing the door, as if someone drew an X on the floor and put the desk right over it. Floor-to-ceiling book shelves faced each other on the side walls with no more than three feet from the edge of the desk to the shelves. The wall behind the desk was a rustic brown blank slate. Everything in the office was some shade of academic brown, even my chair. The desk had only two items on it, a telephone and an ashtray, both brown. The ashtray was the department chair's approval for me to smoke my pipe in the office. There had been pressure not to condone smoking of any kind, and I would have complied if required, but my life was less stressful with a bowl full of tobacco from time to time.

I sat in the chair and swiveled around several times like a child on a carnival ride. Unlike my old chair, this one didn't make a single noise. My new office was completely sterile, no character, indistinguishable from the other thirty or more offices on this floor. It is the modern way, I thought, and boring, horribly boring. It's English.

I put the two books from the library on my desk, noticing the font used for each title when my thoughts drifted off. Will Ireland forgive me? Is my atonement enough? Does God forgive, really? Can I forgive myself? I was going to plunge into Catholic mysticism? Dark Night of the Soul: even the title was depressing, as if the author wanted to teach us that all hope was banished.

I was pretending that life was normal again, visiting my office, riding my bike for exercise and frugal transportation, inviting Mairin to dinner. Why did I invite her to dinner? Was I so desperate for human socialization? Even though I just met her, it was clear she was not like Eileen. I couldn't trust my own judgment about women, Eileen made that clear. The truth was, I couldn't trust my judgment on any aspect of my life, except my sister Caitlin, my niece Brianna, and Mickey O'Shay.

Although he spared my life, I was not even sure about Kieran Fitzpatrick. And now a priest wanted me to study Catholic mysticism to claw my way out of the pit I've fallen into. Is this really my path?

Fear took hold of me and wouldn't let go. I heard the clock in the hall strike half six. I left my office and rode my bicycle on all the back streets to Mickey's. There were two places in Cork everyone knew where I could be seen: the college and Mickey's, and now I would have been at both on the same day. I was sure somebody would see me and report back to the Council that Kieran didn't do his job. I could have waited a lot longer than the three days Kieran asked for and the result would have been the same. I should relax. I've been seen already. The clock will be started.

On a whim, I snuck in the back door of Mickey's, made my way through the kitchen and into the pub. I saw Mairin sitting at my table. By taking the back roads ,it must have taken longer than I expected. I must be late. It was one of the risks of not wearing a watch, but I still didn't want to wear a watch.

"Good evening. I apologize for being late."

Mairin brushed her hair back and smiled. "No problem. I just arrived. What has happened to you? You look exhausted. You didn't look like that earlier. Have you eaten yet today?"

"You're observant. I'm a bit preoccupied with my troubles. And I visited my new office. It's bland. No character. I don't think I want to use it. I'd be more comfortable meeting students here."

"Your role working on the Good Friday Peace Accord is well known here in Cork. It was an outstanding accomplishment. I'm sure Cork is proud of her native son. Soon people will forget that you were a Provie."

"Is that possible?"

Mairin glanced up, a question mark formed in her eyes.

"There's my friend Ian Murphy, and who is the lovely lady?" came a voice out of the blue.

"Mickey O'Shay meet Mairin McCarthy. Mairin is a librarian in the Religion Department at UCC."

Mickey thrust out his hand and gave Mairin his warmest two-handed handshake.

"You're the proprietor?" Mairin asked.

A jowly grin stretched across Mickey's face. "Third generation. This ol' pub has supported a gaggle of O'Shays. Would you like to order dinner? Irish stew is the special; the lamb is fresh."

"Well?" I asked Mairin.

"That would be fine. What could be better than pub Irish stew? A bit of brown bread too?"

"Comes with the stew. What would you like to drink, miss?" Mickey asked like a professional server.

"I must have a pint with the stew, but can you bring it out before dinner."

Mickey nodded his head in approval. "The regular for you, Ian?"

I squirmed in my chair. "Well, well, I was thinking..."

Mickey turned, not waiting for an answer. "I'll bring you both a pint."

Under my breath, my thoughts tumbled out of my mouth. "But I wasn't going to drink tonight."

Mairin stretched her hand across the table as if she wanted to take my hand. "You weren't going to drink tonight? Ian, you look like a man who could use a drink. It's only a pint. I'm curious, what's your "regular" that Mickey was talking about."

"Midleton."

"Well, you have very good taste, Ian Murphy. Most folks can't afford it."

"It's a family tradition. My great uncles started the Midleton distillery. There's still pride for it in the family. But the truth is, I was trying to go on the wagon."

Mairin sat without speaking for several minutes and then blurted out, "I didn't mean to ruin anything for you. I just can't imagine Irish stew without a pint. I could have tea if that would help you."

I shuffled my feet under the table and avoided looking at her. "It's fine, let's just eat. Your offer was gracious and kind."

The pints arrived and we exchanged small talk until dinner arrived. The rich smell of the stew with warm bread and cultured butter aroused my hunger and I ate the entire bowl without saying a word. When I looked up, she still had half a bowl of stew to finish, and she hadn't touched her bread.

"Ian, I believe you were famished. Could you use another bowl?"

Again, I avoided looking directly at Mairin.

"Thank you for not judging me, being a glutton. I usually eat alone."

Her eyes softened. "I do to."

"You're alone, then?"

"Yes, my husband passed over five years ago from pancreatic cancer. It is a cruel death but fast; he was only sick a few months."

I was at a loss for words. This lovely woman, alone in the world. She must have suffered and experienced deep grief. "I'm sorry."

"I have had my own 'dark night of the soul.' It's passed now. I am at peace. Death gives meaning to life. Can you imagine what life would be like if we didn't die?" Mairin looked directly into my eyes and took both of my hands into hers. I couldn't resist her firm, sensitive touch. I felt wetness on my cheek. How embarrassing it was to have tears slide into my moustache.

"By God you did enjoy your stew now, didn't you Ian." Mickey surprised us and broke the moment. He set two glasses of whiskey on the table, one in front of each of us.

"Your private collection of Glencarin whiskey glasses? Mickey, when did you get these?" I asked.

"They're yours. The only person that will be served in my pub with the Glencarin is you and, of course, anyone with you," Mickey explained in his best bombastic voice.

"But Mickey, I didn't order these."

"Since when do you have to order a Midleton in my pub? Don't you insult me, Ian Murphy."

"You are generous to a fault, Mickey O'Shay. I hope my presence doesn't drive business away for you."

"You're joking, of course. You really have no sense for business at all, do you? You're a one man magnet for business. I now advertise that this is Ian Murphy's pub, not your favorite pub, your pub."

I hid my face in my hands and shook my head. "Mickey, Mickey, Mickey. You could have asked. I won't be able to take a meal here any longer. Every tourist in Ireland will want to say hello and have a handshake or sign one of my books or take a pot shot at me, for Christ's sake."

Mickey stepped back from the table shaking his head in disagreement. "Were you bothered tonight?"

"No."

"Are you opposed to greeting your fellow Irishman who wants to wish you well? Don't be a recluse on us, now. You're exaggerating the situation. If you want, I'll run interference for you any time you ask. But I'm not changing my advertising; you owe me that much, Ian." He glared down at me with arms crossed over his considerable girth.

I hung my head, trying to avoid Mickey's glare and Mairin entirely. He was right; when I needed to escape to Kieran's family cabin in County Donegal, he gave me his truck without asking a single question. On occasion I needed to get lost, so to speak, because of the article in the Irish Independent that exposed my role in the IRA. He suspected my secret for thirty years and never said a peep to anyone. Mickey dropped everything to go with me to Belfast when Brianna was injured. He also was indispensable in making it possible for Caitlin and Brianna to move to Cork while I was in hiding.

"Yes, I do owe you that, my friend. I apologize for being so self-centered. I promise to be a gentleman."

A toothy grin spread across Mickey's face. He slapped me on the back with affection and returned to the kitchen. I leaned in close to Mairin and whispered, "I haven't had a drink in three days. I've a bit of a problem with the whiskey."

Mairin didn't hesitate. "I understand. If you don't want a whiskey, that's fine. I won't have one either. I don't want to be your temptress, at least not with the drink. But I must be honest; you look like a man who could use more than just a pint."

"It is fragrant, and the taste is unlike any other Irish whiskey. Have you ever had a Midleton?"

"No. I could never afford this kind of whiskey. Jameson's has always been fine for me."

"Well, tonight we'll celebrate our meeting with Ireland's finest, at least in my opinion, even if there is a family heritage."

We each took a glass and raised them high in the air. "Slainte!"

"To a new-found friend," Mairin whispered as she brought the glass to her nose to breath in the whiskey's fragrance.

"Yes." The amber whiskey slid down my throat with ease, filling me with a special warmth. My muscles relaxed, and I felt mellow and comfortable with Mairin. After Eileen's betrayal, I never expected to feel at ease with another woman in my life.

We talked about this and that as time slipped away, and soon Mickey stopped by the table to let us know he would be closing soon. Another hazard of not wearing a watch, time was illusive. Mairin was an excellent conversationalist and she had a way of making me feel comfortable.

"Ian, didn't you ride your bicycle into town today? How are you getting home now?"

Her practical question hit me like cold water in the face. My jaw dropped and words caught in my throat. "...I ride home several evenings a week, it's not a problem. My bike has a fine torch. But thanks for the offer."

"Now Ian, that's ridiculous. I'll drive you home."

"I am so embarrassed. I don't want to inconvenience you. It's obviously late. I don't have to be anywhere in the morning, but I'm sure you'll be opening the library by nine. You must think I'm inconsiderate. I'm not, really. I was just enjoying our conversation. You are well-read and articulate, which I should not find surprising for a college librarian. Of course, I would deeply appreciate a ride home; I will be in your debt."

Mairin smiled and patted the top of my hand, not in a condescending way but in a friendly, affectionate way. "I've enjoyed my evening, too. The truth is, I've wanted to meet you for a very long time, but I've noticed you don't spend much time in your office."

I shifted in my seat to retrieve my wallet from my back pocket, hoping I had enough cash for dinner and drinks. Carrying cash also wasn't one of my strong suits. Long ago I became lazy and relied on plastic for everything. It meant I paid one bill, once a month along with my standard living expenses like utilities. Cash is easier for Mickey, so I tried to keep enough in my wallet to support my habit. I checked and I only had a few euros, probably not enough.

Mickey came to bus our table and slipped the bill to me. I looked at him with dismay and he picked up on my signal. "Ian, why don't I add this on your tab. Did you enjoy dinner Mrs.?"

"Mr. O'Shay, dinner was excellent and the company even better. And it's miss, not Mrs."

Mickey mocked slapping his wrist. "I should be ashamed. I didn't mean to assume anything, Miss McCarthy, I hope you grace our establishment regularly from now on."

Mairin threw her head back and laughed. "Oh please, call me Mairin, and yes, I'll be back, and I'm hoping Ian will invite me. I'm not keen on visiting pubs alone, even on the weekdays."

"From what I saw from the bar, you two get along well, so I expect I'll be seeing the both of you often enough. Ian, do you have a way to get home safely?"

Mairin jumped into the conversation. "Yes, I'm giving him a ride; it's my fault we're here so late."

Mickey patted Mairin on the shoulder. "Thank you for taking care of our Ian. I'll look forward to seeing you again. Friday nights we have a fried fish and colcannon special." Mickey slipped the bill into his pocket, scooped up the dishes, balanced them on his arm, and walked with a swagger back to the kitchen.

As I expected, Mairin had a modest car, unexceptional in every way. That made me more comfortable. It was another sign that she was a practical person and that we shared values, not needing an ostentatious vehicle to tool around Cork or Ireland's other environs.

The night was perfectly black since clouds obscured starlight from reaching the earth. Darkness felt both comfortable and secure to me. I was convinced that I was now being watched. My thoughts drifted off as we drove west of Cork into the country. At some point, I realized I hadn't given Mairin either my address or directions to my cottage.

"How do you know the way?"

While holding onto the steering wheel with both hands, Mairin shot me a glance. She seemed surprised at my question. "Oh Ian, everyone in Cork knows where you live."

"Oh, I didn't realize."

Mairin followed the road, managing each turn with ease. "Ian Murphy, you are either not self-aware or innocent or some intriguing combination of both. I know you grew up in Cork and you've lived here since college. That must be more than twenty-five years. So, yes, all of Cork knows your cottage."

I didn't know why I wasn't aware of that fact. It made me wonder if that would give me some protection in my current circumstances. I wondered if people also noticed me coming and going. Lord, maybe I even have a routine. Oh God, I hope I don't have a routine. A routine implied a well-ordered, unexciting life. Although, the last year had provided the most excitement I needed for the rest of my days. In a single year my country had seen me as both a terrorist and a peacemaker. That was hard for any one person to accomplish. God, I hoped the common knowledge of my cottage and my routine offered me some protection. I couldn't really expect security. The proverbial sword of Damocles would dangle overhead until the day I find my peace and leave this earth behind.

"Ian, you're so quiet. Are you all right?"

That was an interesting question, and I wasn't sure how to answer her. The truth was, I didn't know if I was okay. The question wasn't as simple as it sounded. I didn't want to be evasive or flippant, so I took my time trying to choose the right words, remembering Mark Twain's admonition about using the "right words."

"I'm a hunted man. Three days ago my best friend was sent by the Provisional Irish Republican Army Council to shoot me for being a traitor to the Cause. They hate the peace; they despise the Good Friday Agreement and blame me for its resounding approval in the referendum. I had nothing to do with the vote, trust me. The people were eager for peace. Thirty years of fighting each other cripples a country, and to put it simply, enough was enough. My best friend, Timolty Doyle, was killed in his first raid in Belfast. My brother-in-law, Brian Lourigan, died trying to save an innocent Brit working too late at night at an equipment depot he was blowing to hell. Two years ago my niece, Brianna, was injured when an unknown unionist tossed a Molotov cocktail over the wall of a peace line, in Belfast. My sister and her daughter lived next to a Protestant part of town. My sister worked for Sinn Fein so they took it out on her daughter. She was just twelve. That poor girl had second degree burns over most of her body. It was her innocence that shamed me. My days in the IRA ended the day she was a target of hatred.

"My friend Kieran Fitzpatrick had risked his life in order to save me – even if it was for a short time. The bond of friendship is deeper and more precious than a person's devotion to any cause, for any purpose. God knows where he is. I doubt if he is in Ireland or would ever be able to return to our shores. He had broken the IRA code, and there was no possibility of redemption." They will kill him. And they will kill me, I thought to myself.

"I remembered, at the start of the civil war in '22, they took out Mickey Collins right here in County Cork, his home. Insiders have told me he could have gotten away but he had to be a cowboy and shoot it out. Everybody knew Collins would go out that way. That was why he was ambushed, to force him to fight for his life. Me? I don't know how it will happen. I wasn't meant to suffer for my transgressions, just to die."

Mairin pulled into the drive, turned off the engine, and sat holding the steering wheel with both hands, staring into the darkness. Neither of us spoke for what seemed like thirty minutes or more. She turned to me and placed her hand gently on my shoulder, looking directly into my eyes. "Would you like me to stay?"

I wasn't sure what she was offering: her comfort, her body, her love. "I'm sorry, I'm not ready." I opened the door and walked into the cottage, forgetting to say thank you. I don't remember Mairin driving away.

EIGHT

The next morning, I woke still dressed, sprawled across the top of my bed, my shoes still on. Literally crashing into bed was becoming an unwelcome habit. I scratched my beard and looked around the room. From my position on the bed, it looked like I had attempted a belly flop onto the mattress. I'm not a swimmer so this could be dangerous. I rolled over onto my back and stretched in all directions at the same time. Everything seemed to be working. I stared at the ceiling, not able to remember how much I had drunk. My self-imposed abstinence had only lasted three days. Mairin said I looked like I needed a drink. What look could that have been? Had I evoked some type of empathy? Maybe she just wanted to taste Midleton. I did recall painful silence as we drove home. God, I didn't know that my cottage was such common knowledge in Cork.

I lay on the bed, letting thoughts fly in and out of my mind, never landing. I pushed my elbows up to brace myself for the first attempt to get up. My mouth was parched, and my lips felt like they were stuck together. A good cup of tea would go a long way to making me feel human again. Every motion was deliberate and slow, but I felt a throbbing at my temples when I tried to slide across the bed to let my feet search for the floor. The pain bolted across my forehead and reverberated between my temples. I rubbed them with my fingers, but the pain didn't subside. As I struggled to balance myself, I began panting and squeezed my eyes shut against the agony in my brain. A normal person would realize the drink had this effect and not have a problem passing it by. Not me; just one little suggestion from an attractive woman and one glass follows another. How was Mairin able to drive? Maybe I only imagined she matched my drinking.

I brewed the strongest cup of breakfast tea I could tolerate and made my way to my writing room. On top of the desk I found the two St. John of the Cross volumes. At least I hadn't left them at Mickey's or in Mairin's car. Their appearance on my desk was the first evidence of a miracle. No wonder the monk was canonized. My recovery would be complete with a full bowl of tobacco. I found my favorite meerschaum and packed it tight with my private blend. I squinted at the hot, sun-like blaze I held between my fingers. I drew the flame deep into the pipe's bowl, the tobacco igniting with a crackle. I could feel the muscles in my back unknot, and I concentrated on smoking and the life-invigorating tea.

My desk calendar was open to 30 May. Seven days since the referendum passed and Ireland embraced peace for the first time since I was in college. During my entire adult lifetime we were at war. It was as incomprehensible as it was true. I looked about the room where I spend at least ten hours a day. My best friends—my books—surrounded me on three sides, and the window at my back looked into the yard, with the sacred oak filling the frame and reminding me of ancient Ireland's history and mythology. The two Catholic mysticism volumes waited patiently for my attention.

Crafting the Good Friday Peace Accord may have been my atonement for being a Provie but it didn't wash away the blood stains covering my soul. Working on the Agreement was for Ireland, not for me. In reality, I was like the lion in the book *The Wizard of Oz*: a coward. Why would Father O'Connell instruct me to read St. John of the Cross? He was more than aware that I was not a religious man. I was a man grounded in the human experience, a man of imagination and words, with no place for mysticism in my life. Yet his demand for atonement did lead to contributing to the Good Friday Agreement, so I should banish my disbelief and ignore my skepticism. I knew if I didn't find redemption, I would never write again. If I never wrote again, I would die a slow, meaningless death and my time on this earth would have been futile. Worse than futile, it would have been a waste. Maybe the IRA assassin's bullet is the right end for me.

I demonstrated to Mairin last night how weak and vulnerable I was. The myth that was my life, was fragile and transparent. I was so ashamed. I don't think I can stand to see her again. In all likelihood, she will not want to see me. I didn't have the courage to test it.

I sat in a cloud of fragrant tobacco as it enveloped me. I can't rely on Mairin or Caitlin or Mickey or even Father O'Connell to guide me out of the abyss I've thrown myself into. I must be my own savior. The idea was sacrilegious for a good Catholic boy from Cork. Taking summers off from teaching was the right thing to do. The isolation of the Dingle Peninsula tugged at my heart. Roaming the hills and breathing in the salt water would cleanse me through and through. I'd even take the St. John books with me. Memories of staying at Uncle Padraic's bed and breakfast wove their way through my mind. I received my middle name from my uncle, and being his namesake, I've always had a special place in his heart. I reached for the phone.

"Hello, Uncle Padraic, this is Ian. I know it's the beginning of the tourist season but I was wondering if I could impose on you for a bit. I am desperate to walk the hills of the Peninsula. I will pay you, it's only fair."

"Ian, I would be proud to have you, of course. By God, you could be a tourist attraction."

"No. Not that. I must be your best kept secret. I'll pay you double, and I won't take my meals at the Inn. I need time to be alone, to contemplate, to…to find myself again."

"My boy, I don't understand you. Sometimes it's a wonder you are Daley's son. Your father enjoyed working with his hands and if he read at all, it was a daily newspaper. You, nephew are a man of books. In memory of my brother, I'll accept your conditions. Your visit will remain a secret. When should we expect you?

"Day after tomorrow, in the late afternoon. Thank you. I will be in your debt."

"Nonsense, Ian. Your Aunt Shioban will be excited to see you again. Goodbye."

"Goodbye."

NINE

True to my word, I took the morning to pack and organize myself, ensuring I had a large supply of tobacco, two large boxes of wooden matches, books to read, a stack of yellow writing tablets, and at least a dozen of my favorite pens. Of course, I included the two St. John of the Cross volumes, which I had at least twenty excuses not to start yet, chief among them that the perfect time to begin was during my Dingle odyssey. I made a decision not to put a time limit on my visit. I would know when it was time to return to Cork. I packed enough clothes for at least two weeks and my hiking equipment, especially my Harpers Head walking stick, a cherished hand-made stick designed specifically to fit me. If I needed more clothes, I could always buy them or use Aunt Shioban's laundry in a pinch.

The drive from Cork to Dingle was normally less than two and a half hours, but I wanted to take my time and take the less traveled R561, which hugged the shore of Castlemaine Harbor. I left the cottage about half one and pulled into Murphy's Bed and Breakfast on Strand Street about five. I found the drive relaxing, and it put me in a mellow frame of mind. The pub for the B & B was on the corner, with a bright red exterior and "Murphy's Pub" boldly painted over the entrance. The lace curtains in the windows were pulled back and stools lined up inside so that tourists could enjoy a stout and gaze at the North Atlantic. The bed and breakfast was attached to the pub and painted a teal-aqua green with white framed windows. I pulled into the car park at the rear of the bed and breakfast and walked to the front door. Even though I was family, I didn't feel comfortable walking in the back door, it seemed too familiar.

"Ian, just in time." Shioban rose from her overstuffed chair near the fireplace and extended her arms for a hug. "You said it would be late afternoon. Did you have a pleasant drive? Isn't it a perfect day for a drive? Are you hungry? We can have supper here or over at the pub, whichever you prefer. What would you like? Did you leave your luggage in the boot? Do you still have the Opel? Would you like me to ask Padraic to fetch your luggage for you?" My Aunt Shioban was always full of twenty questions. Although in her mid-sixties, she only had a few streaks of gray in her brown hair. She didn't wear any makeup and had a few crinkles around the eyes, which she proudly said she had earned. Her dress was simple, with a cloth belt and practical shoes.

She placed the book she had been reading on the table next to her cup of tea.

"I've not seen you in glasses before," I said.

"Just reading glasses, my boy, nothing serious. Can't give up reading, you know."

Absolutely nothing had changed from the last time I visited. Uncle Padraic and Aunt Shioban had owned and operated both the inn and pub for as long as I could remember. Both had grown up in Cork and then decided the city was too big and too fast-paced for them. On a lark they purchased the pub, and after a few years saved enough money to purchase the bed and breakfast. They also lost their traditional Cork accent in less than two years, and most guests mistook them for Dingle folk born and raised. Uncle Padraic was the last of the Murphy brothers since Da died over ten years ago and his older brother, Shemus, has been gone for nearly twenty years. Shioban and Padraic never had children, and being devout

Catholics, the family assumed it wasn't their choice but nature's that left them barren.

"Padraic should be here soon. He likes to make sure everything is ready for early dinner in the pub. Sorry, we won't have a band until the weekend. Then, next week we'll have a session every night. The first week of June the tourists come flocking in, having music draws them like a magnet," she explained.

"That's fine. Which room do I have? I'll bring my things in and unpack, then join you and Uncle Padraic for dinner. The pub will be fine."

"We have your favorite room on the top floor looking out over Dingle Harbor. Take the outside stairs then down the hall. You remember, Ian. You can get to and from your room without ever using the main entrance. That should protect your privacy."

I smiled at her understanding. It took me about an hour to haul my luggage up three floors and unpack enough to feel at home. By that time, I had worked up both my hunger and my thirst. Murphy's Pub was well known in Dingle for well-prepared Irish food, specializing in what came from the sea, especially salmon.

I met Padraic and Shioban at the bar. We each got a drink and found a table in the corner where we could talk. It was early enough that we would be able to have a good visit, a filling meal, and be done before the din in the dining room would require us to nearly shout at each other to be heard.

I imagined my Da would have looked like Padraic, had he lived to the same age. He had a slight paunch from a steady diet of stout and maybe too many Irish breakfasts. Plus he didn't take the time for a hearty hike in the hills around Dingle Peninsula. He combed his hair straight back just like Da, but unlike his brother's, his remained thick like mine.

We placed our dinner order and exchanged small talk to pass the time. Talking about family resulted in tension I didn't need, and I wanted to avoid talking about the last year of my life altogether. I found comfort in the familiarity of the pub. I don't think Padraic and Shioban had changed any of the interior since they bought the pub or the inn. The pub was exactly what both tourists and locals expected in an Irish pub. As you entered, on the left wall there was a large black and white metal sign advertising Murphy's Draught; the name was accidental, no relation. The sign was unique because there was a figure of a man sitting on a board, painting the sign. Anyone entering the pub was immediately drawn to it. I gathered up my courage and finally asked, "Where in the world did you get the Murphy's Draught sign? Did you have that made special?"

Padraic and Shioban looked at each other and broke out into laughter. "It's taken you years to ask hasn't it?" Shioban said.

"Well, yes."

"The black and white sign was on the wall when we purchased the pub. A local painter had worked up a considerable tab, which we also inherited when we bought the pub. He offered to make our sign one of a kind in all Ireland in exchange for wiping his slate clean. We accepted, and you see the result before you," Padraic explained.

"Only in Ireland," I laughed.

I felt a hand on my right shoulder and turned to see Mrs. O'Connelly smiling down at me. "Ian, it's good to see you again. I can't remember when you've been here last for a visit."

"Mrs. O'Connelly, you look as young and robust as usual. How is the boat rental business?"

"Well, I cannot tell a lie. The winter was rough, and I'm ready for the spring tourist season, which I hope starts this week. Shioban, is the inn booked? I wouldn't mind if you sent a few of your guests my way. I've only got four boats to rent now, you know."

"What happened to your other two boats? I hope there wasn't an accident," Padraic asked.

Mrs. O'Connelly sat down in the chair next to me indicting she might be with us for a longer conversation than I really wanted.

"Oh, no accident. I received an offer for two of the boats that was very beneficial. I'm not getting any younger, and handling four boats is about all I can do now. The day will come when I'll want to sack it in. Maybe you two would want to add boats to what you provide to your inn guests."

Shioban raised her eyebrows, "Well, I don't know..."

Mrs. O'Connelly didn't let Shioban finish her sentence before she turned directly to me. "Now, young man, I want to thank you for helping out on that Good Friday Peace Accord. I voted for it, of course. All those troubles were a long way from here, but of course, it was no good, no good at all. People should learn to live together, I think."

I smiled and patted the top of her hand. "Mine was a small part, I can assure you."

"I must be getting on. I'm having take-away tonight. Maybe someone will stop by to rent a boat for a moonlight cruise. Don't be a stranger now, Ian. I can have a boat for you any time you want." Mrs. O'Connelly fetched her food and scrambled out the door to return to her business, which was right across the street.

"She hasn't changed in years," I said.

"Our food should be here soon. People will notice that you're back, Ian. You must expect it," Shioban said.

"It's fine, really."

Just as I finished talking, I felt a sharp slap on my back, which made me tip forward and nearly knocked my glass over.

I snapped my head to the left to see Conor Sweeney's weathered face. I jumped out of my chair and shook his hand with vigor. "Damn, Conor, it's good to see you. Are you still giving walking tours?"

"Tomorrow I lead my first tour of the season. A group of six Irish Americans, who I hope are flush with cash," Conor said.

"You haven't changed a bit, you opportunist," I chided him.

"Now listen, young man, you have some explaining to do. I read that nasty business in the Independent about your role in the Provisional IRA. I can't imagine how that Eileen Donohue scooped the story. You're certainly a master of keeping secrets; that is for sure. I know the Murphy clan has a reputation for being Republicans, but Jesus, you were an architect of the long war?"

I bent my head to avoid his stare and demand for a response. I looked both to my left then to my right to search for an escape route; there wasn't one. I never expected to be challenged in Dingle, back in Cork yes, but not Dingle. Dingle has the good fortune to be far removed geographically from Ireland's civil war and for most of the twentieth century was able to ignore it. Life on the peninsula was different; it was rural and completely dependent on tourism to survive economically. Its scenery was its attraction so it couldn't afford to become embroiled in the travesty of war. The population of Dingle hardly even noticed when Northern Ireland was partitioned in '22.

"So, speak up, Ian." Conor was insistent.

"It was a matter of what's right, isn't it? You may not have noticed but we're an occupied country. Read your history, Conor. By my reckoning, since the Earls abandoned us 390 years ago, we've been British captives. I'm Roman Catholic, as

I'm sure you are, and in Northern Ireland the Catholics have been subjected to cruelty, forced to take menial jobs, and denied the rights of citizenship. I only wanted an Ireland for the Irish. I dreamt of a united Ireland as many true Irish have for decades." I felt my face flush and my pulse quicken. I had no idea this spark still lived in my heart.

Conor pulled out the chair next to mine and sat down. He looked at Shioban, then Padraic, and then at me. "I need a whiskey," he said almost as a plea rather than a request or order to the bar. Padraic got up and returned in a few minutes with a large tumbler filled to the rim with sweet Jameson. He set the glass in front of Conor, who was still staring at me without saying a word. Conor reached for the glass, took a long drink, and set it down again. "Your blood still runs hot, Ian Murphy."

I pointed to Conor's glass and said to Padraic, "I could use one of those too. Put everything on a tab for me. Your business shouldn't have to suffer because of my presence."

"You're family, Ian." Padraic got up again and this time returned with three whiskeys, one for me, for Shioban, and himself. "I suppose it was a matter of time before this subject came up, Ian. To be honest, Shioban and I have been curious too. I know your Da was an IRA man. Never knew what he did, but it wasn't exactly a family secret. You, on the other hand, kept that secret from the world. It's not the secrecy that bothered us. Your business is your business. It's what you did. Writing the training manual for Provies? Can't imagine how you did that. You don't have any military experience. I read in the papers that the war changed because of that manual – the code of silence and all. Was that oath of silence your idea?"

It felt like the temperature in the room had increased by several degrees. My beard felt scratchy and beads of sweat gathered across my brow. I took my time sipping the whiskey. My right hand clenched tight, and I hid it under the table, hoping no one would notice. I felt like a trapped lion at the zoo, pacing back and forth across its enclosure. I didn't feel like Conor, Padraic, or Shioban were challenging me, they were just curious. They wanted an explanation for my behavior. I should have expected this, if not from Conor, at least from Shioban and Padraic. In one of my novels I could have anticipated this, but in real life, I was an innocent.

Conor drew back, his eyes widened. "Those Donohue articles were life-threatening to you, I guess. You're lucky you're not in a British gaol waiting to be tried for treason."

"True."

"Why didn't they arrest you, Ian?" Shioban asked.

"I was a pawn in their political game. Awarding me amnesty was only to make them look good and gain sentiment among the Catholics in Belfast."

Conor took a long drink of whiskey, searching for the words for his next question. I'm sure he could tell I was trapped and at his mercy. "Did revealing your secret in the paper force you to change? Is that why you went from Provie mastermind to author of the Good Friday Peace Accord? That's a dramatic change for one person, especially in a short period of time."

I looked at Padraic, then Shioban and let my stare rest on Conor. Without blinking, I spit out my answer.

"Blood."

The three of them didn't speak for a few minutes. They finished their whiskey without looking at me or even speaking to each other. Conor's chair screeched on the unpolished wood floor as he got up. "It's time I have my supper. Padraic, Shioban, Ian." I didn't see Conor again during my stay on the Dingle Peninsula.

TEN

My first night in Dingle didn't go well, and my sleep was restless. I decided not to bother Padraic and Shioban for breakfast. I could always find something when I was rambling about. I sat on the edge of the bed looking out to Dingle Harbor. The sky was steel gray, and I guessed sunrise was at least an hour away. In my mind I reviewed my favorite walking paths, unable to make a decision on which one to take today. My first decision was to leave soon before the sun became too much higher in the sky. Today I needed to be alone, and hitting the trail early would best ensure not running into a gaggle of open-mouthed tourists, either foreign or Irish. I showered, then examined the growth of my beard in the mirror. It was clear that my beard would be as white as the petals of a daisy, while my hair and moustache remain streaked with a dull, unappealing gray.

I stood back from the mirror and took in the full view. I wasn't sure if I would still be recognized as easily as I had been before I sported just the moustache. I wouldn't need to worry about this if my picture wasn't plastered on the back of every one of my book jackets. I argued with my publisher about including my picture. It wasn't necessary; that, in fact, it was superfluous. Publishers have the reputation of being demanding and insensitive, and mine is the king of them all. So my books contained a frontal picture of my face. Unsmiling, of course. At least I could insist that an author should look serious and not be some smiling goon. As a writer, I insist on preserving both my integrity and authenticity and a picture of a baboon-faced nave is not me, not now, not ever. I took one last look at myself and was satisfied that my beard would provide the anonymity that I needed at this junction in my life path.

I popped on my tweed walking hat and matching cape, sturdy walking boots, and my vintage Harper's Head walking stick. The walking stick offered sure footedness in the hills and protection from scoundrels, not that I had ever had to use the stick as a shillelagh, but it offered me the sense of protection that I craved.

I jumped into the car and it headed north out of Dingle, knowing I was heading for the Annascaul Glen Walk. The need to be alone and avoid all tourists today resulted in selecting the interior walk around Annascaul Lough. Most tourists were not aware that Scotland was not the only Gaelic country with loughs, and that ignorance was what I was counting on to maintain my privacy today. Based on previous walks in the central hills of County Kerry, I could get five or six hours of exercise and contemplation, find someplace for a late lunch, and be back in Dingle by late afternoon to share a pint with Padraic and Shioban. I would lunch at the Teac Seain pub because the owners were lifelong friends of my aunt and uncle, and I could count on them to not wag their tongues about my visit.

I parked my car at the trailhead and was en route before the sun peeked above the horizon. It was the perfect day to take the high path and view the lake from the ragged hill, not a mountain really but high enough to make the hike a physical challenge and an obstacle that could be a metaphor for my life right now. The path was paved with thick grass pods, the blades of grass sharp enough to draw blood if you were wearing shorts. The wind came directly off the North Atlantic and reddened my cheeks. The foot of the hill contained a painter's pallet of spring flowers. The ox-eyed daisies spread out across the landscape, waving their greeting to the morning's first hiker. There was an elegant spring carpet of flowers including spring gentian, with bright blue petals and a white button center, scattered across the field in what appeared to be a random pattern. My favorite was the sherads downy rose, with tiny pink blooms and matching delicate fragrance. The arens provided an almost exact opposite appearance from the daisies, with white petals and a yellow capitulum. The trail became steep after a short distance, feeling like it was a forty-five-degree angle. The morning air chilled my lungs, making me gasp for breath. I wished now I had taken time for breakfast. My stomach felt like it had a hole in it, and it began to ache. Just then, I detected a sweet fragrance that drove my hunger deep. Ahead of me was a patch of furze that smelled like fresh shredded coconut.

As I walked higher, the grasses and flowers were replaced with sharp cut rock formed by thousands of years of blistering, relentless winds. The Dingle Peninsula was raw like a man's soul, surviving exposure against all odds. The stone path had been worn over the centuries by both the wind and the boots of hikers. What draws a man to climb this mountain? Hell, what drives me to climb this mountain. I don't know. There was sadness in not being able to come up with a reason why I was exerting myself to conquer this wretched little mountain. Maybe my life was the same. Could this hill represent St. John's dark journey? We Irish were good at honoring both the dark and light of life, although I felt that most of my days I've wallowed in darkness. I am two men, really. There is the man of light, writing stories of near heroic characters willing to hunch his shoulders and overcome burdens to reach his goals, always ready and willing to make the sacrifice. There is the man of darkness who kept a secret from the world for damn near thirty years. It takes a great deal of work to keep a secret, to live a life no one really knows about.

Kieran Fitzpatrick knew, of course. That explained the depth of our bond. I have not felt I was a man that needed others; I had the people I created in my fiction, and they had always been enough. Not true with Kieran. I needed Kieran because he kept my secret. He also used me. He played with my life, letting me hide in the shadows to do his deed. Without me would there ever have been a Green Book, giving those innocent, high-spirited lad's instructions on how to be terrorists? In 1977 I thought it was a way to keep our Republican boys safe, so if they landed in a British gaol, they could survive, maybe even be released, by frustrating their jailers in not giving up one shred of information.

When Eileen Donohue published her exposé of my life, my first reaction was incredulity. Because I went into hiding rather than face my journalist-accuser, the high hand went to her. What was I to say? She revealed the truth of me. Aren't all humans some mix of both good and evil? I am no different from other souls in that way.

I was so lost in my own thoughts, I didn't notice the summit looming just a short distance away. Sweat collected in the rim of my hat and found its way to my temples where little droplets formed, ready to slide down my cheeks and onto my coat collar. I was breathing in short gasps, trying to fill my lungs. The hill wasn't tall enough to cause light headedness, but my erratic breathing made me close to losing consciousness. Maybe that was what I wanted, to collapse in exhaustion at the summit and let the winds ravage my body, subjecting me to intentional pain and suffering. What an ugly thought for a forty-eight-year-old man to have. That would be giving up, and I was a Murphy, which meant I was a fighter. I won't relinquish myself and just let life happen to me. Murphys have been warriors for millennia. The original Gaelic form of my surname, Murchadh, meant sea-warrior. I had always lived near water and could never imagine not living close to water. I am a water spirit.

When I reached the flat rock summit, my breathing was irregular both because of the strenuous climb and the sight of the lake below. Even from this height, the white waterfalls that fed the lake could be seen without binoculars. I swore that I could hear the water rushing to the basin. My imagination must have been in overdrive; that just couldn't be possible. Alone on this rock, glaring down at the valley and Annascaul Lough was in many ways a metaphor for my life. I am an observer looking out across my native island and every now and then dabbling in the affairs of my countrymen.

My feeble efforts to bring peace to this land did not cleanse the blood that I had accumulated in thirty years with the IRA. I know Father O'Connell had his reasons for demanding I atone for my sins, but the act turned out to be hollow for me. I could feel the blood stain my soul. My God, how do I seek absolution? But there is no priest in Ireland willing to grant me a holy reprieve. It is as if I had pulled the trigger or set the bombs myself. I prayed that St. John of the Cross could point the way for me and my "dark night of the soul."

I looked down the path to make sure others weren't struggling up the hill to join me. I didn't see a single hiker, so I had enough time to stoke up my pipe and have a good smoke, allowing my mind to wander as it would, across the Irish countryside. The wind was brisk enough that lighting my pipe became a major undertaking. I turned my back to the westerly wind, drew my knees up and hunched over to shield the wind. After three or four attempts, the tobacco lit. I packed the bowl tight so that I could enjoy a good long smoke.

The pipe bowl eventually cooled, and I noticed the sun must have been at least thirty degrees above the horizon. My sense of time had always been poor, but I guessed I must have been on the summit for several hours and panic set in, fearing my solitude would soon be lost for the day. I looked down the slope with anticipation and saw four figures relentlessly making their way toward me. I didn't feel in the mood to share my hilltop today, so I stuffed my pipe back into my pocket, got up, and stumbled my way down the hill, only preventing a fall by skillful use of my walking stick.

About two thirds the way down, I met the other hikers. Each of them glanced in my direction and said: "Morning." I responded the same. I was thankful they were Irish and respected another person's privacy, not attempting to engage in any chit chat. In a few minutes I was at the foot of the hill. I looked from side to side, trying to choose between a hike around the lough or returning to the village. Even without breakfast, I didn't feel particularly tired, so I thought a vigorous hike was in order. I wouldn't return to Annascaul until early afternoon and with any luck miss the tourist stopping for their midday meal so I could enjoy a long lunch on my own.

I estimated the circumvention of the lake took about four hours. When I entered the village, the tower clock read 2:00 p.m. Perfect, I should have the pub to myself at this time of day or at least free of foreign visitors; only an Irishman would be in a pub this time of the day. I was glad to see the familiar side-by-side, blue doors, one leading to a bed and breakfast and the other to the pub. The door to the right was the pub entrance. To say it was a traditional Irish pub came as close to an understatement as I could come.

Once through the door, the aroma of stick-in-your-gut pub food overcame me, and my stomach screamed in agony. I ordered a scotch egg with mustard, the pub meat pie, fresh bread, a stout, and the house whiskey. I told my server to bring the stout and leave the bottle of whiskey on the table. The service was immediate because I was alone.

I ate the egg in two bites, followed by a long draw on the stout. My head became light, and I thought I should hold off a bit on the whiskey. I planned to drive back to Dingle later that afternoon.

I was wolfing down the pub meat pie when I heard a familiar voice speak to me as if out of the nether.

"Ian?"

I looked up and saw someone with indistinguishable features standing at the edge of my table.

"Ian, that is you, isn't it?"

It was a woman's voice, one that I recognized but I didn't know why. "Yes, it's me. And...and you are?"

"Ian, it's Mairin – Mairin McCarthy."

"I...I'm sorry, Mairin. There are times that setting and circumstances are blinders. I never expected to see you in Annascaul. Forgive me, please. Would you like to sit? Are you hungry? Would you like to share a bottle of whiskey?"

A cunning smile crossed her face. She pulled out the chair and sat without a sound. She brushed her hair back, first with her left hand and then her right and shook her head from side to side. I don't recall her fussing so much with her hair the first time we met, but my memory couldn't be trusted right now. She looked directly at me a few minutes without speaking with a Mona Lisa-like smile plastered on her face.

"Nor did I expect to see you. I was surprised you didn't call me. I thought we had a pleasant conversation. I actually had the impression you were interested in me, in a man-to-woman way. I suppose I jumped to conclusions. It's not every day that a faculty member, or for that matter even students, asks for works of Catholic mysticism. Oh, God, I'm babbling. I apologize, I don't mean to babble. I haven't eaten yet; do you have time to stay for a bite?"

She was right, she was babbling. I couldn't imagine why. The first time we talked and had supper she was much more reticent. Maybe that was first-meeting behavior. I wasn't happy to see Mairin, but I wasn't unhappy either. "I've eaten already, but I would be happy to stay and chat with you and share a drink, of course. I can recommend the meat pie, if you have an appetite. I spent my morning hiking to the summit and then around the lough, so I had a ferocious hunger."

The waiter materialized at the table, and glancing up at him, Mairin ordered the meat pie with a cup of tea and a large glass of water. She thanked him for coming over to take her order.

"I apologize for not calling you after we had dinner. To be honest, I've been self-absorbed since the referendum passed. I'm glad to see you now, even if it is completely unexpected." I poured myself a whiskey, and to avoid getting under-the-table drunk, added a touch of water to the glass. The water turned the amber whiskey to a light brown. I took a sip, not sure what to expect. I can't recall drinking whiskey except straight up, sometimes with ice, never water. The water gave the whiskey an unexpected, slight sweet taste. Not bad, interesting even.

"What brings you to the Dingle Peninsula, Mairin?"

"At the end of term, I always take holiday before the summer session begins. I've been coming to Dingle for years. It's where I reconnect with myself and my heritage. I have family history here. No family currently, though."

I rubbed my beard, amazed at another coincidence with this woman, who was becoming more interesting as each moment passed. "I too have family connections to Dingle. Murphy's Bed and Breakfast in Dingle is my uncle. My middle name comes from him. I've spent many summers working at the bed and breakfast, with ample time to explore the peninsula on my own."

Mairin sat straight up in her chair. "You're that Murphy?" I've stayed there several times, it's lovely."

My beard was beginning to itch, and I gave it a good scratch with both my hands. "Can you imagine a Murphy not living in County Cork? Uncle Padraic worked at the pub as a young man and fell in love with Dingle. It's also where he met the love of his life, my Aunt Shioban. When the bed and breakfast came up for sale, they bought it and about five years after that, bought the pub. As far as I know, they've never left Dingle. He always says the world comes to him so why should he travel?"

The waiter sat a steaming pie in front of Mairin, a pot of tea, and a glass of water without ice. "Anything else?" he asked.

"No, this smells delicious. Thank you very much. Ian, would you like anything else, dessert maybe?"

In an automatic response, I shook my head. "Don't normally eat desserts; my svelte figure, you know."

Mairin chuckled and turned to the waiter. "Thank you for asking. Nothing for now, but I plan on having dessert later."

The waiter grinned broadly, draped his towel over his arm, and walked back to the kitchen.

"Now, while I enjoy this meat pie, tell me what has brought you to Dingle this week."

I watched her eat, carefully taking a spoonful of the pie, blowing on it, and enjoying each bite. After several bites, she took a sip of water from the glass. She must have been self-conscious because after every bite, she took her napkin and dabbed the sides of her mouth, even though there was no reason to. She looked back at me, raising her eyebrows, waiting for me to begin talking.

Mairin was working hard to be kind and empathetic, and I decided it was time for me to be truthful with myself and her. Learning to trust a woman again would be a challenge but it was very clear that Mairin and Eileen had nothing in common. Taking leaps of faith isn't in my nature, but Mairin was oddly reassuring and I felt safe with her.

"My initial plan was to hike the less-traveled paths and take Saint John of the Cross with me and try to absorb his guidance. After my hike this morning, I'm not sure. I'm not on a spiritual quest, and I don't have any desire to find God. I haven't been a practicing Catholic for years. Don't get me wrong. I'm not agnostic or an atheist; I guess I could best be described as uncertain. My life is about writing first and last. I find all that I need in the writing. Until I said it out loud to you just now, I don't think I have had that conscious thought. Poor self-awareness, I guess."

Mairin scrapped the bowl clean, then pushed it to one side and pulled the mug of tea toward her. She took several sips to test the temperature. She tipped her head to one side and held her face with one hand. It was the first time I noticed her eyes were a deep hazel color. She certainly liked direct eye contact, which often made me uncomfortable for reasons I didn't understand.

"Ian, you judge yourself too harshly. I came to hike. Would you like to join me? We can talk, admire our Irish landscape, and become better acquainted. Maybe we've both been alone for too long. Tomorrow?"

ELEVEN

The door rattled in the frame, the person knocked so hard. "Ian, Ian, there's a woman downstairs asking for you." Shioban shouted loud enough to wake anyone still sleeping.

"Thank you, Aunt Shioban. I'll be done soon. Give her some tea, will you?"

"Do you know her, Ian?" Shioban asked.

"Yes, of course, I do."

"Oh, all right, dear. I'll get her tea. Don't be long now. It's not polite to keep people waiting."

I heard her stomp down the stairs. I was sure she was surprised that a woman would appear out of nowhere asking for me. I rinsed my face with water and brushed both my hair and my beard. It was odd to brush your face, but I had noticed that after sleeping, the beard could appear very unkempt and I was interested in being well-groomed.

I found Shioban and Mairin sitting on the sofa in the parlor in animated conversation and both drinking tea. Shioban was always the perfect hostess. Over the years, most of their business was repeat customers, and Shioban was a large part of the reason, plus the excellent, hearty Irish breakfast that came with the cost of the room.

"Well, you've met." I said, stating the obvious. Mairin looked up and smiled at me. She was dressed for a day of walking, with her rainproof, country walking hat, a matching walking cape, and a blackthorn, knob handled, walking cane sitting next to her. I too have this type of walking stick in my extensive collection. It was clear she was an experienced walker because she was prepared for rain and wind. Very practical.

"So, you two are off for a day walk. You must have breakfast before you leave. Ian, we have porridge with clotted cream, and blueberries and brown bread with cultured butter, just for you. We could have the kitchen make some sandwiches and tea to take with you, too," Aunt Shioban offered.

"Mairin, it is my special breakfast and it's delicious. You won't regret it, and you'll have energy for a long walk today," I said.

Mairin took off her hat and stood to take off her cape, looking for a place to put them.

"Oh dear, I'll take those." Aunt Shioban swept in and took the garbs, disappearing into a side room. "Ian, take Mairin through to the dining room, will you? I'll have breakfast brought right in."

We found a place at the corner table, not wanting to disturb or be disturbed by the other guests. We had no more than sat down when Padraic rushed in. "Good morning, good morning. Ian, introduce your lady friend, won't you?"

"Uncle Padraic Murphy, my friend Mairin McCarthy." I gestured toward Mairin.

"I am so pleased to meet you, Mairin. By the looks of you, you're off for a day walk. Our breakfast is exactly what you need. It's supposed to be a fine day today, but of course, there's a chance for rain this afternoon. It's the Dingle Peninsula; there's a chance for rain every afternoon in June. Do you know our peninsula, Mairin?" Uncle Padraic gushed.

"I am pleased to say I do. This is my regular annual holiday after college term ends."

"And what college would that be?" Padraic asked.

"University College Cork."

"Oh, the same as our nephew, Ian. Interesting. And do you teach?"

"No, I'm a librarian."

"A librarian, now there's a fine profession. Libraries are so essential, aren't they?"

"Padraic, help me with this tray, will you?" Shioban ordered from behind where Padraic stood.

They placed the food on the table with the grace and efficiency of people who had done it every day for many years. The bowls of porridge were mounded with fresh blueberries and smothered in clotted cream made just that morning. Steam rose off the plate of brown bread that must have been just minutes from the oven. The smell of fresh bread in the morning sent memories flooding through my mind of my mother serving breakfast.

"Please, let's start. Do you care for cultured butter with your bread, Mairin?" I asked.

We allowed ourselves to wallow in our breakfast a few minutes before we erupted into conversation at the same time.

"Where would you like to walk today, Ian?" Mairin asked.

"Any place on this peninsula would be fine with me. I doubt if there's a single corner of this landscape I haven't explored."

"How far would you like to walk, or how much time do you want to be on the trail?" She was succinct in everything.

I finished the last bite of porridge and tossed my spoon in the bowl. I took my time slathering the butter on a thick slice of bread and drank half a cup of coffee to give myself time to answer. "Most the day, I would think. Seven or eight hours would be refreshing and soul cleansing, don't you think?"

"Yes."

I pulled my pipe out of my pocket, fidgeting with it and searching for my tobacco pouch, which I couldn't find. I hoped

I had not left the pouch in my room; I didn't want to take the time to do a hunt and search.

I was itching to be on the trail if we were to avoid all the tourists. Rummaging through my pockets again, I found it all scrunched up with only enough tobacco for several pipes. Hiking was likely to be strenuous today so I didn't need to smoke, but having one bowl before our trek began would settle me down. "I like to be close to the ocean. I find myself drawn to it."

Mairin finished her tea and shook the teapot to see if there was enough for another cup. "Well, then I suggest we take the Dingle Trail from here to Dunquin. I'm not sure we would be able to stay the night there. If I recall, there is only a small hotel and a bed and breakfast. I was told the tourist season began early this year, so my guess is that all the rooms are rented."

Did she just say what I thought she did? She's willing to stay the night with me? We've only known each other a week. I don't think I'm ready to leap into another relationship. I should tell her. "Finding dinner will be impossible. We'll need a hearty, savory meal after a day on the trail," I said. "We could hire a car to pick us up and plan on dinner back here in Dingle. Actually, we don't even need to hire a car, I'm sure Padraic wouldn't mind being our chauffeur."

As Mairin sipped her tea, she looked as though she was trying to read my face. Her searching made me uncomfortable, and I felt my right hand begin to clinch, so I put it on my lap before she could notice tension creep through me like a snake. She took small sips of tea and set her cup down squarely on the table. "That would be fine, Ian."

I felt the need to explain myself, but I didn't know how to respond. Mairin was attractive, intelligent, cultured, and an excellent conversationalist—for me an excellent companion. Therein lay the key. For now, companionship was the most complex relationship I could tolerate with a woman. Eileen's betrayal still felt like my trust and love were abused, used exclusively for her selfish, almost narcissistic, need to be a journalist and not a human being. How can I explain this to Mairin? People who identify first and foremost with what they do rather than who they are, is destined to lead a tragic life.

We said goodbye to Padraic and Shioban and headed out the door.

The walk began after crossing the Milltown River Bridge just west of the village. The first leg of the journey was through low-lying farmland with both sheep and cattle grazing on plots outlined by knee-high stone walls.

"Mairin, about your idea to stay overnight in Dunquin. You need to know, it's not you. It's me. Eileen Donohue and I were lovers, for a short time, a very short time. I thought she loved me anyway, but looking back, I'm beginning to see I may have deluded myself. I've been a bachelor all of my life. Relationships with women are not my strong suit. I can write about them, I just don't seem to be able to sustain them in real life." I intentionally didn't look in Mairin's direction as we walked, being much more comfortable gazing off into the landscape.

"Ian, why are you walking so fast? We're not in a hurry, are we?"

"No, of course not, I'm sorry. I didn't notice I had changed pace so dramatically." I tried to glance at Mairin out of the right corner of my eyes with as much discretion as I could muster. Mairin stroked my back with a delicate touch.

"You are a sensitive man, Ian Murphy; trust me, an admirable quality. You should know, I didn't take your response as rejecting me personally. Your response was very kind, in fact. I appreciate your honesty. I never would have guessed. Isn't she married?"

"Oh yes, she's married. That was one of our arguments. I wanted her to divorce. She dismissed the idea by reminding me we were a Catholic nation and Catholics don't divorce. She was willing, even eager to have an extramarital tryst but not make a commitment to love. Oh God, I was…I am so naïve. How can a man my age be such a knave?"

While we talked, we passed through the Pilgrims Route and soon we were descending into Ventry from the north and the smell of saltwater became stronger with each step. I anticipated the beach at Ventry and thought it would be a good place to rest, soak our feet in the ocean, and talk about something else, anything else but me. I couldn't tell if Mairin was reticent to talk about herself or I had dominated the conversation in my unique, self-centered fashion. As we approached the Ventry Harbor beach, I took off my hat to feel the sea breeze ruffle through my hair. "What about a good ol', saltwater foot soak?" I barked out over the sound of waves kissing the shoreline.

Mairin laughed out loud, and with her right hand, she grabbed her hat and threw it in the air. "I would love to. Race you to the water!" She took off at a dead run. I didn't have a chance. A woman with spontaneity was the perfect remedy for a woman like Eileen Donohue. By the time I caught up with Mairin, she had plopped down and was ripping her hiking boots off.

"Damn, you're sneaky."

She threw her head back. The wind caught her hair, blowing it in all directions. She ran to the water's edge and splashed her feet in the water each time it lapped closer; the tide was coming in. I unlaced my boots as fast as I could, yanked off my socks, and stuffed them back into the boots. The water was colder than I expected, and goose bumps ran up my shins. "Mairin, that water is cold. You could have warned me."

Mairin laughed again and wagging her finger at me. "I didn't want to ruin the experience for you."

"Would you let me fall off a cliff too, just not to ruin the experience?"

"Ian, you're being ridiculous. But I must admit, I enjoyed watching the expression on your face when you plunged your feet into the harbor. Priceless, absolutely priceless."

Eventually, we sat on shore. The sound of the water lapping the sand was mesmerizing and lulling me into a false sense of safety and contentment. There was a definite sense of grounding when I was with Mairin. There were those who knew who they were, what their place in society was, and they found satisfaction in living each day, one at a time. I have never had her centeredness. Living a dual life, one in secrecy and the other in books, was mentally and psychologically exhausting. Is it possible that the real purpose for my relationship with Eileen was to expose my life in the IRA and end the duality in my life?

The wind chilled my arms and goose bumps popped up. I drew my coat in, tucked my chin into the collar, and pulled my hat down over my ears. I loved the rhythm of the ocean; it reminded me, in a visceral way, that there were rhythms, patterns in all of life. It made me realize that we all needed to work on our awareness of rhythms and align our lives with the natural ebb and flow of life.

"Ian, where are you? Are you still here with me? You appear completely absorbed in the moment." Mairin put her arm around my waist and tugged me closer.

"Are you cold?" I asked.

"No, I just want to share your inner world with you. Would you allow me in?" Her eyes were soft and inviting.

"I'm dedicated to leading a completely open, transparent life now. No secrets. Never, never again. No hidden life for me. I am an open book."

Mairin rested her head on my shoulder. Then she lifted her head and looked me directly in the eyes, as if searching for something, I couldn't guess what. "What were your thoughts a few moments ago?"

I threw my head back and chuckled out loud. "The first test, is it?"

"No, not a test, Ian. I respect you too much. I would never test you. Testing someone is not trusting, is it?"

"It's not trusting, indeed. I was just wondering if the real purpose of my relationship with Eileen was to uncover my secret and force me to account for myself. I believe things happen in our lives for a purpose. Does that make any sense to you?"

"Hm...I believe big things happen in our lives for a purpose, not everyday things, the big things like having her betray you."

"Interesting."

I put my arms around her shoulder and drew her close to me. Her hair had a faint scent of magnolia, which I found intoxicating. *Mairin McCarthy, you've come into my life for a purpose too, of that I'm sure*, I thought.

Our magic moment was shattered when I remembered that the next section of the hike was along the Slea Head Road. A short distance of about a kilometer, but any vehicle traffic made it treacherous for any walkers. It was an extraordinary scenic drive but not compatible for both hikers and motor traffic. Unfortunately, at this time of the year, about ninety percent of the drivers were foreigners, not accustomed to the Irish way of driving. They would not be expecting to meet hikers wanting to share the road with them. The only safe choice was for vehicles to slow down and hope the hikers would let them through so that both could continue their journey without endangering the other.

I jumped up and offered my hand to Mairin. "This section of the trail is life-threatening for all the wrong reasons, so let's walk quickly."

"Oh, you're right. Excellent idea. Let's practice our speed walking," Mairin suggested.

"Our speed walking? I have no idea what you're talking about."

"Oh, just match my pace."

"Walk on!"

It was a sight to behold, I'm sure. She bolted ahead of me, her arms drawn up to her sides and swinging back and forth wildly. She came close to jabbing me with her elbow with each stride. She took short, quick steps that didn't appear, at first, to be fast, but she out-distanced me in no time. In response, I lengthened my stride and used the tapping of my walking stick on the pavement to make a cadence. I thought I would have an advantage in the length of my stride and my seasoned hiking experience. I was wrong.

My breathing became labored, and beads of sweat collected at my temples. I was amazed at how fast Mairin could walk, and from all impressions, she could maintain that pace all the way to Dunquin. We stayed on the outside of the curve, giving vehicles from both directions the opportunity to see us flying along single file. In minutes, we were back on the Dingle Way proper and near the foot of Mount Eagle. Off in the distance the Blasket Islands came into view as we rounded Slea Head.

The sun was directly overhead and the winds from the Atlantic brought gray-black clouds filled with water like a sponge. Just as we reached the abandoned, stone schoolhouse, there was a thunder clap that made me jump. The winds swept across the crown of the trail and pushed frigid rain at us sideways. "Let's try that building," I shouted.

Mairin broke into a run and held one arm behind her like she was running a relay race and expecting the baton to be handed off. She was so quick, I didn't have a prayer to catch up with her. I ran as fast as I could, but the grass became slick with rain, and I worried I would fall and careen down the hillside. I've never been athletic, and as I've matured, I've noticed my balance wane from time to time.

I rushed in and found Mairin leaning against a wall in the far corner, raindrops falling from her hat onto the straw-covered, stone floor. "Looks like someone has left straw for any sheep that might wander in to avoid storms like this," I pointed out.

"A reasonable conclusion."

Mairin took off her hat, shook off the water, and brushed her hair with her hands.

I was overwhelmed at her plain beauty and leaned close to kiss her lips. I don't know what possessed me. It was very forward and not my normal behavior. After holding the kiss a few seconds, I pulled back. Mairin smiled, blushed, and dropped her head to avoid eye contact.

I stepped back several paces and dropped my arms to my side, ashamed at my boldness. "I...I...I'm sorry. I can't explain what came over me. Please forgive me."

She looked up at me with soft, moist eyes and smiled. She stepped toward me, took my face into her hands, and kissed me as she stroked my beard.

I pulled her close and let my pent-up passion explode. Our kisses deepened and evolved into warm, engaging French kisses. We parted to catch our breath. I listened; the rain had stopped. "Perhaps we should see if we can find a room in Dunquin." I suggested.

Mairin stroked the back of my hair, which tickled all the way to the soles of my feet. "You trusting again, Ian?"

"Who wouldn't bathe in your sensitivity and empathy? I'm not a monster; I guess you accept that now. To answer the question you asked the day we met in your department library, I am ashamed to have led a double life. God knows, my soul will be blood-stained to the end of my days."

"Shhh, Ian, not now. Today is about us. Remember, all that we are in this very moment is a product of our history. We can't change history, and I wouldn't want to change anything that has led us to this schoolhouse in the midst of a typical Dingle Peninsula rain surge."

I took my time and thought about Mairin's viewpoint. Maybe she was right. If I accept my past, I could forge a new future from the rubble of my life. Rather than rambling in narcissistic conversation, I peeked out the window to see a light drizzle that would probably carry on for some time. "Let's have those sandwiches and tea now, unless you want to walk on in the rain."

"This would be a perfect place for a bite. The speed walking's left me famished. The floor doesn't look too comfortable, but it will do."

We sat on top of the straw, opened our packs, and found a feast for two. I sniffed a cheese wedge. "Ah, vintage cheddar, my favorite."

"Oh, Shioban knows you well; here are a couple of meat pies. I can't imagine you hiking without a meat pie to sustain yourself."

"Yes, of course, you're right." I rummaged in the bag and pulled out a package of dried figs and apricots. "Oh, my favorite. Apricots are a special treat. Let it rain, doesn't matter, does it?" I suggested.

"No, this is perfect. Now cut me a chunk of that cheese."

We took our time and savored each of the treats provided. When we finished, I stretched out my legs. I leaned to one side and looked out the window to see if it was still raining. "Ah, the sun is just about to emerge from behind the clouds. If we're quick, we might catch a rainbow." I offered Mairin my hand. She rose and came in close for a sweet kiss. She scampered out of our temporary shelter and looked toward the sky, scanning the eastern horizon for a rainbow. I picked up the scraps of paper and stuffed them into the bag, then went to join her.

"Well?"

"Not today, Ian. But the day is perfect in every other way. I don't need a rainbow." Mairin extended her hand for me to take. "Let's visit the Blasket Islands tomorrow. I'm ready for a good night's sleep."

"You expect to sleep?" I asked, tongue in cheek.

"Oh Ian, you rogue!"

TWELVE

We arrived in Dunquin mid-afternoon and found a room at the Gleann Dearg Bed and Breakfast. Like my aunt and uncle, the owners were seasoned and had made a comfortable living by sharing their abode with travelers for close to forty years.

"We worried we wouldn't be able to find a room tonight without a reservation, Mr. Houlahan."

Mr. Houlahan grinned from ear to ear and brushed back a few remaining wisps of long, white hair. "Over the years, we've learned to keep one room open just for folks like yourselves."

"Do you know the Murphys in Dingle?" I asked.

"I do, though not well. Lord, they've been there as long as we've been here," Houlahan said.

"Well, they're my aunt and uncle. I'm Ian Murphy and my ah...ah...companion, Mairin."

"Now isn't that grand? You must meet the Missus when she gets back. She's shopping for groceries; must have fresh food for breakfast. Here's your key. Room is upstairs on the right," Houlahan instructed.

"Thank you. We're grateful, really, we are," Mairin said and led the way upstairs.

We spent the evening learning about each other in passion and intimacy. For the first time in my life, I experienced what it feels like to love a mature, self-confident woman, who expresses the joy of her body and knows that fulfillment comes from sharing ecstasy. Lacking experience except with one other woman, I found myself comparing Eileen and Mairin. Eileen was always in a rush and could climax before I could, which I understand is rare, almost unusual. Did that make me less of a man?

Mairin was not in a hurry and with her hands, led me to her most sensitive, erotic areas. Mairin moaned with pleasure, a signal I find both alluring and informative. In our first night together, I learned how to be responsive to her breath, heartbeat, and undulations of her entire body. I didn't ask about her previous sexual experience nor did she ask about mine. It was clear that history didn't matter. Mairin was an expert at teaching me how to be in the moment, in all things: eating, hiking, sharing feelings, making love, and even in sleeping. This must be what love is.

†††

"Ian, thank you, I haven't slept like that for years.

It was the hiking, I'm sure." Mairin curled up to my side, placed her head on my shoulder and rested her hand on my chest, curling and uncurling my hair with her fingers.

I glanced at her; she looked so serious the first thing in the morning. "Yes, the hiking. I'm sure that was it. I could get accustomed to sleeping like that without having to guzzle almost a bottle of whiskey. My head feels much better in the morning, too, although my stomach suffers. Do you realize we didn't have dinner last night?"

Mairin snuggled even closer and pulled the comforter up over our heads. "I didn't realize we missed dinner until you mentioned it. I'm not sure I want to crawl out of our warm bed yet. Do you mind?"

My nature is as a morning person. Once awake, my mind kicks in and I'm ready for the day—at least on those days when my sleep isn't whiskey-induced. On those days, I wake in a fog and struggle to find the clearing. There have been too many of those days in my life, more than I will admit to myself. More than I can honestly remember. I think this is love. Dare I tell her?

"No, I don't mind. I don't mind at all. I'm sure you know 'the world is too much with us now.'"

"Mmmm good."

I lay awake listening to her shallow breathing, her skin quite warm to the touch. I spent my time imprinting all of yesterday's memories. What were the chances that Father O'Connell would have known that suggesting that I read a Catholic mystic would lead me to the college religion department, to the religion department library, and to Mairin McCarthy?

At some point though, regardless of my emotional ecstasy, hunger would win out, and I would gently wake Mairin. Maybe I could make a cup of tea in the room and sneak downstairs for a couple of scones. I didn't want her to think I would abandon a beautiful woman in bed. I thought about that for a few minutes and rejected it; she was more emotionally mature than that.

I slipped out of bed, put on enough clothes to be presentable, and tiptoed downstairs to find a small mountain of blueberry scones with orange frosting sitting on a plate on the sideboard. My mouth watered as I picked up the top two and put them on a plate. I was glad the door to our room wasn't like my cottage, which would have woken Mairin with its nails-across-a-chalkboard screech.

Mairin peeked out from beneath the comforter when she heard the soft whistle of the teapot. All I could see was her tousled hair and her enchanting hazel eyes. At first, her eyes had large question marks, which quickly transformed into an alluring smile. She lowered the comforter enough to lick her lips. "Ian, you are so sweet. Did you hear my stomach growling?"

I put two mugs of steaming tea on a tray with a scone setting next to each mug. I sat on the side of the bed in a slow, deliberate way, trying to avoid the embarrassment of spilling the contents. The tray almost toppled over when Mairin scooted up and took one of the mugs.

"There's no better smell than strong Irish tea first thing in the morning. Are those blueberry scones?"

"Yes, blueberry, with a yummy orange glaze. My favorite. A person would have thought I ordered them intentionally, but I can't take the credit. My good fortune continues."

We took the time to indulge in the scones, one small bite at a time, and sip the hot tea without burning our tongues. While good, the nibble only served to make my hunger more intense and my stomach growled out of control. I blushed several shades of red, looking as bright as a stoplight in central Cork City.

"I think we should dress and have a full breakfast. We're still planning on the Blasket Islands today, yes?" I asked.

I took her mug, set it on the tray, and got up without making a fool of myself. "I don't want to rush you, regardless of my gurgling stomach. Do you want to shower?"

Mairin jumped out of bed, threw on the clothes lying on the floor, and brushed her hair. "No, I need a good Irish breakfast, too. Besides, we can shower after breakfast—together."

†††

The ferry ran on the half hour from 7:00 a.m. to 8:00 p.m. during the summer. We had all the time in the world, a brandnew experience for me. We didn't arrive at the ferry launch until early afternoon, when the sun was well past being overhead. The trip to the Great Blasket Island was smooth and uneventful. No cars are allowed on the island so the ferry carried only walk-ons and bicyclists. For June, there weren't many passengers, not a good omen for the summer tourist trade. We stood at the railing at the bow, letting the sea breeze ruffle our coats. I wrapped my arms around Mairin, closed my eyes, and let the gentle rocking and the sound of waves lapping up against the hull lull me into euphoria. Water has a unique, therapeutic property.

Midway between the mainland and the island, I felt that my soul had been thoroughly cleansed by the ocean. I felt refreshed and almost released from the burden of my past. I knew in that moment that I wouldn't find redemption in the Church. Not that the Church wouldn't offer me consolation and forgiveness, but my sin was with Mother Ireland, not Mother Church. Had I pulled the trigger or set the bombs myself, my recourse would be with Mother Church. My sin was both more insidious and discrete. What burden does the instigator bear?

Mairin allowed me to reflect during the thirty-minute ferry trip and didn't bother with conversation. We landed with ease. The plank extended and we followed our fellow travelers onto the bleak island. It was said that at one time as many as 150 people inhabited the island. A few remained through the mid-fifties, fewer than twenty-five, and then the island was abandoned. Today it was beautiful, rustic, and barren.

Mairin grabbed my hand and pulled me off the boat. "Let's start with the ridge trail."

"Damn, you read my mind. It's my favorite, of course. Good thing I have my loyal walking stick; I'll need it. Sometimes the trail becomes a bit narrow for me."

We walked at a good pace until we ascended to the level of the trail. The breeze gained strength and I worried that Mairin's delicate skin would suffer wind burn. "Have you ever stumbled, Ian?"

"No, not on this trail, but I have on the Dingle Way; I've twisted my ankle several times. That's why I changed to these above-ankle hiking boots. I also wear padded hiking socks. A few years back I wasn't so well informed. I've learned that gear can make a difference."

Mairin squeezed my hand and smiled. "A good quality; you are adaptable, Ian."

We walked on for at least an hour, respecting each other's private thoughts by avoiding banter in idle conversation.

"Ian, do you see the donkeys? They're off to our right about a kilometer ahead."

"They have the entire island to themselves. Fortunate creatures—no natural enemies, grass aplenty for grazing, water, and they roam at their own heart's content."

"Sounds to me like you envy them, Ian."

"Oh, I don't know."

We walked on to the farthest western point of the island. A bit out of breath, the wind continued to strengthen and I could feel a chill in my bones. "Let's take a rest. We have hot tea, don't we?" I stared to the west, into the Atlantic Ocean. "This is the most western point in all of Ireland, and it's the closest I'll ever get to America."

We poured the tea, toasted with our plastic cups, and sipped slowly to let it warm us through and through. "That's an odd thing to say, Ian. You've not been to New York or Boston?"

"No, never had the inclination. Not sure why. I'm sad to admit, I don't have much curiosity about our American kin. The Cork Murphys refused to immigrate. That's how my uncles got into the distilling business. My da started on the docks and retired from the docks. It was exhausting work. He worked himself to death, literally."

I felt Mairin tuck her head into my shoulder and take my hand in both of hers. With her other hand she stroked my beard with tenderness. "Thank you for sharing. I don't think you find it easy to talk about yourself. Why is that? Maybe it's an unfortunate outcome of having such a secret life for so many years. I'm not judging, Ian. I'm not that way. You should share more of yourself with the world. You certainly don't have anything to hide any longer."

I wrapped my arms tightly around her as we sat together looking toward the ocean. Eventually, I took another sip of tea, which by then had gotten cold. I dumped it out onto the rocks of the escarpment.

"Ian, you must write your memoir. You can cleanse your soul by sharing your story with your Irish kin."

I leaned her over to my right so that I could see her eyes, which were translucent and beaming with love. It was if I had been struck by lightning and left to sit out on this cold stone to recover. My mind went completely blank. I felt her stroke my beard with her hand and a smile broke on her lips. All I wanted to do was kiss her; I leaned in and lightly touched her lips and became intoxicated with the deep scent of magnolia.

"Wha…what are you talking about?"

"What I'm saying is, you don't need to hike until you drop from exhaustion. You don't need to study Saint John of the Cross. You are a writer; it's not just what you do, it's who you are. If you are serious about redemption for your part in what tore this country apart, you must earn it from your people. From the rumblings at the college, the reaction to your noble efforts with the Peace Accord is appreciation and some admiration. Yet how can a man just exposed as an IRA mastermind become a peacemaker with the snap of his fingers? You are a mystery, Ian Padraic Murphy, and sharing that mystery would begin your journey for redemption."

"Well, I could write an autobiography, give all the details."

Mairin pulled away and looked directly into my eyes for what seemed like at least an hour but had to be only minutes, maybe seconds. "God, that would be boring," she said with painful accuracy. "We're Irish, Ian. We Irish thrive on story. We don't want a detailed account of your life. A memoir shares your motivations and lets you share with us the journey of your transformation."

"Even when I tried to kill myself and take a few Brit soldiers with me?"

"What?"

"Two years ago, I wanted to quit the IRA. Kieran Fitzpatrick told me that wasn't possible; I would be shot as a traitor. There were reports in the paper about children being injured in an IRA raid in Belfast. When children become the victims, the war is lost, all perspective is lost. Kieran Fitzpatrick showed up unwanted at my cottage one night. I asked him for an explanation of the raid in Belfast, and he didn't have one. The movement was out of control. There was no discipline among the rank and file. And when I wanted to quit, Kieran threatened me. I was furious. I got stinking drunk and came up with this outrageous plan to ram my car into a British barricade. If I was going to die, it would be at my own hand, not that of some IRA grunt, and if I could take out a few Brit soldiers, all the better."

Her soft glow changed into paleness as the blood left her cheeks. Her eyes became stark and fearful. She pressed her hands together as if in prayer during morning mass. "Dear Jesus, Ian. I remember reading the newspaper accounts of the unknown IRA attack in north Cork. You?"

"My injuries were minor. Kieran found me in an IRA safe house. Don't know how I got there. He whisked me up to his family vacation cottage near Donegal Bay."

A single tear welled up in Mairin's eye and slid down her cheek to the corner of her mouth. I kissed her and removed her tear.

"Poor Ian, you suffered like no one can imagine. But suicide? Suicide is for cowards or those with mental health issues. I can't imagine that you have either of those in your life. You felt personally responsible for those children? That's absurd. The raid wasn't your idea. You didn't give the order. Being an IRA volunteer doesn't make you responsible for every act the IRA has taken since 1977."

I let her words sink in as the sun slid into the ocean. Explaining events to Mairin was worse than confessing to Father Connelly. I didn't have to look Father Connelly in the eyes as I told of my lies and collusion over the past thirty years. When confessing to a priest, a bargain of sorts is struck; the sinner tells his story and the priest offers absolution with the appropriate penance. Father Connelly didn't require penance, although he also didn't offer absolution. He said in my case only God could do that directly, he couldn't or wouldn't do it as an agent of God.

"Listen, Ian, we need to start walking before the sun sets. I have a surprise for you."

I struggled to lift myself off the cold stone. My muscles were stiff and nonresponsive. As I got up, I leaned on Mairin and she almost stumbled trying to get up herself. When I stood upright, the wind caught my hat. I grabbed it with both hands to prevent it from flying off into the ocean. Mairin broke out laughing at my clumsy attempt to save my hat. Her laughter was infectious and I began laughing, too. Laughing at yourself was a special gift and I must confess, it hasn't always been possible for me. I tended to take myself too seriously.

I think people who have the ability to regularly and easily laugh at their own actions, are well-balanced and not absorbed with their own ego. I have not always wanted to be that way. I've been insecure most of my adult life. When I was honest with myself, I realized my relationship with Eileen was based on my insecurity. My ego was charmed by a young, attractive, intelligent woman who wanted a middle-aged recluse. I don't know if she loved me. Hell, I don't know if I loved her. I did know that my feelings now for Mairin, even in the short time we had known each other, were much different than they had been for Eileen. I had been infatuated with Eileen. I was physically smitten. It happens. I didn't feel apologetic, but I had to be honest with myself. That was the first step to take on my new life path: self-honesty.

"My Ian, you seem so distant all of a sudden. So lost in your own thoughts. I'm not offended but don't you want to know my surprise?"

"Yes, of course. I'm sorry. I'm easily distracted. It comes with too much of a life spent alone. My mind wanders off for I don't know how long. Please, bring me back to this world when I do that. Bring me back to our world."

Mairin took my hand in hers and laced our fingers together. We swung our arms back and forth like school children experimenting with their first affection. "Well, look over the rise, what do you see?"

"The three whitewashed cottages? I believe one of them belonged to Peig Sayers."

"The smaller of the three, off to the right, with a chimney at either end."

"How remarkable you are, knowing a detail like that."

"I'm a librarian, remember. I studied the history of Gaelic literature, and Peig Sayers is a savior of sorts. Her storytelling is epic. We would have lost so much without her. Yet she was so plain. Have you read her autobiography?"

"Read it? I teach it. No college-level course in Gaelic storytelling would be complete without both the autobiography and the collected stories. Peig Sayers embodies what it is to be Irish through and through. We're staying in her home? Mairin, you are a wonder, what a perfect surprise. You know, for all the times I've been on this island, I've looked at the house but never gone inside. I had no idea a person could rent it for a night. God, what an inspiration. When did you make this arrangement? You are a marvel. Mairin, I think you know me better than I know myself. How is that possible?"

I gave her a kiss on the cheek and a wink. We took long strides up the slope, and I was panting by the time we reached the small plateau where the houses had been built. From the bottom of the hill, the three homes looked close together but in fact it was an illusion. I couldn't image Peig Sayers living among people, and with only two neighbors, the scene fit everything I knew about her. I hoped that by staying in her cottage, I would be imbued with her spirit.

We tried the thick oak door. The incessant rain on the island had rusted the latch almost shut. I wiggled it back and forth and showered the ground with orange shavings. The door opened into a large room with sparse wood furniture, a few straight-back chairs, and a table just large enough for two. No curtains on the windows. The walls were whitewashed stone and the floor pounded dirt. On one end there was a brick hearth in the center that took up nearly the entire wall. A neat stack of peat graced the hearth, along with a stack of newspaper to use to light the fire, and a small tin box of matches. At the other end of the room, on one side of the second fireplace, a staircase painted sky-blue led to the upper level. At the foot of the stairs was a four-level wooden shelf painted the same blue as the staircase. I stood with Mairin in the center of the room, imagining what it must have been like when Peig lived in the house.

"Do you think it was this bare when she lived here?" I asked.

Mairin turned around several times, taking in the room, letting it soak into memory. "Well, from what I've read, I think it looked like this the day she left to move to Dingle. To say she was a plain, unadorned woman is an understatement."

I copied Mairin's circling examination of the room. I am a frugal man and live simply, but this home was so lacking it was almost depressing. "Stories must have been the only thing that enriched her life."

We went to the pile of peat, crumpled up several pages of newspaper, and struck a match on the brick to light the fire. A plume of dark-blue smoke filled the room; I had forgotten to check the flu before lighting the peat. I poked my head into the bottom of the fireplace to check for daylight. Not a bit of light; the flu was shut tight. I waggled the lever as hard as I could.

"Damn thing must be rusted." I shouted over the noise I was making. I took both hands and gave the lever a mighty jolt and it snapped open, the smoke rushed up the chimney, clearing the small room. I looked back at Mairin; she sat with both hands over her face holding back laughter as best she could.

"Nice job" she said through her chuckles.

"All in a day's work."

"Are you hungry?"

"I could eat."

Mairin walked to the kitchen and returned a short time later with wine, cheese, charcuterie, rustic bread, and some apples. "Here we go. Do you mind getting us some plates and cutlery; they're on the cabinet in the kitchen."

"I'm impressed. This is an exquisite plan. I'll be right back."

I poured us each a glass of wine—a heavy pour—and suggested a toast. "To a new beginning. To life, to love, and to a memoir."

Our glasses clinked in the small space between us. Mairin's hazel eyes were blazing and I'm sure mine must have reflected the love I felt bathed in. Time stopped as we looked deeply into each other's soul. I felt suspended in this moment and a feeling of completeness filled me that I had never before experienced.

"We need to drink the wine to make the toast come true," I offered.

"Oh, yes." We both just sipped, not breaking eye contact. There was a miracle on Blakes Island that day. We ate our fill of cheese, the thinly sliced meats, and the apples until just a small core remained. The contents of the wine bottle disappeared, and the sun sank away as darkness filled the room, which was now lit only by the peat fire. I fumbled in my pockets to find my pipe and tobacco. "Mind if I have a short pipe?"

"Well, well. A meerschaum. I should have guessed. Of course; enjoy yourself. Pipe smoke can be luscious and intoxicating. I'm sure you have your own blend, handmade?"

A sheepish grin spread across my face. "You do know me well. I've had a tobacconist for years. Through trial and error, he's found a blend that suits me." As I smoked and gazed into the fire, Mairin cuddled close and rested her head on my shoulder. "I can imagine nights with old Peig sitting here, animated as she told stories to her son, who, I imagine, scribbled as fast as he could with a dull pencil in his cheap notebook. Rumor is that once she started, she could ramble on for hours without interruption, except for an occasional sip of whiskey, which was always at her side. Yes, for an Irish writer, this is a sacred place. A good deal of ancient Irish folktales were saved right here. Can you imagine?"

"I honestly don't know if I can imagine it, but it's obvious you can. I'm glad staying here was the right thing to do."

"Perfect. It's perfect."

"Your toast included the memoir. So, you've decided that's the path for you?"

"Aye. And if it weren't for you in my life, I never would have thought about it. I've not been a big memoir reader. The key, as you already know, will be the writing. Writing it will be my journey of 'the dark night of the soul.'"

"Ian Padraic Murphy, I have not known you for very long, but I know that I love you."

I set my pipe on the hearth and pulled Mairin close to me. Our lips and then our tongues found each other. She took her hand and began playing with the back of my hair, which both tickled and excited. "I love you. I know you are my soul mate. We have found each other at long last."

I unbuttoned her blouse to fondle and nibble on her breast. Before I knew what was happening we had joined together, moving back and forth in our rhythm of love. She raised her head, thrusting her hips and bracing herself with her arms. She sucked in air and caught her breath in the same moment I thrust to an explosive orgasm. I stopped breathing.

I felt the ecstatic tension in her body ebb away as she bent her arms and lowered herself onto my chest and rested her head on my shoulder. Our hearts beat against each other in unison. I wrapped my arms around her in a bear hug that I never wanted to let go of. She kissed the side of my neck in soft, delicious pecks, then slid off to my side. We turned toward the peat fire, spoon to spoon.

The long hike during the day had been a challenge and sleep snuck up on us. We drifted off to our dreams and let the fire extinguish itself during the night.

THIRTEEN

"Mickey, do you have the paper?"

"Got a copy back in my office. Go help yourself. When will you want lunch today?"

"I'm not in a hurry. I'm spending the afternoon with Caitlin and Brianna. We don't have any specific plans. You and the Missus could join us."

"I have a pub to operate, Ian, even on Sunday, especially on Sunday in the middle of tourist season. Have you forgotten its mid-August? Give us about thirty minutes in the kitchen and come on out. I'll join you for lunch today."

Mid-August? I thought to myself. It feels like it was just a week ago that Mairin and I were hiking the Dingle Peninsula together; it was more like damn near ten weeks ago. I found the paper spread out on Mickey's desk, all the separate sections separated. The front section was on the bottom of the pile. The headline knocked me back into the chair:

OMAGH BOMBING DEVASTATING
29 Killed, more than 200 Injured

I read through the tragic story. A group calling themselves the Real IRA took responsibility for the slaughter. The "Real" IRA claimed that they didn't accept the Northern Ireland Peace Accord and vowed to continue the war against the British government.

"How do they think killing innocents in Omagh hurts the British government?" I asked myself out loud. When I was dumbfounded or in a conundrum with my writing, I often talked to myself, and reading about this disastrous event plunged me into self-conversation.

For all her sins, Ireland carries the yoke of repeating history. After the separation in May 1921, many couldn't accept Ireland officially splitting up into the Republic of Ireland and Northern Ireland. DeValera declared civil war immediately and the senseless carnage continued for years. Once again, some separatist group wouldn't accept the peace, and their solution was to continue killing.

"Mickey!" I screamed as loud as I could.

"Jesus, Ian, what a blood curdling scream! Are ya having the heart attack or something?"

"Did you read today's headline? The peace has been eradicated already, not even three bloody months after it began. Cancel lunch. I've got to go."

Mickey walked up to his desk with both hands stretched out in front of him, motioning me to stop. "Now you just hold on there, Ian Murphy. Where in the name of Jesus Christ do you think you're going?"

"Omagh, of course. I need to put an end to this absurdity."

Mickey crossed his arms across his rotund belly. "And who elected you? My guess is that Jerry Adams will clean up this mess. He's tryin' hard to make his Sinn Fein party legitimate. It's a cryin' shame really. This bombing will jam up the whole works. The Peace Accord may be swirling down the drain as we stand here."

I leaned forward and put both my fists on his desk to stare him down. "Which is why, Mickey O'Shay, I need to be there. That agreement is our Holy Grail. If it doesn't work, this country will tear itself apart again. Everyone realized the Peace Agreement was fragile, and it would take months, no years, to bring real peace to Northern Ireland. This is an atrocity, and my voice will be heard."

Mickey took several steps back and dropped his arms to his sides. "I hear you. Ian, you are a fool who is both naive and noble at the same time. At least take the time to have lunch with me and I'll help you plan out your trip. Maybe you can sort things out as you drive."

I smiled at how quickly Mickey dropped his resistance to my plan. "I can agree to that. There are a few loose ends I have, and of course, I need to talk with Mairin and Caitlin. You've always been my voice of reason, Mickey, thank you."

"You're welcome. Lunch is served."

† † †

The drive to Omagh was uneventful. I was thankful that Mairin completely understood my need to rush to County Tyrone, search for those responsible for the atrocity, and work with whomever necessary to keep the peace intact and watch over the activities of the Royal Ulster Constabulary. I wanted to ensure fairness, and prevent the British from establishing military rule in the county in retaliation for the violence under the guise of securing the public peace.

Caitlin, on the other hand, could not understand my motivation. This from the woman who worked for peace in Belfast and had been a Sinn Fein stalwart for more than ten years.

"Ian, you're flying into danger, personal danger. Just because you have amnesty doesn't mean you're safe. That was for the past, not the present."

"Caitlin, I'm so surprised. You're overreacting. I'm at no risk personally. It isn't necessary for me to have either your approval or understanding. I just wanted to share my plans with you."

"Have you told Mairin?"

"Of course."

"Did she understand?"

"Yes. Yes, she did."

"At least you were honest with her before you left. No secrets—that part of your life is gone forever, right?"

"I love Mairin with all my heart. Not to be trite but we're soul mates. It's just that simple."

"I am happy for you, Ian. Everyone deserves a bit of happiness in their lives. I'll keep you in my prayers every day. Before you leave, please come back to say goodbye to Brianna."

"I promise."

†††

While driving to Omagh, I listened to the news reports. About eighty percent of the air time was devoted to the bombing. The investigation had begun immediately with interesting and apparently unrelated facts being revealed daily.

The first surprise was that there had been three warning telephone calls. One was made to Ulster Television thirty minutes before the explosion. The message included the location, size of the bomb, and when it would go off. This call was followed a minute later by a second call, this one saying the bomb would go off in fifteen minutes. In both calls, the code word "Martha Pope" was used, a well-known, legitimate, Irish Republican Army code.

The last message was much more specific, telling them the bomb was 200 yards from the courthouse. Each message was passed on to the RUC. About thirty-eight minutes after the messages were received, the bomb detonated. Allowing five minutes for the RUC to receive the information from the three calls and pass them up their ranks, left thirty-three minutes for them to respond. What did the RUC do in those thirty-three minutes? I was puzzled.

A partial list of deaths included a pregnant woman, six children, and six teenagers, illustrating the complete randomness of the act. What were they thinking?

I decided to find a place to stay outside of town and then start calling on a few people I knew about through Kieran. God, how I wished Kieran was here to help untangle this mess. This is so close to his home turf. I found a worn-down bed and breakfast, ironically enough on Dublin Road. I found it ironic a road in Northern Ireland bearing the name Dublin, the capital of the Republic of Ireland.

At this time of year, it was unusual to find a room without a reservation. I guessed that the condition of the bed and breakfast explained the empty rooms. While checking in, I was told there would be no hot breakfast but just pastries and coffee served on the sideboard in the dining room. The "meal" would be available by 7:30 a.m. every day. Also, bedding would not be changed during the duration of my stay unless I specifically requested it.

"How long will you be staying with us, Mr. Murphy?" Mrs. Nicholl, the inn owner, asked. I guessed her to be between sixty-five and seventy years old.

"It's hard to tell. I could pay for a week in advance," I offered.

"Let me check if there's a booking for that room. No, there isn't. A week's advance would be fine. Will that be cash, credit, or check?"

"Check, if you don't mind."

"No problem."

"What do you think of the bombing?"

"Shameful, disgraceful, and my heart goes out to all the families."

"I've heard the Real Irish Republican Army has already taken responsibility."

Mrs. Nicholl took off her reading glasses and set them on the counter next to the registration book. She looked at me directly, and I noticed her eyes appeared clouded over. Cataracts, I guessed. "I don't know who those fellas think they are. I voted for the peace and they're tryin' to ruin it. Personally, I hope they catch them all and hang 'em by the neck. Yes, sir, that would be just fine with me. Here's your key. Remember, breakfast is set out at 7:30."

I went to my room and made a list of four people I would visit to try to find out who the leaders of the RIRA were. I couldn't resist the compulsion to view the bomb site myself. Of course, a three-block area around ground zero was blockaded. I parked and walked in on foot. A constable asked to see some identification. He checked my license thoroughly and called it in on his radio. "You check out, Mr. Murphy. You're THAT Mr. Murphy, aren't you?"

"I guess I am."

"You're a long way from Cork."

"Not that far."

"What brings you to Omagh?"

"The bombing, of course. I had to see for myself."

"Curious. Well, take a look if you must. Keep your nose clean while you're here. I've let headquarters know you're in town. We'll be watching you."

"I don't have anything to hide."

"I hope not. Now, move on. Don't stay more than fifteen minutes. Come back this way so I can see you leave."

"Yes, sir."

I walked the few blocks in long strides to make sure I could see what I needed to see and get back within my time limit. I have never seen a war zone, but the destruction and rubble remaining could only be described as a city like those bombed during World War II; the streets were littered with the remains of normal human lives. As I walked along, I noticed the pavement soaked in deep crimson with a smell that choked me. I pulled out a handkerchief to cover my nose and mouth. The handkerchief couldn't stop the stench of carnage that permeated everything.

I had seen enough. I had no stomach for such things. I did an about-face and returned to my entry point long before my fifteen-minute time limit. I made sure to walk past the constable.

"Thank you. I'm leaving."

"You weren't gone long."

"No. Such devastation, it's hard to imagine. Whoever is responsible is a monster."

"Thank you for stopping back through."

"Just following instructions, constable. I am a civil man."

†††

I remembered that Kieran maintained a safe house in Omagh because it was far enough away from Belfast that the volunteers needed a quick place to go in case they needed to hide from the authorities. Until this event, Omagh didn't have a reputation for being a hotbed of IRA activity. The safe house was located south of center city near Sacred Heart College. In a college area, there were always young men roaming about and moving in and out of housing, so the volunteers would be invisible in the neighborhood. This was another way that Kieran Fitzpatrick was brilliant as a strategist and planner. The home was at the end of a block in a standard row house neighborhood. There was absolutely nothing to distinguish it from all the other houses on the block, as it had to be an effective safe house.

I bounced up the three steps and banged on the Celtic harp door knocker three times. "Is Brigid at home?" I asked, hoping that was still the code word."

A young man opened the door only a few inches and only the front of his face was visible. He had a narrow Roman nose covered in freckles and an unkempt mound of red hair. "Aye, I believe she is. And who would be asking?"

"My name is Ian Murphy."

"You're shittin' me. Come right in." He opened the door wide and stepped back so that I could enter the foyer. "What are you doin' here, of all places? Come to see all the excitement, I guess."

"Part true. I just came from the bomb site; it's stomach churning. I'm searching for information."

"Listen, Mr. Murphy, as God is my witness, we had nothin' to do with that disaster. Kieran Fitzpatrick would hang us by our thumbs for even imagining such a ridiculous scheme. We're all about the peace now, aren't we."

I looked deep into the young man's eyes and found only the wide-eyed, innocent look that only a twenty-something can have. "Kieran Fitzpatrick?"

"Aye, I thought he was a friend of yours."

"Oh, he is, he is. It's just that you speak of him as if you had seen him recently."

"I didn't mean to speak out of turn, Mr. Murphy. I had better shut up now."

"Is there someone in charge of the house, young man? I won't offend you by asking your name. You'd tell me a lie anyway."

The lad blushed deep red. "There is a lady that comes every day to check in. I guess she's in charge. I'm not really sure. They don't tell us much. She hasn't been here yet today. We never know when she's coming. You can wait, I suppose. Would you like a cup of tea?"

I looked around and listened but couldn't determine if the young man was alone or not. I didn't want to ask too many questions because that would invite suspicion. "Yes, tea would be perfect. May I sit in the kitchen as you make it?"

"Sure."

"There ya go, Mr. Murphy." He put a huge steaming mug of tea on the table for me.

"May I smoke? Nothing like hot tea and a smoke," I said, trying to keep the interaction casual.

"Doesn't bother me none. I'll leave you here."

"As you wish. I'll stay right here. Promise."

The young man left without saying another word and disappeared somewhere in the bowels of the house. After the experience of seeing the bomb site, the hot tea was warming and familiar. I pulled my traveling pipe from my jacket pocket, packed it tight, and drew the flame of the match deep into the bowl. I was soon lost in watching the pipe smoke curl up toward the ceiling and form a mini-cloud in the kitchen.

"Mr. Ian Murphy?" I hadn't heard footsteps behind me before the voice blasted out my name.

I flinched. "Yes?"

"You're fine. Stay seated. I'm Fionnoula."

I guessed the woman was in her early fifties, and she wore a traditional Irish matron look with a plain gray dress buttoned up the front all the way to the short, white collar. Her dark brown hair had streaks of white and was pulled back into a bun. She didn't offer a handshake, so neither did I.

"I just came from the bomb site. This could ruin everything. Everything. I want to find out who ordered this. I know it wasn't us. The new group is calling themselves the Real Irish Republican Army according to the newspapers. I assume that information is correct."

Fionnoula stood directly in front of me and didn't indicate that she would sit down. It was clear that my visit would be brief. "As far as we know, it's correct. Why do you think anyone here would have that information?"

I set my pipe on the table and looked up at her to be sure to make eye contact. "I couldn't go to the RUC, now could I? The peace is only a few months old. People know things. Anyone working with Kieran always knew things; it was his stock in trade. I'm looking for the names of the people who did this."

"If I tell you, what will you do with the information?"

"I'm going to find them and confront them. They must be complete idiots. I'll try to convince them to be men and turn themselves in. If not, I may consider giving the RUC the names myself."

Fionnoula shook her head back and forth in unmistakable disapproval. "I'll give you one name and a pub where you can go to inquire, out of respect for you, your service, and bringing us the peace. I warn you against turning any names into the RUC. That's not our way, but, of course, I don't need to tell you that. Ask for Seamus Devlin at Ferguson's Pub. It's on this side of town, just ask around."

"That's it?"

"It is. I'll be saying goodbye to you now, Mr. Murphy. It's been an honor to meet you. May God bless."

I was dismissed with kindness and left the house without a word. As Kieran would have taught them, information was sparse but direct. All I needed was a name and a place and that's all I was given. Because I had been so vague in asking, it wasn't clear if Seamus Devlin was the man responsible for the atrocity or he would know who was. I was not comfortable conducting my own investigation; it's not a strength or skill I possess.

I drove off toward the east and saw a chemist shop on the corner and thought it a good place to ask for directions to Ferguson's Pub. The proprietor was in and gave me succinct directions without asking me questions or wondering about my obvious Cork accent. As it turned out, the pub was a short distance away, and in less than ten minutes, I was parking my car nearby.

From the pub, I could see the steeple of a Catholic church. The neighborhood had all the appearances of a working-class, Catholic neighborhood. It was late morning and only a few people were on the streets; most were working, I assumed. This was one of those times I needed to be wearing a watch, but I was a creature of habit and, of course, didn't have one. My guess was it was sometime between eleven and half eleven, so the noon crowd would be arriving soon. I thought it would be wise of me to order a bowl of traditional vegetable soup, well known in Northern Ireland, with several slices of bread and maybe a pint of the local brew: Belfast Black.

I sat at a table for two next to the front windows so that I could watch people pass by—a writer's habit. I asked the waitress to bring the beer before the food was ready. She bought the steaming bowl of soup and on a separate plate, two slices of warm bread with a slab of cultured butter. My mouth began to water before the bowl hit the table.

"Thank you. I didn't realize how hungry I am. Breakfast was light and many hours ago. Can I ask, is Seamus Devlin about?"

"Mr. Devlin?"

She obviously had been taught to refer to him by his proper name.

"I think so. I haven't seen him myself. Would you like me to ask?"

"Yes, I would appreciate that."

I unfolded the cloth napkin and tucked it into my collar to avoid embarrassing myself. The soup was hot and chocked with root vegetables. The dark bread complimented the soup nicely. I scooped mouthfuls of the soup into my mouth as I watched the number of people passing by increase slowly. After finishing, I pushed the bowl away, leaving one slice of bread on the plate, too full to finish a second piece. The beer was excellent, not Guinness but excellent nonetheless. There was only one Guinness in the world; even a Northern Irishman would have to admit that.

"Mr. Devlin would like to know who's asking about him."

I must have been transfixed by people watching because for the second time today I didn't hear someone walk up behind me.

"My name is Ian Murphy."

"I will pass along your name, Mr. Murphy."

I was just finishing the beer when a too-thin young man came to the table. "Please follow me, Mr. Murphy."

I did as instructed without leaving any money on the table for the meal. I would make sure to stop by the bar before leaving. I followed the young man to the back of the pub and through the kitchen. At the rear of the kitchen, a green metal door led downstairs. The stairs were so narrow and steep, I had to turn sideways and watch my step. There were no lights in the staircase and it took my eyes a few minutes to adjust to the dark. I followed the young man by sound, not sight.

The room we walked into had cartons of food supplies stacked everywhere in a very haphazard manner. The walls were stone with white plaster. At the back of the basement storage area was a gray steel ship door with a metal bar across the front. The young man raised the bar, pushed in the door, and said: "Go in."

The room was the size of a closet; it might have been a root cellar before it was converted to the surreptitious headquarters for the Real Irish Republican Army. The walls were dark-stained oak. The only furnishings were a cheap pine wood desk and a metal chair. A single light bulb hanging from the center of the ceiling provided the only light. A man in a loose-fitting sweater stood behind the metal chair facing the wall when I entered. I was surprised that anyone in such a cramped space would turn his back on a visitor. Either he was trusting, or I wasn't considered a threat. The room was cool and dry.

"Hello?" I said. "Seamus Devlin?"

I could see the man's shallow breathing as his shoulders moved up and down.

"Ian Murphy?" he asked in a voice that sounded like a cement mixer.

"Yes."

Seamus Devlin turned around, placed his hands on the back of the chair, and leaned toward me as if the low-hung ceiling light prevented him from seeing my face. His hands were thick with stubby fingers; it was obvious that he had spent a lifetime earning his living with his hands. My guess is that he worked on the shipyards. His hair was cut very short, the stubble was salt white mixed with black. His eyes were set deep in his head, so it was impossible to see the expression of his eyes with the brightness of the single bulb. I guessed that the inability to read his face was intentional. His lips were so thin it was as if he didn't have any lips at all. The tips of his ears stuck out and curled over. It was the type of typical Irish face that could be painted on the barrier peace walls in Belfast.

"You asked to see me."

"Your name and the Real Irish Republican Army have been mentioned in connection with the Omagh bombing."

"Interesting," he growled.

"I don't know what you think you're doing. Almost 677,000 Northern Ireland citizens approved that Peace Accord; that's 71 percent. You have no valid grounds to continue the struggle. We agreed to decommission all arms and you have done just the opposite. Your country is trying to form an independent government, which your action jeopardizes. How do you think we look to the rest of the world? We look like uncivilized heathens. How can it be that, once again, a minority can't accept the wave of history? Enough! Your actions are abhorrent and repulsive to any civilized human being. You clearly have no empathy for your own countrymen. I demand that you turn yourself in and take responsibility for this nightmare. There is no "Real" Irish Republican Army. The only legitimate army was the Provisional IRA, which is now officially disbanded."

Seamus Devlin stood in silence staring at me. He took a pack of cigarettes out of the desk drawer, pulled one out with his mouth, and after lighting it, blew a plume of smoke in my direction. "Jesus, you're as arrogant a bastard as I was told. Where do you live? Cork? That bloody accent of yours gives you away. What does anyone from Cork know about living in Northern Ireland? Have you ever fought in the streets? Do you have walls separating Catholic and Protestant neighborhoods so you don't kill each other off? Two-hundred and seventy-five thousand citizens turned their backs on your goddamned agreement. I speak for them. And by the way, what is it about County Cork that breeds traitors? In 1921, Michael Collins sold us out for peace and in 1998, you do the same thing. You're right about one thing, history does repeat itself." Devlin turned his back on me.

"You're intransigent?"

Devlin wheeled around to face me. "What?"

I cleared my throat and explained. "You're not about to change, even with twenty-nine innocent lives to account for. You're going to continue the violence."

"Yeah, that's right. Now leave. I'll keep you safe temporarily, but I can't say how long. We have some strong-willed men who will be offended by you butting into our business."

"Is that a threat?"

"Take it how you want. It's just the truth. Don't linger. Leave now. The young man will escort you to your car, and see to it that you leave this part of town. Forget everything you saw here today if you expect to see the New Year."

Trying to carry on the conversation would have been futile. I left as Devlin ordered and drove to the bed and breakfast. I could see a beat-up brown sedan follow me. The driver watched me walk into the inn. I hoped my presence wasn't putting the business in jeopardy.

FOURTEEN

It had been a long day, and I sat down to enjoy a pipe. I needed to call Mairin to let her know about my adventures or misadventures. I watched the smoke from my pipe curl toward the ceiling and escape out the window that I had opened as wide as it would allow. Mid-August was very warm, and I was accustomed to living next to the ocean, where a breeze was constant. I couldn't detect any breeze in Omagh. The city was stagnant and crouching in fear. Maybe that's what Devlin wants, to instill fear in his countrymen.

The door rattled in the frame from a sudden banging. Instinctively, I jumped, and my pipe slipped from my hand, falling to the floor. I scooped up the pipe in an attempt to prevent the spent ashes from falling out and burning a hole in the carpet. I was so intent on preventing a fire, I didn't hear the shouting from the other side of the door.

"Ian Murphy, Constable Liam Taylor. Open the door immediately!" A deep bass voice penetrated the door. I set my pipe on the table and took a single long stride to open the door.

"A bit of patience, Constable. What do you want?"

Liam Taylor was too thin for his height and the body armor he wore hung on his body. His neck was very long, and I couldn't resist chuckling to myself because he looked like a leatherback sea turtle.

"Mr. Murphy, I'm here to place you under arrest in conjunction with the bombing on 15 August on Market Street, Omagh. I'm the only officer sent to fetch you, so we expect you to cooperate. I will cuff you if you resist this request."

"Forgive me, Constable, I don't think this development is funny. Yes, I will cooperate; the cuffs won't be needed. This is the first time in my life I've been placed under arrest."

"Thank you for making this easy on me. Lowest rank got the order today. We're off to headquarters."

The drive downtown to the RUC headquarters took only a few minutes. The building was a virtual fortress, which reflected the military nature of the Northern Ireland police force. Since Britain supplied arms to support the government, the police force had adopted the mission of being the military. The RUC had been able to justify its role since it was established in 1921, after Northern Ireland was created as a separate nation.

Headquarters was a three-story brick building with only one entrance on the main street. The ground floor didn't have any windows and gave the building the look of an ancient castle plopped into 1998. The constable drove around to the back of the building, which was surrounded by a ten-foot chain fence topped with another eighteen inches of barbed wire. A policeman in full body armor, helmet, and assault rifle guarded the gate. He saluted as we drove through. I didn't understand why a constable would be saluted; it must be their unique code. The back of the building also had only a single entrance with a guard outside, and as we entered, we were greeted by another guard.

"You got him, Taylor," the guard commented.

"That I did."

The hallways were brightly lit and painted a drab, nondescript gray. I was escorted to the booking station and asked to empty my pockets. My wallet and a pouch of tobacco were stuffed into a large, brown envelope. The constable never looked up. "Is that it?" Constable Taylor stood to my right, not showing any interest in the booking. I was sure he had witnessed it hundreds of times. Only the top of the booking constable's head was visible. He had a military haircut with close-shaved, whitewall-style cut on the sides of his head. I guessed he was the type to visit the barber weekly to stay sharp. Working in the RUC was obviously just an extension of his military service.

"Yes."

"You travel light, Mr. Murphy. Have you been read the charges?"

"No."

The constable shuffled papers in a file laid out flat on the desk. "Well now, you are being arrested on suspicion of conspiracy with the terrorist act of bombing on 15 August, 1998, at approximately 15:15 in Market Street, Omagh, which resulted in twenty-nine fatalities and 220 injuries."

"Conspiracy?" I whispered. Hearing that word was like being struck by lightning. How can they fabricate a charge like conspiracy? I just arrived yesterday, a day after the event.

"Constable Taylor, please escort Mr. Murphy to his holding cell. You will be provided a legal advisor today who will explain the charges further and inform you of your rights."

Constable Taylor took my elbow and efficiently turned me, leading me to a steel door and down several hallways. We stopped outside a cell that had a small slot for a window. He opened the door and instructed me to step inside. The cell contained a bunk with a thin mattress and a blanket folded neatly at the foot of the bed. Against the opposite wall was a metal bench that was propped by two supports. In the corner was a metal commode without a cover. As I surveyed the first cell I had ever seen, the door slammed behind me.

A ball of fear grew in my belly that wouldn't go away. *Who knows that I'm here? Do I get to call family? Jesus, what a trumped-up charge. They must want something else; the charge is complete fabrication.* I sat down on the metal bench, trying to collect my thoughts and muster a bit of courage. In the tiny room without windows, time didn't just stop, time didn't exist. Both my hands went into spasm and pain raged through my arms. *Jesus, Mary, and Joseph, am I having a stroke? I could die in this cell and no one would know for hours—maybe days.* I forced myself to sit up straight, take in deep belly breaths, and exhale slowly through my mouth. After a few minutes, the pain subsided and my hands relaxed. I rubbed my hands against my thighs to restore some normal sensation.

There was a sharp, hollow knock on the cell door. *Who the hell knocks on a cell door?* The door opened to reveal a man so broad that he filled the doorway. He had a short, well-trimmed black beard and close-cropped hair with a distinct receding hairline. Round metal-frame glasses rested on his nose, giving him an academic appearance. He didn't look like an RUC officer.

"Mr. Murphy, I am Colin Davies, the legal advisor assigned to you. Are you comfortable?"

"Mr. Davies, that is a ridiculous question. I understand your job is to explain this nonsense to me." Mr. Davies looked into the cell and shook his head.

"I will get us a room. Guard!"

A guard who resembled a street thug more than a police official led us to a room that contained a metal table and two metal chairs placed on either side of it. Mr. Davies threw a file on the table, sat down, and pointed to the other chair. "Take a seat, please, Mr. Murphy."

I sat down, hoping Mr. Davies was my savior in disguise. "Now, the single charge against you is conspiracy. It says a constable witnessed you visiting the bomb site earlier today and then visiting a pub that we suspect is the Real IRA headquarters. Based on these actions, you are suspected of conspiring with the RIRA to engage in a terrorist activity. Are the facts correct?"

"The facts are correct, Mr. Davies, but the conclusion is absurd. I've barely been in Omagh for a day."

Mr. Davies leafed through each page of the file. He picked up the papers and shuffled them in order, put them in the folder, and closed it. "There doesn't seem to be any evidence of conspiracy, and you're not denying your actions. I agree with you; the conclusion is weak. The investigation of the bombing is widespread; they're looking under every rock and conducting a mindless dragnet. My hunch is that you were just in the wrong place at the wrong time. However, your visit to Ferguson's Pub is a puzzle. I could ask you the purpose of the visit and who you talked with, but I really don't want to know. If you tell me, I will be under duress to report it. I don't think District Inspector First Class Clarke intends to press charges; he wants to scare you enough to cooperate with the investigation."

I listened with great care to every word the legal advisor said. I was beginning to form a clear picture of my circumstances.

"You understand that my role is with the RUC. I am not a solicitor. Would you like to talk to a solicitor, Mr. Murphy?" Davies asked.

"Do I need to?"

"I always advise those incarcerated to talk with a solicitor."

"Fine."

Mr. Davies chair screeched metal on metal when he pushed it back to get up.

"One final question. If this charge is trumped up to get me to talk…would you relinquish if you were in my shoes?"

Mr. Davies looked down at me as if he were studying a painting in an art gallery. "Mr. Murphy, I would sing like a song bird."

I sat in the room alone for a long time after Mr. Davies excused himself. For my work on the *Green Book*, I had studied RUC interrogation methods. Public opinion forced them to end using physical torture, however, by my treatment, it had appeared that they had converted to psychological torture. How better to weaken a writer than to force him to sit in a box of a room, alone, with zero mental stimulation for a long period of time. What they didn't plan for was my imagination. To endure the silence, I worked on my memoir, in my mind, of course. I refused to ask for pen and paper or anything that would give a signal that I wasn't adapting to the isolation.

The door flew open and jolted me out of my deep thoughts. "District Inspector First Class Clarke." A humorless looking constable holding a nightstick across his chest came into the room; behind him another guard shut the door and positioned himself in the corner. Inspector Clarke sat in the chair directly across from me. Clarke looked like a military man who had retired from active service and found a new home in the Royal Ulster Constabulary. His moustache was trim and neat and appeared to be groomed daily. He cut his sideburns so high that his cheeks appeared higher than they were. He was blessed with a traditional Anglo-Saxon nose that gave him an air of superiority and command presence. He folded his hands on the table.

As he was studying me, I wanted him to be keenly aware that I was studying him, as well. Writers are natural people-watchers and this was an opportunity to examine the Protestant enemy up close, though I forced myself to give up the notion that this man was my enemy. To create a government and learn how to work in a divided society, we must see what we have in common with those we called enemy just a few months ago. I really knew nothing about him except name and rank, which was nothing.

"You don't look like what I expected." Clarke demolished the silence between us.

"What was your expectation?" I couldn't resist asking.

"I thought you would look like you've spent a life on the docks. Jesus, you look like you could be Jerry Adams' brother."

"That's the problem with expectations, they tend to be disappointing. However, your comparison with Adams is a compliment. I've just grown the beard since the Peace Accord referendum; I'm still getting accustomed to it myself."

"Well, enough chitchat, Mr. Murphy. Let's get down to it. You've been charged with conspiracy with the bombing in Omagh on 15 August."

"I'm aware of the charge. What evidence do you have?"

"Of course, the investigation is still underway. However, we have witnesses that saw you visit the bomb site and the suspected location of the Real Irish Republican Army headquarters. Oh yes, I must ask, before we carry on. Do you want a solicitor?"

"Inspector Clarke, I'm going to trust you. I think the charge against me is designed to be an incentive to encourage me to talk frankly with you and tell you what I know. If you knew me, you would know I don't need an incentive to share the truth."

Clarke's face was like a stone wall. "Refreshing. You didn't answer my question. Again, do you want a solicitor?"

"No."

"Why did you visit the bomb site?" Clarke asked.

"Simple, I wanted to see it for myself. You may find this unimaginable, but after thirty years as a volunteer with the Provies, I've never actually seen what happens in a bombing. I stayed in Cork, safe. Just when I thought we had a chance for peace and reconstruction, a 200-pound bomb shatters it and robs families of their loved ones and injures hundreds. So much destruction both physically and metaphorically."

"Metaphorically?"

"Oh, yes, that bomb is a metaphor for how our society self-destructs, even at the moment of our greatest hope. History is rife with those intent on creating mayhem; I was once one of them."

"Listen, Mr. Murphy, would you care for some tea?"

"Thank you, Inspector Clarke, that would be civil."

Clarke turned toward the guard and nodded. In a few minutes, the latter returned with a tray with two mugs and a tea caddy.

"Returning to our conversation. You were curious about the bombing?"

"Curious? I hadn't thought of it that way. I suppose I was."

"The pub that you visited, is it the RIRA headquarters?"

"I'm guessing it is, yes."

"No subterfuge, Mr. Murphy?"

"No, I would like to see the RIRA disbanded and their weapons taken into custody. The new government doesn't have a chance if all their first efforts are devoted to fighting the RIRA. That would be a total waste of time and resources."

"We've suspected that pub is their headquarters but haven't been able to prove it, beyond doubt, that is. So, how did you find it after only a day?"

"I have contacts. That's my business. I've identified what appears to be the headquarters, that's all I'm going to say."

"Fair enough."

"What was your intent in seeking them out?"

"To tell them to publicly take responsibility for the atrocity and turn themselves in to authorities."

"They have issued an apology. Apparently, the job was botched. The target was the courthouse not the market."

"So what? An apology is hollow and meaningless. In fact, it's an insult to the families who suffered the death of loved ones."

Clarke finished off his tea, got up, and paced back and forth in front of me. "I'm going to ask you a very important question now, Mr. Murphy, and I want you to take your time before responding."

"Understood."

"Whom did you meet with?"

I watched Clarke pace and run his index finger across the top of the table. He was intent and didn't look at me. Asking the question made him uneasy, almost nervous. Why would he be nervous? I took my time, as he suggested, before answering. The truth could mean I ran the risk of being a target of the RIRA. I might be the first person in history who was a target of both the Real Irish Republican Army and the Provisional Irish Republican Army at the same time. My life expectancy would become very short, maybe days. But if I would ever find redemption, it could only be through truth. So this is what a lifetime of secrecy and deviousness leads to?

"Before you answer, if you give me a name, I must be honest, I cannot protect you. Only God almighty could protect you. I want all the cards on the table."

"You are an officer and a gentleman. My past brings me to this point. I have no one to blame except myself. Do you believe in karma, Inspector Clarke?"

"I'm not sure I understand karma, Mr. Murphy. I'm a Protestant; I don't understand those eastern religions."

"Would you mind sitting down?"

Clarke stopped in his tracks and stared at me. He dragged the chair across the floor and sat down, then crossed his arms across his chest.

"Thank you. I met with Seamus Devlin."

"Is he the leader of the RIRA?"

"I believe he is the founder of the RIRA."

"Our interview is over. You'll be escorted back to your cell. You've thrown caution to the wind, Mr. Murphy. I respect you."

The guard with the nightstick led me through the hallways back to my cell without saying a word.

FIFTEEN

The guard was efficient and speechless. He didn't say a word, walking the halls or when he opened the door to my solitary cell. I walked in without direction. I sat on the bench and buried my hands in my face. I felt warm all over and my hands were damp with sweat. I had given them Seamus Devlin's name. I didn't claim he was responsible for the bombing although it was implied. He did identify himself as both founder and leader of the Real Irish Republican Army, so that was a fact I shared with Inspector Clarke.

I don't think this was news. The RUC has always had a well-oiled intelligence gathering machine, even after they had to give up their torture practices. There was always a snitch, that's what Kieran Fitzpatrick was fond of saying. It was not that he didn't trust people, but he understood people and their weaknesses. I would now have to live or die with the consequences of my actions. The RIRA would brand me as a traitor for naming Devlin. The Provisional IRA had branded me as a betrayer for my role in developing the Good Friday Peace Agreement.

For more than thirty years, I had been a coward and succumbed to the irrational dream of reunifying our little island under one Irish government for all Irish peoples. Courage had a very high price and my actions were irrevocable. I couldn't claim any delusions or temporary loss of rational judgment. What I had done had been done intentionally, consciously, even if I didn't consider the personal consequences. My experience taught me that was how we behaved as human beings, willing to act without examining the potential outcome. That must be the definition of risk.

Sitting here, I can't know for sure that either the RIRA or the PIRA will be successful in ending my life. Maybe they'll have a bidding war for my demise. That was pure ego talking. I should have been ashamed of even entertaining such bizarre thoughts.

I learned to tell the passage of time by the meals delivered to my cell. During the interrogation, I had no hunger and no idea how long I spent with Inspector Clarke; it didn't seem like such a long time. After our frank discussion, a tray was brought with dinner: a simple meal of boiled potatoes, peas, some indeterminate meat, and a pot of tea. Whoever the cook was had not yet discovered salt and pepper, so the meal was without taste. No one came to collect the tray, so I slipped it under the bench and then lay down on the bunk. *Why isn't there a pillow? I wondered. Do they think I might use it to smother myself? Maybe I could use it to try to suffocate the guard?*

I rolled over onto my stomach and folded my arms under my head. I tossed back and forth trying to find a comfortable position. I fell asleep after giving up the struggle. My tired, aching body had to have sleep.

I woke when I heard the door open. I had slept with the light on all night. I was more worn out than I was willing to admit to myself. The guard had changed. I guessed he might be all of twenty-five and so thin if he turned sideways, he risked disappearing. His head was shaved, but he sported a small, neat, black mustache. The tray he carried in had tomatoes, beans, and two hard-boiled eggs. The beans were white and tasted like paste. I could only manage one spoonful and spit out the small bite I tried. I wasn't allowed a fork or knife so had to cut the tomato with my spoon and scoop it up. The back of the spoon proved to be the perfect tool to crack the egg so I could peel it.

When delivering breakfast, the guard failed to take the dinner try, so when I finished all the breakfast I could tolerate, I slid that tray underneath the bench, too. Soon there was a stench in my cell from the unconsumed food. Other than letting me figure out how long I had been held, there was no point to the meals, because I didn't have an appetite. To pass the time, I relived my walks with Mairin on the Dingle Peninsula and Blasket Island. Sitting in a cell in Belfast, the memories were both a distraction and a painful reminder. The cell was a thousand miles and many lifetimes away from the joy of finding and falling in love with my new-found life partner. The memories proved to be self-torture, so I forced myself to think about anything else.

Working on my memoir was the perfect substitute. As I organized incidents and chapters in my mind, I felt a growing uneasiness, which blossomed into gut-wrenching fear. I might not live to finish this book. My life would be left as a question mark and my search for redemption unfulfilled!

The sound of the door opening shook me out of the spiraling abyss I was trapped in. A deep baritone voice announced: "Visitor."

"Visitor? I didn't think anyone knew I was here?"

I heard Mairin's deep, sonorous voice. "Ian, the world knows you're locked up in this dreary cell, and they are appalled."

I thought for sure I was deep in a delusion. Mairin couldn't possibly be here. I rubbed my eyes and tried to focus.

"I'm here to get you out of here. You're being released immediately. Oh God, you look decimated. Have you eaten? Are those trays on the floor your meals? You should read the stories about your jailing in *The Times* and the *Independent*. I think you'll find the *Independent* particularly interesting."

"Ian, all the charges against you are dropped. We're leaving now. I have my car. Someone called Brennan gave me directions to the coast. He said you'll recognize the drive. I've been told to drive you there. I can't say that I understand any of this. My intuition is that Brennan is concerned for your safety. I do hope you recognize where we are headed. Now, let's go."

Mairin and I followed the guard through a maze of gray, windowless hallways to the back of the building. As we drove away, I saw a group of people standing in front of the main entrance of the police station. They were holding placards that read: "Free Political Prisoners," "Ian Murphy – Innocent," "Shame on the RUC," "Murphy's been framed."

I blinked several times to make sure I was reading the placards correctly. "Interesting," I mumbled.

"Ian, slouch down a bit until we get out of town. It would be better if you weren't seen."

"Where are we going?"

"West, you're supposed to recognize it, remember?"

While Mairin drove out of the city, I looked at the headline in the *Independent*:

Author Ian Murphy arrested in connection with Omagh Bombing

The byline was by Eileen Donohue. As usual, the article was both well written and well researched. It was clear Eileen had some inside contacts at the RUC. Who knew, it may even have been Inspector Clarke. The article predated the charges being dropped and my release. However, in her article, she speculated that there would be no reason to hold me, and she anticipated that I would be released soon. My guess is that she was told I'd be freed and told to not print it unless she wanted to be cut off from her inside sources. I chuckled to myself that

I was still providing headlines for her. Oh, how she must just wallow in that. It took all the self-control I could muster to read the article without displaying some emotion that Mairin would detect. Everyone in Ireland knew that it was Donohue's article that had sent me into hiding and exposed my role in the Provisional IRA. What Ireland didn't know was that Eileen Donohue and I had once been lovers. Just thinking about our relationship sent chills up my spine.

"What do you think of the Donohue article?"

I cleared my throat before answering: "It's accurate."

"Oh, Ian, is that all you can say?"

"Don't you boil over in anger when you read anything by that Donohue woman?"

"There was a time when I was angry. That has passed. She was doing her job."

Mairin looked at me and took her eyes off the road for longer than made me comfortable. "Ian, you are a forgiving person, aren't you?"

I folded the paper neatly and then tossed it in the back seat. "Well, if it hadn't been for her investigative piece on me, maybe you and I wouldn't have met. That would have been tragic."

Mairin threw her head back and laughed out loud. "You're such a sweet man, Ian Murphy. That's why I love you so."

I smiled and looked around the countryside to determine where we were. I noticed by the clock in the car that we had been driving about forty-five minutes when the road landscape became familiar. "We're heading to Donegal Bay," I announced, "Kieran's family home."

"Who's Kieran; I haven't heard you mention that name before."

I sighed, "Well, it's a simple question but not a simple answer. Where can I start?"

"Well, start with how you met."

"We met when I was in my third year at Trinity College."

"Lord, you've known this man a long time."

"Yes, he made it possible for me to join the Provies."

"That's an odd way to say it. Did he recruit you?"

"No. I volunteered, after my first and best friend in life, Timolty Doyle, was killed in a Provie raid in Belfast back in '71. Kieran Fitzpatrick came into my life, was kind, understanding, and offered me the chance to avenge Timolty's death. I accepted his offer. Hand me those directions, I need to study them."

I took the paper from her, unfolded it, and read the list of turns, stops, and roads. They led directly to the Fitzgerald family cottage off Donegal Bay. "Who did you say gave you these directions?"

"Oh, I don't really remember. It was a young man. Came to the library and said I needed to collect you and take you to this place. He said his name was Brennan. Do you know anybody named Brennan?"

"My darling, this is Ireland, we all know somebody named Brennan."

The sky in the west became noticeably lighter. I rolled down my window and took in a deep breath. "Do you smell that? It's the Bay, we're close. The cabin is well off the beaten path, so it will take at least another thirty minutes. Do you want to stop for an early supper?"

"I can't honestly say that I'm hungry now."

"Don't worry; my guess is the cabin will be fully stocked with both food and alcohol."

The road wound around and came close to the Bay and then turned inland again. At the end of the last road stood the Fitzgerald cabin. The door to the car park was open. "Drive right into the car park," I instructed her.

"That's bold."

"The open door is a signal. They want us to pull in. No use noticing an unknown car is at the family cottage."

Mairin pulled in as instructed. "You're kidding me? You spent far too many years in the IRA. You're telling me this is all planned and there's some purpose to coming here?"

"Yes."

I climbed out of the car and grabbed our bags from the boot. As I walked to the rear door of the cabin, I could see the Bay off in the distance. The last time I was here I was hiding from the world and trying to avoid being arrested as a traitor. This time I was here after being arrested and surviving the shakedown for information from the RUC. The irony wasn't lost on me. As I stood in the kitchen, memories came to me like the tide coming in off Donegal Bay. I heard the door slam behind me.

"I didn't mean to be rude. I should have gotten the door for you."

"Don't bother; it's clear this cabin brings strong feelings for you."

"It was the low point of my life. I don't like admitting that I considered ending my days when I was at this cabin. Some days, I consumed two full bottles of whiskey and had little if any food. I was probably too drunk to kill myself, unless of course, I would slip on the rocks and fall into the Bay and drown."

Mairin stood behind me, wrapping her arms around my waist and pulling me tight. I heard her crying and working to muffle the sound so that I wouldn't hear her. "Those were hard times. They're over now." I set down the bags and headed for the kitchen. "Let's check the food supply."

As I predicted, the refrigerator had a variety of meats and cheeses, butter, and casserole dishes. I even spotted my favorite desert, New York-style cheese cake. Mairin opened the cabinets and found a variety of canned goods, coffee, tea, candles, and matches. Everything gave the impression that someone had stocked the kitchen recently and by someone who knew me very well. It was almost as if Kieran Fitzpatrick had done the job himself. Chills ran up my spine just thinking about the possibility that Kieran could have been the mastermind behind this escape.

"How about a walk to the Bay?" I asked.

"After that drive, a walk is in order."

We followed the well-worn path that led to one of the most unique landscapes in all of Ireland. At the edge of a grass field, it ended abruptly and rather than a beach, the ground was a field of stones.

"What is this place, Ian?"

"It's called Bloody Foreland Point."

"It looks both beautiful and hazardous. Can you walk on them?"

"It takes a bit of skill, but it can be done."

"Have you?"

"Yes, when I was here alone, I challenged myself to walk to the water. It's not easy."

"Let's try now," Mairin suggested.

We held hands, working to keep our balance on the stones as we made our way to the shore. Our shoes, with thin leather soles, were not suited to rock walking. We took a series of small steps, beating to windward until we reached the water's edge. Mairin bent down and cupped the seawater in her hand. "It's cold!"

I laughed one of those deep belly laughs, wondering what else she expected. The salt air filled our lungs as the sun slipped to within a few degrees of the horizon on its daily journey into the Atlantic. From behind me, I heard someone shouting my name. At first, I thought it was my imagination. The voice sounded familiar. I heard it again, this time with some urgency: "Ian Padraic Murphy!"

Mairin and I turned around at the same time. I squinted to look at the figure at the edge of the rocks. The man was squat and square-built with wisps of red hair flying in the breeze and a flush, worn face. His hands were cupped to his mouth ready to shout again.

"Kieran? Kieran Fitzpatrick?" I shouted in his direction and began running toward him, disregarding the treacherous stones. I left Mairin standing at the water's edge.

SIXTEEN

I nearly tumbled three times trying to navigate the soccer-ball-sized stones and for a moment forgot my own clumsiness. As I got closer to Kieran, I could hear his hen-like cackle of a laugh as he bent over and slapped his thighs. I spread my arms out, preparing to grab him with both arms. I bumped into him with a rush, my arms clamped tight around his arms, and my momentum forced Kieran off his feet, falling backward into the grass. I landed on top of him with a thump and felt myself bounce off his stomach like a trampoline. His laughter was infectious, and I joined him in a great belly laugh.

"Jesus, I can't believe it. Kieran Fitzpatrick! Did I hurt you? You don't have to worry about the Provies taking you out—you only have to worry about klutzy me."

Kieran wiggled his arms free and pushed me off to one side. "I take it this means you're happy to see me?"

"Ian, you can move a lot faster than I expected," Mairin said as she walked up behind us. "Not bad for a middle-aged man."

I rolled over onto my back to look at her and then took a sideways look at Kieran lying beside me. "It's not me that's full of surprises, it's Kieran Fitzpatrick here that's the grand prize winner of surprises. Oh, yes, Mairin McCarthy, please meet Kieran Fitzpatrick, my friend for thirty years. At first sight, I thought he was a ghost but here he is, in the flesh."

"Mr. Fitzpatrick, a friend of Ian's is a friend of mine." Mairin offered Kieran a handshake.

Kieran took Mairin's hand into both of his and with great care, shook hands. "Yes, it is my pleasure."

I got up, dusted myself off, and offered Kieran a hand getting up. His chubby, freckled hand fit into mine and felt like a vice grip. I yanked with all my weight to help him break the earth's hold on him.

"I don't understand this, Kieran. Why are you in Ireland? I'm excited but also terrified that you've put yourself in grave danger being here. Did you think I needed to be saved again? Didn't think I could handle a RUC interrogation?"

Kieran slapped me on the back and turned me in the direction of his family vacation cottage, while hooking Mairin's arm to walk beside us. "So many questions, my friend, so many questions. I understand how your mind works. Trust me, I'll explain everything. Now, let's put on a pot of tea. Later I've got someone coming to cook us dinner. We can talk until the sun rises tomorrow, if you like."

I hunched my shoulders and looked at Kieran as he peered straight head, toward the cottage. "So we're all staying the night?"

"Yes, you're both my guests."

We entered the cabin through the kitchen door. Kieran filled the teapot and put it on the stove. I grabbed three mugs out of the cabinet and set them on the stove next to the kettle. Mairin found the sugar in the cupboard and looked in the refrigerator for cream.

Kieran was the perfect host. He made the tea and took a tray into the sitting room. He handed both of us a mug and gestured for us to have a seat on the couch while he sat in the overstuffed chair directly across from us. He lit a cigarette, blowing the smoke toward the ceiling. "Might as well have a pipe, Ian, I have an incredible story to tell. Mairin, I hope we don't bore you."

"Before we start, there is one thing I must tend to. Can I use your telephone?" I asked.

"She already knows," Kieran offered without explanation.

"Who knows what? Don't talk in riddles, Kieran Fitzpatrick."

Kieran leaned back in his chair and gave Mairin a wink. "Caitlin, of course. She knows you've been released and you're safe. Couldn't let her know you're here, though—security, you know."

My mouth dropped open. I looked at Mairin and back at Kieran again, then scratched my beard. "Jesus, you do take care of everything. Thank you, Kieran. Did you talk to Brianna, too?"

"Come, come, Ian. I didn't talk to Caitlin myself. I'm still not her favorite person, plus I have my own security to mind. No, someone she trusts implicitly gave her a message in person. It was the safest way."

"Ok, so who gave her the message?"

"Mickey O'Shay."

I broke into a broad grin hearing Mickey's name and knew that Kieran had, in his own unique style, taken care of me once again.

Mairin blew on the mug of tea before taking a cautious sip. "There is nothing about Ian's life that bores me. I'm sure I'll find your story extraordinary."

"Well, Ian, I hate to tell you, but when I left you in your cabin the day after the vote on the referendum and our evening celebration, I intentionally gave you the impression I was leaving Ireland, most likely for the rest of my life. That was for your protection. If you were picked up for questioning by either the RUC or the Provies, you could honestly say I was somewhere overseas and that would pass a lie detector test."

Kieran stubbed out his cigarette in the ash tray on the arm of his chair and lit another.

"Always the strategist, my friend."

"Damn right. Actually, I traveled to a room I keep at the Kilbeggin Distillery, dead center of the country, where no one would expect me. If needed, I could work a few shifts and blend in with the workers, who are always discrete. I have a look-alike I sent off to Scotland. Anyone who knows me knows I wouldn't go to someplace like Argentina or some city on the continent like Brussels. I'm from the rural area and wouldn't be comfortable hiding out in some city. My "double" is enough not like me that someone following me would conclude I was trying to disguise myself. In fact, I hid in plain sight, didn't change a thing about my appearance."

I tamped the tobacco down in my pipe and lit it again. I was so engrossed with Kieran's story I had let it go out. I glanced at Mairin; her tea must have been cold because she set it on the table without finishing it. My guess she too was taken in by Kieran's tale.

"The plan worked so well that in a few days, the word on the street was that the IRA Council didn't want to expend any more manpower searching for me. A lifetime of loyalty had meant something. It was also the signal that they realized the world had changed, and IRA no longer had a mission; it was obsolete."

"How long did you stay in Kilbeggin?" I asked.

"A fortnight or so. I wanted time to watch how things developed in Belfast and to make some decisions for myself. Mairin, I have no wife or children. What was I to do? The Provisional IRA was my life."

I leaned over toward Kieran and dumped out my pipe tobacco into the ashtray. "Oh, Kieran, you must have been so lonely, I wish I could have been there for you. Not that I was any better off. If it wasn't for Mairin, I'd still be a dismal soul without purpose."

"Enough of this tea. I think it's time for a drink. Ian, I've got a stockpile of Midleton for you. Mairin, what can I offer you?"

With a broad smile she answered, "Ian has already spoiled me; a small Midleton would be fine."

"There's a good start to the evening! Midleton all around. I'll give a quick ring to Ryanne to come fix our supper."

While Kieran was out of the room, I took Mairin's hand and stroked it with long, intimate strokes. I lost myself in her hazel eyes.

"I like how you stroke my hand, but Ian, you appear totally distracted by your own thoughts." Mairin leaned in and kissed me gently on the lips.

Mairin dropped her chin and stroked her hair back, avoiding eye contact. A flair of red appeared on her neck and grew steadily toward her cheeks until her entire face was bathed in pale rose.

Kieran came into the room at some point and neither of us heard him. He might have witnessed our whole exchange; I didn't know and wasn't going to ask. "Well now, there's a special moment. Jesus, Ian, you actually look happy. It becomes you. Mairin, I hope that we can become friends, too. I think you have saved my friend's life."

"Kieran, I look forward to our friendship. You mean so much to Ian, and as you tell your story, I'm beginning to understand why. You are a very unique man."

Kieran set the tray with three tumblers on the table. He passed one to each of us and took one himself.

"Now wait, I have a toast. To peace in our time and joy in our lives."

"Here, here!" Mairin and I raised our glasses and clinked them with Kieran's.

Soon mouth-watering smells floated out from the kitchen, and I realized I had not eaten yet. I began to fidget in my seat. I was so hungry and didn't want to wait any longer. A young woman with long red hair came out of the kitchen and placed a traditional white soup tureen with a lid and ladle on the table. Next, she brought out an enormous loaf of fresh baked bread and a plate with a slab of butter the size of a deck of cards. I looked at Kieran, then Mairin, a smile growing on my face. "Only one more dish for the perfect meal," I said.

Kieran swallowed the remaining whiskey in his glass in a single gulp and almost choked as he laughed. "Patience, Ian."

Our redheaded cook burst through the kitchen door and placed a huge bowl of colcannon—traditional mashed potatoes with cabbage—on the table and pushed a wooden serving spoon into the bowl. She turned to us and announced: "Supper."

I couldn't contain myself. I forgot all my manners and jumped up, getting to the table in a few strides. I left poor Mairin sitting in the chair still holding her half-full tumbler of whiskey. Out of the corner of my eye, I saw Kieran stand and motion for Mairin to take a seat. He pulled the chair out for her and then took a seat himself. "Well, I see Ian still has some of the graces of civil life to learn."

"Mairin, may I serve you?" Kieran asked in a soft, mischievous voice.

Mairin picked up her plate and handed it to Kieran, who stood and removed the lid of the tureen. Steam drifted out with the fragrance of lamb, carrots, onions, and peas in a deep, rich broth. He served two ladles. "Oh, that's enough, Kieran."

"Ian, give me your bowl. Why don't you cut the bread for us?" I did as instructed and made sure to pass the plate with cut slices around the table before helping myself. I was ravenous and dug into the stew, not looking up before it was half gone.

"Who is our cook, Kieran?" Mairin asked.

"Oh, Ryanne. She's my cousin's daughter, raised in a pub. Cooks like an angel, don't you think?"

"Yes, this is wonderful. Why don't you ask her to join us?" Mairin asked.

"How kind. I will."

Ryanne brought a plate and utensils for herself from the kitchen, and her broad smile said she was pleased to join us. Kieran was the gentleman and made introductions and led the conversation while I finished one bowl of stew, then helped myself to another without asking. I spooned a large serving of the colcannon into the bowl and mixed the two together. I was aware that Kieran, Mairin, and Ryanne were having a conversation but it was a blur to me. Two days without edible food had been too much. After my stomach was full, I threw my napkin on the table and looked at each of my dining companions.

Ryanne smiled and offered: "I have strawberries and cream, if you like."

"I apologize, Ryanne; I am not usually this unfriendly. Mairin, Kieran, please forgive me if I was rude or inconsiderate. Hunger clouded my judgment, temporarily. Ryanne, you are an excellent cook. Strawberries and cream would be the perfect conclusion to the meal."

"We understand, darling," Mairin said. "Why do you think Kieran arranged for your favorite meal? Even I understand he is taking care of you again, bringing you to a place where you won't be badgered by the press and you can recover from your ordeal with the RUC. I can't remember when I've had the pleasure of eating strawberries and cream. Ryanne, Ian is right, this was a delicious meal."

I noticed Kieran was listening to our conversation intently, and he was definitely intrigued with Mairin. "Mairin, you are a very insightful person. Let me speak frankly. You are exactly the type of woman Ian needs. Jesus, Mary, and Joseph, I wish he had met you long ago; that mess with that Donohue woman could have been avoided. But we can't change history, can we?"

"Now, I need a small bit of solitude. Please enjoy dessert. You two can get better acquainted. I'm off to Murvagh Beach for a stroll." I excused myself and fetched my hat and walking stick from the boot of the car. I walked directly west, letting the sun guide me to the edge of Ireland. Even though Ireland was an island, it had very few beaches and even fewer white sand beaches like Murvagh Beach. I followed the winding walking path from Kieran's cottage to a small woods, the shade giving me a shiver.

The walk to the beach took a short time, and the sun dropped only several degrees on its journey to nighttime. The beach stretched out in an "S" shape to my left and right as far as I could see. It was the time of the evening when tourists retreated to the cottages and struggled to light a peat fire, most unsuccessfully without assistance from a Donegal native. There was a special skill in knowing when the peat was dry enough to catch and hold a flame. It was all in the scent, and when you ran your finger along the edge and a bit crumbled in your hand, you knew it was dry enough to catch a flame. Any other peat is too wet to burn.

Because I have lived on my own for almost fifty years, I'm most comfortable reflecting on my daily experiences by myself or maybe through my writing. I don't keep a journal. I've tried many times, but it just isn't in me. Keeping a journal requires a level of self-absorption I don't possess. Committing my experiences renders them permanent and exposed to anyone who may read it. I couldn't bear that much exposure, it would be worse than lying naked on this beach.

The salt air of the Atlantic on the western edge of Ireland was cleansing for me. It was the same thing I experienced several years ago when I hid from the world after the traitor Eileen Donohue exposed my life in the IRA. It was the only time in my life when I intentionally drowned myself in a bottle of whiskey a day. I was trying to numb the pain of being betrayed. It didn't work. Whiskey was only temporary, and when its numbing effects wore off, the pain was still there, grinding away.

I walked north on the beach, letting the sun warm me on the left and the early evening cool me on the right. The contrast was exhilarating. The tide was coming in, lapping the sand and inching its way up the beach. The wind kissed my cheek like Mairin's sweet lips. Perhaps I should have invited her to walk with me? On the other hand, I did want her to learn to be friends with Kieran; that was important to me.

As I walked, I kicked up sand and watched it fly a short distance and land a bit farther inland. The tide came in and went out every day without any intervention from man. So many things in our world happened on their own, guided by some special intelligence shared by all of life. How was mankind a part of this life magic? Mankind's volition was more of a hindrance than a gift. Mankind was not deft at making good decisions. Even if we were selfish and acted only in our own interests, would we engage in war, would we pollute, steal, cheat, lie, betray?

I felt outrage when I read about the Omagh bombing. It seemed like a personal offense at my contribution to the peace process in Northern Ireland. That was my ego screaming, not rational thought. Rushing to Omagh was foolhardy. All I had accomplished was to put myself in jeopardy of being the target for some dedicated RIRA volunteer to make his mark with my death. How many times could Kieran Fitzpatrick protect me from myself? Kieran's being alive is a message, it must be.

The light began to fade, and the sky turned from light blue to gray. Darkness was not far off. The sky was cloudless, so the array of stars would be magnificent, something I wanted to share with Mairin. The stars were different in Donegal than they were in Cork.

The ocean swallowed up half the sun and darkness was lowering, like someone was pulling down a shade of a window. I quickened my pace because I feared losing my way back if I had to walk only by moonlight. I dashed through the small wood and saw the lights of the cabin like a beacon. From a distance, I could hear music and laughter. Friends, laughter, and music was how life should be. I broke into a slow jog and came to a sudden stop outside the cabin door. My entire future is beyond this door.

"Hello! That was a grand walk! Kieran, we need to talk."

SEVENTEEN

"Ian, was your walk refreshing?" Mairin asked as she sipped her whiskey.

"It was what I needed. I'm a creature of habit, and I needed to be alone to think through some things. I'm sure Kieran's been the perfect host and you've had a chance to get to know each other a bit. That's very important to me. And I'm so relieved that Kieran is safe among us but at the same time, I'm perplexed."

Kieran was entertaining Mairin in full Fitzgerald fashion with traditional music in the background and stories of the Fitzgerald clan that could take days to tell. I noticed the stack of vinyl records piled on the floor in front of the full-cabinet stereo. I picked up the first one, the Chieftains, as was the second and third and fourth. "Are all of these Chieftain records, Kieran?" I asked and winked at Mairin.

"You know they are."

"Do you own every record they've released?" I was curious.

"Indeed," Kieran replied.

"That is remarkable, Kieran," Mairin said.

I sat on the sofa and patted the cushion next to me, hoping Mairin would join me. Always alert, she smiled and sat next to me, gently rubbing the back of my neck as she sat down.

My tobacco pouch had just enough for one last pipe for the evening. I couldn't recall if I had more tobacco, and we were far away from my tobacconist in Cork. I may need to resort to smoking Kieran's cigarettes. Mairin has never seen me smoke cigarettes and I wasn't sure how she would react to it.

Cigarettes have a completely different smell from my hand-crafted pipe tobacco. I may need to call in an order and ask him to deliver it if we are going to stay more than a day. I packed my pipe as tightly as I could. Soon the bowl was glowing red and I filled the sitting room with smoke.

"I am perplexed, Kieran, how can you be so sure the Provies still don't have a price on your head? Could it mean I'm home free as well?"

Kieran bent over the stereo, trying to stack several records onto the changer so he wouldn't need to get up to add a disk each time one finished. It gave me the impression we were in for a long talk. Before now I wasn't aware that Kieran was a fan of traditional Irish music. Although we've been friends for thirty years, most of our time together has been devoted to working on the cause of reuniting Ireland and now that cause was part of history. I hoped that Kieran would be able to make the transition to the brave, new Ireland that must be created. I heard mumbled swearing under his breath and he glanced back at Mairin and me with desperation on his face.

"Oh, Kieran, let me help you with that," Mairin offered.

Kieran sat down and lit a cigarette. "It's damn embarrassing that I can't even work a stereo in my own cottage. I've missed out on most of the mundane parts of life; I hope to have time now to learn a few."

Mairin turned around and smiled at both of us. "There it is, all set."

"Thank you, Mairin. Maybe sometime you can show me the trick."

"Of course."

"Kieran, we all have fresh drinks, there's a half a bottle of whiskey left, and I've got enough tobacco for one good long pipe, so let's hear your answer." I leaned forward, putting my elbows on my knees and holding the whiskey glass with both hands, my pipe clinched between my teeth.

"Well, like I said, I stayed at Kilbeggin for several weeks and melded into the group. I never received a signal from my double in Scotland that he had any trouble or was being watched. It was unnerving. I expected the hit to be made soon after they discovered you were still roaming the earth. You must have remained out of sight for at least three days like I asked."

"Oh, I was very careful. I wanted to make sure you had a chance to get out of Ireland. At least that's what I guessed you were doing," I explained.

"My plan was based on your believing I would leave Ireland. I knew you would stay low to give me the three days. You were superb. I also bet my life that Dolan Halloran and the rest of the Council would also assume that I would weasel off our little island as quick as I could.

"One fine Monday morning, I was shocked to see Dolan at the distillery at the beginning of the first shift. I pulled down my hat, pulled my collar up high, and slid in with a group of the fellas hoping not to be noticed. But my deception didn't work. A voice bellowed above the din of conversation: 'Kieran Fitzpatrick!'

"I stopped in my tracks, turned around to face Dolan Halloran staring directly at me. He wouldn't take the chance of injuring any of the workers, so I knew I was safe for the moment. 'The office, if you please, Kieran.' Dolan pointed toward the back. He walked ahead of me, reaching the office door marked in gold lettering: Mr. Taylor, Floor Manager.

Dolan held the door open for me and shut it with a slam as he followed me in. He sat at the oak desk made from used whiskey barrels and told me to sit as well. For what seemed like an eternity, we stared at each other without speaking. I'll never forget his first words. 'It's over then, isn't it?'

"I held my breath waiting for the bullet to end my days. Nothing happened. My mind raced, trying to figure out how he knew I would be at this safe house. It could have been dumb luck, or maybe he had already searched several others and just happened to find me that day. Dolan was the only other member of the Council who knew the location of all the safe houses. We had to keep security tight, and it worked for thirty years, didn't it? I couldn't figure out what he meant by saying 'it's over then, isn't it?' I began to sweat and it rolled down my cheeks. Without warning, Dolan broke out in an uproar of laughter, 'I scared the shit out of ya, didn't I?'

"What would you expect? I screamed at him. This is a fine place to do it, isn't it? Then I had a flash of insight. Dolan wasn't there to do the job, even though it would make sense for him to give himself the assignment because it would be only right that a member of the Council take out another member. I felt the tension melt away, and I slumped in my chair.

"Dolan explained what he meant was that the Long War was over. He was as tired of the bloodbath as I was, as tired as you too, Ian. In fact, what he called your defection is what made him reconsider everything. He decided that if you could change horses and work with Sinn Fein and peace, then all of us could. He told me he officially disbanded the Provisional IRA and instructed everyone to turn in their weapons. He couldn't promise Sinn Fein that the boys would give up their guns, but he even put it in writing so that he had credibility. You know, he gave me the impression he was relieved that it was over.

"Setting up a separate Northern Ireland government, separate from Britain and not a puppet government run through Britian's Whitehall, was critical. If the two Irelands couldn't be united, at least Northern Ireland had the right to independence. He said he wanted to have time to get to know his grandchildren. Hell, I didn't even know he had grandchildren. He refused to work with Sinn Fein but told the Council that each man must make his own decision. Fergus Cruthers had contacted him, inquiring if he knew my intentions. The purpose of his visit was to pass along the message from Cruthers. With that, he got up, shook my hand, then gave me a bear hug. He never said another word and left the office.

"So, there you have it. I hooked up with Cruthers, and he convinced me I had a place in Sinn Fein. You gave us the framework for peace but there's a lot to do to make it come true. So this old soldier turned in all his weapons to be an example for the boys and prove to Cruthers I was serious. That's about it, then."

I gulped down my whiskey and set my unsmoked pipe on the table. I turned to look at Mairin. "My friend, you are an amazing man. A Sinn Fein man. Another miracle."

I turned toward Kieran.

"Kieran, I'm sure Sinn Fein could use your skills. With men like you, this government has a chance," Mairin said.

"What about you, Ian? What are you doing with yourself besides falling in love with an angel of a woman?" Kieran asked.

I rubbed my eyes and yawned. "Oh, me? I'm going to write my memoir. But I'm exhausted now. I couldn't sleep in that little cell. We can talk more tomorrow."

"Of course, I understand. Until tomorrow. Good night, Ian."

"Good night, Mairin...Kieran."

EIGHTEEN

When I woke, Mairin was lying on her side, head propped up on her hand, watching me and leaning toward me. I blinked a few times to focus. I could feel her breath kissing my face. She looked at me without smiling. I was lying on my back, the way I started the evening before. Sleeping on my back meant I was exhausted, not turning to either my side or my favorite position on my stomach. I touched my face; it felt warm. Mairin stroked my beard.

"You had unsettled sleep, darling. You were mumbling most of the night."

"Did I keep you awake?"

"A bit. I've been up a few hours, I guess. I felt the need to watch over you. Does your restless sleep mean it was difficult for you to return to this house?"

I turned my head toward the wall to avoid eye contact. "I'm not sure I realized it myself, not in depth. I'm good at avoidance."

"Don't be harsh."

Mairin snuggled closer and put her head on my chest. She let me have the silence of the morning, and I was grateful for her kindness and empathy. I let my mind wander freely without direction or focus. My breathing was shallow and my pillow damp and uncomfortable. Only a sheet covered me from my waist to my feet but felt as warm as if sitting in front of a raging peat fire on a November morning. Mairin reached over my chest and took my hand in hers, entwining her slim fingers with mine. We lay in silence. I stared at the ceiling. I felt like I was floating in a chamber cut off from all external stimuli.

I bolted up, pushing Mairin off my chest as I sat up straight. She was startled and caught herself from tumbling sideways off the bed. I propped myself up with both hands, my elbows locked. I looked to the left and then to the right. I felt a gurgling in my stomach.

"I need to get up, now. I need air. I'm going out." I said in a whisper.

"Give me a moment. I'll dress and go with you."

"That wouldn't be wise,"

"This place has demons for you, doesn't it? You have to exorcise your demons before you're consumed. I can't pretend to understand. I'll look for tea in the kitchen. I don't know if we should expect Ryanne this morning. I'll do a bit more exploring to find out what food we have. I could always go into town for a few of the basics. What do you think, Ian?"

While Mairin talked, I dressed without bothering to shower. I don't know why, but I felt like I had fallen into a sand pit and was slowly sinking away, being swallowed by the earth, never to be seen again. And I had an odd premonition that my writing career might be over. As the poet T.S. Elliot predicted, the world, or my world, anyway, was ending with a whimper and not a bang.

"Ian!"

I turned quickly to see a flash of anger cross Mairin's face. "I wish you would listen when I'm talking. It's rude, you know."

"I'll be hiking. Not sure how long it might be. Please, have breakfast. I don't mean to abandon you."

"Take your time, my love. I hope you conquer your satanic spirits and return to me renewed and vibrant again. Maybe too much to ask in a single morning? No matter, it's my fervent desire. Now, don't tarry, be gone." Mairin held my face with both her hands and shared a soft, tongue-touching kiss. I held her hands against my cheeks for a few moments and then left the room.

The day was bright, not a cloud in the sky. A short distance from the cabin, I felt the soft breeze off the ocean and the warmth of the morning sun warmed my back. I walked with purpose but took no notice of where I was walking. I felt like I was on automatic pilot. The world melted to a blur. My feet hit the earth, but I didn't sense I was striking solid ground. I hiked without effort. The French had a word for it—"flaneur." The rough translation was *loafer* or *idle stroller*. The French used the expression for exploring city streets, Paris at least.

While I was not exploring city streets, I was exploring the back roads of my own mind and my recent history. Life moved so quickly in those days, when I fled Cork after Donohue's article in the Sunday *Independent* revealing my clandestine life in the Provisional IRA. Kieran was certain my life hung in the balance as a betrayer to the Cause, to revengeful RUC, or to a British government demanding justice in the form of my trial and incarceration.

When last I ventured to this refuge by the sea, I was oblivious to all of those potential consequences of Donohue's exposé. My heart was pulled from my chest and devoured by the woman I thought I loved with every ounce of my being. My innocence in believing she loved me was like a living Greek tragedy. I had the judgment of a teenager having his first experience with lustful love, imagining it to be the real, life-changing love of a lifetime. There's a reason I've been a bachelor all my adult life. Worse than being a bachelor, I never sought relationships with women beyond casual acquaintances or a collegial relationship with other teachers at the university.

All of my drive, my passion, was poured into words, stories, and creating worlds that existed in my head and on the pages of my novels. In the surreal world, I controlled everything, absolutely everything. There was a great deal of comfort in living in such a world.

I stopped abruptly when I saw my feet had reached the edge of the path, the next step would have been into the Atlantic. I hadn't noticed any of the Irish landscape around me. I took in a deep breath of salt air and held it in my lungs as long as I could. I glared at the undulating water. The tide was going out. I wanted to let the tide take my grief and remorse and let it float away into oblivion. I looked down at my feet. This was the exact spot I sat when I plunged my hands into the water trying to scrub off the blood of guilt just months ago. I can't undo my role with the Provies. That's the curse. My atoning for my role in the IRA wasn't enough? I needed to be redeemed. How does a man buy back his soul? I can't carry this burden and write another word. She wants me to write my memoir? Is there really redemption in a memoir?

I jumped off the rock and fell to my knees in the sand. I thrust my hands into the sea, like I had before. The water was so cold that my hands became numb and turned as white as chalk. I pushed farther up to my elbows. The current splashed around my arms. It was so cold; tears came to my eyes and drifted down my cheeks, dribbling into the water. Chills went up and down my spine. I felt like passing out, letting my consciousness drift away with the tide. I caught my breath and swallowed as much air as I could. I lost focus and felt my weight shift and I doubled over, hovering just over the receding tide. A single thought exploded from the deepest part of my being—WRITE.

I pulled my arms out of the water and let myself fall backward. I landed on my back like a turtle on its shell. I opened my eyes wide. The sky was catalina blue. I couldn't feel my hands. I wailed out loud as if singing a keen for myself. I rolled over onto my side and curled up into the fetal position. I lay there until I felt my breathing normalize, and a tingling sensation confirmed my hands and fingers would work again.

Next, I found myself strolling on Murvagh Beach, and I had no recollection how I got there. Being late August, families were strung along the beach for their last holiday before school resumed. There were sandcastles being built too close to the water's edge that would soon be threatened by the incoming tide. Young women strutted about in bikinis with their too-fair Irish skin, unable to garner even a slight tan after a summer outdoors. The young men were no better off, sporting their Speedo swim trunks. Looking to the surf, I could make out a few surfers with black wetsuits. One had a red flash of lightening across his chest, a symbol reminiscent of a coat of arms.

I walked south along the beach until I reached the path that led back to the Fitzgerald cabin. As the French already know, being on a flaneur isn't idleness or mindless wandering. To the contrary, it's quiet, introspective, and objective. Objective in a way that lets a person observe the world and come to understand his own place in it. My limited excursion had really been a journey into myself, my interior, the dark core that exists in all people. For the past thirty years, I haven't been reflective about my writing. Writing for the Provisional IRA was for the purpose of reunifying our little country, regardless of whether my brethren in Northern Ireland desired it or not.

Working on the Good Friday Peace Accord was an education for me. Northern Ireland citizens didn't want to join the twenty-six counties in a single government, nor did they want to be governed from Whitehall. They wanted to have their own country recognized and have the right to rule themselves as they wished. How had I ignored that fundamental desire for my entire adult life?

I had never had urgency to my writing, like I would have stopped breathing if I didn't write for a day or two. Writing had been a way of life for me. Now I understand! Writing is how I will redeem myself. Being raised a traditional Irish Catholic, I was taught that redemption was something you purchase with your actions, your behavior toward others. That meant redemption was granted to a person from another person, an exchange. That was not my path. Writing is my redemption, and that is why I must pen my memoir. I think that Mairin instinctively understood this; it was her reason for suggesting I write my memoir in the first place. If I have ever had doubts that Mairin is my soul mate, they are banished forever.

I walked briskly back to the cabin, noticing that the sun was overhead and both Mairin and Kieran might be worried about me. As I got near to the cabin, my stomach groaned, reminding me I hadn't had breakfast and lunch would likely be served soon. The inside of my mouth was dry and a tall glass of water followed by a cup of Irish breakfast tea would be perfect.

"Ian! I was just about to call the Garda to begin the search for your body," Mairin blurted out when I came through the front door.

I grimaced. "Don't be melodramatic. I'm fine."

"Just kidding. You know, you look different somehow; I can't put my finger on it. Anyway, you must be famished. I'll put together a plate for you."

"Will you and Kieran join me for a bite?"

"Yes, I will, but Kieran is gone."

"Gone? Where did he go?"

"I don't know, Ian. I'm not his keeper. I hardly know the man. He keeps his own company, doesn't he?"

I collapsed into a chair at the table, too exhausted to help Mairin with the meal and wondered where Kieran might have gone. I shouted to Mairin in the kitchen, "Did Kieran mention when he would be back?"

"Don't try to have a conversation when we're in two different rooms. It's annoying. I'll be in shortly."

Mairin brought me a steaming cup of tea, which brought me back to my senses. "Sorry about trying to talk to you in the kitchen."

"I know. I'll be right back with lunch."

Mairin brought in a bowl of steaming chicken soup, cold meats, bread, and cheese. I fought the urge to slurp down the soup and waited for Mairin to return from the kitchen.

"When did Kieran say he would be back?"

"He didn't. That is, he said he wouldn't be back. He gave us strict instructions. We're to remain here for a day or two and then take our time returning to Cork. He thought it would be nice if we drove along the west coast, down to Dingle and then across to Cork. I like the idea myself. It could be our holiday before the students invade campus this fall."

While she planned my life, I mounded a few slices of meat and cheese on the bread and stuffed the sandwich into my mouth. "My car is still at the bed and breakfast in Omagh."

"No, it isn't."

"What?"

"Kieran said he had a man with a beard drive it back to Cork and park it at your cottage. Kieran said you would understand what he meant by that."

"Mm, yes."

"So, what does it mean, dear? I'm lost."

"He sent a decoy, so that the RUC and most importantly, the Real IRA thought I went home with my tail between my legs."

"Well, are you up for a short holiday?"

"Yes, it would be perfect, my love."

"My love?"

"Yes, my love. I can be packed and ready in less than thirty minutes."

NINETEEN

My lifelong experience had been that when Kieran Fitzpatrick gave specific directions, he intended them to be followed without comment or question. My guess was that he suggested to Mairin to take me on a road trip to keep me away from the press for a few more days. Over the years, Kieran and I have learned to use the twenty-four-hour news cycle to our advantage. By being intentionally inaccessible, I was waiting out the news cycle so that by the time I returned to Cork, most would have even forgotten that I had been arrested and interrogated in Omagh. As usual, Kieran's strategy was brilliant, and once again I owed him my life, literally. Having time with Mairin before our schedules would become unmanageable with the start of the fall term was perfect.

We threw our luggage in the boot and headed south from Donegal on the N 15. The first part of our road trip offered the perfect mixture of coastal landscape and mountain ranges. While I may not have been objective, Ireland was fiercely beautiful, and our trip promised to refresh me from head to toe.

Initially, we drove in silence, Mairin concentrating on driving and taking in the scenery as much as she safely could. Finally, curiosity welled up inside her and she spurted out a flurry of questions. "Where did you go on your walk this morning? Weren't you famished? I bet your memories of the articles in the Irish *Independent* distracted you from eating. Have you thought any more about my suggestion to write your memoir?"

My mouth dropped open. The dam had broken and all her pent-up questions spewed out, nearly drowning me. "Well, we should have enough to talk about. I'll try to answer all of your questions, if I can remember them, that is. You've been holding back on me. You know, if you want to know something, you don't have to wait and attack me with them all at once."

Mairin did a good job of being patient with me, concentrating on the road and not even acknowledging that I had said anything.

"Ian, it's not like you were available to talk. You're the one that spent the first evening listening to Kieran's tale and then the entire morning on your hike. You distinctly didn't invite me to hike with you, did you?"

"You're right. I'm guilty. We're going to have a lot of road time, so I'll answer all your questions. I'll start with why I went to Omagh."

Mairin nodded her head as I explained that I was furious when I learned of the bombing at Omagh. After thirty years of experience, it was clear it was a botched job and innocent people again paid the price for a dispute we just cannot seem to settle among ourselves. The Peace Agreement I worked so hard on was leaking violence like a sieve, four short months after the referendum. Peace had to be given a chance. The government of Northern Ireland must have time to organize itself and learn the ropes of self-government and self-determination.

I rambled on and somehow didn't even notice when we slid through Sligo. I decided to put my explanations on hold because I didn't want to miss Galway's famous bay. The homes in Galway and the famous Galway Bay Hotel hugged the shoreline of the natural bay. A good hard stone thrown from any of the structures along the bay would plop into the Atlantic Ocean. The breeze from the ocean was incessant, giving the town a fresh, clean smell and making the homes weather before their time.

"Let's stop in Galway for the evening. I've never been here. The seafood here must be fantastic."

"As it turns out, this is my first time in Galway too. I must admit, I haven't traveled very much around our island. It's a shame. My world has been so small."

"Have you been on the continent?" she asked.

"Never been off this rock."

"Oh, we've got to change that. I can hear Paris calling very loudly."

"Paris? Romance? Me?"

"Oh, don't be presumptuous."

"Let's see if there's a room at the Galway Hotel. The view should be rewarding. I wouldn't mind a walk along the shore before dinner; we've been cramped up in the car all day."

"Ian, are you tired of my company?"

"Absolutely not. I'm not one much for driving. Oh, look, take a right one block up. There's the hotel. It's larger than I thought. I hope it won't be a problem getting a room this time of year."

Sometimes having some minor celebrity was useful. The clerk had read several of my books, and we were not only able to get a room but were given one on the bay with a view that made both Mairin and me pause. I offered to sign any books he wanted to bring in while we were staying in Galway. While registering, I convinced Mairin we should stay for two nights to have the opportunity to relax and put Omagh completely behind us.

I let Mairin rest in the room while I scouted for a restaurant for dinner. I found it awkward to ask at the hotel for a recommendation when they had their own restaurant, so I solved my dilemma by asking if we could have breakfast served in the room the next morning. While it wasn't their common practice, they were willing to accommodate my request. After making breakfast arrangements, I asked about for a traditional Irish restaurant specializing in seafood. Without hesitation, the clerk suggested the White Gables.

"Would you like a reservation for dinner, Mr. Murphy?" the clerk asked as he straightened his tie, which fit too tightly around his neck.

"I would."

"And what time would you prefer?"

"Oh, let's say half seven. What time is it now?"

The clerk leaned around me to check the clock on the wall, "Looks like about half four, now."

"Good, that gives us time for a stroll. We've been crammed into our car all day. It's not healthy, is it?"

"Would you like a bottle of wine for the room tonight?"

"Young man, you are thoughtful. That would be perfect. Do you have Bordeaux, by chance?"

The clerk's grin spread across his face. "Yes, a fine French wine for the Irish author. It's a new world we have now. Would you like the wine before dinner?"

"No, I think not. Could it be taken to our room while we're out for a walk?"

"Of course. Thank you, Mr. Murphy."

When I returned to our room, I found Mairin staring out the window, mesmerized by the rolling ocean below us and watching several sailboats glide into the bay in search of their berths. I walked up behind her and slipped my arms around her waist. She had the sweet fragrance of magnolia. She took my arms and wrapped them tightly around her and leaned back into my chest.

"It's idyllic here, Ian."

"As much as I've spent a lifetime trying to reunify our island, I haven't seen very much of it. Looking back on it, I think that has been a mistake. I can't really say I know the people in the various regions. I suppose being a city on the water, Galway has something in common with Cork."

"Mm, maybe."

Mairin drifted off into her own thoughts and swayed left and right in my arms. The boat traffic in the bay was brisk; sailors liked to be in dock before the sun set, especially recreational sailors who don't have the experience of how the ocean changes. I thought I would inquire about renting a sailboat tomorrow and surprise Mairin with a little jaunt into the Atlantic. "I inquired about dinner, and there's a traditional restaurant with mouth-watering seafood called White Gables. Interested?"

"Ian Murphy, you have impeccable tastes. I would love fresh lobster drowning in butter and a plate of fresh vegetables."

"Well, I suggest we explore Galway for a bit of exercise and then we walk to dinner. If I understood the hotel clerk's directions, it should be easy to find."

The central city was a pedestrian district, with narrow, brick streets. Shops, restaurants, and pubs loomed up on both sides, allowing the river of tourists to flow through the city. Many of the restaurants staked out a patch of the street with fencing and set a few tables in the temporary enclosure where people could eat, drink, and people-watch as long as they would like. During the summer months, banners were strung between the buildings, giving the street a festival appearance. Buskers, the ever-present street musicians, were playing with their instrument cases open, ready to accept any tip a passerby might leave for the pleasure of their brief entertainment. Mairin and I stopped to listen to a cellist play.

"Isn't that the prelude from Bach's Cello Suite?" I asked Mairin.

Mairin patted me on the back as her smile caught me off guard. "You continue to surprise me, Ian. You've never mentioned that you're familiar with classical music."

I hunched my shoulders, "Well, it's never been a topic before. I'm quite old-fashioned. My preferences are few, traditional Irish music, a bit of Mozart, even a few of the American composers like Gershwin. *Rhapsody in Blue* speaks to the soul."

"As usual, you underestimate yourself."

"So, do you like Bach or the cello or both?" I wanted to learn as much about Mairin as I could. I found everything about Mairin interesting. It was clear she was cultured.

"Oh, definitely both. Actually, with the exception of Gershwin, our music preferences match well. I'm so pleased we share an appreciation for a variety of music. People's ability to sing, play an assortment of instruments, and compose is magical. I believe music makes us human, don't you."

"I do indeed."

The waiter came around to fill water glasses at all the tables.

"I can feel a distinct emptiness in my stomach. Let's go to dinner."

In a few minutes, we were at the restaurant asking for our table. The host was polite but firm: "Mr. Murphy, your reservation is for half seven and it's only seven now. I can check on a table for you or would you like to have a drink in the pub first?"

"The disadvantage of not wearing a watch is never knowing the time of day. I didn't intend to be rude. Mairin, what's your preference?"

"Oh, let's have a drink first."

The pub was intimate and large enough for only about twelve customers—often called a snug—with rich, homey tones, recessed lighting, and mahogany furniture identical to the restaurant. The atmosphere was warm and inviting. We sat at a booth for two. I ordered a whiskey and Mairin ordered something called the 'Pot of Gold,' a name I found disingenuous.

"I've not been one for cocktails. What is a Pot of Gold?"

"Oh, you whiskey drinkers can be stodgy. It's pear juice, several fingers of Jameson, and sparkling champagne with a twist of lemon. It's light and refreshing, especially in the summer, and I still get the whiskey."

I shook my head in wonderment. "I can't imagine why anyone would want to dilute a good snigger of Irish whiskey; it's close to a crime. But if you enjoy it, who am I to judge?"

"That's right, Ian, you shouldn't judge."

It wasn't long until the hostess found us and escorted us to the dining room. If this was traditional Irish, then it was upscale traditional Irish. The walls were wood-paneled, all the tables had fine linen clothes, and formal settings graced each table with wine goblets already set. The furniture was a beautiful mahogany, similar to the pub décor. Windows in the front lit the room, but by the end of dinner, the candles on the table would be needed.

I ordered baked brie for an appetizer that we shared. Mairin ordered the fresh lobster with an extra pot of melted butter. I had both fried oysters and a small plate of six or so oysters on the half shell.

"Mairin, would you order wine for us? From the wine you've purchased for our travels, it's clear to me that your knowledge is superior to mine."

She dropped her chin and blushed. "Thank you, Ian. That was kind of you to say."

"It's truthful. I try to be a man who knows both his limits and his boundaries."

The waiter brought us a wine menu. It looked large to me, but again, I was not the person to pass judgment. As long as there was Irish whiskey, I was content. But Mairin enjoyed a good glass of wine, and I needed to expand my horizons.

"We would like a bottle of the Saint Emillion, please."

"Who's Saint Emillion? I've not been a practicing Catholic, but I'm enough of a Catholic to be perplexed by that name."

Mairin laughed and shook her head. "Oh, you are a novice, aren't you? St. Emillion is a place, not a person. There's a story that a monk named Emillion founded the little town, but who knows. It's in the Aquitaine region of France. Many French wines bear the name of where the grapes are grown; it's the French way, you know."

"No, I didn't know, but I do now. You are so continental, so sophisticated. I can learn a lot from you."

"We're well-matched, Ian. I hope you enjoy our wine."

We chuckled and talked all through dinner. I was constantly amazed; I found Mairin the easiest person I've ever known to talk with. Other than my sister Caitlin, I haven't ever had more than a passing acquaintance with any women, the exception being Eileen Donohue. But that was a childish infatuation; I really didn't know her as a person. That was now painfully obvious.

After dinner, we walked down to the bay to watch the last boats come in, their lights mirroring off the surface of the water. Most drifted into their berths or tied up at a buoy and used a row boat to come to shore. We held hands as we walked and swung them back and forth like lovesick teenagers wanting to spend as much time together as possible before the parental curfew. A slight breeze came in off the ocean, and I could see goose bumps on Mairin's arm. I slipped off my jacket and put it around her shoulders.

"Thank you, Ian," Mairin tugged the coat closed. "I can smell your tobacco smoke."

"Mm, I suppose most everything I own is permeated with the odor of my tobacco. I hope it's not offensive. God knows, I couldn't give it up. I try to control it when I'm with you, however."

"I like it. Anything that brings you closer to me, I adore. You really don't need to change your habits. That wouldn't be fair of me to come into your life and start changing your lifestyle."

"I think you're teaching me about love."

Back in the warmth of our hotel room, Mairin returned my jacket and noticed the bottle of wine at the sidebar. "Oh, what is this? A French wine? Ian, you are a sneak. Are you romantic?"

I popped off the cork on the bottle as best I could and filled both of our goblets. I propped up several pillows, jumped on the bed, and patted the empty space next to me. Mairin kicked off her shoes, sat on the edge of the bed, and extended her arm around my neck while holding the glass of wine in her other hand.

"Shall we toast?"

I raised my glass to hers, "As light is to the eye, as bread is to the hungry, as joy is to my heart, may thy presence be with me, oh one that I love."

Mairin's eyes clouded over as we both took a deep drink from our goblets. She took the glass from me and set it on the sidebar. As she walked back to the bed, she unbuttoned her blouse and let it fall to the floor. She looked directly into my eyes as she removed the rest of her clothes and rolled on top of me. Her lips were eager and her tongue teased mine.

Her breath was hot and erratic. She lifted herself up onto her elbows, looked down at me and shook her head. "This won't do, I need to touch you." She unbuttoned my shirt, pulled off my pants, and threw them to the floor. "God, I want you. I want you, now."

I pulled her down on top of me and she somehow guided me inside her. "I need you in my life, my love," I whispered as our bodies melded together. I could feel moisture on her back, and she flowed over me like the tide lapping the seashore. Each motion was deeper than the last. I wrapped my arms around her back and held her as tightly as I could. I felt myself thrusting upward while she was pushing herself down on me at the same time. I felt like I was in a blast furnace, not able to catch my breath, when everything went black. I feared I might go unconscious. In that moment, time stopped.

Mairin let her body sink into mine, she rested her head in the crook of my shoulder and her arms held my head close. Our breathing became more regular but neither of us wanted to move. I worried that she would get cold, so I pulled the top cover over both of us.

She slid off of me and snuggled into a spoon shape next to my side with one arm draped across my stomach. Her breathing was regular and shallow.

"Mairin, when we return to Cork, I want you to move into my cottage."

Mairin had fallen asleep before hearing my offer for us to live together. She slept peacefully until we woke the next morning to the bellowing of the fishing boat horns as they trolled into the Atlantic for another day of work.

TWENTY

e meandered down the west coast of Ireland for three days before turning east toward Cork. I never mentioned moving into my cottage again. The days were pleasant and passed quickly. Something magical had happened that night in Galway, and our relationship transformed into tender, loving passion overnight. I had learned that wild, lust-filled love was very temporary; Eileen had taught me that.

Enduring love, I believed, required friendship, and Mairin and I were friends who grew into lovers. Friends share interests, life viewpoint, understanding, empathy, and most of all, laughter. Any relationship between a man and a woman that doesn't have the joy of frequent laughter was doomed for self-destruction. For the first time in my life, I felt at ease with a woman and safe to express myself without judgment or hidden agendas. I had always thought of myself as a trusting person, but my experience with Eileen Donohue changed that. Now, my relationship with Mairin was returning me to the Ian Murphy I knew.

Kieran Fitzpatrick told me in my twenties that people needed to earn my trust. His instruction ran contrary to my own natural lifestyle. I trusted people at first meeting and then, based on their behavior and our relationship, I learned if my judgment was justified. Kieran warned me that trusting first would result in my getting hurt. Until I met Eileen Donohue, trusting first had been a successful strategy, although I must admit, my interaction with others was limited. I was a solitary man, not a lonely man but a solitary one. Frankly, I enjoyed my own company. Creating a fictional world and characters was exhausting and working on those relationships was enough for me. Nonwriters often couldn't comprehend that the characters in my books were real, as flesh and blood as I was myself.

Mairin and I agreed, after returning to Cork, we both needed to devote substantial time to our work. Mairin was behind her self-imposed schedule to prepare the library for the fall term. I wasn't concerned about classes; I had gotten into a routine and had used the same material for years. I could walk into the classroom on the first day and begin. I used the Socratic method of teaching rather than lecturing. By college, I believed students were more than capable of reading literature on their own, without my bantering for hours in verbal Cliff notes to summarize the material. In my literature class, I preferred that they learn plot, theme, motive, and characterization by questioning, analyzing, and exploring every facet of the work during class time.

I don't read nonfiction and a few of my colleagues consider that a weakness because I don't give my students the opportunity to read nonfiction in my classes. I was so insistent in this that I have finally convinced the course catalog publisher to state in bold print that only fiction will be read. I didn't want the students to have any surprises.

I also felt urgency about beginning my memoir. Being so strict a fiction writer, I had to admit that I had never read a memoir. Sad, I know, but true. Initially, I really wasn't sure how a memoir differed from an autobiography. Mairin was very clear with me to suggest I write a memoir and not an autobiography. She knew me well enough to know that I would reject the notion of writing an autobiography out of hand.

Eventually, I learned that with a memoir, I could focus on my experience with the IRA and not worry about a chronology of my life events. I want to share my experiences leading a double life—one secretive yet intense—working with the Provies and not just share the events in my life. One concept I did clearly learn from Father O'Connell was that true redemption required a price. In my case, part of the price was to diverge from the world of fiction, and the other part was to be honest with my Irish brethren about my experience of the Troubles. I was no different from other Irish families in experiencing death of both friends and family for a cause, an idea. I learned while working on the Peace Agreement that a unified Ireland was just an idea that ignored the differences between us. In many ways, we didn't accept or respect Northern Ireland for the truth of what she was. This lesson was one I had to express in my memoir, and that would never happen in an autobiography.

I avoided talking with Mairin about my writing process for several weeks after our return to Cork. The energy she devoted to preparing for the term to begin was beyond my comprehension. I used her distraction to avoid talking with her about my memoir and concentrated on sharing cultural events, dinners, sailing, and walks. Among my few friends, I was well known for avoiding things I found difficult, and telling Mairin I may not see her for weeks while I was in the throes of writing, was at the top of my list of things to avoid. For some reason, I had also avoided having Mairin spend much time with Caitlin and Brianna. I should have known that Caitlin would call me to task.

It happened when Caitlin invited me for our traditional Sunday dinner after she and Brianna attended Mass. She didn't ask me to invite Mairin, which was my signal that we would have one of those "family" talks—something else I prefer to avoid if at all possible. Dinner went well. I learned about all of Brianna's summertime activities and her book club, when

Caitlin abruptly dismissed her. "Brianna, do you mind going to visit Brigid for the afternoon? You haven't seen her for at least a week."

Brianna wrinkled her nose and frowned. "Mom, I haven't seen Uncle Ian for at least a month. I can see Brigid in class any day."

"Brianna!"

Brianna shot out of her chair like a kangaroo, nearly knocking it on the floor. "Okay. I know, it's grown-up talk. See you later."

"Well, I suppose we should clean up. You've made me another delicious meal, the least I can do is wash the dishes," I offered.

Caitlin crossed her arms and looked me straight in the eyes. "Well, dear brother, I suppose you just are so absorbed that you didn't even think to at least give me a call when you returned from your little holiday. I thank God Kieran Fitzpatrick was good enough to let me know you were safe in Donegal and that he had given you instructions to take a holiday. Of course, I knew Mairin drove to Omagh to check in on you, but it took Kieran to tell me you two were on holiday together."

I squirmed in my seat and made myself busy hunting for my tobacco and pipe. "After-dinner smoke?" I asked with all the innocence I could muster.

"Of course. Now, I want the truth from you, Ian. Where is this relationship with Mairin McCarthy going? She's not moving in, is she? You're not moving to her place, are you?"

I blew a blue gray plume of smoke toward the ceiling and avoided returning Caitlin's stare. "No, no nothing like that. But I will tell you, I am in love with her and she with me."

Caitlin raised her eyebrows. "Plain, simple honesty from you. You are in love, aren't you? Amazing."

"This is nothing like the unmitigated disaster I had with Eileen Donohue. I know now, that was a middle-aged man, dumbstruck with infatuation for an intelligent, attractive woman. I know she used me."

Caitlin smiled and offered me a cup of tea. "You've learned a great deal about real life, brother. I like Mairin very much; she's lovely, isn't she?"

"She is. She's my lover and my friend. I'm very fortunate to have found her. If it hadn't had been for Father O'Connell's suggestion, I would never have met her."

"All right, then. And what's your future, you and Mairin?"

"Future? I haven't thought about the future. Right now, I have a job, and I'm writing my memoir."

Caitlin hunched her shoulders and shook her head as she sipped the tea, looking over her cup directly at me. "Memoir? You? Jesus, Ian, you write fiction. What possessed you to write a memoir?"

"This deserves a pipe, doesn't it?" I took my time ramming tobacco into the bowl to let me pull my thoughts together. Caitlin could be a demanding critic when she chose to be. Explaining my motivation to her would be critical. I flicked the head of the wood match with my thumbnail. With a deep inhale, I pulled the flame into the pipe bowl, creating a quick, hot burn that would keep my pipe light for an hour.

"As it stands, Eileen Donohue has control of my life's story. I've done as Father O'Connell instructed and atoned for my years with the Provies by hammering out the Peace Accord. It's not enough. For me to live out a normal, creative life, I must have redemption. The price I'm offering up is to write and publish my memoir. I'm going to limit my memoir to my life in the IRA; the secret revealed, if you will. Now, a part will need to include Brian's story and your move to Belfast. That was a double loss, Brian and then your betrayal to work for

Sinn Fein, at least that's how I saw it. Of course, I'll have you read and approve that portion of my manuscript.

"Writing is more than what I do, it's who I am. Writing my memoir will be the sacrifice I offer to seek redemption. I earned atonement by writing the Peace Accord, and I'll do the same to be redeemed. It may sound presumptuous, which is certainly not what I intend. I'll be quiet now. I'm interested in your viewpoint, or I'll try to answer questions you may have."

"Let's go into the sitting room where we can be more comfortable. The dishes can wait," Caitlin suggested. "Now, has your publisher approved this project? Will your readers care or even be interested in a memoir?"

I moved to the overstuffed chair and pulled an ashtray close. "I haven't talked to my publisher yet. I'm not ready."

"That's bold. What if your publisher won't go along with this insanity. What if they won't publish it?"

"I'll find another publisher."

"Just like that?"

"Just like that. It isn't negotiable. I'm writing my memoir. I'll find a publisher."

"Well, I agree, you won't have any problem getting it published. My sense is that the reading public is confused. You're a writer. Then you're a terrorist. Now you're a peace advocate. There are days I'm confused and I'm blood. I don't pretend to explain it to friends."

"There will be no apologies. No groveling. A straightforward memoir, this is my story—period."

Caitlin got up and walked to the sideboard for a bottle of whiskey and two glasses. "We need something a bit stronger than tea."

"You need to understand, I'm not asking for forgiveness from either my readers or the world. This will not be a *mea culpa* memoir." I took a long slow drink of the whiskey, feeling it burn its way down my throat.

"Your message is loud and clear. Will you let Mairin read the manuscript?"

"Of course."

"Ian, this, this wasn't your idea was it?"

"No." I finished off the whiskey and held up the glass. "Another?"

"Father O'Connell didn't instill this idea in you. No, that's not his way. So...Mairin?"

"Yes, it was Mairin's suggestion."

"I give her credit. In a short time, she has learned to know you well. Be careful, that woman can look directly into your soul."

"I know."

TWENTY-ONE

The day after my heartfelt talk with Caitlin, I dove into drafting my memoir. My first thought was to begin with the first time I met Kieran Fitzpatrick or, to be more accurate, the first day he barged into my life. I wrote about three pages and stopped in the middle of a page, in the middle of the first scene. It didn't feel right. It didn't feel in context. I paced back and forth in front of my desk. I've tried to put an area carpet there, but it was useless. I had worn a path into at least three carpets over the years. Now, I left the bare, unfinished wood exposed. The dark walnut had aged well, especially considering the abuse I'd given it.

Back and forth I went, trailing my fingers along the top of the desk and stealing a glance out the window but not seeing, not looking. Then the idea exploded in my head like it should have been self-evident. I would begin my story with the day Timolty visited me at Trinity. That will demonstrate both our friendship and the diverse paths we had taken. I received a general Leaving Certificate when I graduated from secondary school to apply for Trinity, the only college I would consider. Timolty left school with a Vocational Certificate even though he didn't have a clue on what vocation to pursue. After our graduation, poor Timolty was driftless, and I was following my dream with a ticket to Dublin. Timolty followed his da to work on the docks.

I printed out the first few pages I wrote and put them in a file marked "Memoir." Once written, I never threw anything away. I might decide to use it later, I might rewrite it, or I might use it for inspiration. No wasted words, that was my motto. I made myself a kettle of tea and returned to my writing room to relax and recall Timolty's experience when he had visited me at Trinity my first semester.

He was so uncomfortable; he felt he didn't belong. I tried to reassure him that was ridiculous, but I know I wasn't successful. Later I learned it was after that visit that he volunteered for the Cause. We were nineteen. He needed a purpose. He wanted to be useful. His job at the Verolme Dockyard wasn't suited for him. Like his father, he stood no more than five foot one and didn't have the strength or endurance to be a stevedore. Dock jobs ruined a man by the time he was thirty.

Like my family, Timolty's had a long history of Republican activity, at least back to his great-grandfather. Volunteering was in the Doyle family blood. Timolty couldn't help himself.

As I drafted my memoir, I could look back now and wonder why Timolty didn't talk about volunteering during his last visit to Trinity. He let me know how unhappy he was at the docks and his fear that he was just living his father's life, not his own. I must have tried to reassure him that he would find his own way, but to be honest, I couldn't remember.

I had reached a crossroads in my writing. It was both painful and frustrating. Recalling both your omissions and mistakes from college days on was like a public confession, and I didn't intend to make my memoir a plea for forgiveness. Trinity taught me that the best way to learn to write was to read. Read deeply, read extensively. I found myself on a journey to write a memoir and never had read one. I needed to talk with Mairin.

I rang her that afternoon. "How's your preparation at the library going, love?"

"Well, we returned just in time. I'll be ready for the fall term, but I had forgotten how much work it is. You distract me, Ian."

"Oh, I'm sorry."

"Don't be. I'm not that serious. Our time together is precious. I was resigned to the life of a widowed librarian. Now, I'm alive again. I'm in love. I'm in love with you, Ian Padraic Murphy."

"Aye, as am I you. Do you have time this evening to come out for a simple dinner? I need your help with my writing. Of course, I'd like to see you, I mean. You could stay the night."

Mairin didn't answer right away. I worried that I offended her or maybe she felt I was using her and only asking to see her to help me out. That would be both rude and selfish.

"You want my help with your book?" she blurted out in a high-pitched voice.

"Yes, of course. That shouldn't surprise you."

"But it does."

"Well, you need to get over that. I plan on asking you to be read my draft manuscripts, too. There's no one's viewpoint I respect more. Caitlin will be a reader, of course, because she's in it. I should ask Kieran too, same reason. You know, I don't even know for sure if Kieran has read any of my books. Mickey has, of course. He has signed copies on display at the pub. Mickey's a real promoter. Sorry, I digress so easily. Are you coming?"

"Of course."

"It will be a joy. I've realized I've embarked on writing a memoir without ever having read one. For a writer, that's suicide. I would like to hear your thoughts on memoirs you suggest that I read. I don't feel comfortable writing any longer without the experience of reading good works."

"Well, Ian, let me gather my thoughts. What if I come at seven? That will give me time to finish here and think of some suggestions for you. I assume you're interested in diverse works."

"Absolutely, seven will be perfect. This will be simple, just a bit of soup and bread. Maybe a little Dubliner cheese with toast to start."

"It will be perfect. I have to ring off if I'm going to make this schedule."

The wall clock chimed seven times and Mairin strolled through the rear door carrying a basket. She dropped the basket on the counter, then gave me a deep, open-mouthed kiss that could have gone on for the evening. She pulled back and held my face with both her hands. Her eyes danced, and she had the broadest grin I had ever seen. "There's the writer I love."

"I'm not sure we'll get to dinner with a greeting like that."

Mairin giggled. "Oh, we'll be disciplined. The soup smells delicious. Let's have our talk while we eat. I don't think I'll be able to resist you any longer after that, but I know we need to get some work done." She winked at me and turned toward the basket. "I thought I would contribute a few things. I bought an apple amber pie; I know it's your favorite. For starters, I have a smoked Gubbeen cheese and a Tipperary brie. I know one of your weaknesses is smoked cheese, among others."

"My most serious weakness is for you, and it's not a weakness, love never is."

Mairin giggled and flipped her hair back over one ear. "You tease. Now let's have a snack and we can begin talking about memoir as a genre."

I carried the tray into the sitting room and we sat on the love seat together. At nearly fifty years old, I finally knew why they were called love seats. I tasted the brie first; it melted in my mouth and left a delightful smoky aftertaste.

"What do you intend to write about in your memoir? You've never really said."

"I'm going to limit it to my IRA activities, and I've already talked with Caitlin. I'm going to include the fate of her husband Brian. Of course, Kieran will run throughout the story. I haven't talked with him about it yet. I must be careful not to reveal anything that must remain secret. I'm thinking of writing and then asking him to read it both for content and as an editor. I don't want my initial manuscript to be hampered by worrying about what I can and can't say. I'd prefer to get it all out and then cut material if needed."

Mairin took several bites of the Gubbeen before speaking. "Is that your approach to writing novels?"

"Yes."

"Good, I think it's important to work as you always have versus trying to change your work habits to accommodate a new genre. A glass of wine would do well, don't you think?"

I jumped up, embarrassed that I was a lackluster host. "You know, of course, I have no social graces. I think I have a white."

"Fine."

I rummaged through the refrigerator. Mairin had taught me to properly serve white wine, it should be chilled. I had no idea to what temperature; I was just not that sophisticated. On the top shelf in the back I found an unopened bottle of Pinot Grigio. Why did I have this bottle of wine? Had Mairin brought it previously and I never opened it? Some mysteries can remain mysteries. I fought with the cork, as I usually do, grabbed a goblet, and held onto the bottle with the same hand. I found ale for myself and returned to the sitting room.

"Oh, Ian, you are a dear. I love Pinot Grigio, but sometimes it makes me a bit light-headed. We wouldn't want that; at least not before we finish talking about your memoir."

I set the goblet in front of her and filled it near the rim.

"That's a heavy pour. Are you trying to get me drunk?"

"Heavy pour. Interesting terminology. I was just pouring the wine. Did I shatter some convention or wine etiquette?"

"Well, dear, it's customary to fill the glass to no more than half way."

I scowled at her. "Why?"

"I don't know. It's just a custom, that's all."

"My custom is to fill the goblet to the top."

"Don't be difficult, Ian."

"I'm not good at glib bantering. Have you thought about memoirs that would be good for me to read?"

"Yes, Yes I have. I thought you would learn most by reading memoirs of other authors. I also thought it would to your advantage to read authors from other cultures and countries other than Ireland."

"What memoirs should I read?"

Mairin took several bits of cheese and sipped at her wine as if she were avoiding making her suggestions. "There are four. First, George Orwell's *Homage to Catalonia*. The memoir is about his experience in the Spanish Civil War in the late thirties. He's a good writer, and he was able to write about his experience soon after he returned to England. He served on several fronts and saw what war and left-wing politics was like firsthand."

"Sounds like an excellent choice. I've never read Orwell. No particular reason, just haven't. Next?"

"I've selected an author from America, Langston Hughes, *The Big Sea*. It may be more of an autobiography than a memoir; people have different opinions. I chose it because he grew up in the 1920s. He was raised in Harlem but lived in Paris so he knows about European life. He's best known for poetry, but his prose is straightforward and realistic. Some reviews claim his prose is simpler than even Hemingway's. Speaking of which, I think you should read his *A Moveable*

Feast. It covers the same time period as the Hughes book and is his recollection of living in Paris as an expatriate. He was just learning to write, and he lived in a creative incubator. James Joyce was among his many artist friends. Interestingly, it wasn't published until three years after his death. I've always been curious on why he didn't publish it during his life.

"The last one is another American author. That makes three American authors. I hope you don't mind. Anyway, Styron wrote *Sophie's Choice*. Both the film and book are favorites of mine. His memoir is *Darkness Visible*. Interesting title, don't you think? He chronicles his struggle with depression. Hemingway didn't survive his illness, and there was even a family history of suicide in his case. Styron did survive, and in my view, writing the memoir saved his life. His book had a major impact on how depression was viewed. He related both the severe pain and the fact that it's an illness. Frankly, I think you border on depression, and I worry about your whiskey consumption, which, even for an Irishman, is formidable."

I sat across from her, unable to speak. My hands began to clench so tightly that I couldn't hold anything. I buried my useless hands in my lap, pretending that I was hiding my pain. I could feel beads of sweat form on my temples that begin their journey through my beard and down the side of my face. I couldn't believe her diagnosis of my depression. How in the world did she decide I suffered from depression? We had only known each other a few months. I don't recall a bout of depression since we had been together. Damn, that was risky of her to claim I'm depressed.

"Ian! Ian! What's wrong? Your eyes glassed over. Are you feeling well? Can you move your mouth, can you smile? You're not having a stroke or something are you?"

"Jesus, Mary, and Joseph. First you call me a depressive and next I'm having a stroke right in front of you. You've exceeded my boundary, Mairin. Do you think I'm depressive or just a drunk?"

"Oh, God, this conversation is not going the right direction. I didn't mean to offend you. But I have the right to make observations. Maybe you suffer from denial. I love you, and yes, I think you suffer from depression. Alcohol is a depressant; that's common knowledge. You're an artist and sometimes artists struggle with coping."

I buried my face in my still-clenched hands and wept. Truth can be harsh. Love can be just as harsh and sometimes even cruel. I couldn't bring myself to look at Mairin.

"I think I should go," Mairin said in a whisper.

I felt her kiss the top of my head and she was gone.

TWENTY-TWO

I didn't see or call Mairin for several weeks. She didn't call, either. I was embarrassed, not about the fact that I cried but that she discovered my other secret—depression. I know I have depression, but I deny it. Caitlin has never said anything to me, but she knows. Our mother was said to be moody. Today I'm certain the diagnosis would be depression. My mother never drank in public. What she did while we were in school and Da was at work, who's to know? I do remember that there were many late afternoons when Ma stayed in their bedroom behind locked doors. When I asked for something to oat, oho would oayı "Chook tho frig, Ian, that'o whoro tho food is."

Most nights Da came home just before our bedtime. "There's my brilliant boy," he would bellow. "You'll not be on the docks like your da, Ian. Now, off to bed with you. Got to rest that great brain of yours." I never argued or tried to have a conversation with him. I read every night until my eyes scratched and I fell asleep.

I ordered all the memoirs Mairin suggested from Ryan's Bookstore, and within a week all arrived. I took a holiday from writing until I could devour all of the memoirs. I filled my days with research on the Troubles, to fill in gaps and refresh my memory of events as I experienced them. Boole Library had a treasure of resources, and I spent days in the Special Collection Department in the basement. Sitting in the basement is uniquely conducive to research.

All the librarians there were Mairin's friends, and I was sure they reported my presence on campus to her. I could have paid her a visit, but I just wasn't ready. I don't think she was being judgmental; it's not her way. She was sharing her observation. She had taken a chance to be honest with me. Compared with Eileen, Mairin's honesty was refreshing. I needed to be as honest with myself as Mairin had been with me.

I read three of the memoirs in a week but was finding the Styron book challenging because he had the courage to write about depression, when I spent all my days avoiding it. One day in late September, the air cooled soon after supper. I donned a sweater to walk through Fitzgerald Park and along the River Lee. I had been walking about fifteen minutes when I noticed a familiar sign. There, off to my right, was a tarnished broach, the signal Kieran had used for thirty years to contact me. I blinked and rubbed my eyes, convinced I was having an hallucination.

I walked over, bent down to pick it up, and made sure it was in fact a broach—our broach. It was. I looked to my left, then right and turned to look behind me. I almost expected to find Kieran there in the woods. Nothing. Then I held my breath to listen. All I could hear was the soft rush of the river on its journey to the Celtic Sea. I stuffed the broach into my pocket and rushed home, where I could inspect it in the light. I had to make absolutely sure this was the signal broach.

In the lamp light I could tell, it was definitely the tarnished broach we had used as a signal. Kiernan needed to have contact with me. Why hadn't he just telephoned? He could even have posted a letter. Kieran had always been a deliberate man. He was using the broach as more than just a signal to contact him; it was symbolic. I confess, I had retreated into my familiar writer's cave and hadn't read a newspaper or magazine in months. I refused to watch television news; the stories were thirty-second summaries that were repeated many times during the broadcast day and then the next day forgotten. They called it the twenty-four-hour news cycle. It was maddening.

I didn't have a choice. I had to respond to the signal the same way I used to. In two days, I would pay a visit to Ryan's Bookstore and ask for a copy of the *Irish Independent*. If the storekeeper's response was "No matter buying it, mine's upstairs in the office. Help yourself," Kieran would be there waiting for me.

†††

I trudged up the stairs of Ryan's Bookstore with a sense of both anguish and nervous anticipation. Using the old signal for our meetings meant our meeting must be surreptitious, the same as the previous thirty years. Halfway up the stairs, the distinct wrench of Carroll's Major cigarettes made me choke. "If I'm goin' to smoke, I've got to taste the damn things," he would bark at me. I had tried teaching him about the pleasures of decent tobacco and quality whiskey, but to no avail. I hoped he was being respectful of Ryan's office, another politeness for which he didn't have a good reputation. I wondered why Ryan tolerated Kieran all these years. We all made sacrifices for the Troubles, and Ryan had definitely made his.

At the top of the stairs, I pushed the door. It was stuck. Over the years, the building had settled into the soft soil it was built on. Large sections of Cork, including the city center, had sponge-like topsoil and the bookstore was built on it. The land was cheap, and it was a way to encourage businesses to locate downtown.

"Give it a shove, man. Have ya gone weak?" Kieran shouted in an excited tone.

I gave the door one final shove and lost my balance, half falling into the small office. Kieran began to laugh, then choked as he lost his breath.

"Light up another, why don't you?" I stabbed back.

"Bugger you. You're so important with that fancy pipe of yours. Mer...Meer...something or other."

"Meerschaum," I said, sitting down in front of him.

"Right." Kieran bolted up and pulled the shade down on the window.

"What in the hell? Why the sudden secrecy and using the broach again to signal me?"

Kieran sat behind the desk and lit another cigarette while he searched the drawers for the ashtray that Ryan kept just for his use. "Here it is," he whispered to himself, not paying any attention to me.

"The broach was necessary, that's all. You know I'm a cautious man. I've survived thirty years running a guerilla war; that takes some skill. Have you been following the movement to build more peace lines in Belfast City?"

I shook my head. "No."

Kieran pounded his palm on top of the desk, demanding my attention. "Been playing ostrich again. Jesus, Ian, you worry me sometimes."

I leaned in close to Kieran and made direct eye contact. "Listen, I've been busy."

Kieran pulled back and stubbed his cigarette out in the ashtray, blowing smoke directly in my face. "That damned book of yours, the memoir?"

"Yes, now what's this about building more peace lines?"

Kieran lit another cigarette. Chain-smoking was a signal that he was irritated and not feeling in control. "It's bizarre. They want a barrier between Falls Road and Shankill Road in West Belfast and several other locations you probably wouldn't recognize."

"I don't know Belfast, Kieran. I'd have to ask Caitlin. Isn't Falls Road where the Sinn Fein headquarters is? I know James Connolly lived there when he tried to organize workers in the linen mills."

"Your knowledge of history has always been impressive; however, your awareness of contemporary issues is lacking. Yes, Sinn Fein headquarters are there. The Unionists are on Shankill Road. Let me lay it out for you. How are we going to build a country if they build walls to separate the Catholics from the Protestants? What the hell is the meaning of the Good Friday Agreement if we construct walls to separate us?"

For several minutes, I was unable to find words to express the anger and disappointment I felt. My work on the Peace Accord was unraveling in less than a year, in less than six months! The vote proved that the majority in Northern Ireland wanted peace, why did they want to wall themselves off? I slouched in my chair and felt depression descend on me like an early morning fog.

"Why?"

"They're afraid, Ian. They're afraid of violence. They don't trust themselves. They don't trust each other. They've had centuries of practice distrusting each other. I can understand that. Sinn Fein is furious, of course, it's a Unionist idea."

I pushed my chair back and began to pace in front of the desk.

"You have to do something."

I rubbed my beard and stared at Kieran like he had just told me to jump off a bridge or something equally ridiculous. "Me?"

"Yes. You." Kieran demanded.

"Give me one of those cigarettes," I ordered.

Kieran tossed the package in my direction. I shook it until a cigarette dropped out onto the desk. My hands shook as I tried to light it. I drew the pungent smoke deep into my lungs and coughed, feeling my neck tighten. My body wanted to reject smoking, but I resisted.

"Those walls first went up back in '69; this isn't something new. I don't understand Sinn Fein's concern. If it brings safety to both the Catholic and Protestant populations, who are we to judge?"

Kieran jumped out of his chair, screaming at me. "I can't fucking believe you said that. The great moralist, Ian Padraic Murphy, approving building more peace walls in Belfast City. Your sacred Good Friday Agreement is worth shit then. You're the one that added civil rights to the paper, aren't you? That Human Rights Commission you insisted on is already hearing cases; it's beginning to work. They're already enforcing the ban on handguns, and decommissioning arms is happening much faster than we expected. It will be done within a year, even though you negotiated two years to get the job done. It's the damned British Government that wants to build more walls. They want to say to the world: see, we were right, the damn Irish can't govern themselves, and they have to keep them-selves apart with walls." Kieran fell back into his chair and pushed hair out of his face with both hands.

I listened so intently to Kieran's diatribe that I forgot I was holding a smoldering cigarette. I stubbed it out in the ashtray before it could burn my hand. "I see. Forgive my ignorance, my friend. You're right, of course. I'm sure the Brits are behind it all; they are masters at using fear to terrorize a people. I...I just don't know what I can do. I'm willing, of course, but at a loss to know what to do."

"Speak out. Let your voice be heard. You have enormous credibility with both Protestants and Catholics as a man of conviction. You're both an insider and an outsider. It's unique."

I stood up, pushed the chair to one side of the room, and began to pace back and forth in front of the desk again. I could see Kieran follow me with his head, back and forth like he was watching a hurling match. He knows me well enough to not disturb me when I start pacing. It was my own trick for distracting myself, so I can process random thoughts quickly. It came to me in a flash.

"I must move to Belfast."

"What?"

"I just can't rush up there, make a few speeches, visit with some politicians, and come back to the security of my little cottage in Cork. I must walk with them, beside them. I need to experience what it's like living with a wall in my backyard. People have lived like that for thirty years. Now that I think of it, the topic of the walls never came up during our negotiations on the Good Friday Agreement. That's odd. It would have been immensely symbolic to begin tearing down those walls the day after the referenda passed. There was silence. That's interesting. Sometimes I am so dense."

"Gracious Lord, living in Belfast? God, I never expected you to come up with an idea like that, Ian."

"I'll talk to Caitlin, she can guide me, help me understand their mentality. I hope she has kept in contact with some of her Belfast friends. I need to get to know the people, both Catholics and Protestants."

"Are you going to be able to take a sabbatical from University College Cork? This is such short notice."

"I hadn't thought of that. You're right. It could be difficult. How urgent is the effort to start building walls again?"

"Who's to know? There isn't panic or fighting in the streets. They're a fickle bunch, though. Could start next week, could be six months."

"You're not helping," I snapped back.

"No, I'm being honest. Remember, this is all new to me, too. I was asked to convince you to help somehow."

"Someone asked you? I was under the impression this was your idea."

"I never said that."

"So, who's asking?"

"Doesn't matter." Kieran shrugged off my question.

I stopped pacing and squared off directly in front of him. "Kieran?"

"My understanding is that it was John Hume's idea conveyed through Marty McGuiness. There's a rumor that Hume and Trimble are going to share the Nobel Peace Prize. Hell, getting nominated for it is damned near a miracle. Now, building walls to separate the population would give Belfast a black mark beyond imagination right at the time they're burning the midnight oil to form a coalition government."

I turned to grab the chair and sat down. "This is becoming clearer. You still keep things close to the vest, don't you? I suppose it's been a way of life for you for such a long time, it's just second nature. I'm not finding fault. It's your modus operandi, I know that."

Kieran sat down too and pulled a cigarette out of the package with his lips, then offered me the pack.

"No, thanks."

"How are you going to tell Mairin, especially without any idea of how long you'll be living in Belfast?"

"You do think of everything, don't you? I have no idea. We've had a…"

"Jesus, Mary, and Joseph, you haven't screwed things up with her, have you? She's perfect for you. A helluva lot better than Eileen Donohue. I tried to warn you about Donohue, but you were smitten. Well, now I'm telling you, don't let Mairin McCarthy go. It will ruin you."

"I've always appreciated your directness, Kieran. No, she knows me so well that I find it a bit frightening. She sees through me, right into my soul. I love her. With Mairin, I've learned what real love is. I was infatuated with Eileen, dumbstruck; it wasn't love. I'll talk with Mairin. We could see each other weekends. It's not like I'm going to the States or something, and we could call every day."

Kieran blew the last puff of smoke from his cigarette directly into my face. "Ok, I'll let you deal with it, but like I said, don't screw it up.

"I need to report your plans. Any idea on timeline?"

"No. I'll be in touch. So, I'm curious. Who do you report to?"

Kieran bowed his head, fumbling with the pack of cigarettes. He stuffed the package into his coat pocket and drummed his fingers on the desk. He fidgeted in his chair.

"Okay, if it makes you that nervous, forget that I asked."

"Gerry," he whispered under his breath.

TWENTY-THREE

I went to the library to research both the history of Belfast and the peace walls. I was embarrassed to admit that I knew more about medieval Irish history than I did about either Belfast or Northern Ireland. Of course, I'm familiar with the general historical timeline of how Northern Ireland developed separately from the rest of the country. However, I'm ignorant of the people and their culture.

When I took an objective view of my role in the IRA, it was ironic that I just assumed that Northern Ireland should not be separate from the Republic of Ireland. I never imagined that the people and their culture were anything but Irish. Reading history in depth, I learned that a large portion of the population in the north, the Protestants, viewed themselves as British, not Irish. How could I have not known that? The influx of Protestants from Scotland and Britain began in the 17th century. By the time the Government of Ireland Act was implemented in 1920, Ulster had been a Protestant land for over 300 years.

When I reflected on my research, I was disturbed about the question of self-determination in Northern Ireland. The British Parliament created a self-governing Northern Ireland and what we originally called the Irish Free State by that Act. How arrogant for one country to enact a law to create a separate country outside of its own borders. It was interesting that the people of Northern Ireland accepted the Government of Ireland Act without reservation.

I was absorbed in my studies when I heard a familiar voice and the delicate fragrance of magnolia.

"Ian?" a woman's voice whispered from behind me.

I turned to see Mairin standing a few feet away with her arms in front of her and her hands clasped. I pushed the books to one side and let a smile grow across my face. "Dear Mairin."

"I've missed you, Ian."

"And I you, Mairin."

"You haven't called."

"Nor you."

"Ian, the way we left things, I didn't feel it was my place to call. I didn't intend to hurt you. I could never do that."

"This probably isn't the place to talk."

"Oh, of course not. I apologize. Just seeing you again, I'm desperate to patch things up. Whatever it takes. Do you want to talk? I don't want to interrupt you. You look very busy. Maybe, maybe we can find a time—soon."

I couldn't resist getting up and giving Mairin a hug; it didn't matter to me that we were in the research room of the library. "Let me gather up a few of these books I need to check out. Would you care to walk?"

"A walk would be perfect. I'll buy you lunch."

"Offer accepted."

"I find Fitzgerald Park serene and quiet. Would you be comfortable talking with me there?"

"It's not me that needs to be comfortable, it's you."

"Then Fitzgerald Park it is. I often walk through the park when I feel the need to gather myself together and I don't have the time to drive to Dingle."

"I learn something new about you every time we're together. You are a complex man, Ian Murphy."

"Not nearly so as you might imagine."

After lunch, it only took a few minutes to walk from campus to the park. At once we entered a beautiful, serene place with fountains, interesting walkways, and magnificent gardens that had brought peace to my restless soul many times. I took deep breaths to take in all other fragrances I could. I could tell there was a particular flower in bloom, but I wasn't able to determine the type by its smell. It was too comingled for me to distinguish it from the other fragrances. The longer we walked, the slower my pace became. Mairin matched my stride. We walked until we found a secluded stone bench.

"Shall we sit?" I asked.

"If you'd like."

I motioned for her to take a seat, and I sat down next to her as close as I could. I slipped my hand into hers. She gave my hand a slight squeeze. She looked directly into my eyes and gifted me with a faint smile.

"No one's better at killing a story than Kieran Fitzpatrick. It would be frightening for you to know how much of the media the IRA controlled at the height of the Troubles. I was contributing most of the misinformation at the time. I wrote constantly," I explained.

"Attempting suicide is a classic indication of depression in men. The data indicates that about 80 percent of all suicides are men. And then there's..." Mairin retorted.

"I know those statistics. When I made that decision, everything was bearing down on me at one time. That was a one-time journey into hell. But I survived both physically and mentally. You were going to mention something else?"

Mairin squirmed in her seat and looked away.

"Just say it, please. I need to hear it. I need to hear it from you, Mairin."

"The drinking. You drink a prodigious amount of whiskey. I'm guessing you drink at least two bottles a week. Is there a single day without whiskey?"

I could feel the blood rush to my face. Both hands clenched so hard that my nails bit into my palms. "I don't know. I don't keep count. All I know is that Mickey keeps me supplied, no questions asked. I pay my tab every month—never miss. So, what harm is there in a bit of whiskey every day? Remember, the Murphys are distillers; it's probably in my DNA."

"Ian, my dear, you're making excuses. You don't need to be ashamed. It's an illness and like other illnesses, it can be treated."

I tried to unclench my fist by drawing it across my thigh, but it didn't work. "Jesus, you have all the answers, don't you?"

"If you must know, Ian, I've lived with it. My father suffered from depression. In the end, he cut himself off from the world. In his last years, he didn't communicate with anyone. He died silent, alone in a world only he inhabited. It was sad; it was a waste."

I bent toward her and rested my head on her shoulder. I couldn't find fault with anything she said. "I suppose it's in my family, too. We used to say that Ma had her moods. I don't know if she drank. If she did, she hid it well from me and Caitlin. Da, well, he would stop off after work for a few pints with his friends. I don't remember him drunk or loud. Sometimes Ma would retreat to their bedroom and not come out for days. Da would pick up take-away for us kids to eat. It's just the way things were. She died young, my ma, at sixty. Died of leukemia. The doctors said she didn't have any pain."

Mairin sat up straight, massaged my hands, then kissed the palms of each hand. "Do you want to feel normal?"

I searched her eyes, not sure how to respond. "I...I don't know what 'normal' is. I've lived like this since I moved back to Cork after Trinity College. Maybe I have deluded myself. I've always found it difficult to look in the mirror."

"Treatment is completely individual. You need to see a doctor. They can prescribe antidepressants and you might want to consider psychotherapy, maybe just a few sessions to get some grounding."

I felt myself pull away from her. "Now, that's where I draw the line. I'm not subjecting myself to some shrink, whining about my life. My expression, all my expression, is done through my writing. Period."

"My love, I respect that. I've learned that writing is not just what you do; being a writer is who you are."

The tension in my body melted away, and I took Mairin's hand in mine and kissed the back of both her hands. "Thank you. Knowing that about me is to know the depth of who I am, now and forever. I will listen to you because I trust you with my life. Truth be known, I'm fortunate to have you, Kieran, and Caitlin, people I can trust with my life, my soul."

Mairin cradled my head on her shoulder. We sat undisturbed until midafternoon. "Who should I see? I don't have a regular doctor, never needed one."

"I'll ask a few people I know well. I won't mention you, I promise."

"Your love is transforming my life, Mairin. There's one more very important topic we need to talk about."

"What a surprise!"

"Well yes, well, I..."

"Ian, darling, why are you nervous?"

"Mairin, I've been called back into service."

Mairin scrunched up her nose. "Service? Ian, what in the world are you talking about?"

I slipped my arm around her shoulders so that I could speak quietly and not be overheard by folks strolling along the path. "Have you followed the news from Belfast City?"

"You know I'm an avid newspaper reader. Whatever has been in print, I'm familiar with. Where are you going with all this?"

I smiled the most charming smile I could. "Well, that's the point. I'm going. That is, I'm going to live in Belfast?"

Mairin pulled away to look me directly in the face. "Belfast? I...I...don't understand."

I scratched at my beard and searched my pockets for my pipe and tobacco. "Do you want the long version or the abridged version of the story?"

"I think I'd better hear the long version, if you please."

I told her about my meeting with Kieran and how the Brits were working overtime to maintain the fear and distrust between the Catholics and Protestants and thwart the efforts of Hume and Trimble to form a government. "British authorities were using the IRA's refusal to decommission arms to suggest new peace walls needed to be built to protect Belfast residents. After the damnable Real IRA bombed Omagh, the citizens of Belfast begged for more walls."

"Mother of God, will peace ever descend on our island?" Mairin wondered out loud. "What do they want from you?"

"Several things. First, I need to convince the IRA of the urgency to begin decommissioning arms at a greater rate. I developed the strategy during negotiations to allow for a two year implementation of turning in arms. Now, they are refusing to honor that portion of the accord. Not even Kieran knows why they have reversed their position. Then I was charged with persuading the Catholic population that building more peace walls is a symbol of failure and giving in to British manipulation."

Mairin scooted farther away from me on the bench and let my hand drop from hers. "By your explanation, do I understand that you've accepted the charge?"

I cleared my throat and looked directly into her eyes. "I started this conversation by telling you I am moving to Belfast."

Mairin shook her head back and forth and folded her arms in front of her chest. "Have you talked to Caitlin about living in Belfast?"

"No, I wanted to talk with you first."

"Don't be coy with me, Ian Murphy; I just happened to see you on campus. You were busy researching. You didn't come to my library; you knew I would be there this time of day."

I bowed my head and sat on my hands. "I would have stopped by this afternoon. Asked you to dinner."

"Ha! There's a tall tale."

"Be kind. I was working up the courage."

"What about us, Ian?"

"Uh...uh, us. Well, yes there's that. Kieran mentioned that, too."

A scowl of disapproval grew across Mairin's face and her brow wrinkled. "Did you expect we would have a long-distance relationship? Oh, wait. Maybe this is your way of calling it quits."

I bolted straight up and braced my hands on my knees. "No. I love you with all of my heart. I thought you might consider a sabbatical and come with me."

"Oh, Ian, that's so impractical. You just expect me to put my work on hold to follow you to the most dangerous place in Ireland and do what? The term has started, do I need to remind you? The administration is not likely to grant a sabbatical unless the circumstances were dire."

"Mairin, the circumstances are dire. Peace is at risk. Lives are at risk. A country is at risk. I might be able to help, if you would be willing to ask for a sabbatical."

"You're serious."

"I couldn't be more serious, my love. I want you with me. I need you," I whispered.

As silence grew between us, I concentrated on the birds I heard singing overhead in the trees. I heard a robin distinctly, then I think I r ecognized a siskin and a house sparrow. I needed to distract myself and let Mairin own the silence between us and not let it grow into a wall that might damage or end our relationship. It was obvious that I didn't handle the situation well. Kieran was so aware of such things and I am in a cave, a cave of my own making. When Kieran mentioned it to me, I should have spent some time thinking about Mairin's possible reaction and the meaning of a major move on our relationship. Instead, I began researching the details of Belfast's history and catching up on the news of the current impasse. I am my own worst enemy. It reminded me of the quote from Pogo, 'We have met the enemy and he is us.'

"You've wandered off again, Ian. Lord, I do wish you could be more attentive. I need a few days to think this over. You are asking me to turn my life topsy-turvy. I don't know if I can sustain that much change and the stress of living in a different city—especially Belfast. Has your department approved a sabbatical for you?"

"Yes, with no time constraints. Probably a year."

Mairin stood up and walked away without saying goodbye or looking back at me.

TWENTY-FOUR

y conversation with Mairin couldn't have been more disappointing. It was likely that I had been a bachelor for too long and expecting to develop a normal, healthy relationship with an intelligent, mature, attractive woman just wasn't my life path. I don't consider myself old, even though I hadn't inherited genes that pointed to longevity, I had a reasonable expectation of at least another twenty years, even with my lifestyle.

As I watched Mairin walk away, I decided to shift my focus back to preparing for life in Belfast. I found myself torn between two paths. One was to do only limited preparation: take care of finding my replacement for my lecture at UCC and determining what I would take to Belfast. I would live as the innocent in a foreign city and learn as I experienced their unique life and culture. My comfort level with this approach wasn't great.

The opposite would be to bury myself in reading history, literature, poetry, newspapers to try to soak in as much of the culture and way of life as I could. I had no idea how long that would take me and Kieran impressed on me the sense of urgency to move, although he didn't give me a deadline. I'm sure he thought a deadline wasn't necessary, that I would come when the business matters of my life were in order.

I made an appointment to talk to Professor O'Flaherty to use his reputation to garner my replacement. We had known each other for years, at least as colleagues, and had a professional respect for each other, but would not be considered friends outside of college. When I called the next morning, his secretary said he was expecting my call and that I could come in after lunch today. *How could that be*, I wondered. Once again there was hidden machinery working behind the scenes to influence my life. As long as I was in town, I decided to call Caitlin and share my decision with her and ask for her guidance in my assignment and some of the details of a man from Cork living in Belfast. Her ten years there was proving to be quite an advantage and would help my comfort level. My sister is one of the few people I trust unconditionally.

I arrived promptly at Professor O'Flaherty's office at half one. By his office alone, even a novice could see that he was a senior professor. Six-foot-tall stained-glass windows provided a view of the green where students lounged and studied at all times of the day and night. Two walls were floor-to-ceiling dark walnut bookcases that were too small for his Jeffersonian -sized collection. He sat behind an enormous, matching dark walnut desk that served as a barrier between him and any guest to his *sanctum sanctorum*. It was well-known that if he stayed hidden behind his desk, the meeting would be brief and formal. If he got up and walked to the leather couch in the corner next to the door, it would be a friendly meeting without a time limit.

I was surprised that he stood and greeted me with a warm handshake when I entered. "Ian, let's go to the sofa; we'll be more comfortable. Can I get you a whiskey? Oh, it might be too early. I don't intend to offend you. At my age, no time of day is too early for a nice whiskey."

"Thank you, Professor O'Flaherty, a whiskey would be nice." I responded with intentional deference.

"Please, Ian, let's dispense with the formality, and please call me Padraic."

"That's my middle name, sir."

"Ian."

"Yes, I understand. Mm, this whiskey has a unique nose to it. I definitely detect peat," I said.

"You are a discerning man, Ian. It's a blend of my own design, and I am of the opinion that any Irish whiskey must have a touch of the peat. How could it be otherwise?"

"I don't want to waste your time. I've been called to help out with the mess in Northern Ireland. I worked hard on the compromise on decommissioning arms and now what's left of the IRA isn't cooperating; the renegade Real IRA is presenting overwhelming obstacles. I hate to ask, but I need a sabbatical, certainly for this term and maybe the spring term, too."

Professor O'Flaherty took a long sip of the whiskey and slurped it like a professional taster. "Yes, I'm aware. Gerry called me yesterday and explained the circumstances. He's counting on you for a lot. I wouldn't want the burden you've been given."

"You, you talked with Gerry Adams?"

"Known him for years; don't be surprised."

I took a moment to understand what was being orchestrated in my life. Kieran made it sound like I had a choice, but I think he was just creating an elaborate illusion for me.

"I've wanted to get back into the classroom for a long time and this will give me the opportunity. I became a professor to teach, not to be an administrator. The Chancellor will have no choice but to accept my offer. I owe you a debt of gratitude for providing me with this opportunity."

"The students will definitely benefit from this switch in instructors. I really can't express my gratitude."

"I've also decided to make this a one-year sabbatical for you. I seriously doubt if you will be able to patch things up by the start of the spring term. They've been at this for 400 years," O'Flaherty said.

"I have immense appreciation for the history of their differences. Thank you for your support. It is more than anyone could expect."

"Well, there's one person who expected it, and people don't often say no to Gerry. Godspeed, Ian Murphy."

I set my empty glass on the table and left without saying goodbye. Goodbye didn't seem appropriate.

†††

It was a short walk to Caitlin's office in the student center. She said I could come by any time after talking with Professor O'Flaherty. She would be in until four this afternoon. She was the college's freshman activities coordinator and in her short time in the position, she had demonstrated a special flair for the job. I was amazed at her ability to form relationships quickly with a wide range of students from throughout Ireland and the continent. Several people I knew in administration thanked me for bringing her to the college. There had been talk for several years of the need for someone in her position but never an effort to create a job description and recruit staff.

When I introduced Caitlin to the student center director, Doreen Finnegan, her face lit up like the rising sun. I simply made introductions and then left Caitlin to make her own case. That very afternoon she walked away with a new job. It wasn't common for college administrators to hire so quickly, especially when the job hadn't been formally advertised. Ms. Finnegan dodged that hurdle by making the position interim to access the need for the position. Clever, I thought. Caitlin didn't mind that it wasn't a permanent job to start with. She has the Murphy family confidence in herself.

Her office reflected her lack of official status on campus. It gave all the appearance of being an enlarged closet. She had a pine-wood desk with two matching chairs, one hers and one for a guest; a computer that took up most of the space on the desk with a telephone crowding one corner. There were no windows, and I couldn't find a vent for either air conditioning or heat, not that she would need it.

The door was ajar and I knocked.

"Come in, it's open."

"I can see that. Thought it would be polite to knock anyway," I responded.

"Oh, Ian, do you want to stay here and talk or take a walk out to the Commons?"

"The Commons will be more comfortable."

"Don't you make any comment about my office. It's enough. Most of my time is spent with the students or in meetings making connections. I don't need a big, fancy office like you have."

"My office is not fancy. I'm just a lecturer, remember. It is comfortable; I don't admit anything more than that. I can't remember the last time I met with any students in my office. I much prefer Mickey's."

"And that's common knowledge. I do want to thank you again for getting me this job. You've been too kind, the house, the car, and a job."

"I didn't have anything to do with you getting this job. You sold Ms. Finnegan on the idea. Everything I've heard about on your performance is exceptional. You have real talent, dear sister."

Caitlin stretched her arms out in the sunlight and spun around. "Oh, it is such a beautiful day. I don't miss Belfast. I think Belfast is fast fading in Brianna's memory, too. I let her call a few of her friends there once a month. Oh, Lord, stop me from babbling. You wanted to talk. There was some urgency in your voice. What did you want to talk about?"

I pointed toward a nearby bench, "Maybe it would be best to sit down." As we sat on the bench, Caitlin's eyes filled with eagerness. "Well, I'm being called back into service. I'll be moving to Belfast, and I need your insight into the people, the culture, the problems there, from your perspective, from all the years you were with Sinn Fein."

Caitlin jumped backward, almost falling off the edge of the bench. "Holy Mother of God, Belfast! Ian Padraic Murphy, you have lost your mind. Your life won't be worth the price of a tin whistle there. You absolutely cannot go to Belfast. I sure Mairin won't tolerate this ridiculous notion. Have you told Mairin?"

"I told her yesterday and it's not a topic I want to discuss. What did you mean about my life not being worth the price of a tin whistle?"

Caitlin crossed her arms in front of me and leaned in close to whisper. "You are so naïve. The Protestants will hate you because you got rid of the British Army, their protectors. The Catholics will hate you because you made the IRA give up their guns. Of course, there's your attempted intervention with the Real IRA in Omagh, that didn't win you any points. Since when have you decided you're Ireland's savior?"

I sat up straight and grabbed her by the shoulders, looking her directly in the eyes. "Dear sister, this wasn't my idea. I would be just as happy to stay here in Cork, teach, write my memoir, and bask in my relationship with Mairin. Who knows, I might not always be a bachelor."

"I'm listening. Has someone in Belfast specifically asked for your help?"

"Kieran is working with Sinn Fein now. They recognized his ability to organize and need the relationships he's built up over the years. Kieran paid me a visit several days ago. Your observations are correct. The RIRA is refusing to turn in weapons as our agreement demands, and the Brits are talking about building more peace walls in an effort to avoid violence. They haven't been able to form a stable government, there's still no trust. Agreeing to peace doesn't mean as much as I thought it would."

Caitlin drew her arms around her body, hugging herself, and she began to rock back and forth. She looked to the left and right as if worried that someone might overhear our conversation. Her behavior made me uneasy.

"It's Gerry. Gerry has asked you to go to Belfast, hasn't he?"

"How did you know?"

"I worked with Sinn Fein for more than ten years, Ian. Gerry is a clever man and a master working behind the scenes. He has a keen sense of the right resources needed to further Sinn Fein objectives. Your work on the Peace Accord gives you credibility and some level of trust with both factions. I may understand, but that doesn't mean I agree it's the right choice for you."

"Choice. I didn't feel there was a question of choice. Who knows, maybe it's my path to redemption."

"When are you leaving?"

"Soon, no date set yet. O'Flaherty approved a year sabbatical for me this afternoon. I have a few things to sort out with Mairin."

"I can imagine. Okay, let's schedule some time together in the next few days and I'll share my Belfast years with you in detail. You need to spend some time with Brianna, too."

"Thank you, Caitlin. I really didn't expect you to under-stand, but I desperately need your support."

Caitlin opened her arms wide and stretched her arms around my neck and whispered. "You're my brother; I love you, in all times, in all circumstances."

TWENTY-FIVE

It took three days to complete the rest of my preparations, listen to a thorough briefing from Caitlin about life in Belfast, make some special time to spend with my niece, Brianna, and wait to hear from Mairin. Brianna had a hard time accepting the news. The logic of a twelve-year-old is impeccable. She and her mother had just moved from Belfast to Cork at my insistence. The fact that I would turn around and move to Belfast myself simply didn't make any sense. From her perspective, her reasoning was excellent. Point of fact, from an adult's perspective, her reasoning was excellent. I didn't bother refuting her, I just told her I was needed to help the people living there and that was that.

Brianna didn't have a choice in accepting or not accepting it was going to happen, so she decided to be angry with me. I'm not sure what anger means to a twelve-year-old girl, but she decided not to talk to me any longer and refused to say goodbye. By the third day, I concluded that Mairin had made the same decision Brianna had about my Belfast move.

The last person I shared my decision with was Mickey. I called him and made some excuse to order a case of Midleton that I would pick up. He knew that I could have picked up a case at the distillery because they claimed I was their most famous patron. Mickey even suggested that for me, they would deliver it.

†††

I went to pick up my whiskey order midmorning before the lunch rush at the pub. I walked into the empty pub to find Lorna setting tables and Dolores wiping down tables. "Where's the boss this morning? He's not helping you?"

"Oh, he's downstairs taking inventory. You know he won't let anyone take inventory. I don't think that man would let the Lord himself take inventory," Lorna said as she moved from table to table.

"I'll just go down."

"Have a good day, Mr. Murphy," they responded in perfect unison.

The wooden stairs needed some work, and I took one step at a time to keep my balance when a familiar voice blasted me back a step, "I told yous, I don't need help!"

"I didn't come to help, I just came for my whiskey," I shouted back.

"Damn, I thought you were one of the ladies."

"I can't understand how you take inventory down here. It always looks the same to me."

"You didn't need to come down. I have your case sitting upstairs in my office."

"That's fine. I'm glad you're down here; we need to talk."

"Ian Murphy, I'm your friend and barkeep, not your confessor."

"Relax, Mickey, I just wanted to tell you that I'm moving to Belfast for a while."

"Jesus, Mary, an' Joseph. I'm looking right at a dead man. I would bet half of next year's wages there's a price on yer head. Have you told Caitlin and Mairin about this or are you just trying it out on ol' Mickey first?"

I finished walking down the steps and walked to where Mickey clung to his clipboard. He tucked a pencil behind his ear.

"I've told both of them."

"An' you're still here able to make yer announcement to me?"

"Look, Mickey, you've helped me out when I had no one else to turn to. I know I haven't always made good decisions, but this is different. Things are not going well in Northern Ireland. The IRA's refusing to turn in any more of their guns; there's talk of building more peace walls; and that damn Real IRA group is making a mess of things, like the bombing in Omagh. Some people there like my work on the Peace Agreement and they think I can help now."

Mickey scratched his head. "Can you?"

"If they have the confidence to ask me, then yes, I think I can help. I need to do more, Mickey. That peace agreement won't be worth the paper it was printed on if they can't form a government and until the British army goes home."

"Amen to that," he said under his breath. "How long will you be gone?"

"I don't know, my friend, I hope not more than a year."

"A year?"

"I have a year sabbatical from college."

"Oh."

The cellar became quiet, and I'm sure I heard mice scratching in the walls. Mickey shuffled his feet back and forth in a struggle to find a few words.

"Wha...What can I do for you? Help out, I mean?" Mickey asked.

"You could watch my place."

"Done."

I gave him a bear hug and slapped his back several times. "I'll be fine, Mickey. I'm sure I'll get protection the entire time I'm there. Kieran asked me to come, and you know he has the best security network in Ireland. I'm not worried about my safety. If it makes you feel any better, Caitlin had the exact same concern for my well-being as you did. You've been a great friend."

"I know when you have your mind made up, well, nothing can be done. Of course, I'll watch the cottage for ya. Give me a ring from time to time, will ya?"

"Of course. Now, let's get that case of whiskey."

TWENTY-SIX

All my goodbyes were now said and I took another day to finish packing, call Kieran to expect me on Friday, and wait one more day for Mairin. I tossed and turned Thursday night, replaying my last conversation with Mairin over and over. I didn't expect her reaction to my decision would be so harsh, and I couldn't comprehend her silence these last three days. Maybe she thought I was devaluing her idea for me to write my memoir. Working in Belfast didn't mean I wouldn't work on the draft, although, if I was going to be honest with myself, I didn't think I had the capacity or the energy to work with Sinn Fein and write. Writing consumed me, as it should. There was no deadline for writing my memoir, and if it was delayed a few months, a year, what would it matter? No, that can't be it. Does this mean our relationship is over? Does she expect me to contact her before I leave? She walked away from me. I'm conflicted. I don't want this to shatter our relationship; it's so promising.

† † †

I thought I got a few hours of sleep, but I wasn't sure. Most important, I didn't drown myself in a bottle of whiskey. Whiskey is a depressant, at least in the quantities I normally consume; my doctor has warned me many times. Knowing that intellectually and acting on it in your life were very different. I needed to start revising my vision of myself, who I was, and what I stood for. I would express what I stood for with my work in Belfast. As Shaw said, "Life is about creating yourself" and that was my new life mission—I was going to create a new Ian Padraic Murphy by revealing myself in the memoir and, God willing, I would find redemption for my past, as I do.

The drive to Belfast took about four and a half hours, for me a very long drive. It was a lot of time by myself, idle time, time to think, dangerous time. Kieran told me to meet him for lunch in a snug just off Falls Road, guaranteed to be a safe place. I was instructed to find a seat and wait; most likely he would arrive shortly after me. I shouldn't expect anyone else to be there for lunch and there would be one man at the bar, but I wasn't to talk to him. These were unusual instructions, even for Kieran. As he reminded me, safety first, so I followed his instructions to the letter.

† † †

The snug was smaller than I expected and could accommodate not more than six customers comfortably. The man at the bar kept his back to me and was absorbed in reading a newspaper. I took a seat in the corner, facing the door so that I could see whoever came in. No one came to wait on me; I couldn't tell if anyone was actually working. It was unnerving. To pass the time and make sure I didn't appear uncomfortable or out of place, I loaded up my meerschaum pipe and started a long, slow smoke.

The door opened, letting a rush of light stretch into the small room, and Kieran came in, walking directly to the table. "Ian, Ian, have ya been waiting long?"

"About half a pipe, not bad."

"Only you would tell time by how long it takes you to smoke that pipe. It is a fine-looking pipe though, I must admit. Anyone bother you?"

"No, it's just like you said it would be. Does anyone work here? I would have liked a pint while I waited."

"I've already ordered for us. It will be out directly. Now, we need to review a few things."

Kieran lit his cigarette then looked from table to table for an ashtray. He got up and asked the man at the bar to fetch him one. The man disappeared into the back and returned with an old-fashioned glass ashtray and set it directly in front of Kieran.

"Anything else, sir?" he asked with noticeable politeness.

As I looked at him, I decided he had his job because he was the picture of average. His brown hair was cropped short so didn't need to comb it. He wore a gray jacket with an open-collared white shirt, matching slacks, and black shoes. His hands looked like he wasn't a stranger to manual labor. He could walk down the street of any city in Ireland and disappear. Kieran watched me absorb every detail of the man's appearance.

"His name is Dominic; get used to him. He's going to be your shadow. He was named for the saint but believe me, he's no saint."

"Is this necessary?"

"Ian, my friend, you're in Belfast. Believe me, it's necessary. I also have a car and driver for you. I don't want you walking about unless either Dominic or I am with you."

"This is worse than Caitlin told me."

"Things have changed since Caitlin lived here with Brianna. It's a powder keg, and the fuse is very short. There's a hard-core group that wants peace to fail and the government is unable to get itself together."

A man appeared as if by magic balancing two plates of food on one arm and two pints in his right hand. He placed the food on the table and addressed Kieran. "Will ya be needin' anything more, sir?"

"No, this is fine, fine, thank you. You are, as usual, very prompt and efficient."

"Thank you, sir." The man turned on his heel and retreated to the backroom where he came from.

"Sir? Do they all call you sir?" I asked Kieran.

"Yes, most do. You will be called Mr. Murphy or sir, too. It's the way it is in Belfast, it's a formal place. It's as close to civility as they come. Now, let's eat, and then we can continue with your instructions."

I ate as ordered, without any small talk. Even eating lunch was a job, not a pleasurable social experience. In a few minutes Kieran pushed his plate to one side and finished off his pint in one gulp. He looked at me, raising an eyebrow as if he wanted to ask me when I expected to finish. I have been a slow eater my whole life and I wasn't about to change now. I put my knife and fork across the edge of the plate and pushed it toward Kieran's plate. I really didn't know what we ate, the food was completely nondescript. I hope that this wasn't going to be how all the food in Belfast would be. I rubbed the glass pint between my hands, watching the brown liquid swish back and forth. "I'm ready. What other instructions do you have?"

"I have an apartment for you on Falls Road, near Sinn Fein headquarters. You'll be able to walk there, but Dominic will be close by—even there. When you have meetings, your driver will come and fetch you, take you to the meeting, and wait for you. At many of your meetings, you'll be on your own. Your credibility is based on your independence. Gerry will expect a briefing after every meeting. The immediate task is to get the holdouts to turn in their weapons—we want everything, not just the small arms. They're using the two-year deadline to drag their feet, but we have to turn in more weapons to show good faith. The damned Real IRA group has made things very difficult for us. Dolan's not in charge anymore, and the Council disbanded after the referendum on the Peace Accord passed so overwhelmingly."

"So who do I work with?" I asked.

"We're working on that. Now, let's get you settled into your apartment. I'm having your car taken away for safekeeping; you won't need it here. I'll drive with you to the apartment."

Dominic put down his newspaper and watched us walk out of the snug. When we parked on the street outside the apartment, I noticed Dominic was already there, sitting in a car, smoking a cigarette.

The apartment I was given to use was at the end of a row of six attached, two-story brick buildings. The two-inch oak door was painted black with gold number 18, with a plain knocker. There were two narrow windows on the main floor and two matching windows on the second floor. The roof was shiny black steel. My guess was that the windows were also bullet-proof.

Kieran unlocked the door to let me in as I retrieved my luggage from the boot of my car. The hallway was narrow with polished, solid wood flooring. To the left was another locked door. As we walked down the hall, Kieran pointed to a door about halfway down the hall. "Toilet." At the end of the hall there was another door that Kieran pushed open with a nudge of his shoulder. "This will be your bedroom."

There was only one window at the top of the room above the bed. A rod hung down one side that was attached to a crank on the window that would open it a few inches to allow a breeze. A standard bed filled the center of the room and a closet stood on the wall behind the door. "This is Spartan," I commented.

"No need for luxury. You'll only sleep here. There are two other rooms, I'll show you. Toss your luggage on the bed; you can unpack later," Kieran said.

He shut the door behind us when we left the bedroom. There was another door on the opposite side of the hall, which opened into a kitchen with a gas stove, cast-iron sink, and painted white table with two chairs. "Good thing I'm not much of a cook," I said.

"You'll be taking your meals out. This is only to make a cup of tea or have a snack."

We left the kitchen and walked toward the front door to another door on the right side of the hall. That door led to a postage stamp sized sitting room with two overstuffed chairs, a cast-iron fireplace, and one lamp. While the windows were at least six feet tall, they were narrow, probably about a foot and a half wide and didn't let in very much light. They were covered by full-length, lace curtains.

"Another sparse room, Kieran."

"It's for your reading, nothing more. You won't be having visitors here."

"I appreciate the accommodations but there's a strange air of a prison about this apartment. Why does each room have only one separate entrance, none of the rooms are connected. I hope I won't be living here long."

"It's a special design for safety. Each room is independent and could withstand a petrol bomb or a hand grenade, the window in the bedroom is high to make it difficult to lob something into the room. This isn't an apartment to live in; this is an apartment to be safe in. We're only about two miles from Sinn Finn headquarters. It's common knowledge Sinn Finn owns this block of apartments, has for years, so they are a target, of course. Even through the Troubles, not even the British Army had the audacity or stupidity to attack these apartments; it's why you've been put up here."

I sat down in one of the overstuffed chairs and found an ashtray on the floor near the fireplace. I lit my pipe and tossed the wooden match into the ashtray. I sat back in the chair and took a few moments to absorb my surroundings. "I'm learning already, my friend. I've been naïve about how important personal safety is. It explains the walls, doesn't it? In this city, safety is paramount. Certainly not like Cork. It feels closed in to me. How do people live waking up every morning worried about their safety and the safety of their families? The stress must be unbearable; it would be for me."

Kieran flicked a cigarette butt into the fireplace as he sat in the chair opposite me. "It's become a way of life. They don't know anything different. They couldn't imagine walking down the quay along the river in Cork like you do, any time of day or night. Generations have lived in a war zone. That's why they don't mind if another wall goes up. They see wall and think "security." You see a wall and think division, maybe even insecurity and certainly the political price. They don't care anything about the political; it's their families that matter. Can you blame them?"

I didn't want to answer Kieran, so I busied myself with enjoying my pipe.

"Can you blame them, Ian?"

"Well, it's not about blame, is it? I do hope I can enlighten a few about the political implications. Peace is the greatest security, not walls."

"Aye, maybe so. But you haven't lived here. This will be a much harder assignment than drafting the Peace Accord. A large part of that was writing—what you do. This job will be one of negotiation and building bridges of trust that have never existed before. I'm going to let you settle in. Don't worry, Dominic will be close by. Tonight, we'll have dinner with Gerry and a few other influential folks; we'll talk strategy. Take a nap maybe. We'll likely be up until the next morn."

I raised my eyebrows at Kieran's explanation of the evening events. "I get to meet Gerry?"

"Of course, he's the brains, you know. You'll get along well with him, don't worry."

I knocked my pipe of ashes out on the fireplace floor. "That nap sounds like a good idea. I really do appreciate all you've done for me. I feel sorry for Dominic stuck with babysitting me."

"Don't worry about Dominic, he's a professional. Have a good rest. I'll be back at half six tonight."

"Goodbye, see you then."

I tucked my suitcase into the wardrobe and tested the bed. It was hard and had two oversized pillows, another sign Kieran made all the arrangements personally; he is well aware of my idiosyncrasies. I kicked off my shoes and lay down on my back, crossing my legs at the ankles. I thought about opening the window but wasn't yet comfortable with even that much exposure. My thoughts drifted off to Mairin, wondering if I had accidentally destroyed the only mature relationship with a woman that I have ever had.

Not seeing each other or even talking before I left Cork wasn't a good sign. A lump formed in my throat and an uneasy fear settled in my bones. I had no idea if repairing our relationship was feasible or if she had any desire to see things through. For me, not communicating is the worst of all, it's torture, it's hell on earth. Maybe I'll write her a letter this weekend. That would be quaint, maybe even romantic. I'm at my best with the written word, so that's what I'll do. My body relaxed and soon I was asleep.

✝✝✝

How long had I slept? There wasn't a clock, not even a small alarm clock in the bedroom. I assumed that when it was time to go to dinner that faithful Dominic would be knocking on the door. There wasn't a knock, or if there had been, I slept through it. I walked to the WC and doused my face with cold water to completely wake up and be alert. I then explored the kitchen and noticed a plain wall clock above the sink. It was already half five so I had an hour to idle away.

Unexpectedly, I had an urge to call Mairin, an urge like an itch that had to be scratched. I scanned the kitchen walls and countertops: no phone. I checked the sitting room: no phone. I couldn't remember seeing a phone in the bedroom but checked in case my powers of observation were weak from driving. No phone. While unlikely a phone would be in the WC, I checked just to be thorough. If this were a writers' retreat, that would be perfect, but it wasn't, and I felt isolated in a city of over 250,000 people, at least 50,000 more than Cork.

I unpacked, not because I was filling the void of time, but because I was searching for writing supplies. I had a few of my favorite pens but no paper—none. How could a writer ply his trade without paper? Not everything could be done on those damn computers, and I had resisted the transition for years. Even now I used the computer only for the second draft of a manuscript; the first must be written in hand. Why didn't I have any paper? Damn, my mind had been distracted and this was proof. I would ask Kieran to pick up several tablets for me; he knew what I needed.

I heard the front door open and jumped off the bed. Had I been so absorbed in my own thoughts that I didn't hear a knock? I stood still, listening. I listed to firm determined footsteps, which stopped just outside my door.

"Ian, are ya awake?" Kieran bellowed.

"Jesus, Kieran, did you knock? I didn't hear a knock. Come in. You shook me up, you have."

"Well, I suppose you have no idea what time it is. It's time for me to pick you up for our dinner meeting."

"Surprise, surprise, I know it must be about six because I found a clock in my little cloister and it was half five then."

"Good for you. Let's go, I don't want to be late. We're not ready to go public with your presence in Belfast so tonight we dine privately. Sinn Fein has an office on Antrim, so we'll have food brought in there. Don't worry, I took care of you. I have a bottle of Midleton waiting, but after tonight, I don't want you to drink anything but Bushmills."

"Bushmills is a fine whiskey, that's no sacrifice. Listen, I need a favor. I don't know how but I forgot to bring writing tablets. Could you pick up half a dozen for me?"

"Of course."

"Why isn't there a phone in the apartment I'm staying in, Kieran?"

Kieran ran his hands through his hair and gave me his famous exasperated look.

"Okay, stupid question."

Dominic was sitting in the car parked in front of the apartment. I barely shut the car door before he peeled away from the curb. He glanced back to see me pull the door shut and catch my cuff in the door. "Sorry, Mr. Murphy, old habits. I'll be more careful next time."

"Thank you, Dominic."

The rest of the drive was uneventful. We took a direct route to the office on Antrim, which was also located on the corner. I was beginning to discern a pattern. The home was plain and didn't give the appearance of being a Sinn Fein office, but I doubted that it was much of a secret for anyone in Belfast beyond the age of eleven or twelve.

Dominic parked on the side street, bolted out of the car, and was opening my door before I could even grab the inside handle. I noticed he used his body to block me from the street and escorted me to the door. He knocked and a short, square man with brown hair opened the door a few inches, peeking out to see who was there. He opened the door wider and motioned with one hand for us to enter. I saw the man make eye contact with Dominic, but he said nothing.

I looked around my shoulder to see if Kieran was coming. He was still sitting in the car, but watched us with intensity. I could feel his eyes drill through my head. The three of us stood in the hallway without speaking or having eye contact. Then Kieran was standing next to us like a magician who materialized out of thin air.

Kieran took me by the elbow and led me down the hall. "This way, Ian." At the end of the hall, he pushed through a panel that turned out to be a door leading downstairs. The stairway was pitch black, and I groped my way down one step at a time and put one hand on Kieran's shoulder. When we reached the bottom, Kieran whispered, "Wait."

I heard three sharp raps on a door, which then opened and flooded the stairwell with light. I shielded my eyes.

"Come," Kieran ordered. I stayed close to him, and someone slammed the door behind me as soon as I was in the room.

Three men stood directly in front of us in a semi-circle. "Ian, I'd like to introduce you to Kerry Abbot, Morgan Ellison, and Tomey Robb." He pointed to each man from left to right. In unison, they said: "Mr. Murphy," and we each shook hands. Kieran sat down at a table with six chairs in the center of the room. The rest of us followed his lead and sat down. I didn't notice the smell of any food and the table was completely bare. There was no evidence that we were having dinner.

Kerry Abbot got up without a word, disappeared into an adjoining room and returned with a bottle of Bushmills's and six glasses. He sat a glass in front of each of us and one in front of the empty chair. I took my glass in my hand and brought it to my lips, eager to have a sip of Northern Ireland's pride. Kieran cleared his throat and shook his head at me. Then I noticed that each of the men sat, holding their tumblers, but not drinking.

It was clear that we were waiting for the person who would take the last chair. I took a moment to study each of the men.

Abbot had a narrow face with stubble that looked like he hadn't shaved in several days. The collar of his shirt was soiled and turned up at the ends.

Ellison was a surprise; he looked like the product of an English finishing school. His black hair was parted neatly and combed so that each hair lay back perfectly. His Roman nose gave him a royal appearance. I could smell the faint scent of aftershave, so he must have shaved just before the meeting.

Robb looked like a picture of the average Irishman with a round face, pug nose, and rosy cheeks. He was bald with a bit of short, gray hair in a ring around his head. Kieran must have noticed me studying the men because he cleared his throat again.

A distinguished man appeared as if by magic, standing behind the empty chair. "Gentlemen," he said and sat down.

"Mr. Murphy, I'm pleased that you're joining us. Your work on the Peace Accord was instrumental in completing that task; words are a gift with you. Now, your task is to make those words come alive. Mr. Murphy, Sinn Fein is an idea. I've been working for fifteen years to make the idea of Sinn Fein have meaning in our daily lives in Northern Ireland. What do I mean by that? *Sinn Fein*—we ourselves—means self-determination. Yes, once there was a dream of reunifying Ireland, but we are, in fact, two countries, in our economy, our culture, and our religion. By Sinn Fein, we now mean self-determination.

We are on the brink of creating our own country, independent of Britain after more than 300 years. I know I'm preaching to the choir, but you need to understand, to have context for the work ahead of you. I don't know if Kieran told you but the IRA leader, Dolan Halloran, had left the country. His dream, his IRA is dead and it has to be. I'm told he's somewhere in Denmark, and that's good both for him and for us. Yet, there are those in the old Provisional IRA that cling to the dream.

"I honestly thought that when Kieran joined me, others would follow. Some did. Some didn't. There is a core group that's incorrigible and view me and Sinn Fein as traitors. It is this group that refuses to turn in arms. So our conundrum is that the leaders refuse to form a government until the RIRA at least begins to turn in arms, and the hangers-on just refuse because they don't agree with forming a separate Northern Ireland government. Before leaving our island, the Brits are threatening to build more peace walls to demonstrate to the world that we can't live with each other. Ironically, there are both Catholic and Protestant leaders who agree with building more walls; they call it "the price of peace." As politics have always been in Northern Ireland, our issues are woven together like a Celtic knot. The men at this table can be trusted. They will help you. They know what I want done and have the skills to make it happen. Depend on them. This is the only time we will be speaking directly. Questions?"

I sat there, absorbed in the speech I had heard. I now understood how this one man had led Sinn Fein for fifteen years. He had a commanding presence and an air of informal dignity and authority. He was the type of man people liked to follow. When he talked to you, he looked directly at you without making you feel uncomfortable. His smile was shy, charming, and inviting. When I thought of people I would like to have dinner with, his name was on the top of the nonliterary group. I understood we wouldn't be having dinner together and that was fine.

"Questions, Mr. Murphy," he asked again.

I looked directly into his face. "No, you've been very concise, thank you."

"Then let's raise our glasses," he said as he stood up.

All of us stood and raised our glasses as directed. He broke out in a wide grin. "*Sliocht sleachta ar shliocht bhur sleachta.*" (Blessings on your posterity.)

"*Slainte!*" we shouted in unison at the top of our voices and downed our whiskey in a single gulp. When our glasses hit the table, the leader of Sinn Fein was no longer in the room. His toast struck a chord deep in my soul. It was the maiming of children in the Peace Zone two years ago that forced me to question the morality of the Troubles and my responsibility for innocent deaths. I now understood; we were all working for posterity, to give them a life we had never had, but desperately wished for them. All parents wish to leave their children a better world than the one they were born into. The great sadness was how infrequently that happened, an Irish world view for sure. Yet, we strove. We must.

I shared dinner with my new friends, and they briefed me, in detail, about the current stalemate. It was a critical point that both Catholics and Protestants agreed with building more peace walls, and the fact that they frankly didn't care what world opinion was over their inability and unwillingness to coexist. They gave me a list of people I could talk with, both Catholics and Protestants, about the proposal to build the walls. Having contacts with the former Provisional IRA members was more difficult.

Dolan wasn't available. He elected to retire in Denmark because it was thought that the Danes were the most content people in the world. I don't know how that was measured, and it probably didn't matter. All that mattered was that Dolan had completely washed his hands of leadership. And it was clear he wanted to be left alone, which after thirty years at war anyone, especially me, understood. His absence created a vacuum that left the organization within the IRA in a shambles and that none of us that had been part of it could recognize. What was incomprehensible to me was that Kieran Fitzpatrick no longer had any influence with the remaining IRA activists.

"So now that you've had a briefing, what's your plan, Mr. Murphy?" Ellison asked me as he leaned forward on his elbows. I stroked my beard a few times, which Mairin says I do absentmindedly. This time, it was intentional. I looked at each man in turn, except Kieran; I avoided eye contact with him. Did they really expect me to give birth to a detailed, intricate plan right in front of them? I needed time to digest all the information they had dumped on me this evening.

"Honestly, gentlemen, I don't know. You've given me a lot of information. What's missing is the soul of it all. I need to get to know the people here, both Catholics and Protestants, and I need to embed myself with the remaining dissidents. I'm beginning to feel that having my sister, Caitlin, here would be very helpful, but I don't know if that's feasible or practical. I don't want to appear arrogant and impose myself on this situation, boasting of all the answers."

"We respect your judgment, Mr. Murphy. We would have been a bit disappointed if you would have shown up with ready-made solutions. It's complex and you've grasped that," Tomey Robb explained.

"What about his sister coming up?" Morgan Ellison asked Kieran.

Kieran hunched his shoulders. "Don't know."

"Will you explore it?" Kerry Abbot asked Kieran.

"If Ian feels it would help, of course I will. If, and I say again, if she's willing to come back to Belfast, it will take some time. I won't make a commitment on when she would be here."

As usual, Kieran was cautious. Before this meeting, I never would have imagined that I would want Caitlin's help, but her experience living here for more than a decade was suddenly a huge asset in addressing these problems. Tiredness descended on me like Mahon Falls. My eyelids felt heavy, and I could feel my body slump in the chair.

"It's been a long evening. It must be late. I need to sleep. For me, a four-hour drive from Cork to here is an eternity. Thank you for your time and all the information. I will depend on each of you in the coming months."

Kerry Abbot pulled a railroad-man's watch from his pocket and flipped open the cover. "I'll be damned; it's nearly one in the morning. We should be tired. Let us know how we can help, Mr. Murphy."

"That I will, thank you."

I was anxious to get Kieran alone in the car. There were questions burning that I had to ask but was uncertain about asking in front of the group we had just met with. Dominic was waiting in the car, which he parked on the curb outside the Sinn Fein regional office. The motor was running. Kieran motioned for me to get in the door that was curbside, and he walked around to the driver's side and slipped in before I could even open the car door. It was a small car and with two of us in the back, we were shoulder to shoulder.

I grabbed Kieran's arm to get his attention. "Kieran, I don't understand this renegade group of old Provies who are refusing to turn in their arms. Don't you control them?"

"Shhh." He tried to cut off my question before I was fin-ished. His eyes flared, and he turned ruby red. His signal was unmistakable, so I shut up and stared out the car window as

Dominic took a very indirect route back to the house. I didn't know what to expect when we arrived. I wanted Kieran to come in so that we could continue the conversation, especially because he wouldn't allow it in the car. Kieran didn't give me any clues. When the car stopped, I looked at Kieran, raising an eyebrow as if to ask if he would be joining me. He grunted. I opened the door, got out, and wiggled the door handle to the house and found it locked, when I heard from behind me, "Sorry, Ian, forgot. I've got the key." Kieran scooted in front of me. The latch clicked open, and I turned around to see the car drive off.

"Good, you're staying; I have a lot of questions for you."

"That's obvious, but never in front of others," Kieran instructed.

"You don't trust Dominic?"

"It's not a matter of trust, more a matter of exposure."

"Kieran, I don't understand."

"You don't need to understand; it's my job. Now, let's find the whiskey and a couple of tumblers and I'll answer all your questions. I planned to stay on the couch tonight, anyway."

With glasses full, we made ourselves comfortable in the sitting room. I lit a peat fire, kicked off my shoes, and filled my pipe to the brim, expecting to see the sun rise.

"Ian, after Dolan left the county, everything went to shit. No one expected him to leave. It was even a surprise to me."

"You were surprised; I've never heard you admit that before."

"Everyone felt abandoned and angry with him for running away. I worked with the man shoulder to shoulder thirty years but never really knew him. Hell, I don't even know if he has family—can you imagine?"

"When did he leave?"

"The day after the resolution vote. He slithered into the office and announced he was moving to Denmark. He shook everyone's hand and walked away. That simple, that direct."

"He didn't offer an explanation?"

"Nope."

"What about the rest of the council?"

"They just evaporated, like they had never existed. Not one of them has been in the office since the day Dolan left, except me, of course."

"Incredible. So why can't you reel in the misfits who won't cooperate?"

"The truth is, I'm not even sure who they are. I don't know the Belfast gang. My job was always outside Belfast. Of course, we never had a list of names. You know the rule of six; each man knew only six others in the organization. I only knew the other members of the Council."

I puffed away on my pipe, downed the whiskey, and poured myself another. "It's ironic, isn't it? Our strength is also our weakness. Doesn't Sinn Fein know who they are?"

"That's an interesting question. My brain tells me they do, or they should, anyway, but my gut tells me they're clueless. The relationship between Sinn Fein and the Provies has always been complex and secretive. The British army is laughing their arses off about the situation; we're incompetent from their viewpoint. For Christ's sake, Ian, share that bottle. I'm parched."

I noticed the bottle was already half empty when I handed it to Kieran. He lit a cigarette and took in a long draw, blowing it out as he sipped his whiskey. Our conversation reached an end with neither of us knowing what to say. I finished my pipe and dumped the ashes into the fire. "Where do we start?"

Kieran leaned forward covering his face with his hands.

"Well, I'll start by making arrangements to have Caitlin join us. That was a good idea. I assume you know she'll be willing to give it a go. You, my friend, start with that asshole in Omagh. At least you've met him. All we want from him is information, names of the Belfast gang."

"I'm exhausted, Kieran, I'm going to bed. Thanks for your honesty. I was full of hope driving up here, now—now, I'm not so sure. Looks bleak."

"Don't make any premature judgments, my friend. Go to sleep."

TWENTY-SEVEN

I went to my bedroom but didn't sleep. I couldn't sleep. Many nights, the whiskey lulled me into a dreamless sleep, and I would wake the next morning wet with sweat. That night the whiskey was ineffective. I longed for the case of Midleton that was in the back of my car, which was who knows where. Whiskey produced in Northern Ireland was no good for sleep; it was my first lesson in living in what I was quickly learning was a foreign country. While we all share one island, Northern Ireland might as well be on a different continent. I wasn't prepared for the dismal assessment faced by this new-found country. I erroneously expected to have contacts I might be able to negotiate with to delay building more peace walls and someone in authority among the rebels to convince them it was in their interest to turn in all their weapons.

I paced back and forth in the cell-sized room to tire myself out but it didn't work. The walking made me more alert and my brain felt like it was part of the Beltane fires that are lit to celebrate the coming of spring. I kept reviewing all the information I had been given tonight, searching for an angle, a strategy, just someplace to get started.

The best idea was to ask for Caitlin's help. I knew it would be a sacrifice for her to leave Brianna in Cork. I never would have imagined that I would need my sister to help me tackle the overwhelming problems of this tiny country. At least they had not asked for my assistance in forming a government. I knew absolutely nothing about how to form a government, which, on reconsideration, might have been a wonderful advantage.

Caitlin would be shocked when Kieran talked with her and asked her to return to Belfast City. She left the city defeated, her ideals shattered, and her daughter severely wounded by some thug that tossed a Molotov cocktail indiscriminately over a peace wall with no idea of the damage it would render. Caitlin would also be confused by Kieran's making the request and not me. I had told him to make the request in my name, but I must admit she will wonder why I didn't talk with her myself. Actually, I can't answer that question even for myself. I wanted to call Caitlin, but Kieran wouldn't allow it.

There would be a lot of arrangements to be made for Caitlin to return to Belfast. She must get a release from her job and decide if Brianna will stay in Cork or join us in Belfast. To join us here, Brianna would need to be in school, which wouldn't be fair to her. We no longer had relatives in Cork so Brianna would need to stay with friends, and I don't think they had lived in Cork long enough to find a friend who would be willing to have Brianna move in with them for some indeterminate time.

While I had lived in Cork for most of my life, I couldn't boast of any friends who would take care of her, except for maybe…Mickey. There it is! The perfect solution, if Caitlin would agree. Brianna called Mickey uncle and would be comfortable in his home. His wife would dote on having a child in the house again. I hoped Kieran thought of that solution. When I see him in the morning, I'll make sure to mention it to him.

I paced with such determination that beads of sweat rolled off my face and onto my shirt collar. I collapsed on the bed and shut my eyes, but still couldn't sleep. Was I misled on how difficult it would be to take on this job? Kieran never mentioned that he had no contacts in Belfast City or that he didn't even know who was leading the rebel IRA leaders. As for the peace walls, it was easy to blame the British for making a display of their former colony.

Could fear be so engrained that people would willingly build walls to separate themselves? It was like the Tower of Babel in the twentieth century. The Chinese built the Great Wall for defense, using slaves; it was a wall of death, used to keep the Mongols out of China. The Russians built the wall in Berlin after the war to keep people in, enslaved in their own country and separated from their kin. It didn't last. The walls in Belfast are unique in the world, they separate two peoples with the consent of the people themselves; self-imposed apartheid. How absurd. A purely Irish solution to a social and political impasse.

I swirled into a deep depression, realizing that my likelihood of success for the RIRA to hand in their arms or stop the new walls from being built was remote, if not impossible. Why did they choose me? I'm a writer, not a politician. I don't have the constitution to take on Northern Ireland. This is a mistake. I don't belong here. I left Mairin in Cork for this? I gave up writing my memoir for this? I have no one to turn for guidance; I'm alone in a foreign land, staring failure and rejection in the face. My right hand clenched so tightly I couldn't pry my fingers from their tight curl. I could feel nails digging into my palm with blood seeping from beneath them. I fell back on the bed and cried.

I didn't know if I fell asleep or passed out; it didn't matter. When I opened my eyes again, rays of sunlight danced on the ceiling. I was spread-eagle on my back with my feet dangling over the edge. When I tried to move, my back wrenched. With extraordinary effort, I got up by propping an elbow on the bed and rolling off to one side. I dug my elbows into the edge of the bed and pushed myself up with my feet. I looked like an inverted V, a ridiculous sight. Inch by inch, I stood up straight.

I needed to talk to Kieran, now. I edged my way down the hallway, shuffling my feet. I peeked into the sitting room where I expected Kieran to be asleep, but the room was empty. Damn, gone. I didn't have the strength to check in the kitchen and knew to regain anything resembling normalcy, I needed a very hot shower.

After the shower, I dressed and went to the front window to peek out. There, in a black sedan, sat Dominic, smoking a cigarette and reading a newspaper. I could depend on Dominic to always be close by.

I opened the passenger door and slid in next to him.

"Mr. Murphy, good morning, sir."

"Morning."

"You look a bit rough, if you don't mind me sayin'."

"You're honest. I never mind honesty, Dominic."

"Where will it be then, sir?"

"That's a good question. Where will it be, then?"

Dominic folded the paper into quarters and tossed it into the back seat. He smashed his cigarette between his thumb and finger, then flipped it out the car window.

"Cork would be nice."

"I'm not authorized for that, Mr. Murphy. Belfast is my limit. Outside Belfast, you need to talk to Mr. Fitzpatrick."

"Don't be so literal, Dominic. I wasn't serious."

"Literal?"

"Never mind. Please, call me Ian. We're going to be spending a lot of time together and there's no need to be formal. What time is it?"

"Half eleven."

"Have you seen Kieran yet?"

"His car came to pick him up about eight."

Jesus, I don't know how he does it, I thought to myself.

"Were would you like to go, Ian?"

"Truth be told, I could use a drink, and I slept through breakfast. Do you have a favorite pub?"

"Aye."

"Then we're off. Can you have lunch with me?"

"That's not allowed, sir."

"No more sir, if you please. Listen, I need to get to know some people here, people who have lived here for years, regular people, working people; people who would be willing to talk with me, teach me what it's like to live here day in and day out; people who have experienced losses during the Troubles."

Dominic started the car and drove slowly down the street. "There's plenty of folks like that, Ian. I want you to meet my friend Vern O'Flahertie, he runs a pub on Ballymurphy Road. You'll be at home there, and many speak Irish."

"Perfect, let's drive there straight away. I'm thirsty and my stomach is beginning to churn."

I don't know how long we drove, but I thought it must have been more than thirty minutes; Dominic disregarded my need for both drink and food. Clearly his first priority was my safety, not my creature comforts. To calm myself, I loaded up a pipe and filled the car with blue smoke as we drove. Dominic rolled down his window but said nothing about smoke clouding the windows and obscuring his view. I was learning that there was no direct route to anyplace in Belfast, by design. I needed to learn their ways, and I could only do that by keeping quiet and observing—natural for a writer. *Maybe that's why they chose me for this job*, I thought.

TWENTY-EIGHT

Dominic parked directly in front of a pub, as if the spot had been reserved for our car. That had to be impossible, I was sure, but how likely was it that there would be a free spot directly in front of a pub during lunch time? I think it unlikely. I suspected Dominic had ways of communicating that were totally unknown to me and so secretive that I would never be given access to their surreptitious ways.

There was an oval sign hanging above the door in a traditional Gaelic font with gold lettering on black background. The first line read: O'Flahertie's, and just below it, but not centered: Irish Public House. Curious, I thought, that the establishment would be called an Irish Public House. In this section of Belfast, there would be none other. Maybe in East Belfast, there were British public houses. I would need to learn.

"This is it then, Ian," Dominic said. "I want you to meet the owner. Our families have been friends since my granda. Our sons play on the same hurling team. O'Flahertie, he's grand, he is."

The pub could have been used as a picture for those tourist guides to show what to expect in a traditional Irish pub. When you entered, there was a long mahogany bar with twelve matching stools. Behind the bar was a full-length mirror with shelves mounted in front holding every type of hard liquor a soul could ever desire. Sprouting out of the center of the bar were two brass spigots. One would be for the black, I'm sure, but the other was a mystery. I would ask.

Behind the bar stood one of the tallest Irishmen I had ever seen. He looked like Michael Collins might have looked had he lived into his sixties. His gray hair was slicked straight back and pointed in the front like the V formation of geese flying overhead. His eyes were bright, steel gray with a hint of the mischievous and lines at the edges of his eyes. He had the full, broad face of an Irishman with a bit of a pug nose for a man his size. He must have stood at least six and three. He wore a crisp white shirt, open at the collar, sleeves rolled up to above the elbow. The shirt fit tightly around his pear-shaped middle. His face broke into a grin when he saw Dominic walk in behind me.

"Good lad, Dominic. You've brought one of your fares for lunch. That's grand," he said.

"Mr. Murphy, I'm proud to introduce my lifelong friend, Vernon Brady O'Flahertie."

O'Flahertie looked me up and down. "Murphy, the writer?" he asked.

"One and the same, Vern," Dominic said.

"*An bhfuil Gaeilge agat?* (Do you speak Gaelic)?" O'Flahertie asked.

"*Ta* (Yes)," I said looking directly into his eyes.

"Welcome to my humble establishment, Mr. Murphy. Any man who speaks Irish is a friend. Dominic, you've done well. Can I serve you both a pint of the black?"

"Aye," Dominic smiled. Thirst was growing in him.

I sat on a stool and folded my hands in front of me on top of the bar. "I'd rather a whiskey; it's early but I could use one."

"I've never refused a man a whiskey because of the hour of day and I'm not about to start. I'll pour you a glass right after I draw Dominic's black," O'Flahertie said.

Dominic pulled out the stool next to mine and sat down. "How about two specials, Vern? I could hear Mr. Murphy's stomach growling on the drive."

O'Flahertie set the drinks in front of us. "I have a room in the back where we can talk. It will be more comfortable there," Dominic said and grabbed his beer and led me to the private room.

"If you want to learn about Catholics in Belfast, this is the place. You've passed the test by speaking Irish. It's safe for us here. We often speak in Irish to protect ourselves and honor our heritage," Dominic explained.

"Did you know I teach Irish through Irish literature at University College Cork?"

"I did not. How fortunate for us."

Two young women came in with steaming plates, setting down two bowls and some type of bread that smelled fresh from the oven.

"What is our pleasure?" I asked.

"You need to become accustomed to our traditional meals, Mr. Murphy," Vern said "Here is a bowl of fresh potted herring and wheaten bread just out of the oven. There's a slab of cultured butter on the plate next to the bread. There's nothing better. You won't find food like this in the south," Vern boasted.

I dug in with full vigor and didn't look up until I was sopping up the last spoonful of the fish broth with my bread. When I did look up, both Dominic and Vern were watching me with a note of glee in their eyes.

"I told you he was hungry, Vern. For a man his size, he's a healthy eater."

"He's proven that," responded Vern.

"Gentlemen, I'm sitting in front of you. Please don't talk about me in the third person."

They looked at each other and hunched their shoulders. "Third person?" they said in unison.

"Never mind, just talk to me directly. Now, I'm here to learn about Belfast, and Dominic suggested this was the place.

There must be a reason you asked if I spoke Irish at our first introduction."

Vern pushed back his chair and extended his legs out to the side of the table. "It's a code."

"A code?" I asked.

"The British want to believe that Irish is like Latin, a dead language, so we speak Irish to tell our secrets and keep our culture thriving. The sign on the front proclaims this is an Irish Public House, which means Irish is spoken here. Every person who passes through the front door is expected to speak Irish," Vern explained.

"We teach Irish in school; it's not a dead language, everyone knows that," I said.

"In the Republic yes, but this is Northern Ireland, Mr. Murphy. My understanding was you were the one who insisted the Good Friday Agreement include the right to acknowledge our Irish heritage and speak our language openly," Vern said.

"I did."

"You are our hero, Mr. Murphy. That Peace Accord, it was fine and officially gave us our language back. No, you won't be forgotten."

I bowed my head, uncomfortable being called a hero. Then I looked up into his smiling face and scrunched my face into a sideways grin.

"Dominic here says you're lifting heavy weight here. I don't see how we can be any use to you, but we'll try. What do ya want?" Vern raised his eyebrows in question.

I leaned toward Vern, putting my arms crosswise on the table. I looked deep into his eyes to measure the depth of the man. "I'll be blunt. I need two things. First, I need names. I need to know who's leading the gang refusing to turn in their weapons. Second, I need to talk to folks about the threat of building more peace walls to separate the Catholics from the Protestants."

Vern looked at Dominic, then at me and then studied his hands resting on his lap. "That's a lot," he said without looking up.

"Can you help?" I asked in a pleading tone.

Vern's face changed into a painful, twisted expression, as if someone was wringing his arm.

"I don't mean to put you into jeopardy or risk harm of any kind," I said.

"Your second request is easy. Most of my customers, friends really, live within the shadow of a peace wall. Those walls have been both our defense and our safety for thirty years. You won't understand that, Mr. Murphy. Dominic can bring you to the pub to meet the locals. Spend all the time in my pub you want. Drinks are on the house; food you'll need to pay for. Ask the gents you meet here about the walls. There's an education in it for you. Where you from again?"

"Cork."

"I thought I knew that accent. All yous from Cork have a peculiar way of talking, at least to my ear."

I rolled my head back and let out a deep, gutteral laugh. "So it's said, Vern, so it's said. What about the names?"

Vern pulled his legs in and leaned forward, placing his elbows on his knees with his head down. I looked at Dominic, wanting some sign from him. It was clear this was a sensitive topic, and I wasn't sure why. This was a Republican bar, a safe place for the soldiers of the Troubles. People knew things; it was how it had worked for decades. I didn't think my request was unreasonable. Everyone knew about my history in the Provisional IRA. I was one of the brethren, not an outsider, and yet...I gave Vern all the time and space he needed.

If I insisted, I would lose his trust before earning it. I wanted to let him off the hook and tell him to forget it, yet, he or one of his customers had to be the best source there was.

None of them was talking with anyone at Sinn Fein, but I was not connected to Sinn Fein, at least not directly. My guess was that they all knew Kieran Fitzpatrick. Should I use his name to encourage cooperation? Of course, Kieran had said he didn't have good connections here, but surely he was a known person, a trusted person. Did they know Kieran had been given the job of killing me and chose friendship over loyalty to the Provies? It seemed like minutes passed without Vern or Dominic speaking.

"Look, Mr. Murphy, I'm no miracle worker. The truth is, I don't know who's behind it and I haven't asked, not sure I want to know. I understand there are some who see the Good Friday Agreement as a sell-out. I'm not sayin' I think that. We ought to try makin' our own government without the Brits and without the Republic. That's fair. We can take care of ourselves, given the chance."

Vernon O'Flahertie surprised me. There was a real depth of character to him and a keen sense of what was happening to his country. This country could have used men like Vern by the thousands.

"Would you be at risk if I ask the regulars?"

"Not me. I've made it known it's none of my business. If they ask me, I'll share my views, but that's where it ends. Most won't be asking me. All they ask of me is good whiskey, good food, and a safe place. I've been doing that almost forty years and my father and grandfather before me. There's no question of that. You? I can't guarantee your safety if you start asking a lot of uncomfortable questions. That's your choice. Be prepared to live with any consequences. Make sure Dominic is always close by; that's all you can do."

I looked toward Dominic. He winked at me and patted the side of his coat. I understood.

"I can ask no more of you, Vernon O'Flahertie."

TWENTY-NINE

very evening for three weeks, I visited with the patrons of the Irish Public House, with Dominic always close at hand. I'm not sure how many people I talked with. It must have been close to two hundred or more. One unusual aspect: they were all men. I didn't talk to a single female, which I found curious. Women came to the pub and appeared to enjoy it just as the men did, but only men were sent to me to talk. Northern Ireland is more conservative than the Republic, and I concluded that one feature was the lack of women involved in public and political issues. It may have helped to explain their radicalism; there was no balancing contribution from women.

Of the hundreds I talked with, three stood out and especially one, Francis Farrell. He was the only person to insist on meeting back in O'Flahertie's office.

Dominic escorted me to the office without anyone in the pub noticing. Farrell was sitting behind the desk, a pack of Major extra-size cigarettes with the message "smoking kills" written in both Irish and English in dark, black letters on the front was sitting in the center of the desk next to a glass ashtray and a cheap, American Zippo lighter. Farrell watched me with unexpressive, light blue eyes. He didn't appear to blink, which I found unnerving. He noticed me looking at the cigarettes and broke into an open-mouthed smile, revealing two teeth missing in front and the bottom row stained like brown pavement tiles. He reached into his pocket, pulled out a revolver, and slammed it on the desk next to the ashtray. "This fucker kills too, so what. Anything can kill a man if yous think about it, eh?"

I turned around to check if Dominic was in the room. He had closed the door in silence and was standing with his arms crossed in front of him directly behind me.

"I guess that's true, Mr. Farrell."

We took account of each other across the desk. Farrell's nose was bent to one side of his face and looked as if it had been broken more than once. As a result, his breathing was labored, or as I learned during our talk, it may have been from chain smoking. Farrell had an edge about him that was both mysterious and noticeable. This was not a man I wanted to meet in a dark alley or for that matter in an alley at lunchtime. His hands had huge knuckles and he wasn't able to straighten his fingers out, yet he was too young to have arthritis set in.

His knuckles were the result of a lifetime at the shipyard or a lifetime fighting or both.

"Ol' Vern let it out you wanted to talk to some locals."

"That's correct."

"I'm local."

"Excellent."

"Whadya want, I mean talk an' all."

"I don't want to waste your time, Frank."

"Francis be my Christian name, not Frank. Time, time, I got."

"No offense, I didn't intend to be so informal."

"Do I look poor? Keep yer money, Mr. Murphy."

"Ian. Please call me Ian."

"Jesus, Mary, Joseph, and all the Holy Martyrs on a first name way, I am with Mr. Ian Murphy. Ok, how can ol' Francis Farrell help ya?"

"I'll be direct. I need names. I need to find out who's leading the old Provies and convincing them to not turn in arms. The Brits are already saying the ol' boys are not to be trusted. They're saying the Peace Accord isn't worth the paper it's printed on."

Farrell lit a cigarette, the end glowing like the noonday sun as he drew in a deep breath and held smoke in his lungs longer than I thought feasible.

"No names." Farrell blurted out. "You know the pledge. The pledge is good to the grave, thought you already knew that."

"I know the pledge. These are different times, Francis. I'm not turning anyone in. I spent too many years as a Provie myself. I only want to talk with them. I want to convince them it's a mistake to resist. Forming a government is our task now. We need to show the Republic, the Brits, and the rest of the world that Northern Ireland can govern itself in peace. To do that, we need a government."

Farrell picked up the pistol in the center of the table and stroked it as if it were his lover. He opened the chamber and emptied six bullets out on the table. He picked up each bullet and fingered it a few moments. He shook the bullets in his hand as if he were rolling dice and then slammed them down on the desk. He looked up at me, one tear escaped from his eyes and trickled down his cheek.

"You can start with me. God knows my family has suffered enough. I lost a brother and two cousins. It's only by the grace of God that I'm talkin' with you now. I've robbed death three times myself. At least we're rid of the Brits. I knows you helped with that, Ian. I respect that. So, take this fecking pistol, turn it in. Tell them you got it from a real soldier."

My mouth dropped in disbelief. Farrell's response to me was completely unexpected. I felt I had found a comrade who was as tired of the struggle as I was and came to the same conclusion: Enough is enough. My respect for the stranger sitting in front of me swelled. I looked back at Dominic; his face was like stone. Looking back at him must have been an unintentional signal. He moved quickly around me and scooped up the pistol and bullets off the desk and stuffed them into his jacket pocket. Farrell didn't flinch at Dominic's swift action.

"Thank you, Francis. I will be proud to let the authorities know. I won't reveal your name."

"They knows me well. But you're right; they don't need to know it was me."

"I hope you will let your comrades know about the brave action you've taken this morning. Trust is hard, I know. Trust must begin with a leap of faith, like the leap you've just taken."

Farrell stubbed out his cigarette and lit another in one continuous motion. "Ain't got nothin' to do with trust, Ian. I don't trust them bastards now and don't expect I will before I'm planted. It's what yous call mutual interest. I get that, don't I?"

His words gave me a lesson I hadn't expected. I wanted to build trust between the Catholics and the Protestants and those trying to put together their first independent government. Government based on trust is a political theory, a political ideal, not political reality. Francis Farrell was my teacher about how the world really works.

"Well, this has been a very productive meeting and quite a life lesson for me, Francis Farrell; I want to shake your hand," I said.

"I thought you wanted names?" Farrell asked.

"You've relinquished your pistol, a huge symbolic gesture I never expected. I don't want to pressure you for names. I don't want to jeopardize your safety."

"Well, there's a couple a other fellas you can talk with, like you talked to me. Colum Boyle and Neil Daly, they're friends of mine. Look, these boys are not leaders, but it would be in your interest to talk to them, if you get my meaning."

I jumped up and took Francis Farrell's knotted hand in both of my hands and pumped his arm. "Bless you and all yours, Francis Farrell, you are a man among men." I felt the need to leave immediately. The meeting had given me more than I could have wished. Dominic winked as he opened the door for me. The stone face had actually broken his own code. We left the pub without speaking to anyone and sped away in the sedan without my telling Dominic where I wanted to go.

After driving through the streets of West Belfast for at least fifteen minutes, Dominic broke the silence. "I guess you want to talk to Boyle and Daly."

"Absolutely."

"I know them," Dominic said without emotion.

"I'm not surprised."

"Do you want to see them together or separately?" Dominic asked.

I thought about his question and was surprised that he even asked. "What do you recommend?"

Dominic glanced in the rearview mirror and concentrated on what he saw before answering my question.

"Together would be fine. It would need to be in private, like today."

"That's fine, of course," I said without hesitation.

"It will probably take several days to arrange."

"That's fine. I hope I don't have to be imprisoned in the apartment waiting for a meeting. Those walls are closing in on me. Do you always have to be with me?"

"It's for your safety. I got a job. I can't be arranging for meetings and watching you at the same time, can I?"

I felt a surge of anger swell up in me like a volcano ready to blow. "Dominic, I refuse to be caged like some animal!"

"No disrespect, Mr. Murphy, but hollerin' at me does you no good. I ain't your jailer, I'm just your protection. You got issues, you take it up with Kieran Fitzpatrick."

I let out a long sigh and took a few breaths to compose myself before speaking. "I apologize, Dominic. Whatever you can do to get those two gentlemen together will be appreciated. As you know, I'm available anytime. Maybe I should talk to Kieran. Can you let him know?"

"Of course."

We pulled up outside the apartment and our protocol was for me to wait for Dominic to come around, open the car door, then watch him bound up the steps to unlock the apartment door and open it for me. I ducked and bolted up the stairs in just two steps and fell into the hallway. Dominic slammed the door behind me and it shook in the frame.

THIRTY

realized I had been so excited about Francis Farrell's decision to turn in his pistol to me and give me two more names, that I didn't eat lunch. Dominic whisked me away from the pub and planted me in the apartment before I realized my stomach was in revolt. The refrigerator was a barren cave. I checked the cupboards and found only a bag of Caffrey's snowballs and Thompson's Family Punjana tea. I was definitely in Northern Ireland, Indian tea just like you would find in England. I suppose it was unreasonable to expect the kitchen to be stocked with Barry's Tea, even though Kieran was well aware it was my standard brew. I was being forced to expand my horizon, even if I wanted a cup of tea.

I brewed the tea and found it had an unusual but not unpleasant aroma. I put the mug of tea and bag of snowballs on a tray and settled into the sitting room. There was a stack of books on the table that I would examine once I had a bite. I finished the entire bag of snowballs, and I slurped down the last bit of tea. The tea wasn't bad; I just wasn't accustomed to it. Given enough time, I could learn to drink it on a regular basis, at least for the time I lived in Northern Ireland.

I was distracted by the stack of books on the table when I heard the front door open and shut. "Ian, are ya about?" I heard Kieran scream.

"Where else would I be, you eejit?" I screamed back.

"Don't be mean, Ian Padraic Murphy. I bring good news."

I smiled at him. "Oh, you brought me carry-out—how thoughtful."

"Carry-out? Why would I bring you carry-out?" Kieran asked.

"I assume Dominic let you know he yanked me away from the pub so quickly after our meeting with Frances Farrell, I didn't have lunch."

Kieran broke out into one of his belly laughs. "That explains the bag of snowballs. I didn't think you had much of a sweet tooth. There's not much food in this apartment, is there?"

"That's an understatement," I snarled.

Kieran looked around for the chair and plopped down without taking off his coat and hat. He searched through his coat until be brought out cigarettes and a box of matches. "Well, then I have two pieces of good news."

I followed Kieran's lead and sat down across from him, tossing the empty snowball bag on the floor. I packed my pipe tight and soon was enjoying plumes of smoke and the tobacco's sweet aroma. "Now, it's two good things. I like the direction, please share, my friend."

"Well first, I'll have a woman come by to cook your meals. You'll need to let me know what time you want your meals."

"I'm stuck eating alone? Jesus, it's like being back in Cork. I thought maybe I could use at least dinner to meet some of the locals; it wouldn't be quite so lonely."

"You complain about being alone? I must have misunderstood you."

"There's a difference between being alone and being lonely. I'm accustomed to being alone in my cottage but this is different. I'm lonely here. I'm the proverbial fish out of water."

"The cook can eat with you, if you like."

"Better than eating three meals by myself, isn't it? Fine. What's the second piece of good news. While I'm appreciative, so far I'm underwhelmed."

"You've become difficult in middle age, Ian. Well, the good news is that in a few days, Caitlin will be here."

I couldn't resist clapping and shouting, "Hurrah!" Then I became somber as I thought about Brianna. "What about Brianna? I know Caitlin would never let her come back to Belfast under any circumstances."

Kieran threw his cigarette in the fireplace. He was inattentive and it singed the tips of his fingers. "Her teacher has agreed to take her in for as long as Caitlin is here."

"That's perfect, isn't it? I guess for security reasons, you won't allow Caitlin to stay here with me."

"You're catching on, Ian. She still has friends here; she'll stay with them. I had to promise her she would be away no more than a month. You understand that, don't you? She didn't want to tell you herself. I got the dirty job, always do."

"A month is fine, of course. I'm surprised her visit wasn't limited to a fortnight. She's going out on a limb. That's my sister. A Murphy family trait, if I don't mind saying so myself."

Kieran wiggled in his chair. "Now don't be asking me what day she'll arrive. The less you know, the better, just in case."

I gave myself a few minutes to let Kieran's words sink in. "I understand. After just a few weeks in Belfast, I understand a lot of things. You didn't happen to see Mairin while you were in Cork, did you?"

Kieran cleared his throat and coughed like a man who had smoked for forty years. "Let's not talk about Mairin."

My pipe nearly dropped out of my mouth. "That bad, is it? Have I lost her, Kieran?"

"Not for me to say, Ian."

Kieran's face changed as quickly as a chameleon changes color. "I won't be able to have a cook here until tomorrow. Look, let's go out for a late lunch, then we'll take a driving tour of Belfast. I want you to see the peace walls up close, get a feel for them, smell them, see how they block the sun. I think even the Jews and the Arabs tolerate each other without walls. As a race, there are times we're despicable."

"We are a strange people and we get stranger when we're starved. Let's go eat. I have news for you, too."

As soon as we got into the car, I told Kieran about the incredible meeting with Francis Farrell. I learned that Kieran didn't know Farrell or the other two men I would be meeting with. He wasn't joking when he told me he didn't know the Provies in Belfast. It was proof again that the IRA organizational structure was so tight and limited that the leaders were perfectly insulated. It was how Kieran had survived. It was how we all survived thirty years of war.

Kieran didn't understand why Farrell didn't give up his pistol without more resistance. I had talked with at least seventy-five men before Farrell, and it certainly wasn't a secret what I was asking of them. The real lesson was what men are capable of doing when they think it's in their own interest. It's what drives the world.

After lunch, we drove to the peace walls. There's only one wall, which delineates the political and religious demographics of the city east of River Lagan. All the other walls were in West Belfast, the Catholic side of the city. It was painfully clear to me that the Protestant wall builders intended to fence in the Catholics like cattle. Now, the mystery to me was why the Catholics had accepted this treatment willingly and now even clamored for more walls to protect them.

My niece, Brianna, had been burned from a Molotov cocktail thrown over a wall into a children's play area. It was a well-known play area, so whoever threw that cocktail knew what the result would be, which made that person a heartless monster by any standard of civility. I wish I could understand the psychological damage done to generations of Catholics who were born, lived, and died behind Protestant-constructed walls. The walls weren't effective at either keeping the Protestant rabble-rousers out or the Catholic population safe.

From talking with West Belfast residents at the pub, I learned that the vast majority have never even met a Protestant their entire lives. For them, Protestants are the devil incarnate. In Cork, I know both Church of Ireland Protestants and Catholics from my own parish, but they don't share the animosity that the two groups do here in Belfast.

It's not that Cork wasn't touched by the Troubles in the twenties, with Michael Collins, a son of Cork. Of course, he was assassinated in his home county by rogue IRA soldiers angered that the price of peace was separating Northern Ireland from Free Ireland. I've always thought his assassination was political expediency, not betrayal of Irish Catholics. He understood better than most how Northern Ireland was tied economically, culturally, and historically to Great Britain. He recognized it as a fact, a fact that couldn't be changed, and especially in 1921 when Irish Catholics were a minority without any power base. Creating Northern Ireland eventually allowed for creating our Republic of Ireland. That, too, is a fact.

In historical perspective, Northern Ireland having its own government, separate from Whitehall, was political evolution. The problem was that the population had no experience in governing themselves and most of their history was warped by the abyss between Irish Catholic and Scots-Anglo Protestants.

Although I've been a Provisional IRA member for thirty years, I finally understood the need and importance of Sinn Fein, which was working frantically to give Irish Catholics a political power base not dependent on guerilla fighters, who wanted to force their way onto the public stage.

I became so lost in my own thoughts as we drove through the city that Kieran and Dominic disappeared from my little self-contained world. Kieran leaned over and whispered into my ear. "Ian, did ya forget I wanted to know about Boyle and Daly?"

I jumped, startled to hear his voice so close to me. I turned to look at him and blinked several times, trying to focus. "Boyle and Daly?"

"Jaysus, man, you do have a way of gettin' lost in your own thoughts. Even when I witness it myself, it's amazing. Where the hell were you?"

I smiled. "Here, my friend, right here, throughout history."

Kieran pulled away from me as if I were a leper and hugged his door handle. "You ought to find this embarrassing that I have to jog that incredible mind of yours back into our century. Boyle and Daly are the two fellas that Francis Farrell is bringing to you for one of your little talks. Do you know when?"

I straightened up and forced myself to be in the present moment. "I have no idea. I go to the pub every day and talk with whoever shows up. The locals are comfortable with that, and I'm a visitor in their land, so I accept how they want to or need to do things. That's reasonable."

"Ok, ok, I get it. What's your guess, though? Are these the rogue leaders we've been worried about?"

"I definitely think Francis Farrell is one of them. He has an air of confidence about him and impresses me as a natural leader of men because of his life experience. He's tough both physically and psychologically."

Kieran sat huddled next to the door and held his hands together between his knees. Then he turned his head toward me and arched his right eyebrow. "So, what made him give up his piece? Are you that persuasive?"

"My friend, it had nothing to do with me. It was just in the course of our conversation, he discovered that disarming was more in his self-interest than the protection he thought he bought with a pistol in his belt."

Kieran turned away and stared out the window, watching sections of a peace wall as we drove by at a crawl. "I don't get it."

"What's the alternative? If the Catholics and Protestants can't form a government, what happens?"

"The fucking Brits get a big chuckle and come rushing back to save the day."

"My friend, I knew you were politically astute.

That's exactly what Francis Farrell understands now. The one and the only one thing the Catholics and Protestants can agree on right now is the chance to have a go of it on their own—independent of Great Britain. How they do it will be like walking on broken glass, probably for years. The Protestants see armed IRA men as a threat; in my opinion, they should, history supports their fear. So, to have any chance of forming a government, out of self-interest, the Catholics give up their guns. A *quid pro quo*."

"What the hell is that *quid...*"

"An equal exchange, Kieran."

"You college guys still slay me, can't talk plain," Kieran complained.

We drove for a few more minutes without any more conversation, which was more to my liking.

"I need a drink," Kieran exclaimed.

"I wouldn't say no to a tall glass of whiskey," I answered.

In a few minutes, Dominic deposited us back on the apartment stoop. The next morning, I woke slumped in the sitting room chair, woken by the aroma of a mug of Barry's tea. The empty bottle was sitting on the floor next to my chair. I must have dropped the glass on the fireplace mantle; it lay shattered on the red brick. Another night I slid into a whiskey-induced sleep. Oh, God, I wondered, could I sleep without the whiskey? It had been a good day, I didn't need the whiskey. It went down so smooth and well, habit was habit.

Kieran shouldn't have let me finish off the bottle. Maybe he wanted me drunk to shut me up. I don't know if I'm a quiet drunk or not. I didn't feel dark last night when we got back to the apartment. Maybe it was the prison-like environment of this apartment that plunged me back into the dark place. It always happens at night, the dark place bubbles up from the depths of the earth to swallow me. I'm afraid of the night.

I rubbed my eyes and squinted at a fuzzy figure standing not three feet from me holding a tray with a steaming mug of tea and a plate of toast and jam. The fuzzy shape spoke in a deep Belfast brogue, "Tea an' toast, Mr. Murphy?"

"Oh, bless you, goddess of the new day. Yes, please set it down."

"None of your fancy talk with me. Do ya want more than this for yer breakfast?" she asked.

"A bowl of porridge with honey would be nice."

"I'll make it with milk; you seem like the type that don't have it made with water."

"You are kind, my angel."

The longer we talked, the more my vision cleared, like the fog lifting off the peat bog in the morning. My benefactor was dressed in a red, pinstripe dress buttoned to the top and plain black shoes. She wore no makeup and appeared never to have spent her money on such an extravagance. Her hair was curly brown with a large tuft of white on both sides over her ears. She had a traditional, pudgy Irish nose and thin, expressionless lips. Her eyes were pale gray and looked out onto the world with accepting weariness.

"I'm nobody's angel, Mr. Murphy."

"Then, what is your name?" I asked.

"Sophie Campbell."

"Good morning, Sophie Campbell."

"Good day to yous. When will you be wanting yer lunch?" she asked in her unique business-as-usual style.

"Half twelve would be wonderful."

THIRTY-ONE

That evening Dominic picked me up at six as usual to drive me to O'Flahertie's Pub as he had done for the past three weeks. Once again, he didn't speak during our short drive. Dominic, a man of very few words, was paired with a man who made his living with words. In some ways, Kieran was cruel to assign Dominic to me. However, I knew that thought would have never crossed Kieran's one-track mind; he only cared about my security and for that I had to be thankful.

Dominic stopped at the curb and I jumped out without waiting for him to stop the car and escort me to the door. Over the past few weeks, I had become a fixture at the pub, and in this Republican neighborhood, there was no fear of harm coming to me. If Dominic allowed me to exit the car by myself, I knew it was safe.

I walked straight to the bar and joined a group of four men engaged in lively conversation. When they saw me, I was greeted with, "Well now, boys, it's our friend from the south. Must be in need of a Bushmills and a little light conversation."

"And have I come to the right establishment for such a thing?" I responded to the balding man with deep furrows along his nose and a straight mouth that could be taken as sinister.

"Aye, that you have, Mr. Ian Murphy," said a young, frail man that looked as if he was carrying some disease inside him. A tall glass of Bushmills appeared in front of me, my passion for the whiskey was now common knowledge in West Belfast.

I listened to the men describe their work day without interrupting them or having a need to share with them my day of reading to fight off the blackness and the wound in my heart from missing Mairin.

Since my time in Belfast, I hadn't received a letter or a telephone call from her. I wanted to break the silence but when she walked away from me in the park, she made it abundantly clear that if she wanted to talk, she would let me know. I had decided to respect her request and hope to God I was making the right decision.

From nowhere, Dominic appeared at my elbow. He leaned in close and whispered into my ear, "They're here."

"They?" I wondered.

"Boyle and Daly. Back room."

After my experience with Francis Farrell, I understood what was expected of me and followed Dominic to the back office without a question. Once in the room, I looked around but didn't see anyone. As usual Dominic was standing in front of the door. "So?"

"They wanted you to arrive first. It's their way."

I sat in one of the chairs in front of the desk. "Then I shall wait."

I didn't wait long before two men entered from a side door that was hidden behind a wall panel. I should have suspected this office wasn't ordinary. It had multiple entrances and exits, hidden from view. Both men walked directly to me and shoved a hand in my direction. I stood up as they approached. "Ian Murphy," and I extended my hand.

In unison they replied, "Boyle," "Daly."

I stroked my beard in confusion, unable to determine who was who. They looked at each other and then recognition of the problem flashed across both of their faces.

The man on my left was short and must have not been more than five foot. He wore a blue denim shirt with a vest, soiled trousers, and brown shoes that were scuffed and in need of repair. The man on the right was my height with curly brown hair and a walrus moustache. He wore a clean striped shirt with a vest and his pants were held up with suspenders. His black shoes were worn but polished.

"Colum Boyle," said the man on the left.

"Neil Daly," said the man on the right.

I shook hands with them and said we should find a third chair to sit down and talk. Again, Dominic was alert and brought a chair for us.

"Would you gentlemen like a pint of black? We could have it brought in."

"There's not a day goes by that I'm not thirsty," said Colum.

Three perfectly poured glasses of Guinness were brought in by O'Flahertie himself. "Would you care to join us, Vern?" I asked.

"Sorry, Mr. Murphy, but four's a crowd."

"Francis told us we should talk to you. Says you really want to listen to us," Neil said.

"That's right," I said.

"He left his piece with you. Jaysus, now there's a miracle. You must be a miracle worker, Mr. Murphy. Farrell has had that pistol on his person since he was a teen. Never thought he would walk the streets of Belfast without it."

"To be honest with you, gentlemen, it surprised me, too. I learned a great deal from him. I'm beginning to understand the need for the peace walls even though to me they represent failure of the human spirit. I've learned to you it means safety, and in the priority of human needs, safety is in the top five."

"You use a lot of words when you talk, Mr. Murphy," Neil said. "Look, we're here because Francis Farrell told us to see you, to look you in the eye and see for ourselves."

"See what, gentlemen?"

"That you're honest. Francis said if this government thing is going to get off the ground, we got to turn in our guns an' stuff – that you wrote that in the Good Friday Agreement," explained Colum.

"Listen, I've been a Provie for thirty years. I may not have used weapons, but I used words to fight with. I penned the *Green Book*. I wrote stories about our battles for newspapers across the country. I know you. I know you well. The days of fighting in the streets are over.

Colum and Neil looked at each other and then at me. "This ain't easy, Mr. Murphy. I don't know any other way to live," Colum said.

"It was a simple deal. The IRA turns in its guns, the Brits get out of Northern Ireland, Sinn Fein and the Protestants put together a government separate from Great Britain. If you want any chance of having your own government in Northern Ireland, give up your guns. I'm not asking you to trust the Protestants, I'm just asking you to try to rule your own country.

"I know it's a risk. Think of your children. Don't they deserve the chance to grow up in a world without violence in the streets?"

"Francis said you got a way with words. He is right; when you put it like that, it makes some sense. As God is my witness, I'm tired of fighting. It ain't got us nothing," moaned Colum.

"I got a boy and girl at home. They be ready to go try it on their own in a few years. I get your meaning. They deserve a chance, don't they? Fightin' up to this time hasn't gotten me anything but grief. I'm tired," Neil added.

"Ok," they said in unison. Both of them leaned forward, reached behind their backs, and brought out their pistols. Neil reached down his pant leg and pulled out a snub-nose pistol.

"In three days, a note will be passed to you here at the pub. The note will be an address. Give it to Sinn Fein, nobody else.

They'll find a stash there, but Sinn Fein must take the credit for turning it in," Neil instructed.

I stood and patted each man on the back. "You won't regret this. Let's have a whiskey to toast." Dominic came back with a bottle and three tall whiskey glasses on a round, wood bar tray. I poured all of the glasses full and raised mine in a toast. *"Erin go bragh!"*

"Erin go bragh!" Colum and Neil repeated. They slammed the whiskey glasses on the desk with a thud that only an empty glass can make, then turned and disappeared out of the room through the hidden panel they had used to enter.

I was left alone in the room with Dominic. I raised my glass to him in a silent invitation to join me in good cheer. He shook his head and opened the door for me to join the patrons in the pub. I couldn't decide if I was extraordinarily persuasive or possessed Irish luck in succeeding in half my Belfast mission. It wasn't clear to me if Francis Farrell filled the leadership gap in the Provincials when Dolan surreptitiously left the country the day following the referendum vote, leaving a leadership vacuum, but it was clear that Colum and Neil specifically followed Francis' direction. It wasn't clear if they had a choice or they came to the same conclusion Francis did once they met me in person. Looking a man in the eye was critical for the Irish. For hundreds of years, we have known that the measure of a men could be found in the eyes.

Maybe they agreed to turn in arms because I was an outsider. I come from the land of Michael Collins, and thanks to Eileen Donohue's betrayal, the whole damned country knew my part in the Troubles over the last thirty years. Kieran's told me that the *Green Book* has saved many lives and taught men how to keep our secrets when they were interrogated, sometimes for months at a time. I could feel my ego flying and I was certain I was giving myself too much credit.

The one mistake I didn't make was to demand that they turn in arms because that was what the Peace Accord required, although I hoped they knew that I was the one that convinced the Brits to allow the Provies two years to get the job done. Protestant leaders Ian Paisley and Robert McCartney didn't fall into place, but their resistance was more over including Sinn Fein as a partner in forming the new government.

For some reason, these men turning in their guns felt more important to me than drafting the Good Friday Agreement. Kieran had been right, as a man of words, being involved in the work necessary to create a government was critical in offering the children of Northern Ireland hope and peace in their lifetimes. Theirs could be the first generation in this century to live without violence. If I made just a small contribution to this end, it's more important than any book I've written or will write ever again.

I carried the whiskey bottle with me to the bar and shouted out: "O'Flahertie! Vernon O'Flahertie, I want every patron in your establishment tonight to drink on my tab."

The pub fell silent and all eyes turned toward me. I looked around the room. Surprise registered on every face. I began to laugh. "Can't a man buy his new Belfast friends a drink? Good times are coming to Belfast and Northern Ireland, mark my words. Watch the papers in the next few days, then you'll understand. Until then, join your relative from Cork in a hooley tonight!"

One by one, the faces transformed from disbelief to smiles, laughing, and toast after toast. I looked over at Vernon, seeking his approval. He motioned for me to lean in close. "I hope to God you know what you're doin', Ian Murphy. I'll be sure to put every drink on your tab, and I'll expect your payment in full at the close of the month."

"I'm confident, Mr. O'Flahertie. Now pour those drinks."

At some point, a plate of butcher's sausages, a bowl of champ, and a slab of wheaten bread with a golf-ball-sized dollop of fresh butter appeared. Once again, I had distracted myself and forgot to eat. I was thankful that Vernon was sensitive to my needs; in fact, he was more sensitive than I was myself. Many evenings my dinner consisted of a bottle of whiskey, either because the darkness came or, rarely, like tonight because of a joy felt only once or twice in a man's life. I let the crowd continue with the hooley and turned to devour every bit of food placed before me. I was so full that I didn't feel like another drink. I looked around the room and it was clear the party could carry on without me. I looked around for Dominic and saw him sitting in the corner by himself with a mug of tea, waiting patiently, as always.

He noticed I was looking in his direction and he understood the signal. He got up, carried his mug to the bar, and walked past me out the door. In a few minutes, I followed him and found the car running in front of the pub with the rear door open.

"You done good today, Mr. Murphy," Dominic said. It was the first time he had spoken to me after one of our evenings at the pub.

"Thank you, Dominic. The truth is I think it was more luck than my persuading them to give up their guns. I've learned an important lesson; men can act out of self-interest or without trust and their actions still benefit everyone.

"I'm sure Mr. Fitzpatrick will want to see you. Word will fly fast; it always does here."

"Yes, I can't wait to see Kieran."

The car came to an abrupt stop outside the apartment, and before I could open the door, Dominic had jumped around the car to open the door for me. "Good night, Mr. Murphy. God bless you."

"Good night, Dominic. Until tomorrow."

When I walked into the hallway, I was overcome by the familiar fragrance of magnolia. I missed Mairin so much I was hallucinating her being with me to celebrate this evening.

"Ian?"

I thought sure I heard Mairin call my name. One of the stranger aspects of being a writer was that I was capable of imagining any scene with all the senses. Often, when I wrote I found myself actually living in the scene with the characters, like being a part of a Woody Allen movie. I imagined Mairin's fragrance and now her voice calling me.

"Ian!" This time there was urgency in the voice calling my name. I stopped dead in my tracks to listen. Again, "Ian!" with the exact same inflection. I turned and walked to the sitting room and peeked in. The fire was robust. I felt a wave of heat strike me in the face.

Mairin stood by the chair in front of the fire. She chuckled when she saw me look into the room. "Yes, darling, it's me. I came to be with you."

I rushed into the room and took her into my arms; tears of joy fell down my cheeks. I felt her soothe the back of my neck. "Oh, my God. Oh, my God," I whispered through my tears. "You're here. You're really here."

"I just can't imagine my life without you, even when you do completely irrational things like moving to Belfast. You are a crazy man, but you've taken my heart."

We spent the evening together laughing, exploring our secret places, and wallowing in our ecstatic lovemaking.

THIRTY-TWO

The next morning, I stretched in bed, searching for Mairin. I patted the bed in several places and didn't find her. I bolted up, looked around the room, and then listened for the shower. The bedroom was as quiet as a cathedral before Mass. The urge to relieve myself got me out of bed; I didn't find Mairin in the bath. Did I miss her so much that I dreamed she came to me last night? I picked up the pillows and sniffed, yes, the faint but distinct fragrance of magnolia. I was wide awake and Mairin's scent in bed proved we shared love last night. I slipped on slacks and a shirt and walked barefoot into the kitchen.

"Good morning, my love. Tea?" Mairin sat at the table holding her tea mug with both hands, her hair a bit ruffled. She was wearing my robe.

"Mornin', sir!" Mrs. Campbell said in her curt, formal way.

"Ian, darling, you forgot to tell me about Mrs. Campbell. We've introduced ourselves and had a nice conversation this morning waiting for you."

I looked at Mairin, then at Mrs. Campbell, and back again. For some reason I couldn't comprehend the scene in front of me. Why would I mention Mrs. Campbell to Mairin? I didn't want to be rude to my cook so I opted for silence.

"Tea would be perfect." I sat across from Mairin and a mug appeared in front of me. I picked it up, but it was too hot even for a sip. I blew on it until I guessed it was safe to drink.

"Ian, you are so lost in your thoughts; I don't think you're in the room with me. You must be thousands of miles away," Mairin said.

I looked over at her to find her eyebrows twisted into a question mark across her face. I reached for both her hands and held them tenderly in mine and let myself get lost in her hazel eyes.

"I don't mean to interrupt somethin' so sweet, but will you two be wantin' breakfast this morning? Yous both look like ya need the full Irish," Mrs. Campbell suggested.

"Yes, that would be fine. It's going to be a busy day, and I'm not sure when we'll be having lunch today," Mairin responded.

Mairin wasn't aware that I was a prisoner in this apartment and I hadn't been busy during the day for weeks. Most days Dominic didn't pick me up until six in the evening.

"Busy?" I asked Mairin.

"I've never seen Belfast and I intend to, especially those peace walls that I know you're so concerned with. Did you know Caitlin will be here this week?"

"You know about that?" I wondered out loud.

"We talk, Ian."

"Of course, you do."

Mairin fetched us both another mug of tea while Mrs. Campbell busied herself cooking breakfast. While she cooked, she hummed some song I wasn't familiar with. Soon plates appeared on the table with eggs, both black and white pudding, sliced tomatoes, fried potatoes, and brown bread with our choice of cream butter or jam.

"Mrs. Campbell, this is quite a spread; there's enough food for a family of six. Please join us," I begged.

"You are kind, Mr. Murphy, but me and mine had our breakfast hours ago. None of mine ever leaves the house without a full stomach."

"We'll never eat all of this," Mairin quipped.

"I'll box it up for Dominic; it will be his lunch." Mrs. Campbell suggested.

"Dominic? Who's Dominic?" Mairin asked me.

I chewed on a mouthful of eggs and potatoes before answering. "My driver."

"Your driver? Well now, aren't you important? A driver."

I shook my head. "It's for security. Kieran insisted."

"Oh, I understand now. I was just punching your ego a bit this morning."

"Darling, my ego is intact. This is Belfast. You'll learn things are different here. I need to find out how you arranged to be here. I am so relieved. It was so long since our talk in the park; I thought we were history."

Mairin looked directly into my eyes, patted my hand, and whispered as if she didn't want Mrs. Campbell to hear what she said. "Yes, I need to explain how this happened but later. For now, let's just finish breakfast. Can we drive around the city?"

I shoved the empty plate to one side and patted my full stomach. "Well, the truth is, that's problematic. Usually I get picked up in the early evening and I don't know how to contact Dominic."

"You don't?" Mairin asked.

"I'll be takin' care of that, Mr. Murphy. When you want him here?" Mrs. Campbell waited for instructions.

"Mairin?"

"Half eleven would be lovely. Ian and I need to get ready and have a chat before embarking on my sightseeing tour."

"Done. Now, you two be off. I'll clear the table and wash up. It was grand to meet you, Miss."

"Please, call me Mairin."

Mairin and I met in the sitting room. I enjoyed a pipe while waiting for her. She shut the door behind her when she came in and kissed my forehead before sitting in the chair across from me.

"I've been thinking, my love, I just don't understand how you're able to be here when the term has started at UCC," I asked.

"I confess, it wasn't easy. I'm on sabbatical. Dr. O'Keefe proved to be less than understanding when I asked for time off. He thinks I'm fickle following you here. I didn't know what to ask for. I've never taken sabbatical even though I've earned one. I didn't even know what the process was to ask for time off. Of course, I knew it would be a major inconvenience, but I'm a librarian, I'm not in the classroom. It took me weeks to negotiate with him. He could have simply refused but he did insist on his terms."

"Terms?"

"Yes. First, my sabbatical is for the full academic year. He didn't think he could find a replacement for me that would take the position for less than a year with such short notice. Also, I couldn't argue my leave was an emergency. Lord, I didn't even take any additional leave when my husband was ill. It's how he wanted it. I still have guilt about that. I'm Catholic, after all."

"Your pay?

"With my years, it's a full-pay leave. That's policy, I learned. O'Keefe couldn't do anything about that, HR wouldn't let him. If he had a choice though, I know he wouldn't have granted me any salary. That man has a mean streak I didn't know he had. But there's one more condition. I won't be returning as Director of the Religious Studies Library. He wouldn't commit to any position. All he would say is that I could return to a position commensurate with my education and experience, but he won't let me return to the Religion Department."

I fell back in my chair, overcome both by Mairin's sacrifice and by Dr. O'Keefe's harshness. "Oh, dear, you've jeopardized your professional standing just to be with me." My right hand cramped into a fist, shooting pain up my arm. I felt tears slither down my check, wetting my beard. My eyes clouded over. I lunged out of the chair and lay my head in Mairin's lap. Her sacrifice was complete; she may have ruined a notable college career—for me? Mairin stroked my head.

"We need to be together for all time. Whenever we can get back to Cork, I want you to come live with me."

"You're giving up your independence, your privacy?" Her questions were challenging, not loving.

"I'm taking a risk on love. I'm taking a risk on you. That's what life is, taking a risk for all the right reasons. I love you, Mairin McCarthy. I can't imagine waking up without you. Without you there, it's only darkness. This is my choice. You've brought light back into my life after a long, long time of loneliness. I was like a zombie going through life, making the motions, not really feeling. Does that answer what I want to do about this?"

"I love you, Ian Padraic Murphy, and I also can't imagine life without you. This journey you're on now will end. All it took was to not have you in my life for a few weeks for me to realize how I've come to love you. I admit, when you told me your decision, without any discussion, I was very angry. I felt abused. You just expected me to accept the choice you made and that was to leave me. Love doesn't have room for anger. After I calmed myself, I was able to view the situation more clearly. The truth is, I think you're courageous to help the people of Northern Ireland as they struggle to create their own nation."

I raised my head off Mairin's lap and cleared my throat. "I'm not altruistic. I still fight the darkness every day. I hoped taking on this challenge I could fend off the darkness for a time, maybe even cleanse my soul and fulfill my searching for redemption. I have to outlive my past and I have no idea how to do that. What I do know is that I am blessed with you and your love, and that is enough."

I sat with my head in her lap until I heard the front door open and familiar steps walk down the hall to the kitchen.

"Dominic?" Mairin asked.

"I'm sure." I stood and guided Mairin out of the chair into my arms. We held onto each other, never wanting to separate.

"Mr. Murphy?" shouted Dominic as he walked down the hall toward the sitting room. He barged into the room holding a brown paper sack with the leftovers from breakfast.

"Oh, shit." Dominic whispered under his breath.

Mairin and I both broke into laughter. "It's all right. Let me introduce Mairin McCarthy. She'd like a driving tour of Belfast City, if you have the time," I said.

"Welcome to my city, miss. It would be a great pleasure for me to show you our little town. I've had the pleasure of showing Mr. Murphy our humble home. Do you want to see the walls too? It upset Mr. Murphy something terrible to see 'em."

Mairin glanced at me and I glanced back at her.

"Yes, I need to see the walls. I won't pretend to understand how the people of Belfast can wall themselves in, but I need to see them, all the same. Those walls are symbolic."

Symbolic. She's right, I thought. Mairin was so insightful. Symbolism. Maybe there was a chance I could grasp the true meaning of the peace walls. My guess was that Caitlin could complete the picture.

I escorted Mairin to the car with my arm wrapped around her shoulders. "Drive on, Dominic."

THIRTY-THREE

Kieran gave Mairin and me a few days to ourselves. He gave me the credit for convincing the Real IRA to turn in weapons. It was impossible to know what portion of their stockpile they would relinquish, but the fact that they acquiesced to the demand was sufficient. Kieran claimed I snatched victory from the jaws of defeat. A well-worn adage, but coming from Kieran it seemed original. I protested that the Real IRA's announcement was coincidental to my talks with Farrell, Daly, and Boyle. I told Kieran I had no idea that they would also take responsibility for the bombing in Omagh. He claimed I tweaked Seamus Devlin's conscience. Of course, I didn't have any moral authority then or now and would never claim to have any.

On the morning of 7 September, Kieran sent Dominic to the apartment with an urgent message. He invited me and Mairin for lunch. Dominic was instructed to have us leave immediately. When Kieran sends an order, it was obeyed, without question. Dominic drove out of the city—west. As usual, our route was circuitous. In a few minutes, the city was behind us and we were in the countryside.

Belfast was ringed by small villages where people live simply and travel into the city for work six days a week. I strained to catch sight of a sign as we entered a village. Mairin and I held hands; she was content to watch the country landscape. A large gold sign with black letters and a black border read: Ballymagarry. From there, Dominic turned east and drove back to West Belfast, the safest place for a Republican. Dominic drove down an alley, where we parked. He escorted us through the back door and into a private dining room, just large enough for a table with six chairs.

When we entered the room, Kieran slammed his cigarette into the ashtray and jumped up. "Mairin! You are a beauty. Better than when I last saw you in Cork. Reuniting with Ian has been good for you." He gave Mairin a hug and pulled a chair out for her to sit down.

"Listen, I hope you don't mind but I've ordered lunch. Hope salmon is ok with both of you. Pints and a couple a fingers of whiskey will be here directly."

"Kieran, why all the cloak and dagger?" I asked.

Kieran lit a cigarette. "I wanted to give you the news myself. There's going to be an announcement today." Cigarette smoke rolled out of his mouth as he spoke, and I couldn't help but notice his eyes were as bright as the Beltane fires in spring.

"Please, don't make us wait, Kieran. What announcement?" Mairin begged Kieran to reveal the news.

"Okay, look. There's going to be a press conference this afternoon." Kieran pulled back his sleeve to check his watch. "Right about now. The Real IRA's chucking it in."

Mairin blinked several times and looked at me for translation. "Chucking it in?" she asked.

"Yeah, they're going to put an end to their campaign. No more shootings, no more bombs. Their war is over at long last. Jesus, Ian, I don't know how you did it. Drafting the Good Friday Agreement was big but this, this is the biggest yet. I didn't think those fellas would ever give it up. You're one son-of-a-bitch to deal with, I guess. And all these years I've never known it."

Mairin burst into a grin, pulled me toward her, and gave me an open-mouthed kiss right in front of Kieran. She grabbed my shoulders with the strength of a dock worker and wouldn't let me go. I heard muffled sobs as she buried her head in my shoulder. "Your quest is over, my love. This is your redemption. We can go home soon, very soon."

I pushed Mairin away and stared at Kieran. "Mairin, I love you with all my heart, but you don't know what you're talking about. I have nothing to do with this. Nothing."

The drinks arrived and broke the mounting tension among the three of us. "Look, Ian, we're going to toast and that's that," Kieran demanded. "We're toasting the end of violence and civil disobedience in Northern Ireland. From the bombing in Omagh in mid-August to peace the first week of September—there is a miracle by any standard."

"We can toast the end of violence, but not because I had anything to do with it, that's my condition," I insisted.

"Oh, Ian, your humility is sometimes embarrassing," said Mairin.

I lifted my whiskey tumbler. Mairin and Kieran clinked my glass: "To abolishing violence and bloodshed on our sacred island for the rest of time!" I toasted.

"Amen," Mairin and Kieran responded.

THIRTY-FOUR

wo days after the Real IRAs announced the end of their campaign of violence, my sister, Caitlin, arrived in Belfast. Dominic brought Mairin and me the news and shared Kieran's instructions that we would all be meeting at Sinn Fein headquarters at half two. As usual, I had no idea what time it was when Dominic arrived. It meant no more to me than I would be reunited with Caitlin and maybe she could help me crack the mystery of why Catholics and Protestants would agree to building more peace walls now that violence was in the rearview mirror and the politicians were busy patching together a plan to share power at the government compound called Stormont. My suspicion remained that the idea to extend the peace walls came from Whitehall, to demonstrate to the world that the fledgling Northern Ireland wasn't capable of governing its own citizens, which both explained and absolved Great Britain of their intervention in Northern Ireland.

"Ian, we'll have time for a leisurely lunch before seeing Caitlin. That is, I assume I'm invited to go with you," Mairin said.

"It goes without question, my love. I wouldn't confine my worst enemy to these Spartan accommodations. I understand that Sinn Fein must be frugal with its public funds but this apartment borders on cruel confinement. It's not a gaol but it has the same psychological effect on a soul."

"Do you want me to say somethin' to Kieran, Mr. Murphy?"

Mairin threw her head back and laughed out loud. "Oh, Dominic, Ian is being melodramatic. Writers have that tendency, at least this one does. Take him away from his precious cottage near Cork and he complains as if he's mortally wounded. Pay no attention to him. The apartment is fine. Can you return to pick us up about half eleven?"

"Yes, ma'am."

Dominic turned on his heel and marched down the hall like he had just been given a command as when he served in Ireland's army.

"Now, Ian, could you ask Mrs. Campbell for a bit of tea? Let's relax and read for a bit. You seem tense this morning and it's making me uncomfortable. There's absolutely no reason for you to be anxious."

"Yes, ma'am." I saluted Mairin.

"Ian!"

"I'm off to the kitchen and I'll return with two mugs of tea."

I dawdled in the kitchen while Mrs. Campbell made a full pot of tea. She was a woman of incredible efficiency. Everything she did was clean and slick with no motion wasted. When she worked in the kitchen, she was in complete command, never needing assistance. It was a joy to spend a few moments observing someone who enjoyed her work and was as committed to her duties as Mrs. Campbell.

The Campbells of the world go on from day to day. They were authentic people with integrity and a forbearance that was both common and remarkable. It was because of the likes of Mrs. Campbell that the Irish spirit hadn't been tarnished in eight centuries and never would be. *Maybe I should ask Mrs. Campbell to explain the need for the peace walls*, I thought.

"May I ask your opinion, Mrs. Campbell?"

She looked over her right shoulder at me, leaning against the kitchen cabinets.

"You can ask, but don't expect an answer. Depends on the question, don't it now."

"Well, in many ways Belfast City is a mystery to me. I'm wondering, why do the people support the peace walls? There's been a proposal to build additional peace walls yet this year. It demeans both Catholics and Protestants in my view."

Without turning around, she responded, "And that would be your view. You who lives down in Cork City."

"Where I live isn't relevant, Mrs. Campbell."

"What?" she turned to face me as she twisted a hand towel into a rope.

"My opinion has nothing to do with where I live, is what I was saying."

"Look, Mr. Murphy. I knows yous are an important writer an all that. Can't say I've read any of your books. Readin' just isn't for me, is it? But them walls. It's just what it is, that's all. They been there thirty years, and I suspect my grandchildren will grow up in their shadow."

"The kettle's boiling," I said.

She turned like a spinning top, grabbed it off the flame, poured the gurgling water into two mugs, and swished the tea caddy in each cup. She put the mugs on a tray and turned to hand me the tray. "Enjoy yer tea, sir. Would there be anything else?"

"No, Mairin and I will be having lunch out today. I'm not sure of our plans for the rest of the day. I'm sure you have family to tend to; we'll take care of our own dinner."

"Thank you, sir. I don't mean to be rude about them walls. That's just livin' in Belfast."

Mairin and I enjoyed our tea and read until Dominic burst through the door. The man was incapable of making a normal entrance. His bulk and stolid determination made him a unique force of nature.

"Thought I'd find you two here. It's half eleven."

We left our empty mugs on the fireplace mantel, and I knocked the ashes out of my pipe into the fireplace. "I need to get another pouch of tobacco."

"We appreciate your promptness, Dominic," Mairin said.

Without saying a word, Dominic left through the front door. He was waiting outside, holding the car door for us when we stepped out of the apartment. I was never sure if he did that out of courtesy or for security, to guard our exit from the apartment.

"Where's lunch?" Dominic asked.

I looked at Mairin and she looked back at me with raised eyebrows. "Why don't you choose for us, Dominic," I answered.

†††

Later at the Sinn Fein headquarters, Dominic escorted Mairin and me to a second-floor room. The room was empty except for three straight-backed wood chairs. Caitlin stood in the middle of the room waiting for us.

Caitlin and I ran to each other and hugged. I picked her up and turned in a circle, setting her down in front of Mairin. Tears fell down my checks and I laughed a hearty belly laugh at seeing Caitlin in Belfast, knowing she was there to help me. In turn, Mairin stroked Caitlin's face and then held her tightly.

"A sister couldn't wish for a warmer welcome," Caitlin said. None of us noticed Dominic standing in the corner of the small room with bars across the single window.

"Now, there's a fine family welcoming. I'll leave yous alone to talk. If you need anything, just open the door, someone will be in the hall to help you," Dominic instructed.

"Always vigilant, Dominic, thank you. Maybe some tea would be nice?" I looked toward Caitlin and Mairin. They both nodded and Dominic left promptly, making sure to shut the door without a sound.

We sat our chairs in a circle and waited for someone to start talking first. Of course, I was impatient and broke the silence.

"When did you arrive in Belfast, Caitlin?"

"Just now, actually. I had a driver pick me up in Cork and we drove directly here. The driver didn't say a single word to me the entire trip. I took in the scenery and recalled the trip when I brought Brianna here as a baby. I was so headstrong then. My Brianna nearly died because of my decision to sketch out a life in this city that God has turned his back on."

I sat up straight and slapped my knees with both hands. "I'll have none of that, Caitlin. You followed your heart. You couldn't have foreseen that after twelve years, misfits would still be tossing things over the peace walls. Hell, there was a report in the paper yesterday about golf balls being thrown over the wall on North Howard Street."

"Ian's right, my dear, it's pure chance. You're not responsible for Brianna's injuries. Besides, she's fine now and has new friends in Cork."

"Well, you might as well know, Ian, I'm not sure I disagree with putting up more walls. I've lived here. I've lived the fear that people stow away deep in their hearts, not just today but for generations. I will help as I can. All I want to do is learn what my friends think of the idea and share it with you," Caitlin explained.

I stretched out my legs and looked toward the door, expecting someone to deliver our tea at any moment. I didn't want to be interrupted, but I also didn't want to hold up our discussion.

"That's exactly why I want you here, dear sister. I understand the political implications of building more peace walls, and I understand Sinn Fein's position that it's an international embarrassment. Those are objective, intellectual considerations. I'm in the dark about what it's like to live in the shadow of a peace wall, but you do, and you know people who are living there now. I'm afraid that if I would ask about it on my own, I'd get laundered answers. I don't want to hear what people think I want to hear. That serves no purpose. I want the truth of living in Belfast with those walls. If the new government has a chance of succeeding, it must start by listening to its citizens."

Mairin nodded in agreement. "I must say from my short time here, my impression is that the walls bother outsiders and not those living in Belfast. I know some of them have been here for thirty years; that's two generations."

"Ian, I'm glad you want to listen. Even in Northern Ireland, you're a familiar name. I'm not sure you would get the truth on your own. I hope this doesn't take long; I'm already missing Brianna," Caitlin said.

"Oh, Caitlin, I'm so sorry. I don't mean to be insensitive. I haven't asked about Brianna. What arrangements did you find for her?"

"Oh, she's grand. Of course, she loves living in Cork. The atmosphere is free and engaging. She's made friends easily in school and she's even picked up the Cork accent already. Children are remarkably adaptable. At first, she was angry with me for not letting her join me on this trip. She still exchanges letters with several friends here. After a long, heartfelt talk, she understood my fear of this place. She's staying with Miss O'Donovan, the principal of the school. It's a good arrangement. How long do you think you'll need me here?"

"A few days should do it, I would think. It's not really complex. I intend to do what's right for the people of Belfast, with no regard for the politics," I explained.

"Good. That will give you credibility."

The tea arrived and we continued talking, learning Caitlin's feelings about returning to Belfast and hearing stories about the time she moved here shortly after Brianna was born that I had never heard before. I saw my sister in a different light, who she was thirteen years ago as a new mother and today as an experienced woman with a thirteen-year-old daughter.

Our conversation was cut short because Mairin and I were scheduled for a private dinner and were to be escorted to someone's home. I hoped that Kieran would be able to join us but he didn't arrive. After dinner, Mairin and I were to be driven back to the apartment. We were told Caitlin would be taken care of, but weren't told the arrangements for her, again for security reasons.

I was never able to judge if the level of security we were given was justified or not. Compared to living on my own in Cork, the security was harsh. My guess was that to some extent, it was the way life was in Belfast. Certainly, Gerry Adams had not been able to steer Sinn Fein for fifteen years without living in intense high security at all times. To be honest, it was a type of prison. The price to bring the end of violence and some level of peace to Northern Ireland was to willingly give up your own freedom.

I didn't have the stamina to do that myself, I had learned during my short stay in this city. Being a writer required that I didn't live in fear, that my movements weren't watched by others, and that I had choice daily in my life. I had learned that working for the people in Belfast also meant you relinquished personal choice in your life. While I didn't know the details of Gerry Adams' life, my guess was that it was not too much different from what I had experienced here. I didn't know if he had a private life, a wife, children? Wasn't that odd, for someone who was such a public figure for so many years, to not have known the most common things about him?

My personal mission, to find redemption, was still in limbo. I had learned that having Mairin at my side had changed my life forever. Her unconditional acceptance of my life, with all my misjudgments and mistakes, let me wake up each morning looking forward to what the day would bring. It was sad, but since my days at Trinity, there had not been a lot of those days.

Why was it that so many in the arts, especially writers, suffered from depression as I did? It was only with the drink that I could sometimes fend off the blackness. Yet in my head I knew that alcohol was a depressant. Human psychology was a conundrum, or at least mine was. A reasonable person would expect that by midlife, a person would have figured things out, understood themselves and the motives for their actions. Yet, I still struggled. With Mairin in my life, at least now I had hope. Mairin sensed I was seeking redemption even before I was aware of it myself. There were lessons I needed to learn here in Belfast. That I knew. I believed Caitlin would be the messenger of what I was to learn.

THIRTY-FIVE

e left Caitlin at Sinn Fein headquarters and were greeted by a gust of wind with rain striking directly at our faces. Neither Mairin nor I were prepared for rain, our Cork jackets hanging in the wardrobe in our bedroom at the apartment. Dominic threw a wool blanket over us as we rushed to the car, as if a bit of rain would mortally injure us. We both laughed as we scrambled into the back seat.

I saw Dominic throw the blanket over his head and rush around the front of the car. He left the headlights on. There was a fine mist with the rain and drops spattered off the warm hood. Dominic had left the engine running, not common procedure, I was sure.

"I don't recall the newspaper forecast mentioning rain today, Dominic." I commented as he tossed the blanket on the seat next to him.

"It comes from the west from Lough Neagh and has a mind of its own. Then the wind off the North Atlantic pushes it over Belfast, horizontal to the earth. It's one of a kind, I'm sure."

"It must be. Does this happen often?" asked Mairin.

"Often enough."

"Maybe we should have dinner in tonight," I suggested.

"Is that possible, Dominic?" Mairin asked.

Dominic eased the sedan down the street, not wanting to test the brakes on rain-soaked pavement. "Of course. Mrs. Campbell is off for the evening, so it will be take-away."

"That's fine. It can be simple, not elaborate," I said.

"And what would satisfy both of you on a night like this?" Dominic asked.

With no hesitation, I said, "Liver and mash for me." I looked toward Mairin, expecting she would answer as quickly as I had.

"Give me a moment, Ian, I'm thinking. Well, lamb chops and champ would be wonderful. Dominic, why don't you join us?"

"Thank you, but it's been a long day. The rain aches my bones, and I'm feeling the need for a warm whiskey and seeing my missus."

"Missus? You've never mentioned a missus or family, Dominic," I said.

"No, and I shouldn't have now. Rule is, the less yous know, the better. For all of us. Now, I'll take you to the apartment and pick up the take-away. I'll be back in less than an hour."

† † †

I expected Caitlin to be in contact with me, but I was disappointed. She didn't contact me the next day or the day after. Anxiety grew in me like a noxious weed invading my rose bed in Cork. I felt the darkness like a shadow following me from room to room. Even having Mairin near me didn't fend it off this time. I was worried about Caitlin's security.

The area of the peace wall near the Falls Road had a reputation for repeated violence that was well-known beyond Belfast City. I asked myself why I ever agreed to let Caitlin stay with friends in that area, even if it was her idea. Her fact-finding mission should have been mine. I was usually an excellent, attentive listener, and expert at reading facial expressions and noting tone of voice. The only advantage Caitlin had over me was that she knew these people; they were her friends. Of course, they would be open and honest with her.

It shouldn't have taken more than a day to learn from them their views on building or even needing additional peace walls. It was a mistake to let Caitlin live there, even temporarily. Once again, I was being selfish. I was intent on being the hero of Northern Ireland, fighting those who wanted to use walls to impose peace on a people who had been at war with each other for centuries. Caitlin could have refused. She should have refused. I needed a drink. The bottle sitting next to my chair was empty. How full had it been when I had my first drink tonight? Where was Mairin?

"Mairin!" I screamed at the top of my voice.

I heard footsteps running down the hall and the door of the sitting room flew open and crashed into the wall behind it.

"Jesus, Ian. You're drunk. Can't I just take a hot bath without worrying about you?"

I tried to focus on Mairin's face, but it was blurry and wouldn't clear up no matter how hard I tried. "It's Caitlin. She's come to harm, I'm sure. It's been three days, Mairin. Why has it been three days? Three days is too long. If something has happened to her, I'll burn in hell for sure because it's my fault. I'll have to care for Brianna; I don't know a damn thing about caring for a twelve-year-old girl. Oh shit, this is the worst."

"Ian Padraic Murphy, you should be ashamed. It's the whiskey talking. Do I have to hide the stuff from you? No, that wouldn't do. When I've stayed over at your cottage, I've seen what happens. The shadows attack you and you sink into an abysmal depression where you experience a terrifying loneliness. I can see it on your face." Mairin sat in my lap and pulled my head to rest on her breast. She stroked my hair and beard. "My darling, if I could take this from you, I would. I don't know how. I don't know how."

We heard the apartment door open, followed by two familiar voices. "Do you want me to wait, Mr. Fitzpatrick?"

"No, Dominic, you need to spend time with your family. Your loyalty is obsessive. I can call another driver when I'm ready, and I don't know when that will be."

"Thank you, sir." The door slammed shut.

Kieran filled the sitting room door, his double-breasted coat wrapping him in a cocoon. "Well, it looks like I'm interrupting something here."

"You are, Kieran, but it's not what you think," Mairin said. She picked up the empty bottle of Bushmills Black waving it in the air.

"Oh. Can he talk, Mairin?"

"He can. He's a functional drunk, at least. Lord, I would like to know how to rescue him from his darkness."

"Aye. I've had the same desire for years. But I must confess, there have been times that he and I have downed more than one bottle of his precious Midleton. So, I guess, maybe I've contributed to the problem a time or two. I'm not innocent."

"I'm not looking to place blame, Kieran Fitzpatrick. Ian, Kieran wants to talk. Can you talk?"

"As glib as any Irish bard. Talk away, my friend Kieran. Mairin, will you stay?" I asked.

"Of course. I'll need to be your memory tonight, just in case."

"I have news from Caitlin. Very thorough, that woman," Kieran said.

"Is she safe? What's taken her so long? Three days is too long without some communication. Is she safe?"

"Yes, she's fine. I told you, she's thorough. She's talked to a lot of people, more than thirty I would guess. She's very well-respected, I've learned. Having her come has been brilliant."

"What did she find out?" Mairin and I asked in unison.

"You need to hear that from her. I've only had maybe a ten-minute briefing.

"Can't you give me a hint?" I begged.

"No. I'm just the messenger, Ian. That should be no surprise. You look exhausted. Mairin, do you need help getting him to the bedroom. He'll need a good night's sleep."

"Oh, Kieran, I would so appreciate your help. He's a bit much for me sometimes."

"It's not my first time," Kieran said.

They each put a shoulder under my arm and guided me down the hall, weaving from side to side. I felt an illness swell deep in my stomach. Kieran kicked the bedroom door open with his foot and I was plopped down on top of the bed fully clothed.

"I can handle it from here," Mairin said.

"Aye, I let him sleep it off fully dressed more than once," Kieran said.

"What time will you pick us up tomorrow?"

"Let's say half nine. Will that give you both time for clean-up and breakfast?"

"Yes, Kieran, that will be fine. We'll be ready. Good night."

"Good night, Mairin. You're an angel of a woman. He doesn't deserve you."

They talked as if I couldn't hear every word.

Kieran's footsteps faded away down the hall and the front door slammed shut, his usual exit. I didn't recall anything else.

THIRTY-SIX

ominic was prompt, a habit from his military days that continues to serve him well. He wasn't his jovial self but performed his duties with the ease and comfort of a self-confident man. He drove directly to Sinn Fein headquarters rather than the roundabout route he drove every other day I had been in Belfast. His seriousness was disarming and put me on alert. Apprehension hung in the air like the morning fog on the bog in County Cork. Mairin slipped her hand over mine and squeezed with a delicate touch. Her eyes held question marks, but she attempted to smile with reassurance. I know she could feel the sense of danger creep up my spine. My right hand squeezed into a fist. I tried to pry my fingers loose with my left hand, but it was no use.

Dominic led us into the building and up the back stairs to the second floor. This was my first time on the second floor. The building was divided into sections that formed separate compartments. I would have thought the number of times I had been in the building, I would have seen Gerry Adams, but not once. I didn't even know which section of the building contained the offices. Their level of security was not second to the Stormont. I wondered how people worked every day in an environment that always had a certain level of paranoia. In its entire history, the headquarters had never been attacked, even in the darkest days. But there was always the first time—a uniquely Irish view of the world. The door opened into a large room already filled with people talking and laughing. When

Mairin and I entered the room, everyone fell silent and looked at us. Kieran's familiar voice chided:

"Our guest of honor. Mr. Ian Murphy himself, and the lovely Mairin McCarthy."

I looked around the room and didn't recognize anyone. From behind me, I was greeted with a familiar voice. "Good morning, dear brother," Caitlin said. I gave her a quick hug. I had never seen her dress the way she looked today, with a plain blue dress, flats and her hair pulled straight back into a ponytail. She also didn't have on a bit of makeup. Dressed this way, she reminded me of our mother. I hadn't realized how much Caitlin resembled Ma; I found it disconcerting.

"Who are these people?" I whispered in her ear. She swung around to face the group of people sitting in a semicircle.

"Well, as usual, Kieran stole my thunder; you know this is my brother Ian. Ian, I'd like to introduce a few of my Belfast friends. I lived with these folks for over ten years. On your left are Kiley and Barry Boyle, in the middle Nola and Egan Gallagher, and on your right, Tulia and Malachy McNulty."

"Good morning," I said.

"Join us, please," Kieran insisted and pointed to chairs for Mairin and me. "Would everyone like tea?" Kieran asked.

Everyone nodded.

"Ian, in addition to being my friends, all of these people live near the peace wall that parallels North First Street. Tulia and Malachy moved here from County Donegal just at about the same time I moved to Belfast. Egan and Nola Gallagher moved here with their families from Derry when they were teenagers. The Boyle family has lived in Belfast for generations. I don't think they can even remember a time when their entire family didn't live in Belfast. Barry's great-grandfather worked on the *Titanic*. How about that for Irish history?"

As Caitlin introduced each couple, I took notes as writers do. The Boyles appeared to be in their mid- maybe late-thirties. Kiley had the kind of gentle, attractiveness that women get when it was said a woman got the face she deserved in her thirties. Both were dressed like they were accustomed to working in an office environment. The Gallaghers were closer to my age. Egan's hair was thin on top and combed to one side to cover up the bald area. Nola wore an attractive wool sweater that hid her weight gracefully. Tulia was pregnant. I couldn't determine how many months, but I noticed her feet were swollen, so I guessed she would deliver in the near future. Malachy had clear blue eyes and upward curved lips that gave him the appearance of a permanent smile. Caitlin had attracted a variety of people as her friends, which I expected.

"The best way for you to understand the peace walls and why the idea of building more peace walls is important now is to listen to the people who live here. I know you find the peace walls abhorrent, but except for college, you've lived your entire life in County Cork. The politicians were brilliant to ask you to fight against building more peace walls. Your role with the IRA during the Troubles and your work on the Peace Accord gives you unique credibility. But I don't want you to just express your viewpoint. You have responsibility to represent the residents of Belfast."

I looked toward Mairin, searching for her support. Then I looked toward Kieran for his direction. Both of them had poker faces, not giving me any type of signal.

"Well, Ian?" Caitlin asked.

"It's quite a charge you have for me. I confess, I find the peace walls an embarrassment to all of Ireland and to Belfast in particular. I am dumbfounded by people who willingly embrace and even create an apartheid-like community in the name of peace. No one has ever said that I represent the people of

Belfast. I'm not sure they want to be represented, especially by the likes of me."

"It's simple, Mr. Murphy, people will listen to you. They won't listen to us. We're invisible," Barry Boyle explained.

Three people came into the room balancing trays with mugs of tea. A fourth person brought a tray with three teapots, ensuring we didn't run out of tea the entire morning. I used their interruption to gather my thoughts and decide how I would respond to both Caitlin and Barry Boyle. I noticed that Kieran didn't help with any direction whatsoever; he just observed. That Kieran was a cunning man.

"Your request is fair. I owe it to you to listen with an open mind and set aside my own views. I don't want to propose something that you don't want. I am painfully aware that I'm a Cork man here, and while I may have a private opinion, I don't have the right to have my views affect your lives in any way. I'm honored that you have faith and trust in me to represent you. To be honest, I don't deserve it. I will listen to you, I will work very hard to understand and be empathetic. Please be patient with my ignorant questions, I will have quite a few questions; it's my way."

The small group of people broke out in spontaneous applause and laughter. "Jesus, who would have thought a Cork man would be our champion," shouted Egan Gallagher above the jovial clapping.

"Who would like to begin? I know the Boyle family has the longest history, which gives a special perspective. Barry and Kiley, would you mind starting?" I asked.

They looked at each other and smiled, pleased their family's history was acknowledged. "Sure, why not," they said in unison.

"First, I've always lived behind those walls. The first walls were built the same year I was born. I've never really questioned why they are there—it's a fact of life. So how can I even imagine them not there? Simple, I can't. I don't have a need to."

"Do the walls protect you and your family, Barry?" I asked.

"They must."

"Why must they?" I challenged Barry.

"It's ok, Mr. Murphy. I guess I understand why you would ask. Let me ask you a question. Let's say you lived on the same street all your life. That street never changed, only the people living in the houses. Would you wonder why you lived on that street?" Barry asked.

"I see your point. But what about building more walls?" I wondered.

"The walls protected me growing up and now they make my children safe. Everyone wants to feel safe. If another wall would keep one Catholic family safe, then I say don't waste any time, build it now."

Kiley nodded her head in agreement. "I moved here from County Donegal, looking for work after school. I know what you mean. I didn't understand the walls either. I still don't understand them, but I do know one thing. The walls work. My children have never been exposed to violence like children in the past suffered. The walls are for the children really, it ensures their future."

"Do you both feel that the walls are necessary to stop the violence?" I asked.

"Oh, it doesn't stop the violence. Look at your niece Brianna. The walls didn't stop her from being injured. No, the walls don't stop violence. I'm not sure anything can totally stop violence, it just means less violence," Barry said.

"It also means when there is violence, it's not as bad as it could be. In Brianna's case, without the walls, maybe a dozen or more children could have been hurt. I know that sounds harsh, but we're a practical people," Kiley said.

"Now that's absurd." I shook my head.

"Ian, dear brother, you promised not to judge, just listen. Actually, I agree with Kiley. Of course, Brianna's injury was a tragedy, but it could have happened to more children. Don't you dare judge parents; you don't have the right," Caitlin admonished.

I put my hands up to fend off her verbal attack. "I promised. I won't judge. I shouldn't have said anything. It's just that..."

"Ian." Kieran wagged his finger at me in warning.

"So, who else would like to weigh in?" I asked and looked at the McNultys and the Gallaghers. Malachy shrugged his shoulders and looked toward Egan.

"Go ahead, Malachy," Egan said.

"Well, as you can see, we're in the family way," Malachy said.

"Is this your first," I asked.

"Yes" Tulia answered as she rubbed her belly in a circular motion and smiled at her husband.

"Have you read the quote on the Bobby Sands mural on the outside of this building, Mr. Murphy?" Malachy asked.

"*Our revenge will be the laughter of our children,*" I said, reciting the famous quote.

"I want my children to laugh out loud. Now that we have the peace, there's a chance that can happen. I may get to see my children laugh and I will laugh with them. I can't risk them not laughing. Those walls are my insurance that my children will laugh. If it takes building more walls to give my children a chance to laugh, then so be it."

"Don't you laugh now, Malachy?" I inquired.

"Today was the first time I've laughed this year, and to be honest, for me, it was out of nervousness mostly," he explained.

I bowed my head and clasped my hands together. "That is very sad, Malachy, very sad. Have you both always lived in the shadow of the peace walls?"

"Oh no. When we found I was pregnant, we found a house here. Before we lived south of Belfast City," Tulia said.

"You moved here when you became pregnant?" I wondered out loud.

"Of course. We want our baby to grow up safe. With the walls, our baby will be safe. It's that simple," Tulia explained as she looked at Malachy and squeezed his hand.

"Good decision," Egan said.

"Dear, sure they don't need your approval," his wife scolded.

"It's all right, Nola, I don't mind," Tulia said.

"Did you ever consider moving to another county in Northern Ireland?" I asked Tulia and Malachy.

"Oh, no, Mr. Murphy. Belfast is our home and we want to raise our family here. The jobs are here. Good Catholic schools are here. Isn't that right, Tulia?" Malachy said.

"Oh, yes. This is definitely where we want to raise children. There's opportunity here. Outside of the city, there's poverty and not many jobs. So those walls, they're important. Without those walls, we would probably move away, maybe try Dublin or something."

Malachy nodded his head in agreement.

"Are you gettin' a picture here, Mr. Murphy?" Egan interrupted again.

"Well, so far it is unanimous, but for very different reasons. Interesting," I responded.

"Tulia, Malachy, do you have anything to add?" I asked.

"We've had our say, I guess," Malachy said, and Tulia smiled.

"Egan, that means it's your turn." I pointed to Egan and Nola.

"I helped build the first walls back in '68, when I was in my twenties. Best damned work I ever did," he said.

"Did it pay well?" I asked.

"Best job in Belfast for a workin' stiff like me."

"You worked for the British?" I wondered.

"Hell, no. I was considered a city employee then. Don't insult me, Mr. Murphy. I would never stoop to work for the fuckin' Brits," he sneered.

"Maybe I have my history wrong. I thought the British army built the first peace walls," I said.

"Oh, poor Egan didn't explain very well. He didn't mean he built the very first wall. They started out experimenting with just fencing and barbed wire. When we found out they worked, then they built real brick-and-mortar walls. Egan, he worked on the permanent walls," Nola explained.

"Okay, so the walls meant work for you. That was then. What about now? Is there still a need for more walls?" I asked.

"Do you read our newspaper or listen to the radio, Mr. Murphy? Something happens every week. The politicians are busy tryin' to make peace but the people, the people got their grudges," Egan said.

"Grudges?" I asked.

"That's right. Those words on paper, the Peace Accord, those are just words. I hope they mean more in the future, for my grandkids, but right now, right now, we need walls so we don't kill each other. It's just that simple."

Egan said in simple words what everyone in the room knew was true. I couldn't think of another question. Truth was truth, even if it wasn't what I wanted to hear. I looked at Mairin, Caitlin, and Kieran in turn.

"I'm sorry, Mr. Murphy, Egan can be brash sometimes," Nola said.

"Nola, do you agree with your husband?" I asked.

"I do, Mr. Murphy, I do."

"Well, you have all given me quite an education today. We Irish are an odd lot, aren't we? In no other country in the world do people build walls so they don't murder each other," I said.

"No, in other countries, killing is a lot easier, Mr. Murphy. Which would you rather have? Our solution is civil, don't you think," Barry asked.

I looked at Barry and words wouldn't come to me. I buried my face in my hands, not wanting to accept their truth. "I don't know, Barry. I just don't know. Thank you for your honesty and your time. This has been exhausting for me. I need time to reflect on what you've told me this morning. I need time to reflect. Kieran, I need to go now, I'll send you a message through Dominic when I'm ready and not a moment before. Mairin, I need you. You've heard everything today too, so you can help me sort through all this. I reached out and took Mairin's hand and she smiled.

"Thank you, Caitlin, for organizing this meeting. You've done your job, dear sister, now go home to Brianna. I'm sure she misses you."

I stood up and thanked all of Caitlin's friends for their honesty.

THIRTY-SEVEN

Back at the apartment, I was unable to calm myself and paced around the bed. "People who actually want walls to separate them from their neighbors, just because of their religion. I'm incredulous. It rankles me. It's in direct opposition to everything I believe to be right. Jesus, it's immoral. I thought there was more to our Irish character than that? Don't the priests in Belfast teach forgiveness? Can fear be so overwhelming it rules people's lives from cradle to grave? Why don't they want to live without walls?"

I felt my face turn red and my breathing become ragged. I turned around several times. I thought Mairin was in the room. I thought she was listening to my rant. Having an audience was essential. I couldn't see her. I couldn't see her anywhere. The heat off the fireplace made me sweat. I plopped down in the chair next to the hearth, exhausted, unable to move.

"Are you finished?" Mairin's calm, reassuring voice asked. There she was, sitting in the chair opposite mine.

"Have you been here the whole time?"

"Yes, darling."

"Oh."

Mairin leaned toward me and stroked my beard with slow, gentle strokes. "I've never seen you this emotional. This has shaken your core. I didn't think you were even capable of such deep emotional response.

I held her hand against my cheek and looked into her eyes, searching for understanding and with luck, acceptance. Maybe acceptance was too much to ask, even from someone who loved you, but understanding was essential. *How can I make her understand?* I thought.

"Listen, Ian, maybe we should try to talk this out. I'm not going to try to convince you of anything, but we did hear the same thing, not in the same way, that's clear. I'm going to ask Mrs. Campbell to leave. Maybe she should stay home for a few days. I'll give her a shopping list and Dominic can bring us some supplies. I can certainly cook. In fact, I'll enjoy making us meals. If you're not careful, I'll even have you help me in the kitchen. You can at least chop vegetables or something."

I leaned in, held Mairin's face with both my hands, and gave her a warm, gentle kiss. "You are remarkable."

Mairin gave Mrs. Campbell instructions and let me spend some time alone gazing into the fireplace. Soon the room was imbued with the earthy smell of peat. Heating with peat was a unique Irish practice and it grounded me to have a peat fire. I've always been amazed at how our island provided for our meager existence. Not blessed with forests to provide warmth, we had our peat bogs that could provide both shelter and heat. It's a miracle how quickly a peat bog could replenish itself. With only moderate care, it was a resource that kept giving if we only managed our use. We've relied on peat bogs for centuries and understand our land. *If we could only understand each other as we have come to know and understand the land*, I thought to myself.

It was a perfect time to enjoy a pipe and let my thoughts drift away with the tobacco smoke. The fragrance of the tobacco and the peat fire blended together into a sweet concoction. I let my overactive mind go blank, and I enjoyed a few moments without thoughts racing around in my mind. I didn't notice Mairin return to the sitting room with our tea.

"Ian, I thought I needed the fire extinguisher. There's smoke in the hallway. Did you open the chimney flue?"

I stretched to the lever and gave it a waggle. "Seems to be open."

"How many peat logs are on the fire? You don't need more than two or three. Are you cold?" Mairin asked.

"No. I just like the fire."

Mairin waved her arms back and forth to break up the smoke in the room. She walked to the window and yanked on the handle until it came open, at least a few inches.

"This is supposed to be a safe house. If that window opens, it's not too safe. We should tell Kieran the fireplace needs attention. I'm sure he's not aware. Is the smoke clearing?"

Mairin looked around the room then walked back and forth waving her hands. "That should do it. I can breathe now. It's a wonder you didn't suffocate yourself. I worry about you, Ian. I'm surprised you've survived living alone all these years. I think you need me, I really do."

"Oh, my love, I do need you. Not to watch over the stupid things I do, but to share a life with. You're teaching me that the bedrock of love between a man and a woman isn't romance or passion, though those are fine. The bedrock is deep, honest, abiding friendship. It's in friendship that unconditional love resides. Honest love is not contentious. I can spend days with you and always be at ease."

Mairin walked up to me and shared a deep, loving kiss and stroked the back of my neck. I wrapped my arms around her, holding her as close as I could without making her uncomfortable. I rested my chin in the corner of her shoulder.

"Now, my love, let's talk this through like two mature, consenting adults," she whispered into my ear.

I chuckled. She talked like we were going to make love for the first time, not have a conversation about the fate of Belfast City.

"Let's start with the truth. Were you given a specific mission for this undertaking?" Mairin began my interrogation.

"Yes. My mission was twofold. First, to find out who is leading the Real Irish Republican Army movement and to convince them to give Sinn Fein a chance to form a government by turning in their arms. Second, to convince the locals that building more peace walls is a British plot and will mean a blemish for all of Ireland. Plus, it makes us appear uncivil in the international community."

"Why were you surprised that the three families you met all agreed that additional peace walls are needed for the safety of their families"

I glared into my cup of tea and stared at the bits of tea leaves floating at the bottom. "Do you believe in reading tea leaves, Mairin?"

"Ian, you're avoiding the subject. It won't work. I asked you a direct question."

I stared into the fireplace to avoid Mairin's eyes. "Because, because, knowing the Brits built the walls, I thought the Catholics would hate them. I assumed that no one wanted to live separated by walls."

Mairin leaned back in her chair and gave me her "*aha*" look. "So that's it. You assumed they didn't want the walls. You assumed."

"I said it, didn't I? I think it's a reasonable assumption."

Mairin laughed out loud. "Oh, you intellectuals. How many I've had to babysit over the years at university. Don't you see the fallacy?"

"Fallacy? What fallacy?"

"When you start with an assumption, it renders you incapable of listening, really listening. You've made up your mind before the conversation began. It's your assumption that's made you surprised. If you truly would have had an open mind to listen to those families, you wouldn't have had the reaction you did."

"Okay, I was surprised. So what?"

"We, Mr. Intellectual, we've had to waste time dealing with your emotional reaction of surprise to their viewpoint rather than dealing directly with the issue at hand."

"Mairin, I've asked you not to chastise me or judge me. Need I repeat myself?"

"All I am saying, Ian, is let go of your emotional response and think about what those families shared with you. They are terrified. They've been the brunt of senseless violence their entire lives. I think it's understandable that security would be the first priority for these families. They just want to feel safe in their neighborhoods. Why should they have to move to feel safe? They have the right to live where they want to live. If brick and mortar and a bit of barbed-wire fence gives them the security, the feeling of safety they crave, they deserve it." Mairin took a breath after her long speech.

"Don't they care about how it looks in the international community?"

"No. Why should they? The walls have been there for thirty years already. Nothing new to the international community."

"Ok, I'll concede that. But building more walls is something else entirely. The international community will ridicule Belfast residents. More walls will prove we can't govern ourselves," I shot back.

"Quite the contrary. More walls will prove that both the Catholics and the Protestants are serious about ending the fighting. We would rather build walls than continue the ridiculous violence. Those walls are a physical manifestation of the commitment to peace."

I let myself sink back into my chair. Mairin gave me a perspective I never would have developed on my own. I wondered if she had been a debater when she was in college. I wanted to remember to ask sometime.

"One more thing," Mairin exhorted.

"More?"

"Yes, aren't you a proponent of the principle of political self-determination?"

I raised my eyebrows and looked directly at Mairin. "You know I am."

"Well, based on that principle, if the residents of Belfast, both Catholic and Protestant, feel the need to erect additional peace walls for safety, that should be their choice and theirs alone."

I was startled. "Bulls-eye. You've hit the target, Mairin. Who am I to tell our Irish brethren they can't have peace walls? Even if I don't approve of the outcome, the principle of self-determination is paramount. I've fought my entire life for all Irish to have that choice."

We both sat still gazing into the dwindling fire. I slurped the last bit of tea and set the mug on the hearth. I let our conversation sink into my consciousness.

"Ian, you need to chop some vegetables if I'm going to make us soup for dinner."

"Has Dominic delivered the groceries?" I wondered.

"Yes, dear, more than an hour ago. You didn't hear him?"

"No, I was totally absorbed by our conversation."

"I'll accept that as a compliment. I hope I can trust you with a knife in your hands."

THIRTY-EIGHT

The next morning, I woke to the smell of strong coffee, my guess, French roast. I stumbled into the kitchen to find Mairin drinking a cup of coffee and reading. She looked up and smiled. "Coffee?"

"Oh, it smells so good. I'll get it; you don't need to serve me. I appreciate that you took the time to make coffee this morning." I grabbed a cup off the dry board and filled it to the brim, then joined Mairin at the table.

"Did you sleep at all last night?" Mairin asked.

"Why do you ask?"

"You tossed and turned for such a long time. You're not a restless sleeper, at least so far, in my experience. I worried our discussion was unsettling."

I took in a strong breath of coffee and savored it. Taste comes from smell, I've read.

"Ian, dear, are you avoiding my question?"

"No, not really. You know how I process things. There's nothing quick about me. I need to write today. Nothing will be settled for me until I write. It's how I think."

"Do you need to be alone?"

I looked at Mairin with the best pensive expression I could muster. I was self-absorbed enough to not even consider what she would do for the day. Was that selfish? I hoped not. There was a distinction between being self-absorbed and self-ish. Even those who knew me best, Caitlin and Mickey, have never called me selfish. It would stop me in my tracks if that ever happened.

"You don't need to leave the apartment, really."

"That's sweet, Ian; both of us know it would be best if you are alone when you write. I don't expect you to change a thirty-year writing habit."

"Would you like me to call Dominic? He'll take you anywhere you would like to go," I offered.

"I've read Dunluce Castle is spectacular. That would be a pleasant drive. I would like to get away from Belfast."

I set my coffee mug on the table and gazed at this marvelous woman who was in my life. "You are so resourceful. I can't wait until Belfast is in our rearview mirror. My hope is we can leave tomorrow."

Mairin sat across from me and stroked the top of my hand. "You've made a decision?" she asked.

"I need to write. Of course, you'll be the first to read my article; you're my personal editor, aren't you?" I teased.

"If you say so.

"Your article?"

"I'm compelled to make a public statement. I'm not one for press conferences, so I'll write an article for the *Belfast Telegraph* and the *Ulster Herald* and whatever other publications Sinn Fein wants to publish in across Ireland."

Mairin got up, then washed her cup in the sink. "I'll shower now. There's a few hard-boiled eggs in the fridge and you can make toast if you like. You'll be on your own for lunch. I don't expect to be back until late afternoon. Would you like to dine out tonight?"

I turned in my chair and rubbed the small of her back. "Dining out will be perfect. I won't need lunch; I'll be deep into it by then."

Mairin bent down and gave me a soft, warm kiss. I didn't hear Dominic arrive to pick her up. I was hunched over in the chair by the fireplace, a yellow tablet balanced on my knees.

An Imperfect Peace
By Ian Padraic Murphy

In the few short months since both Northern Ireland and the Republic of Ireland approved the Good Friday Agreement, true peace has been elusive. August witnessed the violence in Omagh.

A group of dissidents founded the Real Irish Republican Army (RIRA) and there has been a proposal to build additional peace walls to separate Catholics and Protestants in Belfast.

I was asked to help usher in the era of peace following the Good Friday Agreement and quell the activities of the RIRA. To help understand the discontent that still resides in the hearts of RIRA members, I visited Omagh within several days of the explosion. I didn't learn anything other than the fact that they took responsibility for their actions and acknowledged it was an egregious and regrettable error.

I have met with RIRA leadership in Belfast and challenged them to give Stormont the opportunity to form an independent government. The RIRA has reasoned it is in their self-interest to live in an independent Northern Ireland. They have announced cessation of the campaign of violence. This must be accepted as an act of faith, that the politicians can hammer out some structure to govern this country.

I set my pen down and reread what I had just written. Peace was not defined as just the cessation of violence and Northern Ireland was deep in the throes of learning that lesson. In part, just the end to violence was what made current events in Northern Ireland best described as an imperfect peace. This country had known violence for so long that by having the RIRA declare an end to their campaign of violence must have felt like an enormous victory. Seeing people in the streets when Dominic drove us from place to place, there was a calmness and dreariness in their faces. Maybe it was not calmness I saw but just a certain level of safety or a reduction in fear that individuals can walk down the street day after day with reassurance that they will arrive at their destination without harm.

I gave Sinn Fein credit for understanding that what this country needed was more than independence from Great Britain. This country needed self-determination and not union or re-union with the Republic of Ireland. In my short stay here, I had come to understand that there were many Irish, not one Irish. Most of the Protestant families had lived in Northern Ireland for centuries so they were as Irish as the Irish Catholics. I wondered why the Protestant Northern Ireland residents didn't see themselves as Irish but rather as English or Scots-Irish. It is a mistaken identity. There were English Catholics in Britain, just as there were Irish Protestants in the Republic. Nationality alone didn't determine religion.

I got up to stretch and thought that the above paragraph would most likely not make the final draft. I was musing, which can be dangerous because I wander off track. I have a nasty habit of thinking out loud as I write. I reread the last paragraph and slashed a big X across it.

I made myself a cup of tea and scrounged through the refrigerator to find something to quiet my growling stomach. Mairin knew I would need a snack and had a plate of sliced beef, a bit of smoked salmon, and Irish cheddar waiting for me.

I felt a chill in the room owens I returned to the sitting room, which I hadn't noticed while I was drafting my newspaper article. I balanced the plate on my knees while leaning over to add a few peat logs to the fire. The food, tea, and fire warmed me to the point of feeling drowsy. The time after lunch was dangerous for me, especially after nights of restless sleep like I had last night. I relaxed into the chair and stretched my legs out. Soon I was dozing, hoping the words I would need about the peace walls would be given to me in my sleep.

I woke because of my poor posture in the chair. My neck was so stiff and sore, it would have woken the dead. Another cup of tea was in order. The caffeine would jump-start my brain. I soon settled in with the mug of tea and reread the first sentence I had scratched out before lunch. I started again.

Whitehall's proposal to build additional peace walls presents unique challenges.

That was a bland sentence. I tore the page off the pad and tossed it into the fireplace. I needed a new approach.

I interviewed three Catholic families who have lived close to the existing peace walls for years. Living my whole life in Cork and Dublin, I have no concept of how people live behind walls.

I put my pen down and read the new introduction several times. At least it explains that I had attempted to understand the walls from the perspective of the residents. I might be criticized for talking only with Catholic families, but I guessed it showed I was willing to show I have bias just like anyone else. *I wonder if my perspective would be different if I had talked with Protestant families*, I thought. I decided that in the future, if I was challenged on that point, I would offer to meet with Protestant families out of fairness and equal opportunity. I began to write again.

I must confess that I consider the existing peace walls to be a form of self-imposed segregation. Only those of us who are foreigners call them "walls."

All of the families I talked with are adamant that the walls are absolutely necessary for their safety and well-being. Without the walls, they would be forced to move—somewhere.

I put my pen down again and looked out the window to see what was going on in the street outside. I noticed a black sedan parked directly opposite of the door to the apartment. While Dominic was playing tour guide to Mairin, it looked like someone new had been given the assignment to watch out for me. That said everything about the desperate need for safety and security in Belfast. I need to capture that in my article.

When I met with the three families, I promised to set aside my prejudice and just listen, without judgment...I did listen and I learned.

All of the families agreed that the peace walls have worked the past thirty years...Compared to shootings and bombings, these are minor infractions that can be tolerated. Just because violence is in abeyance, there is always a risk that it could erupt. By separating themselves, both Catholics and Protestants are committed to doing no harm....

The current truce is tenuous. Sinn Fein and the Democratic Unionist Party must learn to create a relationship and forge a government based on shared power....

So, walls have two functions. First, they provide a necessary measure of safety for people to have routine everyday lives. Second, they prevent violence.

I put my pen down, rubbed my eyes and stretched my arms out in front of me. I stared into the embers of the peat fire. It would need more fuel soon if the fire would last into the evening. Dusk was creeping into the room through the small window. I didn't know what time it was but thought Mairin and Dominic would be returning soon. I filled my pipe with as much tobacco as I could stuff into the bowl and still be able to draw through it. The match flame dove into the bowl when I drew in deeply, and I blew smoke out the side of my mouth as it caught. I left the tablet with the draft of my article on the floor next to the chair.

As I smoked, a cloud formed above my head. *If I live here long enough I'll create a round stain on the ceiling like I have at home in my writing room*, I thought.

"Hello, Ian" Mairin said loud enough to be heard from the front door. I jumped up to meet her in the hall, throwing my arms wide open to greet her with a tight hug.

"Oh, you missed me," she whispered in my ear.

"Always."

"Did your writing go well?"

"It took the entire day. I just finished a few moments ago."

"May I read it later?"

"Of course. You're my editor-and-chief."

THIRTY-NINE

An Imperfect Peace
By Ian Padraic Murphy

In the few short months since both Northern Ireland and the Republic of Ireland approved the Good Friday Agreement, true peace has been elusive. August witnessed the violence in Omagh.

A group of dissidents founded the Real Irish Republican Army (RIRA) and there has been a proposal to build additional peace walls to separate Catholics and Protestants in Belfast.

I was asked to help usher in the era of peace following the Good Friday Agreement and quell the activities of the RIRA.

To help understand the discontent that still resides in the hearts of RIRA members, I visited Omagh within several days of the explosion. The RIRA took responsibility for its actions and acknowledged it was an egregious and regrettable error.

I have met with RIRA leadership in Belfast and challenged them to give Stormont the opportunity to form an independent government. The RIRA has reasoned it is in their self-interest to live in an independent Northern Ireland. They have announced cessation of the campaign of violence. This must be accepted as an act of faith that the politicians can hammer out some structure to govern this country.

I interviewed three Catholic families who have lived close to the existing peace walls for years. Living my whole life in Cork and Dublin, I have no concept of how people live behind walls.

I must confess that I consider the existing peace walls to be a form of self-imposed apartheid. The language used to describe the walls is interesting. I have heard them described as "peace lines" and as "intersections" by those who live in Belfast. Only we foreigners call them "walls." The reluctance to call the structures what they really are is an insight into the psyche of those living in their presence. What you call a thing, defines it. If you don't call the structures a "wall," then it isn't. To the rest of the world, however, they are walls.

All of the families I talked with are adamant that the walls are absolutely necessary for their safety and well-being. In fact, they argue that the walls allow them to continue to live in their homes; without the walls they would be forced to move—somewhere.

I worry about the suggestion to build additional peace walls for several reasons. First, because it was proposed by a British government that incorrectly believes it has the right to intervene in Northern Ireland's affairs. Simply said, if it's a British idea, it's bad for Northern Ireland. Second, I view it as a way of announcing to the world that the citizens of Northern Ireland are incapable and unwilling to govern themselves and create a civil society—they need walls.

When I met with the three families, I promised to set aside my prejudice and just listen, without judgment. The families represented older, middle-aged, and young families. One family had young children at home, one had adult children who had moved away from Belfast, and one couple didn't have children. One family had lived in Belfast for generations. I did listen and I learned.

All of the families agreed that the peace walls have worked the past thirty years. Yes, there has been some violence. On occasion, golf balls are tossed over the wall or bottles, even bricks and stones. Compared to shootings and bombings, these are minor infractions that can be tolerated. The walls have not brought peace but they have provided security and reduced violence to a minimum. Just because violence is in abeyance, there is always a risk that it could erupt. By separating themselves, both Catholics and Protestants are committed to doing no harm. For now, that is an accomplishment.

The current truce is tenuous. Sinn Fein and Democratic Unionist must learn to create a relationship and forge a government based on shared power. For that to happen, there must be absolutely no violence. Walls are the guarantee to prevent violence.

So, walls have two functions. First, they provide a necessary measure of safety for people to have routine, everyday lives. Second, they prevent violence.

Representative democracy is based on the principle of self-determination. I do not have the right to impose my views of these walls on the citizens of Belfast. Self-determination means choice and if the people of Belfast chose to have additional peace walls constructed to feel safe—so be it.

†††

I collapsed after dinner and went to the bedroom to lie down while Mairin meticulously cut and pasted my article together from the sheets of notepaper I left on the sitting room floor. I stared at the ceiling, not able to relax enough to fall asleep but too tired for any other activity.

Mairin walked into the bedroom carrying the patchwork draft in her hand.

"There's my man," Mairin said in her Lauren Bacall voice. She curled up next to me on the bed. She lifted her head and looked directly at me for a few minutes without saying a word. She plopped the pages on top of my stomach.

"I'm your man. That sounds like a line from the movies." We both giggled like teenagers in bed together for the first time.

"I made some minor edits. Sometimes you need word tense changes."

"That's fine. Thank you for the improvements."

Mairin rose up on one elbow and kissed me. "So what does tomorrow bring."

"Tomorrow we meet with Kieran. I'll give him my article. I don't want to meet with anyone else. The words speak for themselves. My job here is done. Then we go home to Cork. Let's start looking for a place to live as soon as we get back. Do you want to live in town or the country?"

"Right, now, I just want to be in your arms. I can feel that you're exhausted. We both need sleep. We can talk on the drive home. You are one amazing man, Ian Murphy. I'll love you for all of my days."

In the quiet of the night, we drifted off to sleep, still fully dressed, on top of the bed.

The next day, Mairin went with me to Sinn Fein headquarters to deliver my article: *An Imperfect Peace*. She insisted that I copy it over on unblemished notepad paper rather than turn in the cut-and-paste version she had edited for me. I had her read over the final copy to make sure I captured all of her edits.

Kieran was not happy with me. It was more accurate to say that he was angry with me.

"Watch out, Mairin, when Kieran's face turns that shade of red, we're going to get blasted," I warned her.

"Jesus Christ, Ian, is this it? You weren't supposed to agree to build more peace lines. Hell, we thought you might be instrumental in tearing down the ones we already have. What a fucking disappointment." Kieran threw the pages in my face.

"It's honest, Kieran. Sinn Fein leadership might do well to listen to their constituents rather than worrying about international perception. I admitted in the article I didn't personally agree," I argued back.

"Who cares?" Kieran shouted his face now as red as a fire truck.

"Don't have a heart attack over it, my friend."

"You're going to have to talk to Adams," Kieran snapped.

"I'm not. Mairin and I are leaving immediately for Cork. We're going to be moving in together, and we have a lot to discuss on our trip." I turned and grabbed Mairin by the elbow. "It's time we leave Belfast behind us."

FORTY

Back in Cork, Mairin set to work finding a home for us. We agreed to find an apartment near the UCC campus. An apartment best fit the lifestyle we wanted to share together. Mairin understood that I needed to return to writing and the memoir that I had set aside months ago to make the Belfast trip.

Before resuming writing, I felt the need to talk again with Father O'Connell. I shared an affinity with Father O'Connell that I didn't understand but yet needed. Besides Mairin, he was the one person with whom I was comfortable being completely honest and did not fear judgment. Unlike my experience growing up in the Catholic church, he was a priest who wasn't compelled to give advice. When I asked specific questions, he responded, but he refrained from giving unsolicited advice or direction. For a priest that must have required unimaginable discipline and devotion to unconditional love, as in the commandment to love others as yourself. I called and made an appointment in the first week after Mairin and I returned to Cork.

"Go right through, Mr. Murphy, Father is expecting you." The parish secretary was noted for her efficiency, even if she was a bit formal.

"Thank you."

Father O'Connell walked around his desk. "Good to see you, Ian. From the newspaper accounts, you've been busy in Belfast the past few months. I appreciate that you detest personal press coverage but your contribution to helping create a working peace was impressive. Would you like tea?"

"I would rather stroll in the garden. I didn't come to talk about Belfast."

"Of course not. I didn't intend to be presumptive. Let's walk."

As we had months before, we walked in the inner garden for some time without speaking. One of the reasons I was drawn to Father O'Connell was that he didn't need to talk all the time and was comfortable with silence. I took in a deep breath. The flower garden was like a living painter's pallet with yellow and white roses, meadow saffron, marigolds, St. John's wort, pansies and other varieties.

"The garden is immaculate and perfect for solitude," I said.

"Yes, it is very special, Ian. I sense that you have found peace since we talked several months ago. Did you find solace in St. John of the Cross?"

I shuffled and then stopped to smell the roses. "Well, it's complex."

"Complex?"

"I believe that Saint John of the Cross led me but not in the way you imagined. I...I never actually read the works you suggested. I did find two of his books at the UCC Religion Department Library, but most important, I met the librarian, Mairin McCarthy."

Father O'Connell also bent down to smell the fragrant roses. "Interesting."

"If I hadn't searched for those particular books, I would never have met Mairin. That is clear to me."

"Quite by chance, several weeks after meeting Mairin, we accidently met again on the Dingle Peninsula. I had gone to stay with my aunt and uncle who own a pub and rooming house there. I planned on hiking for several weeks. Every year after the spring term is over, Mairin vacations on the Dingle Peninsula. Her love of hiking is as great as mine. We hiked together and it has altered my life completely."

"That's quite a coincidence. So has Mairin become special in your life?"

"Yes, she's agreed to be my wife. Would you marry us?"

"Would you both consent to marriage instruction?"

I'm sure a look of horror crossed my face and I stumbled, nearly falling into the rose bed. I hadn't planned on asking Father O'Connell to marry us. Mairin and I hadn't even discussed which church to be married in or if she had a priest in mind to perform the ceremony. The words had tumbled out of my mouth without thought.

"It's not required, of course. I'm afraid it's an automatic response when I'm asked to preside. I would be happy to serve as your priest. I assume Mairin has agreed to this."

"I should talk to her. You, of course, need to meet her. I may have been premature." I stammered for an explanation.

"I understand. That's not why you're here, is it?"

"No. I had the illusion that if I could make the words of the Peace Accord spring to life, to have real meaning in the everyday lives of Northern Ireland citizens, I would earn my own redemption. I was naïve. Instead, I concentrated on learning about the people of Belfast and how they would go about creating their own community for the first time in their history. I abandoned my search for redemption and by doing that, found another path."

Father put his hand on my back and massaged gently. We took small steps on the grass path. As we approached a bench tucked away in a corner of the garden, I motioned for us to sit down."

We sat down in the shade. "Tell me more, Ian."

"We always have choices in our lives. Too often we're not aware of the choices we have and blunder through as if everything is predestined. I have shouldered the burden of guilt for encouraging and training young men to do horrible things in the name of reunifying Ireland. That was my choice. What I've come to realize is that those young men had a choice, too. I may have persuaded them to take up the Cause, but the final choice was theirs. The world cannot impose guilt on me or anyone. Guilt is born in the seed of my soul. There is no guilt in the world." I paused to reflect.

"Guilt, a very Catholic concept," Father O'Connell said.

"This is a new world view for me. I've always thought the world controlled how I felt. I decided to atone for my mistakes in the Long War; it was my choice even if you did inspire the idea. I could also have chosen to do nothing. Your words rang true to me not because you are a priest but because I accepted the truth. I now understand I have choices. We delude ourselves that we have a notion of the consequences of our actions but in truth we rarely do. What we do have is intention. We select our path by what we intend."

Neither of us said anything for a long time. "I've been listening. Your heart is calm, Ian."

"My heart is content. I have choices now. I'm going to write my memoir and let writing be my path to redemption. Writing is my path, it always has been."

"Your journey has been one of seeking self-knowledge and self-acceptance. Thank you for sharing with me."

A sense of relief flooded over me with Father O'Connell words. "Well, I suppose we need to find a time for you to meet Mairin, soon."

"Frankly, Ian, I can't wait. I sense you've found your life partner."

"Oh, I have. I have indeed."

FORTY-ONE

airin found a three-story house for us close enough to campus that we could both walk to work. "Why three stories?" I asked. "There are only two of us."

"I have a plan. The top floor will be your writing room, the entire floor. The second floor has three bedrooms and the main level has the kitchen, living room, and dining room. It's perfect."

"Ok, give me the tour tomorrow."

I wasn't aware but Mairin was already negotiating the terms with the auctioneer, which was best; I wasn't interested in business arrangements. The third floor was like a library room with windows on two sides, book shelves on the opposite walls, and a fireplace at one end. It was perfect.

"Mairin, the writing room is a dream come true. I want both of us to work in this room."

Tears welled up in Mairin's eyes as she jumped into my arms. "You dear, dear man. Do you mean that? You'll share your writing room with me?"

"We're sharing a life now. I wouldn't want it any other way."

† † †

Soon after returning, we learned changes were underway in the library system at UCC. When Mairin received a letter in the post with the Chancellor's crest on the envelope, we were both puzzled and apprehensive. "What do you think this means? It doesn't take a chancellor to fire me; the Department Chair can do that."

"There's only one way to find out. Here's a letter opener."

Mairin read the letter and turned white as new fallen snow. She gasped and choked trying to breath. "Dear Mother of God." She handed me the letter.

Ms. McCarthy:

In your absence, your position as the Director of the Religion Department has been filled permanently. We will not be able to reinstate you to that position.

We have been working for months to examine the operation of the various Department libraries and have found unsettling redundancy. It is clear that it is time to reorganize the departmental library system.

As a result, we have merged the Literature Department and the Theatre Department libraries into a single library which will move to a yet-to-be determined location.

Based on your previous performance, we have come to the conclusion that you are the most appropriate staff member to be the new Director of the Arts Library (our designation for the combined libraries). This position is a permanent academic appointment with compensation of €79,000 per annum.

I have scheduled an appointment to discuss this offer with you on Wednesday at 9:00 a.m.

Anticipating your acceptance, we are looking forward to working with you in this new capacity.

A.Maloney,
Chancellor
University College Cork

"Ian, did you have anything to do with this?" Mairin asked in a suspicious tone.

"We've been together night and day. Of course not. But I'm thrilled your talent has been recognized. Now, you will definitely need to share the third-floor library with me."

†††

For the next few months, I devoted myself to writing my memoir while Mairin concentrated on merging the Literature and Theatre libraries, meeting with faculty, hiring staff, and forming a committee to select the best location for the combined collection. Soon it was September of 1999 and we hadn't had a break. I convinced Mairin to spend a long weekend in Dublin, to take in a concert and a new play I had read about.

After dinner on Friday evening, we took a walk through Temple Bar. "Ian, this is so unlike you. Temple Bar? Really? Since when do you want to spend time in the shopping district? You don't value material things at all."

"Oh, relax, it's a James Joyce remembrance walk," I lied.

We strolled through the streets for about an hour, and then I led her into a jewelry store.

"Good evening Mr. Murphy. Glad to see you," The clerk said in greeting.

"He knows you?" Mairin asked.

"Oh, I'm sure it's from a book jacket," I lied again.

"I must go to the back room. I'll return shortly," the clerk said.

The clerk returned with a red velvet bag drawn closed with a gold thread tie string. I walked to the counter and took the pouch from him. I took Mairin's hand and held it palm up, then took a gold claddagh ring from the bag.

"The claddagh ring: the heart held by two hands represents love, and the crown resting on the heart signifies loyalty. It's the perfect symbol of our love, our friendship, our life. I want you to be my wife; I want to be your husband."

Mairin drew her hand into a fist, clasping the ring. Tears streamed down her face. "I didn't think I could be surprised, but you've succeeded, Ian. I want to be your wife with all my heart."

We had a small wedding in Saint Vincent's Church, officiated by Father O'Connell, which Kieran and Mickey almost ruined. Both thought they deserved to be my best man. I wasn't prepared for that type of bickering and was disappointed with both of them.

Mairin was able to draw a truce between them by convincing them that a distinction wouldn't be made between best man and groomsman. Each was allowed a toast at the wedding feast and then they offered one in unison. Getting married at the age of fifty-one was agonizing, not because of the marriage but because of my friends.

The school term began a month after our wedding.

Mairin was swamped in her new duties. I elected to take the semester off to finish my memoir and would return to class in the spring term. Every afternoon about 4:00 p.m., I finished writing for the day and walked to Mickey's pub for a pint and conversation with the patrons.

On Monday, I strolled into the pub as usual. "Congratulations, Ian. God, what a fine thing. You are the most deserving man I can think of. I'm going to have to post yer picture on the wall now, to let the tourists know this is yer pub."

"Mickey O'Shay, what are you babbling about?"

Mickey held up Monday's *Irish Independent* with the headline: "Ian Murphy wins first Irish Pen Award."

"What is the Pen Award?" I asked out loud.

"Here." Mickey shoved the paper in my hands.

This is the first year the Pen Award has been established and it rightfully goes to Cork author Ian Padraic Murphy. The purpose of the Pen Award is to recognize outstanding Irish writers who have made a significant lifetime contribution to literature. Mr. Murphy has yet to be notified by the Pen Award Committee of his recognition. This reporter will attempt to interview Mr. Murphy in the near future for his response to this honor.

I slammed the paper down on the bar. "Well, I suppose that means drinks are on me today."

"Did ya notice the byline, Ian?" Mickey asked.

"No."

"Eileen Donohue scooped the story," Mickey said with a sneer. "Will ya talk to her if she calls?

I scratched my beard and thought before answering. "I don't know."

"It's just like her to get a big headline before even talking to you. I wonder how she found out about it before you were notified."

I shook my head and chuckled. "Mickey, it's her job. Now, go down to the cellar and bring up that case of Midleton I know you have in storage. Everyone in the pub will drink the best tonight. I need to borrow your office. I want to call Mairin."

"Jaysus, Ian, I thought you gave up the Midleton. I thought you were drinking only Smithwick's ale."

"This is a special occasion that deserves Midleton. I'll be fine. I've conquered my demons."

I walked from the bar toward Mickey's office. He followed me and slapped me so hard on the back I lunged forward.

"Aye, anything for you, my friend, anything at all."

ACKNOWLEDGMENTS

"The meaning of life is to find your gift. The purpose of life is to give it away."

I must first acknowledge Dr. Laurel Yourke for suggesting to me that I had the ability and skill to write a novel. Second, I must mention my friend and mentor, Marshall Cook, who was kind enough to read drafts of this book and share his unique insights. Christine DeSmet taught me about story and story arc and provided encouragement to continue writing. Finally, my son, Tim Owens, who brought me Irish newspapers that were the spark for two novels.

ABOUT THE AUTHOR

In 1997, novelist Rex Owens began attending the first of many annual UW Madison Writers Institutes. Featured speaker author Robert Moss explained conscious dreaming as a way to explore the writing life, which inspired Rex to write. In 1999, he joined a critique group led by Dr. Laurel Yourke where he learned the craft the old-fashioned way—by writing. In 2003, Dr. Yourke suggested he had enough material to consider writing a novel. In December 2009, he was unexpectedly laid off from his management position with a healthcare organization. The author interpreted this event as the universe sending a message: it's time finish the novel.

Three years were devoted to polishing his first book, *Murphy's Troubles*, which was released in November 2013. The second novel, *Out of Darkness*, continues Ian Murphy's story and Northern Ireland's struggle for nationhood.

CONTACT INFORMATION:
Rex Owens
rexowens00@gmail.com
www.rexowens.us
608.513.1951

OUT OF DARKNESS